I AM A KILLER

MATTHEW HATTERSLEY

VINCI
BOOKS

Vinci Books

vinci-books.com

Published by Vinci Books Ltd in 2025

1

A CIP catalogue record for this book is available from the British Library.
Paperback ISBN: 9781036700676

Printed and bound in Great Britain by Clays Ltd, Elcograf S.p.A.

Also by Matthew Hattersley

Acid Vanilla

Annihilation Pest Control Series

John Beckett Series

Chapter One

Thelmastone House stands in its own grounds in the countryside, ten miles outside of Hastings. Having no close neighbours, the luxurious villa-style rural mansion is free to host lavish parties that go on late into the night, and where the rich and powerful guests – financiers, actors, members of Her Majesty's Government – can live out their most decadent fantasies, safe in the knowledge their debauched behaviour won't be caught by a paparazzi lens or a rogue iPhone camera.

Bought in the mid-nineties by the Italian-Hungarian billionaire, Brutus Farkas, the country house was now the go-to venue for those so rich they could no longer find enjoyment in mainstream pursuits. Or, indeed, in legal or moral pursuits. Being only a thirty-minute drive from the coast, where guests could make a quick getaway across the English Channel if needed – and with its own helipad – it was the perfect setting for those eager for rare and nefarious experiences. Since 2015 a secret underground tunnel coming out close to the A21 provided an even swifter exit if ever required.

To date, Farkas had been able to keep the goings-on at Thelmastone House free from any police investigations; but, like anyone who made money in illegitimate ways, he understood the need for well-planned escape routes. He had a packed go-bag always to hand, a detailed eight-page contingency plan, plus multiple passports, bank accounts and properties in Eastern Europe and South America. Staff were briefed regularly on what to do if MI5 or the CIA ever came calling.

Up to now, this had simply been an exercise in risk assessment and forward-planning. But Farkas knew that, with each year that passed, he was under increasing pressure to make the next event on the calendar more daring and more depraved. Luckily for his guests, Farkas was more than happy to oblige. An Aleister Crowley obsessive from a young age, he subscribed wholeheartedly to the arch occultist's singular commandment. *Do what thou wilt shall be the whole of the law.*

He couldn't have put it better himself. Over the years, Thelmastone House had hosted multi-level sex orgies, drug parties, a Fight-Club-type evening where none of the immigrant 'contenders' survived, tramp racing, something called 'The Hunt' and a real-life murder-mystery weekend with a million-pound prize for the person who cracked the case. But if the guest list was anything to go by, tonight's event was the first of its kind and one that would no doubt be repeated in Thelmastone House's yearly schedule (available for an undisclosed seven-figure fee to those in the know). Tickets for the night had sold out within hours and guests had travelled from all over the globe to experience Farkas' latest otherworldly event.

But why wouldn't they?

There was nowhere on the planet they could experience the same multi-media, multi-faceted experience that Thelmastone House offered.

Because another reason Brutus Farkas was the promoter extraordinaire when it came to these kinds of happenings was that he put such zing into the marketing. Guests would never have paid a million dollars a head to attend a run-of-the-mill sex orgy or kill party, but bill these occasions as a *Morality-Morphing Sex Quest For The New World Order* or *The Great Eugenics Extermination Experiment* and people were falling over themselves to get a ticket. Both of those evenings sold out within a few minutes. Similarly, tonight's event would never have drawn the same attention listed merely as a sex-slave auction, but as an *Intergalactic Pleasure Sale For The Sexually Progressive*? Now, that was clever marketing.

In his master bedroom on the top floor of the house, Brutus Farkas leaned into the mirror, finishing off the last touches of his make-up. In line with the theme of the evening, he'd painted his face bright green, and along with his black goat beard he had more than a passing resemblance to Max von Sydow in the Flash Gordon film – albeit a little more round of figure and portlier of chin than his wiry equivalent.

He straightened up at a knock on the door. "Who is it?" he called out. "Don't you know I'm busy in here?"

There was no answer. Maybe he'd imagined it. He could already hear the music pulsing through the floor. Hard, fast and electronic. His favourite kind; designed to add an extra layer of anarchy and depravity to the experience. He stared at the door for a moment before shaking his head and turning back to the mirror. It was probably one of the guests, having taken a wrong turn. Selecting a

3

black kohl pencil from his make-up box, he leaned into the mirror until his breath fogged the glass and applied a line of black under each eye, smudging it into the green with the side of his thumb. Satisfied, he placed the pencil down and shifted his attention to the bureau where another smaller mirror lay flat, ten grams of the finest quality cocaine in a pile in its centre. Farkas smiled eagerly at the white mountain, which he'd so far been able to resist. The night was still young and he didn't want to overdo it. But one cheeky line wouldn't hurt. A little pick-me-up.

With thick, eager fingers, he picked up the razor blade beside the mirror and portioned off a decent amount. A Goldilocks. Not too big. Not too small. Just right. Using the edge of the blade, he chopped up the white powder before deftly forming it into a line about two inches in length and resembling a fat white slug. Maybe this is what slugs looked like in space, he thought to himself, still on-theme. Chuckling, he picked up the thin gold tube he used for such activities and obliterated the space slug in one vicious snort.

Reeling back, he pressed his thumb down on his left nostril as the party powder shot into his system. What a rush. Now he was ready. He stepped back and turned toward the door as more knocking emanated through the thick antique wood.

Rolling his eyes, Farkas swaggered over to the large mirror at the end of the bed. "Who is it?" he asked, elongating his vowels and his voice rising from tenor to mezzo-soprano as the space slug went to work on his mood. He grinned at his reflection. He looked great. The black latex bodysuit along with the silver boots and cape perfectly complemented his green skin. And that kohl around the eyes – didn't it just make them POP!

He tutted as the knocking came again. Louder this time and more frantic.

"Fine. I am coming." He marched over and yanked at the handle. "Yes? What is it?"

The woman on the other side recoiled as the door swung open. It was one of the waiting staff Farkas had hired for the event. Hiding behind her blue wig, she held up a bronze tray, on top of which was a bottle that Farkas recognised straight off as Russo-Baltique vodka. The seven-thousand sparkling Swarovski crystals covering the sides of the bottle were a dead giveaway.

"Please. Is from a guest," the girl mumbled.

There were twenty-five staff working here tonight. All female. All beautiful. But this one seemed more timid than the ones they normally sent over. The agency that procured the girls for him would never divulge where they found them, but none of them had English as a first language and all had that slightly glassy-eyed look that came from a life-time of trauma. It was easier that way. You could buy a traf-ficked girl's silence for a few dollars and a threat of worse to come.

"Bring it in," he ordered, stepping aside and holding the door for her. "Put it over there on the table."

As she shuffled into the room, he tilted his head to take her in. He didn't recall seeing this one before, but why would he? Tonight's staff had only been on site for a few hours and, for obvious reasons, Farkas never used the same staff twice. In fact, for the last two events held here, he'd gone even further. In a bid to protect himself and his guests, he'd had all the waiting staff exterminated as soon as the last guest had left the premises. The agency was well compensated for their inconvenience and the bodies were taken out to sea and disposed of. Farkas felt it a shame to

5

destroy such beautiful, fragile creatures, but needs must. And, really, it was only like killing a baby lamb or a calf. No one would ever miss them.

He closed the door and watched her slide the tray onto the round table on the far side of the room. As per his stipulations (and in line with his glorious space-age theme), tonight's serving girls were all dressed like Jane Fonda in Barbarella and this one certainly lived up to the brief. She had curves in all the right places and wasn't too skinny – unlike some of the deprived wenches the agency supplied who looked like they hadn't seen a decent meal in years. The girl turned and lowered her head as he walked over to her. He could almost see her shaking as he approached the table.

"Do you know who gifted me this exquisite drink?" he asked, running a finger down the ice-cold bottle.

The girl shook her head but didn't look up. "No. I sorry. I do not." She waved her hand over her face. "A man. With… err… beard."

No one specific came to mind, but Farkas was thankful for the offering. The cocaine had made his skin tingle and he felt buoyant and ready for fun. He picked up the vodka and pulled out the stopper before pulling two cut-glass crystal tumblers towards him and pouring a large serving into each of them. He held one out to the girl. "Here, have a drink with me."

The girl was startled as he shoved the glass at her. "No. I cannot. My boss…"

"Fuck your boss. I'm your boss. Here you go."

Nervously, she took the glass, slender fingers snaking around the heavy-based tumbler. As she pulled it close, holding it with two hands, Farkas stepped around the front of her and grabbed her by the chin. She flinched, but had to relent as he lifted her face. He was the boss, after all.

"Lovely," he mused. "Really lovely."

It was true she was a sight to behold. Not as young as he'd first thought, but she had wonderful bone structure and delicious puffy lips that returned to their original fullness as she bit and released the bottom one. They reminded Farkas of his new memory foam pillow.

"Where are you from?" he asked, letting go of her face.

She bowed her head. "I am from agency."

"No. I mean originally. Croatia, is it? Serbia?" He narrowed his eyes. "Or Romania, maybe?"

"Please," she muttered. "I do not… My family…"

He stepped back for a better look, sipping at his drink as he considered her. She certainly was a nervous thing. Coy, frightened. Subservient. But that's how he liked them. He could have some fun with this one, he thought, taking another drink from his glass. He could picture it now, him on top, hands around her throat. Her gasping for air, begging him to stop. But he wouldn't stop. He never did. It would be a shame to get rid of this one – and so soon in the evening – but there were plenty more serving staff where she came from. They'd all end up in the same place by tomorrow.

A shiver of excitement ran up Farkas' spine as he eyed the woman. "Have a drink," he told her, taking a large gulp himself. It tasted like chemicals, but neat vodka usually did. Plus, he could also put that down to the thick line of Bolivian marching powder he'd just inhaled. He could still sense remnants of it in his nasal canal and down the back of his throat. It was quality stuff, and as he looked at the woman his vision blurred and dizziness washed over him. His lust was growing with each second in the attendance of this quiet, humble peasant woman dressed up as a space goddess. She was looking more and more uneasy in his presence and that was a big turn-on for him. They always tasted better scared.

"Drink the damn drink," he told her. "That's an order."

"Please… I don't want…" She looked at the floor, face veiled behind the wig.

Farkas growled.

What the hell was going on?

What was this insolent girl playing at?

The room spun as he stepped forward and an intense rush of indignation threatened to overwhelm him. His skin tingled and his back molars ground against each other uncontrollably. It happened that way. One minute he could be the most charming and placid person you'd ever meet and the next a demonic figure, so ferocious and blinded by anger he'd murder you for the slightest of infractions. Only three weeks ago he'd bitten the nose off his broker at Black Rock Capital after receiving some bad news about his recent investment. That time he had to be dragged off the man, but there would be no one to help this pathetic wretch tonight. He closed his eyes as another wave of dizziness rocked him. Breathing through it he grinned, picturing himself, green-faced and naked, showing this insolent girl who was the boss.

No, not the boss.

The king!

He was the king of all he surveyed. King Brutus. People bowed to his majesty. He'd created a high-level world of profligacy and libertarian decadence. He was a self-made man. A true visionary. An artist. That's why his events always sold out and why the rich and powerful flew thousands of miles to attend his parties. He was king.

King of the World. And this wretched *bitch* was still defying him.

His eyes snapped open. "Drink your fucking drink," he snarled. But he was struggling to focus. He felt woozy and sick and it was her fault. She'd done this. She had to pay.

"Why you want me to do this?" the woman mumbled to the floor.

"Because it will help you enjoy what is about to happen to you," he replied. "And because I fucking said so."

He grabbed her hand, shoving the drink towards her mouth.

Grunting, she struggled against him. She was stronger than he'd anticipated.

"I said, drink."

The woman remained steadfast as he dug his fingernails into the skin on her wrist. What the hell did she think she was doing? She was his employee, for fuck's sake. This didn't happen. Didn't she know who he was? She raised her head and he glared at her. The room spun.

What the…?

The dizziness shot down both arms and legs, leaving him weak and unstable. His body shivered with anger and confusion as he stared at the woman.

"I told you to drink," he snarled.

"I told you I didn't want to."

Farkas released his grip on her as she spoke. Gone was the thick, guttural Eastern European peasant accent, and in its place an English one that could cut glass. It was slightly husky, as though she'd smoked too many cigarettes or drunk too much liquor, but she was well-spoken, with consonants as sharp as knives.

"Now get the hell off me."

As she fixed him with a hard stare, he became aware of

her eyes for the first time. They were wide and crazy-looking, but not in the way many women's eyes were when they looked at him. There was no meekness in her soul.

She didn't blink. That was what perturbed him the most. Her eyes were wild and intense. And up close he saw they were different colours. One blue. One brown.

"What the fuck?" Farkas cried.

The woman shoved him away, stalking him across the room as he stumbled backwards. The energy in the room had shifted. Even in his drugged, confused state, Farkas could sense it. He was no longer the predator and that terrified him.

"What do you want?" he gasped, as his shoulders hit the wall. He glanced left and right. It felt like the door, his only way out, was too far away. His legs had turned to jelly and his heart was beating faster than it ever had before. He held one hand up as the woman got closer, but she slapped it away. "Who are you?" he spluttered.

"Who am I?" she said. "I'm your worst fucking nightmare."

"Go to hell."

He lashed out with his fist, but she grabbed his wrist and twisted his arm down, swiping her hand across his throat. He saw a flash of steel and a second later his head felt heavier. As the woman stepped away, there was blood on her cheeks and forehead. Bringing his hands up to his throat, he felt at the open wound. Warm blood gushed out over his fingers from his severed jugular vein.

No!

He grasped at the wound, desperately trying to hold his neck together. But it was no use. He was bleeding out. Fading fast. He made to yell, but no sound came. As all the sins of his past came rushing back to meet him, he sank to his knees, struggling to focus on the woman as she knelt in front of him.

"What a pathetic man you are, Brutus Farkas. You thought you were untouchable, didn't you?"

"Who sent you?" he gasped.

All he could think was this was a hit from some rival. But even that didn't make sense. He'd always been a trailblazer and anybody who might have made life difficult for him was paid off. But now his consciousness was slipping away, like sand through his fingers. He tried to speak but felt a sharp pain in his chest. Looking down, he saw the woman was holding a short dagger, the blade protruding out from between her fingers. The pain exploded through his torso as she stabbed him again. He tried to scream, managed a wet gurgling sound, and fell face down onto his seventeenth-century Persian rug. As his eyes closed and the darkness whisked him to hell, he heard a snort of derisive laughter.

"No one sent me, sweetie," the woman's voice echoed in the darkness. "I do this sort of thing for fun."

Chapter Two

Acid Vanilla watched the sick bastard bleed out all over his
vintage rug, before striding over to the gold-framed mirror
hanging next to the door. Standing in front of it, she
removed the blue wig and shook out a mound of tangled
waves. She'd been growing her hair out recently and she
liked how it fell over her shoulders. She liked the blood
spatter on her face, too. Wiping her finger across her forehead and cheeks, she drew lines in Farkas' blood and
grinned at her reflection. She looked insane. As if she was
wearing war paint. The blood was a signifier of her indignation and craving for righteous vengeance. Although, who
she was avenging here was up for discussion. There were the
girls she'd liberate tonight, of course, the ones being held
against their will before being sold as sex slaves to the
highest bidder. But she suspected it was much more than
just a rescue mission. There was probably a legion of
reasons behind her renewed desire for blood, and no doubt
Spook would be pecking her head soon enough, trying to
get to the bottom of it. Right now, though, all she knew was

that she felt more alive than she had done in years. She was back to doing what she excelled at. It felt good. It felt right.

She tossed the wig on the floor and adjusted her costume. She was wearing shiny silver leggings and black boots that she'd got from Sasha, the girl who was supposed to be working this shift tonight. On her top half, she was wearing a black tank top and a silver harness that came over her shoulders and joined across her midriff and around her back, like some kind of space-age bondage gear. The straps were attached to a wide silver belt, which she now unfastened, lifting the harness over her head and tossing it onto the floor next to the wig. Sasha hadn't wanted to miss out on her wages when Acid and Spook had first approached her, but once they'd paid her double the amount and explained their reasons for wanting her costume, she'd been happy to oblige. Like the other serving girls, she'd need to find alternative employment (the owner of the agency she'd signed on with was face down on his own Persian rug a few hundred miles away), but there were better jobs than serving drinks to rich sickos. Ones with a longer career trajectory.

Acid adjusted the belt she'd been wearing under the costume. It was the same one (made from black nubuck leather) she'd worn on hundreds of assignments. The one Caesar had ordered custom-made from his top weapons man soon after she'd joined Annihilation Pest Control. Until recently she'd kept it locked away in a chest under her bed, but now, with Caesar gone and having made peace with her past, she felt ready to wear it once again. She walked over to Farkas' motionless body and rolled him onto his back before pulling the push dagger out of his chest. Wiping it on his cloak, she stood and rehoused the small, t-shaped weapon in the concealed sheath on the back of her belt. As she straightened, she heard noises from downstairs. Laughter and jeering, followed by a woman's cries.

Slipping out of Farkas' suite, she moved along the corridor to the landing and the wide flight of stairs that led down to the main part of the house. She'd already scoped out the building and knew an armed guard was on patrol in each wing of the large mansion house, four of them in total. Like Farkas, they too had green painted faces and were dressed in black except for silver belts like the one she'd been wearing. The fact each was carrying an MP5 submachine gun only made their appearance more surreal.

The plan now, as they had discussed it, was to find Maria Waddington and get out of here.

With minimal fuss and no fatalities.

She could hear Spook's voice in her head as she hurried down the staircase, but Acid already knew that wasn't going to happen.

Maria was a seventeen-year-old runaway, whose parents had come to Spook and Acid after the police had all but given up hope of finding her. Reading between the lines, Acid had surmised that the ambitious teen had dreams of becoming a singer and had run away after her strict, religious parents tried to send her to boarding school. But soon after arriving in London, Maria had fallen prey to one of Farkas' procurement teams and ended up here. Her parents were paying good money for her safe return and Spook had expressly asked Acid to find Maria and remove her from the situation with as little bloodshed and risk to herself or the client as possible. But screw that. If Spook was here, if she could see these other girls in the same situation, see what these sick bastards were planning, she wouldn't think that way.

At the bottom of the steps, Acid found herself in a wide

entrance hall with doors on either side. The one on her right led through into the main banqueting space where the sex auction was taking place. But as she got closer to the open doorway, there was no sound coming from the room beyond. Just a few minutes earlier – before she'd slipped away to find Farkas – the room had been full of loud, lascivious men in ridiculous space-themed costumes, all of them braying at the drugged-up girls in white robes being paraded in front of them.

Acid pressed herself against the wall and threw a cursory glance around the side. It was empty of guests, but one of the silver-belted security guards was standing with his back to her a few feet into the room. He was holding his submachine gun loosely at waist height, and from the way his bald green head was angled to one side he appeared lethargic and bored. Like he didn't expect any trouble. In front of him, the banqueting table, which had been used as a makeshift runway for the macabre human market, was strewn with empty bottles and wine-soaked robes that had been ripped from the poor girls onstage. Loud music drifted into the room from the corridor beyond. Fast, industrial electronic music, with a throbbing bassline you could feel in your stomach, and occasional high-pitched arpeggios the only concession to actual music. It was the sort of track you might hear in a club in Berlin's underground and anathema to Acid's taste. But the pulsing beats would assist her in what came next.

She drew back, sliding the push dagger out of its sheath before moving into the room. Up on her toes, she advanced silently and got up behind the tall guard without alerting him to her presence. She raised the dagger, the tip wavering millimetres from the skin on the guard's neck as she assessed the bumps and folds. One. Two. If she got this wrong, she was a dead woman, but get it right and she severed his spinal cord and neutralised him instantaneously.

She sucked in a silent breath. Time was ticking away. The women on sale here tonight no doubt had been whisked away to one of the many bedrooms and boudoirs that spanned the east side of the house.

What happened to them next was up to her.

She bit her lip and went for it, plunging the push dagger into the guard's neck. She felt resistance but jammed it in harder. The spine is protected by impenetrable vertebrae and tough, spongy discs that cushion the joints between the bone, but with skill and brute force, you can get between the vertebrae. The guard made a sound like a surprised goat and shuddered as she pushed the blade deeper into his spine. He jerked once, then his body went limp. Once the brain stem is severed, all body function ceases and the victim is unable to speak or move. He was heavy as hell, but Acid leaned into him, yanking the dagger out of his neck as he dropped onto the stone floor. He landed on his back. His eyes remained open, but he was staring at something only he could see. His god, maybe. Or the devil. His breaths came in short, laboured bursts. Death was close.

"I'll take this," Acid whispered, grabbing the MP5 from out of his grasp. "There's a good chap."

She checked the magazine, pleased to see it had the full thirty rounds. That was more than enough, but she had to move fast. Six girls were part of the sick auction tonight, sold to the highest bidders out of the ten guests. She even recognised some of them. One was a social media billionaire, another a British government minister. All affluent, all using their privilege to inflict immeasurable pain on others. It only made her more committed to wiping them out this evening. The pricks deserved it.

Raising the gun to her shoulder, she moved across the room, aiming in front of her. A chorus of invisible bats screeched in her head the moment she stepped out into the corridor, and her muscles burned with tension as she marched up to the first door and listened at the wood. But over the music it was difficult to hear anything. She stepped back and was about to kick open the door when she heard a shriek to her left. Quickly shifting her aim down the corridor, she saw two of the female serving staff staring at her.

"Shh!" she instructed, before tapping her hand to her chest. "Friend. Here to help you."

She lowered her aim and stepped towards them as they looked at each other for reassurance.

"The people you are working for are criminals," she whispered. "*Kryminalista. Zločinec.* Do you understand?" The women nodded in unison. "They plan to kill you and the other girls. You need to gather up everyone who is working here tonight and get out of here. Now. Do you understand?"

"But... please... we don't..."

"Listen to me," Acid said. "Get your friends and get out. Now." She glanced between the two frightened women. They were in their early twenties. Maybe even younger. But they seemed to get the message. Holding onto each other, they hurried back the way they'd come. Acid watched them go before returning to the door. With the bats screaming for blood, she raised her aim and kicked it open.

A cool wave of sangfroid washed over her as she stepped through into a room containing two enormous beds. Three women were standing naked in the centre of the room, attempting to cover their breasts and genitals with trembling hands whilst two middle-aged men watched on from the beds. Acid threw her aim over to the first one, who she recognised as the government minister. He was gangly and long-faced with round glasses and side-parted hair. She couldn't remember his name, only that he dressed and acted like he was from the Victorian era. A silver eye mask hanging around his neck was his pitiful attempt at dressing for the occasion. Squeezing off a single round, she shot the evil prick between the eyes and shifted her aim over to his accomplice. This man was short and round and wearing a bright yellow latex bodysuit that highlighted every lump and roll of blubber. Another perfectly placed shot retired this pig man from the world. As his grotesque form slumped to the floor, she became aware of the three women crying and holding onto each other.

"Don't worry. I'm here to help you," Acid told them. She reached into her back pocket and pulled out the photo Spook had provided. She held it up to compare, but none of these women was Maria. "Stay in this room," she told them. "Keep the door shut. Someone will come for you when it's safe. Do you understand?"

The women appeared to be in shock, but one managed a curt nod of acknowledgement. Good enough. Acid left the room and closed the door behind her. The next door was less than twenty metres away. She approached it as before, kicking the door open and letting the MP5 make the first introductions. A tall man with sandy hair was standing in the centre of the room with his back to the door. At his feet knelt a young woman. She was looking up at him with terrified, watery eyes as he undid his costume. When the door slammed against the wall he spun around.

An expression of anger distorted his chiselled features. "What the hell do you th—?"

Two rounds shut him up. One in each eye, straight into his brain. It was a brutal and ritualistic kill (one of Spitfire

Creosote's signatures) and it sent a ripple of excitement up Acid's spine.

The woman cried out and shuffled back towards the far wall. Acid stepped over to her, holding a hand up. "Please be quiet. No one is going to hurt you. You're safe, but I need you to stay in this room. Understand?" She narrowed her eyes as the woman nodded and smiled meekly. She had blonde hair and Slavic features. Not Maria.

"Stay here," Acid reiterated, moving over to the door and out into the dark corridor beyond. The blaring electronic music echoed down the chasmic corridors, mixing with the noise of the chattering bats in her psyche. In front of her the corridor veered around to the right, leading to the next part of the building. Shifting the MP5 back up to her shoulder and gripping the barrel, she followed the corridor as it veered around to the right, leading to the next part of the building.

Shit.

Two green-faced guards were walking towards her. They saw her at the same time she saw them and raised their weapons, yelling at her in Russian. Acid dropped to one knee, shooting a zip line of bullets across the centre mass of the two men and opening up their chests in a flurry of tiny crimson explosions. Their bodies jerked and twisted with the abrupt trauma, both squeezing off a flurry of bullets from their semi-automatics that pockmarked the sides of the wood-panelled corridor. But neither were neutralised. As they fought through their pain and confusion, Acid jumped up and strode toward them, shooting as she went. She got the first man with a kill shot through the top lip, and the second caught a round in the neck that ripped his throat out before the job was finished with a shot above his right eye.

A smile spread across her lips as she stepped over the

mangled bodies. The hours of target practice Angela Masters (a new alias) had been putting in at the shooting range over in North London were very much paying off.

She headed along the corridor, bursting into the next room she came to. Three fat, sweaty men stared at her like frightened meerkats as the door smashed open. There were no women in this room, but the men were clearly gearing up for some sort of illicit encounter, if the piles of powder and blue pills on the table in front of them were any indication. This time Acid didn't need to rely on accuracy. Squeezing the trigger, she trailed a zipper of bullets horizontally across the scene, delighting as the hot metal tore through the men's chests and had each one dancing a terrible jig before they hit the wall and slumped to the ground. Another ripple of heat energy shot up Acid's spine as she left the room and continued down the corridor.

In the next room she found a naked man chasing a young girl around a large wooden table and took him out with a single shot to the head. The poor girl was traumatised but also eager in her thanks as Acid calmed her for a moment and told her to stay put.

But it wasn't Maria.

Where the hell was Maria?

Further down the corridor, she found two older men with white hair drinking from a bottle of expensive scotch. She killed them both without breaking a stride and raced out into the corridor, allowing herself a brief assessment of the situation. By her reckoning, she'd rescued five women and taken out nine guests. Ten, if she included Farkas. That meant there was one more guest and one girl left to find. Maria. Almost five minutes had passed since she'd left Farkas' suite and begun her killing spree. This should have been handled by now. She was on borrowed time.

A door at the far end of the corridor hung slightly ajar and a shiver of electric heat ran down Acid's arms. That didn't bode well. As she got close she heard heavy grunting noises, just audible above the aural chaos of the music.

"Who's there?" a voice yelled out.

Bollocks.

Whoever this was, he'd got the jump on her. A high-pitched wail, loud enough to cut through the sound system's pulsing bass drum, pierced the air.

Maria.

It had to be.

At least it meant she was still alive. But whether she stayed that way depended on what Acid did in the next few seconds. She held the MP5 up to her shoulder and moved her aim into the room.

"Don't come any closer or I'll fucking kill her!"

Acid froze. A young woman stood in the centre of the room, looking so vulnerable and fragile in her long white robes that one might think she was just a child. Her hair was ragged and hung over her face, which was wet with black mascara tears. She stared at the ground, shoulders clenched up to her ears as though readying herself for pain. Acid recognised her at once as Maria Waddington. She wasn't a child, but at seventeen she wasn't yet a woman.

A wire-framed man with thick salt and pepper hair hunkered down behind her, bony fingers clutching at Maria's upper arm, holding her in front of him like a human shield. In his other hand he had a steak knife pressed to the girl's throat.

"Don't move! I mean it!"

Acid tightened her finger on the trigger of the MP5, squeezing it to biting point but not quite.

"Let her go," she told the man, keeping her voice calm and steady. "Maria? Are you hurt?"

The girl looked up but didn't speak. Her eyes told a story of sedatives and despair. A red droplet of blood formed as the man pressed the tip of the knife into her skin. It swelled to the size of a small beetle before the surface tension became too much and popped, leaking blood down her neck. Acid moved her focus back to the man, noticing his costume for the first time. He was dressed as a purple space alien, with long tentacles protruding from his midriff. They bounced up and down as he struggled to remain shielded behind Maria's petite frame. Acid steadied her aim. She didn't have a clear kill shot, yet she wasn't going to risk leaving him alive long enough for him to slice through a vital artery in Maria's neck.

But time was running out.

She narrowed her eyes. "It's over. Let her go."

"Go to hell. I'll kill her."

Nobody moved. The bats screamed in Acid's head, telling her to fire. To take the shot anyway.

Kill him.

Kill them all.

"Who are you?" the man snarled.

Acid sniffed. She was tired of being asked this question. What was it with these people?

"My name is Acid Vanilla," she replied. "I'm here for Maria. That's all. Let her go and I'll let you live."

The knife trembled at Maria's throat. It was a micro-movement, hardly there at all, but in her heightened state Acid clocked it. He was losing his grip. Quite literally.

"Let her go."

"Please!" Maria wailed. "I just want to go home."

The man squeezed her arm as the knife quivered against her neck.

"There's nowhere to run," Acid told him. "Let her go."

The man shook his head. He wasn't going for it. But she didn't need him to. She just needed him to move his head half an inch to the left. This was taking too long.

"Let her go."

"Go to hell."

"Pleeeeease…."

The tension in the room was unbearable. Acid stepped to one side, moving into the room but keeping her aim fixed at the side of Maria's head. The young woman began to sob as the man gripped her arm, pulling her with him towards the door. But he wasn't fast enough. A sonic crack reverberated through the room and Maria shrieked as the man's head flew back, his brains painting a pink and claret halo on the wall behind him. As he released the young girl from his bony clutches, she stumbled forward.

"Oh my god, thank y—"

She stopped as Acid raised her hand. Her heightened senses had picked up a new sound in the corridor outside. Footsteps. Someone running in heavy boots.

Pissing hell.

The fourth guard.

With a rush of manic energy prickling the hairs on the back of her neck, she shifted to stand in front of Maria. Positioning herself with her back to the door, she placed her arm around the young girl and pulled her forward into a tight embrace. In her other hand she held the MP5, pressed between the two of them. The hard metal was cold against her stomach but concealed from view.

The footsteps grew louder and then came to a stop. Acid tensed as she felt a new presence enter the room.

Without turning around, she squeezed Maria close and sobbed loud enough so that whoever it was could hear over the music.

"What the fuck?" the guard barked. "What happened? Who did this?"

"A man came," Acid wailed into Maria's shoulder, using the same heavy accent she'd been employing all evening. "He had a gun. Was very angry."

"Where did he go?"

Maria was rigid in her arms. Acid stepped back a half step, allowing herself enough space that she'd be able to swing the gun up and around in a swift arc. A second went by that felt like a minute. Through the chaos in her head, she heard the static crackle of a radio transceiver. It couldn't have been one of the guard's colleagues trying to make contact because they were all dead. But it was unexpected, and just the distraction she needed. Spinning around, she swung the barrel of the MP5 into her other hand as the stunned guard shifted his focus from the radio on his belt to her. But he was too late. Finger down on the trigger, she fired a barrage of punishing rounds up his centre-line, sending him dancing backwards through the open doorway like an epileptic mannequin. As he dropped to his knees, she finished him with a single shot to the head.

Job done.

All threats neutralised.

"Right then, let's get out of here," she said, turning back to Maria. "Oh, shit..." The young woman was cowering in the corner, eyes filled with panic as they flitted between the mangled, bloodied bodies of the guard and the man who'd purchased her from Farkas. "Maria, I'm here to rescue you. You're safe. No one's going to hurt you. But we need to go. Now."

She rubbed her palm on her leggings, attempting to remove some of the blood and grime before holding out her hand. But Maria only stared at her with eyes like saucers.

"Go where?" she whispered. "I don't understand."

"You're in shock," Acid said, getting behind her and helping her up, leading her out of the room. "Trust me. I've got this."

As they reached the end of the corridor, Acid pulled out the burner phone she'd stuffed inside her left boot. There was only one number saved in the contact list. She hit call as she yanked open the large wooden door in front of them and ushered Maria through into the mansion's immense entrance hall.

Spook picked up on the first ring. "Acid? We're good?"

"We're good," she replied. "I'll see you outside in two minutes."

"I'm on my way."

Chapter Three

Spook shoved the stick into first, grinding the gearbox as she did and whining at the unpleasant sound of metal on metal. The black Toyota Prius Acid had commandeered for the evening wasn't the first manual drive car she'd driven, but it was certainly the biggest. Having learnt to drive only a few months earlier, and in a small Nissan, she was still wary of being in control of a vehicle. But it was imperative she get to grips with it if she was to hold her own in this new world she'd created for herself.

The Avenging Angels Agency was now – finally – a going concern. Finding Maria Waddington and bringing her home safely was their first proper assignment and Spook knew she had to bring her A-game from the start. Acid had made her concerns about their new line of work clear on more than one occasion, so to make this work, she needed to be an integral part of the operation both behind her laptop and out in the field, despite her own anxieties. After all, the agency was her vision.

Given everything that had happened over the last few

years, she could never go back to her normal life, but that didn't mean she had to lead a life of crime. This agency was her concession to that belief. The Avenging Angels would help people in trouble. People who, for whatever reason, had found themselves in a situation where the authorities couldn't or wouldn't help them. It was a good vision, Spook thought. And the perfect way for Acid to atone for her past sins.

If only she saw it that way.

It wasn't just the name that her acerbic friend objected to (although she had made it abundantly clear how much she despised it), but more so the idea that she might become a 'do-gooder' – a concept that seemed to be a fate worse than death to Acid.

With all that had gone on since the two women met, Spook had hoped this 'atoning for one's sins' idea would appeal to her. Acid had started using her real name on occasion, which led Spook to hack into the relevant records departments and reinstate her identity in the necessary databases. But whilst the enigmatic and frustrating woman now had a passport and National Insurance number in the name of Alice Vandella, it seemed her persona was still very much Acid Vanilla.

That didn't mean Spook was ready to give up on her friend's salvation, though. Acid had been a ruthless assassin, but the very fact she'd spared Spook's life and then helped her escape proved she'd changed. A series of terrible circumstances had led the young Alice to become the terrifying Acid, but who was to say a series of positive circumstances (like, say, helping people who needed help) couldn't flip that around? Plus, she had agreed to the talk therapy sessions, so that was something.

One thing was certain, however, she was still good at

what she did. As Spook neared the rendezvous point at the end of Thelmastone House's sprawling driveway, she saw Acid with her arm around a young woman. Maria Waddington. She was safe.

"Good job," she whispered to herself. "I knew you could do it. I— Ah, Acid. What the—? No!"

As she got closer, the headlights picked out more detail and she saw Acid was covered in blood. It was in her hair, on her clothes, completely coating her face. Spook stopped the car a few feet from them, keeping the engine running as Acid led the young woman to the car.

Don't make a scene, Spook told herself, gripping the steering wheel like she was holding on for dear life. We can talk about this later.

"I thought you'd forgotten about us," Acid said, opening the back door.

"It was further than I thought. Hi Maria, are you okay?"

"She is," Acid answered. "Just about."

Spook twisted around as Acid helped the shaking woman into the car. "Hey. I'm Spook," she said, as they made eye contact. "We're taking you home. Everything's going to be okay."

"Tell that to Brutus Farkas and his friends," Acid said, before slamming the back door shut.

Spook faced forward, composing herself as her errant partner walked around the front of the car and opened the passenger door. As Acid climbed in and closed the door, Spook kept her eyes fixed on the road ahead. It was a two-hour drive back to London. Something told her she was going to feel every single minute of it.

"Come on then. Let's get moving, shall we?"

Easing up the clutch, Spook steered the car around in a

one-eighty turn. As they left Thelmastone House behind, she kept one eye on the speedometer, watching as it rose from thirty to forty to fifty. Once there, she eased off the gas. Fifty was fast enough. Country roads had brought them here, and without streetlights visibility was bad. It would be twenty minutes before they reached any major roads, over an hour before they got to the M25.

"Everything okay, sweetie?" Acid asked, opening the glove compartment and rooting around inside.

"Absolutely," Spook replied, determined not to take the bait. "What are you looking for?"

"These wet wipes." She held up the packet and grinned in that manic way she often did. "I think I might have got a spot of blood on me."

Spook shook her head. "I thought we agreed. No bloodshed. No unnecessary deaths."

She spoke in a low hiss, for Maria's benefit. Like when her parents would argue on family holidays expecting her not to hear, but she always did. Spook glanced into the rearview mirror. Maria was fast asleep. "Is everyone dead?" she asked.

Acid flicked on the interior light before pulling down the sun visor and examining her face in the small mirror on the back. "Yes. Every single one of them." She sucked in her cheeks and dabbed at her face with a wet wipe.

"But we said—"

"And every single girl is safe. So I chalk that down to a big win. Don't you?"

Spook let her shoulders relax. "Yes. I suppose so. But, Alice, we—"

"*Acid.* It's Acid. Especially when I'm on a mission." She flung a pink wet wipe on the dashboard and yanked another from the plastic packet.

"Sorry. But the mission was to get Maria back, *covertly*. It was to be a rescue mission, not a massacre. We agreed, no unnecessary deaths."

"Yes, Spook, you already said. But I don't remember agreeing to that. And, besides, they weren't *unnecessary* deaths. All those bastards deserved what they got."

Spook's hands tightened on the wheel. "Not all of those men were killers."

"No, some of them were just rapists. Jesus." She snorted and flicked off the light. "A rescue mission. Fuck that. There were five other terrified girls in there, none of them out of their teens. Did you expect me to leave them in that viper's nest simply because their mothers hadn't had the where-withal to hire us?"

"No. I… I don't know." Spook rubbed her lips against each other. She understood Acid's point. But if they flagrantly killed all the bad people they came across – without at least trying other avenues – didn't that make them as bad as they were?

"Once we're clear, I'll make an anonymous phone call to the police. Let them know how they go about closing six missing person cases. I'm sure they'll be very grateful for my assistance. Even if it means a shit-ton of paperwork on the fourteen dead creeps they'll find when they get there."

"You killed fourteen people? You told me it'd be a stealth mission."

"Did I?"

Despite keeping her eyes on the winding roads in front of her, Spook could sense the eye roll coming from Acid. It was either that or a sneer. Typical. There was a time she'd found Acid's cynical ways endearing. But over recent months the arrested teenager that lived inside of Acid had shown up too frequently. It was a defence mechanism.

30

Spook understood that. But it didn't make it any less annoying.

She glanced over to see Acid had rested her head on the side window. "Yes, you did tell me that," she said, instantly mad at herself for taking the bait.

Acid sniffed. "Well, it's a good lesson for you, Spooky. Never trust an assassin when they're on a mission. They'll tell you anything to get their mark."

Spook stiffened. "You didn't have a mark. You had a young woman who you were supposed to rescue. That was the mission. I'm glad the rest of the women are safe. But you can't go off-book like this without telling me. It's not cool."

"Okay. I get it," Acid muttered. "I guess I got carried away."

That was the understatement of the year.

"You're not an assassin anymore, Acid. I thought you'd made peace with that. I thought it was what you wanted." It was as direct as Spook ever got and, as soon as the words left her mouth, a ripple of nervous energy shivered down her spine. But she was glad she'd said it. It needed saying.

She adjusted her grip on the steering wheel. Over the sound of the engine and the gentle snoring coming from Maria in the back seat, she thought she heard Acid aping her.

"*You're not an assassin anymore…*" Then the retort. "Aren't I?"

Spook opened her mouth to respond, but what was the use? The conversation was over and she knew from experience that to push Acid now would be a dangerous move. She was strung out. In a few days, her moods would have levelled out and maybe then they could talk sensibly about what had happened.

Yet as they drove on through the night, with the fields and country lanes soon turning into villages and then dual carriageways, the words played on Spook's mind.

Aren't I?

Aren't I... an assassin?

After all this time and with everything the two women had been through together, this sentiment alone bothered Spook immeasurably. She'd believed Acid to be on an upward trajectory in terms of her morality and empathy. But maybe she was wrong.

She shook it off.

No.

She didn't want to think about that. A few days' rest and all would be well. Besides, Maria was safe. Acid had seen to that. Did it matter that she'd taken her role a little too far?

Spook exhaled her bodyweight in emotion. It was fine. She'd put tonight down to a blip. It happened to the best of them.

Chapter Four

Acid exhaled a long breath as her gaze drifted around the front room of the Soho apartment she and Spook had shared for the last year. There was nothing like having *The Most Boring Conversation In The World* for you to suddenly find your environment exceptionally fascinating. Her eyes landed on a large, colourful print Spook had hung over the fireplace a few months earlier. It was a cut-out style print, showing a white cat dressed in a flapper dress, with the words, *Let's do the ca-ca-cat*, in bubble writing down one side.

Jesus.

It pained Acid to look at it, so she turned away. They said there was no accounting for taste, but she'd always thought that to be an excuse, adopted by those with no taste themselves. There was a time before she'd met the nervy young American, Spook Horowitz, when she'd surrounded herself with the finer things in life. A pair of van der Rohe chairs in soft tan leather, a Dordoni-designed Minotti sofa in ruby, a Brabbu coffee table resembling a Sequoia redwood stump wrapped in eighteen-carat gold. All gone. All left behind when she ran from her old life.

What a waste.

Acid had never thought of herself as materialistic and even now she didn't miss these things. But she didn't not miss them either. Not only were these items exquisite pieces, but they also signified her growing refinement and taste. Proving to the world how far the young Alice Vandella had come. From a humble East End schoolgirl who didn't pronounce her H's to a stylish young woman with eloquence and class and her foot on the world's throat. She'd do anything to have those pieces of furniture back. Not least because each item alone cost a small fortune and, for the first time since before she met Caesar, money was scarce. Back in her Annihilation days, every job she took, every hit she made, brought in more cash than she'd ever known. But now her two Swiss bank accounts had dried up and it wouldn't be long before she used the last of her savings held in the Cayman Islands. This new agency (she loathed to use that silly name Spook had decided on) was designed to bring in new revenue, but the fees they'd agreed on were nothing compared to what she used to get for a job. And the jobs were nowhere near as exciting.

"Are you even listening to me?"

The room snapped back into focus. Acid turned to see Spook leaning forward, wagging a pen in her face.

It was a rainy Tuesday morning, three days after the rescue-mission-turned-massacre at Thelmastone House. Acid and Spook were in the front room, sitting opposite each other on chairs that Spook had dragged through from the kitchen. Each chair had a small round table next to it, with a glass of water sitting on top. It was Spook's idea of a professional set-up, but to Acid it felt ridiculous. This was the second of what Spook had imaginatively dubbed their *talk therapy sessions* and she was even more irritated than she had been the first time. Why the hell she'd agreed to do this was anyone's guess.

"It's not helping anyone if you're closed up," Spook told her. "Come on. You said you wanted to try this."

Acid sighed. She had said that. Damn it. It was in an uncharacteristic moment of weakness on her part. Spook had been nagging at her again, saying she thought it would help if she talked about things. She'd recently read some books on trauma and PTSD and wanted to try to *untangle the knots that were keeping Acid trapped in her past*. Something like that anyway. Total BS. Acid had never had any truck with therapists, ever since Jacqueline all those years ago. But Spook meant well and she had been a good ally (hell, in another moment of weakness Acid might have even said friend) these last few years. So if nothing else, she should at least accept that this entire pointless rigmarole was more for Spook's benefit than it was her own.

The kid was still staring at her, bottom lip hanging open in that way it often did when she was disappointed. "Can we please try?"

"Okay." Acid straightened her back. "What was the question?"

"I was asking if you could think back to the time when you decided cynicism was a better coping mechanism than loving yourself."

Acid choked on an in-breath, making a noise halfway between a cough and a snort. "Jesus, Spook." She cleared her throat. "You're going in with the big guns straight away? Is that how this works?"

Spook shrugged. "No point beating around the bush.

Not with you. And I thought you wanted me to be bolder. You're always saying that."

"Correct. I do. And it's good. Just unexpected." She frowned. "What was the question again?"

"You know what the question was, Alice. Stop deflecting."

Acid chewed on her bottom lip, resisting the urge to flip the table over and kick Spook through the window. "Back to Alice, is it?"

"I spent a lot of time and effort reinstating your old identity. At your request, if you remember. A part of you must have wanted to return to being Alice, even if as soon as it happened you got scared."

"Scared? Is that what you think?"

Spook tilted her head to one side and shrugged. When she didn't respond, Acid shook her head. "What's this, using silence against me? Did you read that in your books? Shut up and let the patient fill the gaps?"

Another shrug. One more and she'd walk. A strong drink was already calling her. She sat back and met Spook's gaze, flicking her eyebrows up into fight mode.

When Spook spoke, her voice was quiet and calm, her words slow, which only made Acid more annoyed. "When did you decide that cynicism was a better coping mechanism than loving yourself?"

"Well, let me see now, that would probably have been when I saw Oscar Duke standing over my mum's broken and bleeding body."

Normally Acid had her words cued up, already having run them through the filter of her persona, but these tumbled out of her mouth as if from nowhere. She looked down into her lap. "She looked so frail and fucked up. I guess I vowed to myself at that moment that I'd keep the world at arm's length, never let anyone hurt me like that. Never let anyone hurt her like that again, either

There was a long pause. Acid kept her head lowered. She picked at a yellow callus on her palm with her thumbnail.

"What happened?" Spook asked.

She glanced up into the American's concerned face. "You know what happened."

"Tell me."

"I killed him. I found an empty wine bottle. I smashed it off the side of the counter and I attacked him. The police said I was in such a frenzy I almost decapitated him."

"Who was he?"

"Oscar Duke. My mother's attacker. You know all this. You knew all this about me before we even met. That's how you—"

"I want to hear you say it. I think it'll help you move on. Please."

Acid glanced out the window. At the sea of umbrellas on the street below. People with their heads down and shoulders up, weaving around each other like bacteria in a petri dish. It was curious, she thought, how the weather always seemed to match one's mood. Spook would probably tell her it was a projection of her internal thought system.

The kid reads one book on psychology…

She turned back to see Spook squinting at her through her thick glasses. She wasn't going to let it go.

"Oscar Duke was a client of my mother's," Acid told her. "He'd come around maybe once or twice a week and pay her to have sex with him. Okay? Is that good enough for you?"

Spook blinked. "What did you think of him before that night?"

"I hated him. I hated all the men who came around to see Mum. Some of them – a lot of them – left bruises. She tried to hide them from me. But I saw them." She turned back to the window. "She was only doing it to try and give me a better life. And I went and fucked everything up."

"You did?"

Bloody hell.

Acid arched her spine, stretching the aching muscles in her lower back and filling her lungs with air at the same time. It took her the length of the exhale to form a response.

"I suppose you think I blame myself for what happened?" she said. "That somehow this persona is me trying to deal with the guilt or shame of my actions when I was younger. But you'd be wrong. The only way I fucked up was by killing Oscar Duke the way I did. I should have waited, stalked him, hidden in the darkness, killed him with stealth. But the fact remains he deserved to die. Just like every single person I've killed since."

"Really? You can say that?"

"Yes. I can."

They stared into each other's eyes, neither one of them wanting to look away first. Acid placed her hands on her lap, her thumbnail going to work on the callus.

"Do you feel any remorse at all?"

"Are you asking me if I'm a psychopath?"

Spook's left eye twitched. "I don't think you are. But then you go and kill fourteen people without even breaking a sweat."

"We've gone over this," Acid rasped through gritted teeth. She rolled her head back. "None of those creeps at Thelmastone House deserved to be spared."

"Still, I think there are aspects of your life and your past you need to deal with. You've done a lot of bad over the years and now you don't know how to deal with being good. I think you're confused."

"I think you're full of shit. Most people aren't bad or good. They exist in a moral grey area of their own making. It's only the media and societal norms that decide what's good and evil, and often to appease some similarly nefarious aim. The line separating good and evil doesn't pass through country or class or even politics, but through the heart of every human being."

Acid flicked her eyebrows at Spook's twitching reaction to her words.

"Do you know who said that, sweetie? Solzhenitsyn. You're not the only one who can read a bloody book."

Spook pushed her glasses up onto the bridge of her nose. "This isn't me trying to get one over on you. I want to help you, Alice. You're not a happy person. I can see that."

"A happy person? Jesus, Spook. Who gives a shit about happiness? No one's happy in this modern world, are they? The only thing we can hope for is to have some semblance of self-respect." She snickered to herself but stopped almost immediately. "Solzhenitsyn also goes on to say how this line of good and evil shifts inside of us and oscillates with the years. What we find immoral in our youth can often change as we get older. Everyone becomes a conservative eventually. If they live that long. But one thing is for certain, Spook. Today, the same as back then, I'm glad I killed Oscar Duke. He deserved to die for what he did. And if I hadn't, I would never have met Caesar and had the life I've had. Duke made me who I am. He set in motion my metamorphosis from Alice to Acid and Caesar finished the job. And yes, I may not be a happy person. But I can live with myself. How many people can say that?"

She dropped back in the chair. The room felt like it was closing in on her. The chatter, which had been quiet since Thelmastone House, now swelled in her consciousness. Over the years, she had learned to hone her cyclothymic disorder into something approaching useful. Her heightened awareness and fast, creative thought processes were often a bonus, especially as a high-end assassin. She had dubbed the surges of manic, teeth-tingling energy as the bats. It was a way of separating her condition as an outside force from who she really was. It made good sense to her and, most of the time, she sensed the bats were on her side.

But sometimes they could be a real pain in the arse.

"I think you can be happy."

Spook's words lingered in the air like a bad smell. When Acid sat back with a sneer and folded her arms, she went on.

"I have a theory. I think you're feeling displaced since Caesar died because you don't have any purpose. That's what people need to feel happy in their lives, a purpose. For a long time it was your job. You know… at Annihilation Pest Control. And then after that, you were so focused on having vengeance on your old colleagues, that became your purpose. But since then you've had nowhere to place your focus. You've got no…"

"Purpose?" She'd trailed off, so Acid finished the sentence for her. "Wow. Thank you, Tony Robbins. I'm unfulfilled and directionless. What a wonderful summation of my life. That's nice to know."

"But what I'm saying is——"

"Fuck. I can't believe I thought this bullshit talk therapy nonsense might help. I'd say you might need a few more lessons."

"But you can have purpose again," Spook said, her

voice quaking with emotion. She caught herself and sniffed back. "Helping people can be your purpose. This agency can be your purpose. No more killing. No more pain and bloodshed. Salvation, for others and yourself."

"Jesus Christ," Acid muttered. "I've had enough of this, Spook. Can we stop now? Please."

She glanced up through her hair. Spook's face was a picture of concern and compassion. She wanted to slap her and hug her all at once. She did neither.

"If that's what you want. We can pick this up next session."

"Yeah. Sure."

She said it convincingly enough, but inside she knew there wasn't going to be another session. She'd done enough navel-gazing for one lifetime and, as she'd always expected, it did no good at all. It only brought up terrible memories of a past that were better left where they were, locked away in the dark basement of her psyche.

She sat upright and rolled her shoulders back. "Right then, your turn." She slapped her thighs and got to her feet. "Come on, kiddo. We agreed. You might not like it. But those are the rules. *Apparently.*"

Chapter Five

Spook placed her notebook and pen on the table next to her and blew out a heavy breath. Acid was already up, bouncing from one foot to the other with her fists raised.

"Do we have to do this?" Spook asked. "I'm tired."

Acid stopped and tilted her head to one side. Her face shifted into an expression of mock dismay. "Are you seriously questioning this? We *agreed*, Spook. You get an hour trying to deal with my issues and I get an hour teaching you how to look after yourself."

With another heavy breath, Spook got to her feet. "But you're the tough one. I'm better at the tech stuff."

"Yes, you are. But that doesn't mean a little self-defence – or even offence – training is a waste of time. And, unfortunately, you don't always get to choose whether you stay safely locked away behind a laptop. If you'd been better prepared in Paris, or on that fucking horrible island, or back in Montana, maybe I wouldn't have needed to save your perky little arse."

Spook looked at her feet. It annoyed her how after all

this time a mere morsel of friendly flirtation from Acid sent her cheeks burning. "I suppose if we are going to make a go of the agency, I need to be on top form," she mumbled. "That reminds me, actually, we might have a—"

"Come on, kid," Acid said, bounding towards her and tapping her on the side of the head. "Raise your guard. Let's see what you've got."

She did as she was told, but she wasn't a fighter. She never would be. Her shoulders sagged and making a fist felt clumsy and ridiculous. Acid grabbed her wrists, positioning her into what you might call a fight stance. But Spook's heart wasn't in it, and as Acid stepped away she shook her head.

"What are we going to do with you?"

Spook didn't take her eyes off Acid as she chewed on the inside of her cheek while assessing with dismay Spook's posture and lack of aggression. Shifting effortlessly from being in such a dark mood to being so focused and in control was textbook Acid. It reminded Spook of a rhyme from her childhood.

When she was good, she was very good, but when she was bad, she was rotten.

A part of that was down to her friend's condition, Spook knew that, but the bigger reason, she suspected, was that at times like this she stepped fully into Acid Vanilla mode. Sharp, sarcastic, full of piss and vinegar, ready to take on the world. The Acid persona Alice Vandella had constructed for herself over the years wasn't concerned with the past or even her own feelings. She was strong and unbreakable in both body and spirit.

Yet Spook had noticed chinks in Acid's armour, especially since Caesar died, and even more so after they'd returned from Montana. She'd even allowed herself to believe – to hope – that Alice Vandella was about to re-emerge into the world. Spook had done what she'd asked, reinstating her identity where she could, but all the while conscious of being too eager. She worried that making her do too much too soon would have her retreat inside of herself. Unfortunately, that was exactly what had happened. The hints of Alice became fewer and far between. And when Acid showed up, so strong and forthright and with an answer for everything, it was hard to argue with her. Not that Spook believed her friend to have a split personality or anything like that. Distinguishing between the two names, the two personas, was her way of trying to make sense of the whirlwind of madness and mayhem that was her friend's personality. The woman had been through so much pain, had seen so much misery, it was easy to understand why she was the way she was. But day to day, living with her erratic moods and chaotic nature, was another matter entirely.

"You're not even trying," Acid mumbled, walking behind Spook. "Let's try something different. Get on your knees."

Spook twisted around to look at her. "What are you going to do?"

"I'm not going to do anything. You are. Now get on your knees." She placed her hands on Spook's shoulders and pushed her down.

"Fine."

She acquiesced, telling herself Acid wouldn't hurt her. She'd often reminded herself of that when they'd first met – back when Acid was known as one of the deadliest assassins in the world. Except Spook hadn't thought about her that way for some time. The fact she needed to reassure herself now was troubling.

"Hopefully you'll never find yourself in this position," Acid continued, moving around the front of her and standing with her arms around her back like she was a drill sergeant. She was wearing black leggings and black boots, which made her shapely legs seem spindly in comparison. On her top half, she wore a faded black Motorhead t-shirt with a rip in the collar. Her hair was shorter than it had been when she and Spook first met, but her bangs, which had once skimmed her eyelashes, had grown out into a messy side parting. She looked good, despite everything. The punk-rock, hot-mess chic was still working for her. But then, Acid always looked good. Despite all her shitty moods and troubling aspects of her personality, she was charming and attractive and bitingly funny when she wanted to be. It just made her more of an enigma and so much more infuriating.

"Now, if you are ever captured and placed in this position, chances are you're about to be executed," she said, eyes flashing with devilment as a manic grin peeled back her lips.

Spook met her gaze with a sneer. "Great. Lucky me."

"But that means you've got the upper hand," Acid continued. "You've got nothing to lose, right? If they're going to kill you anyway, then you might as well try anything to stop that happening. Imagine I've got a gun on you. What could you do?"

She mimed a gun with her index and middle fingers and pointed it at Spook's head.

"Umm. Pray?"

Acid narrowed her eyes. "Bang. Too late." She jerked her finger gun in the air to show the recoil. "No. Praying is for losers. But you can get them talking. Get them close. It's a Hollywood cliché, I know, but in my experience people in positions of self-imposed power often like to wax lyrical about their plans and goals. So let them. Buy some time.

"I remember being held captive in some horrible smelly bunker somewhere outside of Manila once and I began muttering to myself so that the guard had to move close to hear what I was saying. That was his first mistake. As he put his head towards me, I reached out and bit his ear, tearing most of the cartilage away in one bite. After that, I sprang to my feet, barged him against the wall, ripped the cable ties from my wrists – there's a simple technique for doing that, I can show you – and grabbed the gun from him. An Uzi, if I remember correctly. He was dead before he could get his breath back."

Acid's face lit up like she was reliving the memory, but Spook huffed. "That's you, Acid. I could never do anything like that. I'm a nerd. I'm weak and ungainly."

"If you say so." She stepped around the back of her. "What about now? Imagine I'm a sleazy drug baron who's discovered you infiltrating his underground complex. You're here to assassinate me and, as you can envisage, I am not happy about that in the slightest. But the thing is, I'm a cocky bastard and a sadist. I want to make you squirm before I kill you. I want to enjoy the experience. A lot of them are like that." She pressed her fingertips to the back of Spook's head. "So? What do you do?"

"I don't know. Scream for help? Cry. Pee my pants."

Acid lifted her hand with a dramatic tut. "You're pathetic, you know that? Forget good and evil, Spook. This is life or death. See how close to you I am now. Maybe I'm telling you how great I am, explaining what I'm going to do to you. Maybe, as you're tied up and on your knees, I've let my guard down. So…?"

"I don't know. What would you do?"

"Well, I'm a man, aren't I? And your head is the perfect height for my groin area. What I'd do now is dip my head forward and then swing it back with as much force as possible. Headbutt the prick in his bollocks. Catch him in the right place, you'll neutralise him for a few seconds. Long enough that you can scramble to your feet and run. Or, even better, grab his weapon. Shoot the fucker with his own gun."

"But what if it goes wrong? What if there's more than one gunman? What then?"

"Then you get creative," Acid snapped. "But my point is you're probably a goner anyway, so be bold. Lash out. Do what you can to give yourself a few vital seconds. In which time you can escape or overpower the enemy. And a good headbutt to the balls always works a treat."

Spook leaned forward onto all fours and leapfrogged to her feet. "Ah, man. I feel like I'd just fuck it up. I'd probably end up missing and flying backwards into thin air."

"All right, look, I'll show you. You be the sleazy drug baron." She turned and lowered herself to her knees. "Stand behind me, pretend you're telling me how great you are, how it's a shame to kill me. That's another one they always like to roll out. Especially the sleazy ones. Come on, don't be scared. I won't hurt you. I'll do it in slow motion so you can see."

Spook hesitated for a second before stepping closer. She knew Acid well enough to know she wasn't going to leave this alone until she'd got her way. Making a gun with her fingers, Spook pointed it at Acid's head, feeling even more foolish than she usually did whenever the spotlight was on her. "Okay, punk. I'm going to kill you."

Acid snorted. "Jesus, what accent is that? You sound like

a fucking muppet. An actual Muppet, I mean. Fozzie Bear, eat your heart out."

"I don't know," Spook replied, still in character and lowering her voice even more. She'd been going for something guttural and South American sounding. "This is my accent. Now shut up or I'll shoot you dead."

Acid shook her head before composing herself, flicking her hair over her shoulders. "Right then, so you're there, I'm here. I've got nothing to lose, right? So, with that in mind, I'm going to go berserk. And I mean berserk, Spook. You do anything you can to shift the play back into your hands. As I said, I'd dip my head like this, maybe make out I'm sobbing to throw you off. Then... snap my neck back as hard as I can, slam the back of my skull into your fleshy regions."

She did as she was describing, throwing all her weight back against Spook.

"Oof, shit..."

Even without testicles, even with Acid moving with more control and less speed than she would have in real life, the force of the blow caught Spook unawares. She stumbled backwards. Before she could right herself, Acid had leapt to her feet, spun around and raised her hands together above her head before snapping them against her waist, breaking the imaginary ties.

"Okay... Yes..." Spook gasped, holding up her hand. "You got me... Hey...!"

But Acid wasn't finished. She leapt forward like a black flash and a sharp pain shot up Spook's arm. She felt pressure on her legs and lower back as the room went from being horizontal to vertical. Her glasses slipped off her face and her vision distorted in a blur of colour and confusion. Air whizzed against her face and her stomach did a full three-sixty flip before she hit the floor with a thud that knocked all the air out of her. A second later Acid was on top of her with a sharp knee pressing down on her chest.

"Fuck you, Fozzie Bear," she snarled, shoving her finger gun against Spook's forehead. "Bang. You're dead."

"All right, get off me." Spook struggled to push her away, but Acid waited a moment longer then climbed off her by pressing her knee into her chest. It could have been an accident, but it probably wasn't. "Jesus, why do you always take things too far?" she said, hand skirting the floor, searching for her glasses.

"Here." Acid knelt and picked them up.

Spook took them and put them on before accepting Acid's offered hand. As she pulled her upright, they bumped chests, Acid barging into her a little more than was friendly, she thought.

"You hurt me," Spook said. "That wasn't cool."

Acid threw her head back. "Oh god! I was showing you how to get out of a life-threatening situation. Sorry for being a good friend."

Spook let out a bitter laugh. "A good friend? Are you serious? You haven't been a good friend for months. Maybe ever."

She hadn't meant to say something so audacious, but as the words left her mouth a frisson of excitement ran down her arms. It didn't feel at all bad.

"Is that what you think?" Acid placed her hands on her hips, her demeanour shifting from petulant teen to angry headmistress. "Everything I've done lately is for you and this ridiculous agency. The Avenging fucking Angels. Jesus."

"Yes, I get it. You don't like the name."

"It's not just the name. I don't like the lack of ideology or anything remotely resembling a business model. I don't like how it's open to abuse from a load of whining snowflakes who can't sort out their own problems. Yes, I know you're going to say people will pay for our services and I agree, we need some income, but at what cost? I keep asking you what the agency stands for, what we do, but all I get is fluff and bluster."

"Bluster?" Spook repeated. "This, coming from the queen of bluster."

"Fuck you."

"No, fuck you. The Avenging Angels offer help to those who the authorities can't or won't help and—"

"Yes, I know all that, but it's just a nice mission state-ment. What does that look like in the real world? How do we find these strays and runaways whilst staying out of the way of the authorities? How do we keep our work under-ground if civilians know about us? Right now we're using our real names, for Christ's sake."

Spook placed her weight on her back leg and crossed her arms. This was the first time Acid had ever voiced any of these opinions and she didn't know how to respond. Prickly heat that felt a lot like rage swelled in her chest and into her back.

"Why didn't you convey any of these thoughts to me sooner?" she said. "We could have talked about them. Come up with solutions to your concerns."

"Oh, piss off with the corporate talk. It's just not me, that's all. It's not how I operate."

Spook held her ground despite her anger turning to nausea. "What does that mean? *How you operate*."

"Caesar trained me to stay in the shadows, to be unde-tected, a silent force that struck before anyone knew I was there. The moment my marks knew about me, it was already too late."

"You left that life behind. You didn't want to do that anymore. Even before we met."

"Yes, well…" She walked over to the couch and slumped onto it with a heavy sigh. Back to being a petulant teen.

"I'm sorry you feel that way," Spook said. "But I'm afraid you're going to have to snap out of this. We've got a new job."

"A new job? Why am I only finding this out now?"

Spook's arms remained crossed. She raised her chin, demonstrating confidence physically and hoping her mindset would catch up, like the books said it would. "I was trying to tell you earlier. I got an email yesterday from a woman who's worried about her father. She thinks he's got himself into a dangerous situation that he can't get out of."

A nasty sneer curled Acid's lip. "Why does she need us? What's this guy done that the police can't help her?"

"I don't know yet. That's why I've arranged to meet with her tomorrow morning at ten. Up in East Finchley."

"Jesus, Spook. That's early. And face to face? That's risky."

"She's legit, trust me."

Acid shook her head, starting on one of her infamous eye rolls. The second Spook saw it, she dropped her arms and stepped forward.

"Hey! Listen! Despite what you might think of me, I'm not a naïve fucking idiot. I've done a hell of a lot for you these last few years. I've risked my life, my freedom. Don't forget that. You need to start taking me more seriously and realise I'm an asset. To you and this agency."

Shiiiiit!

Where was this coming from? She rarely spoke to Acid like this. It thrilled her and terrified her in equal measures.

Acid stared at her with a neutral expression on her face. "Who's this woman who emailed you?" she asked.

"She's called Fiona Zoto. She didn't want to say too much via email or over the phone. I get the impression she's scared of someone."

"I see. How incredibly intriguing." Her voice was thick with sarcasm, but Spook ignored it.

"So? Are you available?"

"I'll have to be."

Spook stepped to one side as Acid got up from the couch and barged past her.

"Where are you going?" she asked, as Acid reached around the back of the door. She grabbed her leather jacket off one of the hooks and slipped it on.

"I'm going out. For a quiet drink. That okay with you?"

"Oh yeah, sure. Run away. Go drown your anger in a gallon of whisky. Like you always do. It only dilutes your problems so much, Alice."

"Fuck you." She'd already disappeared into the hallway, but her head appeared back around the doorframe. "The only problem I have is you going on at me all the bloody time."

"Is that so?"

"Yes. It is. Now don't wait up, will you, *sweetie*?"

Spook made to yell her response, but Acid left, slamming the apartment door. Heavy boots descended the stairwell, then the door to the street slammed a few seconds later. Sinking onto the couch, Spook let out a cry of existential anguish, which only went a short way to relieving her frustration.

That exasperating woman.

What the hell was Spook doing, still putting up with this shit? Maybe it was time to move on. She could go back to the States. There were plenty of jobs going in the tech world, especially for women. She could make good money within six months, live a decent life without all the pain, terror and frustration that came from being friends with Acid Vanilla.

She closed her eyes and lolled her head back onto the soft cushion of the couch. One step at a time. If Fiona Zoto had work for them, then she'd deal with that first and assess where her head was once the job was done. Who knows? Working together on another mission could be just what she and Acid needed to get back on an even keel. Weirder things had happened in the last four years.

She raised her head and nodded to herself.

Yes. That was it. For now, she'd focus all her energy on the upcoming meeting. A new job for The Avenging Angels.

Hell, it might even be fun.

Chapter Six

The Bitter Marxist was dark and foreboding and the jukebox was playing *Gimme Danger* by The Stooges as Acid made her way down the stone steps that led to the windowless room. It had been almost eighteen months since she'd last visited the place, which was unfathomable, considering the nefarious basement bar in Chelsea was once her home away from home. It was where she'd always come after a mission to decompress and settle her nervous system. The décor was basic (black walls, black floor, black ceiling too) but was the perfect foil for her chaotic sensibilities. After a few drinks, and with loud rock music blaring from the sound system, she was able to ground herself.

The barman clocked her as she headed over to him. "Evening." His left eye twitched in a knowing half-wink. "What can I get you?"

"Ooh, now there's a question." She leaned over the countertop, surveying the excellent selection of liquor bottles standing majestically on three illuminated shelves up the back wall. "I'll start with a classic Chivas Regal, please. A double. One chunk of ice."

She leaned back and smiled, eyeing the barman as he nodded in agreement. She hadn't seen this one before. He was tanned, with shaggy blond hair that fell over pale blue eyes. Perhaps a tad too muscular and healthy-looking for her taste (and to be working at The Bitter Marxist, come to that), but she liked his crooked smile and would happily take him home later if the desire took her. She hoisted herself onto the nearest bar stool and breathed in the place.

Stale beer and sweat. You couldn't beat it.

When Spitfire had first introduced her to the Marxist, she was a wide-eyed twenty-one-year-old, and it being prior to the smoking ban it was so full of cigarette smoke you could barely see the person in front of you. Times had changed, but she was glad to see nothing else had in the subsequent years. There were still the three small round tables opposite the bar, with the same badly framed album covers hanging on the wall above each one. The Ramones' first album, Bowie's *Diamond Dogs*, and the Warhol-designed *Sticky Fingers* complete with working zip, by The Rolling Stones. She smiled to herself. It felt damn good to be back where she belonged. And she didn't only mean in terms of location.

Since returning from Montana, it had dawned on her how out of alignment she'd been these last few years. For a long time, she'd put her intense feelings of confusion, as well as the decline in her mental health, down to her past catching up with her. She knew trauma had a way of lying dormant for many years, only to fuck you up later in life or when you slowed down enough for it to catch up with you. And Spook had done little to dispel this notion. So, for a while, it had made sense to try to deal with who she was and what she'd done. And she had bloody well tried. She'd gone to great lengths, distorting her personality and sensibilities so people might class her as an upstanding citizen. A real, dyed-in-the-wool civilian. Only, she'd found it so crushingly boring, this too had made her depressed.

It was time to admit she wasn't cut out to be anything other than what she was. An outcast. An outsider. A shadow on the cusp of society.

"Here you are, miss. Enjoy." She looked up as the barman slid a heavy-bottomed tumbler in front of her. "Do you want to pay now?"

Acid frowned, glancing at the clock over his shoulder. It was a few minutes after nine. "God, no. Open a tab for me, will you? I imagine I'll be here for a while yet."

A smirk curved the corner of the barman's mouth. "No problem. Give me a shout if you need me."

"Don't worry. I will." A wink and a pout sent him drifting away to the other side of the bar.

Kids today. No staying power.

She picked up her glass and held it to her nose, letting the heady aromas from the whisky invade her sinuses. Yes. It smelt like home. She took a sip and closed her eyes as the opening bars of *Welcome To The Jungle* thundered out through the speakers. It had been a crazy few years out in the wilderness of her psyche, but today she felt grounded and stable. She felt like herself and she knew why. It had little to do with Spook's pathetic talk therapy sessions. The kid could wax lyrical all she wanted about coping mechanisms and feelings of guilt or blame driving Acid's personality, but she didn't get it – she thought Alice and Acid were different facets, and that by nurturing Alice back to the fore, she'd grow into a reasonably upstanding member of society. Except that was bullshit. Alice was the person who killed

Oscar Duke. Alice was the person who relished the sight of that evil prick bleeding out on the kitchen lino. Alice Vandella had always been Acid Vanilla. There was no line separating them.

"Good evening, miss. Is anyone sitting here?"

She looked up, already on her guard as she regarded the man standing beside her. He was dark-skinned with thick black hair swept back with pomade. On his chin and top lip he wore a few days' worth of stubble – which normally did it for her, but his was so neatly clipped, and the trim lines so angular, it looked overdone.

"It's a free country," she replied to his question. "But a word of warning, I'm not here to make friends. And I don't do small talk."

The man smirked, perhaps perceiving her response to be a challenge or even a come-on. But didn't they all?

"Can I buy you a drink?" he asked, flicking back his shirt sleeve over his wrist as he beckoned the barman over.

"I've got a drink," she said, returning to it and taking a swig. It was sharp and nutty and she tasted a hint of apple and honey on the finish. This was another plus point of her condition. When the bats were in flight, her heightened senses made even a standard seventeen-year-old scotch taste like it had been aged for much longer.

"Come on," the man said, leaning on the bar to try to make eye contact with her. "What's your name?"

She placed her glass down and faced him. As she did, he smiled. "Listen, mate. I'm a woman on her own, in a bar like this. Do you really think I'm here to meet the man of my dreams? I'm here for a quiet drink. Alone. So why don't you order one for yourself and leave me to it?"

The man straightened, his mouth twisting into a distorted 'O' of bewilderment. She watched him for a moment, but when he had no comeback she returned to her drink.

"Stuck-up bitch."

And there it was.

"Excuse me?"

"You heard me. What are you, some liberal cow who thinks she's better than everyone else?"

"Liberal. There's a thought."

Acid held no belief or interest in politics. Even current affairs passed her by unless they affected her first-hand. Likewise, creed, colour, race, none of these things mattered to her. They never had. She viewed everyone the same. Which was that they were an annoying prick until they proved otherwise. And this waste of flesh was a long way from disproving anything of the sort. She glanced around. Making a scene was never a good idea, even in somewhere like The Bitter Marxist.

"Chicks like you think they're better than everyone else. But guess what? I'm taking this seat here and there's nothing you can do about it. Twat."

She cricked her neck to one side.

Too far, pal.

The stool next to her scraped along the floor as he went to sit down. With a flash of her boot, she sent it skidding across the floor. The man cried out as the seat he'd expected to be there disappeared from under him.

"Shit! What the fuck?"

He tumbled over and scrambled to his feet in haste, grabbing at the side of the bar for leverage. He was up and in her face in the time it took her to sip her drink.

"Stupid, pathetic bitch," he growled into the side of her face, spittle hitting her cheek. "I'm going to—"

"What?" Acid snapped. "What are you going to do? Hit

me? Go on then, sweetie. Let's dance." She turned, fixing him with her best John Lydon stare. Eyes wide and unblinking, jaw rigid and still. The man stared back, but then shook his head and made a snorting noise.

"Whatever."

She didn't take her eyes off him. But neither did she respond. She didn't need to. Her face said it all.

Don't dare fuck with me.

The man pushed away from the bar with another snort. "Do you know what? This place is dead anyway. I'm out of here. Enjoy your drink, bitch."

He sauntered away, trying to claw back as much kudos as he could with his swaggering exit. Acid stared after him, intense with fury. She hadn't blinked since he came at her. Only now, as the man walked up the stairwell to the door, did the muscles around her eyes relax and her awareness return to her surroundings. She saw that the man sitting three stools away at the bar was laughing to himself.

"Is there something funny?" she asked, the red mist not yet having left her entirely.

The man glanced away, a look of terror on his face. "No. I wasn't... You know... It's just... It's cool to see a guy like that get his arse handed to him. And so eloquently. I like your style." He raised his glass to her.

Acid held his gaze. He was slim, with unkempt hair and good bone structure. Plus, he seemed sincere. "Fair enough." She raised her own glass. "Cheers."

Chapter Seven

Over the next hour, safe in the shadowy cellar bar and buffered by a veil of strong liquor and heavy rock music, Acid settled back into a groove. Pleased the scruffy-haired guy keeping to himself on the nearby stool hadn't been so dumb as to pursue the meagre frisson of connection that had transpired in their initial greeting, she finished her drink and ordered another - and then another - playing the altercation with the mouthy idiot from earlier in her mind. She was only slightly annoyed she hadn't done the rotten prick more damage. She should have made him bleed. That would have really made her night.

This was what Spook didn't understand about her. She wasn't like other people. She relished danger and conflict. She needed death and destruction to never be too far away. It was the very act of living on the edge of society that made her feel so alive. Whether she called herself Alice or Acid had nothing to do with that. And yes, it might seem weird to someone like Spook, who craved a safe life in a just world, but her way wasn't realistic either. As the alcohol teased at her nerve endings, Acid was more resolute than ever. There was no pretending she could be anything other than what she was.

As she called the barman over and gestured for him to pour her a fourth double Chivas, she considered the fact that she'd wasted these last two years running from the troubling (in society's eyes, at least) aspects of her personality. But that only meant she'd been confused and now she wasn't. For the first time in a long time, she felt poised and capable. She was being true to herself and that's all she could do. If the world had more to throw at her, then bring it on. She was ready.

That said, as the barman brought over her drink, he nodded towards the door and her heart sank as she saw the prick from earlier swaggering down the stairwell. His dark hair was now hanging in lank strands over his forehead, and it was clear from his gait and the way he held his face that he'd had a few drinks since scuttling out of here an hour earlier. She had to give him his dues. To get in such a mess in such a short amount of time was good going. But if he was returning to the scene of his humiliating stand-off, it meant he'd talked himself into causing more trouble.

As he reached the bottom of the steps, their eyes met across the bar. His bloodshot and full of impotent fury. Hers wild and unflinching.

He pointed at her, his finger quivering with tense rage. "You," he mouthed.

Acid sighed. "Here we go again."

She downed the contents of her glass and swung her legs around the side of the stool. But before she could get up, the scruffy-haired guy at the other end of the bar was off his stool and standing in between them.

"I think you've had enough, fella." His voice was bold

enough that she could hear it over the sound system, but her heightened awareness detected vibrato in his tone. He was nervous. Putting on a front. He raised himself to his full height in front of the greaseball, but the other guy had at least three inches on him.

"Who the fuck are you?" the greaseball spat, stepping back to take the guy in. "My beef is with that bitch, not you."

The man didn't move. "I think it's best if you head on home. She's made it clear she doesn't want to talk to you."

"Get out of my way, you little shit stain."

"Turn around. Walk away."

At that moment the atmosphere dropped. The music didn't scratch off, like in an old Western movie, but it might as well have done, as every person in the place shifted to watch the exchange, which was growing more heated by the second.

Acid slipped off her stool but held her position by the bar, assessing the tension in the big guy's posture, waiting for a sign he might attack. He was drunk, but the seething rage coming off him was palpable.

And here it was.

She pushed off against the bar just as the greaseball lurched forward and smashed his neanderthal forehead into the bridge of the smaller guy's nose. The poor guy crumpled, his nervous system giving up the ghost immediately, and landed in a heap by the wall. He looked like a punching bag that had all the sawdust knocked out of it. He was done. Except the greaseball wasn't finished. Acid grasped him by the shoulder, but he shrugged her off, stomping down hard on the smaller guy's stomach.

Okay. Enough.

As the greaseball raised his fist for another attack, she grabbed his wrist with both hands. Using her forward momentum, she twisted his elbow joint back on itself. He yelled out, more in surprise than pain, but his hand relaxed and Acid shifted her grip, grabbing the index and middle fingers of his right hand in each of her fists. With a swift pull, she yanked them apart, snapping the bones with a sickening crack. Now the pain arrived. He cried out and barged her with his shoulder, but she side-stepped him and grabbed a handful of hair, yanking his head down before kneeing him in the face.

She felt something crunch beneath her kneecap. His cheekbone, maybe, or his jaw. The pain was enough to cripple him, and this, coupled with his inebriated state, said it was unlikely he would retaliate. Yet experience had taught her that if you assumed something like that, it could be the last thing you ever did. She knelt beside his fallen body, sliding the push dagger out of her belt and pressing it against his neck.

"Now listen, pal," she growled, leaning in and pressing her weight onto the blade. "You don't know me, but you picked the wrong girl to mess with tonight. Hopefully, that's clear to you. I could slice your throat open with a flick of my wrist and you'd bleed out in under three minutes."

The man groaned but didn't move. A swollen, bloodshot eye spiralled back into focus and stared at her.

"Do you understand?" she asked. Her voice was calm, almost sinister. But her entire being tingled with hot bat energy.

Kill him, they screamed.

Finish the job.

"I could kill you," she went on, positioning her body to

conceal the blade from the other people in the bar. "But no one wants that. Not tonight, at least. Not here." She looked up as the messy-haired guy made a groaning noise. He sat up and wiped his hand across his mouth, spreading blood over his cheek. Acid turned back to the greaseball, lifting the blade from his throat. "Go home," she told him.

She got to her feet and rolled her shoulders back, sliding the dagger into its concealed sheath in the same movement. As she glanced over her shoulder, she saw The Bitter Marxist was back to the way it had been moments earlier. Two old guys at the far end of the bar were laughing together. The barman had his head down, slicing a lemon.

Keeping watch on the greaseball, she held her hand out to the other guy. "Here. Let me help you."

As his eyes met hers, she saw relief and perhaps amazement in his expression. He grabbed her wrist and she hauled him to his feet.

"Th-Thanks," he stammered. "He caught me completely unaware. I could have handled him if he'd fought fair."

Acid closed one eye and leaned back. A smirk spread across her face. "Yes, I'm sure that's what it was."

She looked down at the greaseball, now on all fours. He got to his feet and brushed himself down, glaring at her through bruised, swollen eyes. Acid clenched her fists, but despite the man's conceit, the fight had left him. His jaw looked dislocated. Acid raised her chin at him and he nodded in mute submission before shuffling over to the stairwell and hauling himself up the steps, using the handrail for balance.

She watched him leave before walking back to the bar and settling herself on her vacant stool. As the chatter of the bats subsided and her adrenaline levels dropped, a shiver of nervous energy shot down her arms.

"I think I owe you a drink."

She looked up to see the messy-haired man leaning on the bar next to her.

"Excuse me?"

He smiled, seemingly unaware the blood around his chin and across his full lips made him look like he was wearing clown make-up. He held up his hand. "I'm Freddie. Freddie Pearce."

Acid arched one eyebrow. "Nice to meet you, Freddie." She looked away but sensed him staring at her, waiting for more. She sighed. "My name's… Alice."

"Nice to meet you, Alice. And thanks for your help with that meathead. You were amazing."

"Don't mention it. I suppose you were trying to help. Not that I needed it." She turned and hit him with a firm look. "Or ever need it."

"Yes. I can see that." He frowned and bit his lip. "So… a drink? Can I get you one?"

She shook her head and laughed. "How about you go make yourself pretty first?"

"What?"

When he frowned, she leaned in and whispered. "You've got blood all over your face, sweetie. It's not very becoming." She sat back and jutted her chin at the bathroom door in the far corner. "Go wash. Then you can get me that drink."

"Oh, right. Yes. Of course." He smiled. "Back in a minute."

He sauntered off and she turned to watch him go, catching the barman's eye as she did. They exchanged a look before Acid returned to what was left of her drink. It was another typical night in The Bitter Marxist, but she wouldn't have had it any other way. Even if she suspected the nervy yet inarguably attractive Freddie was about to become another bad idea on a long list of bad ideas.

Chapter Eight

Once Freddie had cleaned himself up and returned from the bathroom, Acid broke one of her golden rules and allowed him to buy her a drink. She never normally let men do this, on account of the messages it sent, but there was something about Freddie's stray dog demeanour and nervous disposition that warmed him to her. And the unkempt hair and sharp cheekbones helped. As they sipped at their drinks (another Chivas Regal for her and a dark rum for him), the conversation flowed easily. Freddie was rather funny and much more erudite than she'd first presumed. He even shared her cynical world view, and after a while she found herself weighing up the possibility of something happening between them. The last thing she wanted was another needy character in her life – another Spook Horowitz – though one night wouldn't hurt.

But then he asked her *that* question.

"So, Alice, what do you do?"

She paused, her drink hovering in front of her lips. She

lowered the glass to the bar and shrugged. "What do I do?" She stared into the amber liquid. "What *do* I do?"

"Sorry, is that a contentious question? I didn't mean to—"

"No. It's fine. I suppose it's hard to explain, that's all. My partner and I have set up a kind of consulting agency. It's early days. I won't bore you with the details." She picked up her glass and swallowed back a mouthful of whisky. "How about you?"

He smiled and his eyes crinkled up at the corners. The way good eyes did. "I'm a writer. Freelance mainly, a few magazines and the like, but I had my first novel published by a small press at the start of last year."

"Would I have heard of it?"

"Probably not. It's not selling that well. It's called The Sunchasers, about a western reporter who tries to integrate herself into a South American tribe in the late eighteen-hundreds..." He trailed off and snorted. "Yes, it does sound dreadful, doesn't it?"

Acid laughed. "Did my face give it away?"

"A little. But it's fine. It's not my best work. I actually prefer writing non-fiction. True crime. I've got a book on East End gangs in the fifties that I'm currently seeking representation for and I'm writing another on the under-ground art world in London. There are a lot of nefarious characters involved, so it can get rather dangerous. But it's how I heard about this place, The Bitter Marxist. Quite the den of iniquity, isn't it? A lot of the key players in London's underbelly frequent the place, I'm told. Which was why I was a little taken aback to see someone such as yourself drinking here."

She held his gaze. "You don't think a feeble woman can hold her own amongst the dubious clientele?"

"No, I didn't mean that. You've already proven you can. But you're clearly a woman of taste and substance."

"Ha. Sometimes. But I like dens of iniquity, too." She gave him her most devilish smile. But for poor Freddie, that seemed a step too far. He looked away, his Adam's apple rising and falling as his hand grasped for his drink.

"Yes. Me, too," he said. "And exploring the more dangerous and shadowy aspects of the city is a genuine thrill. But there are times when... well, I shouldn't say too much. I can't. But I've had a few scrapes recently in my search for the truth."

Wonderful.

Despite his ungainliness, the guy was basically an investigative journalist, specialising in true crime. She could certainly pick them. This was the last person she should be talking to. Give it a few more hours and she could end up being the subject of his next book. She finished her drink.

"Can I get you another, Alice?"

"No. I should get going."

"Ah, really? Stay, please. One more drink?"

She was about to say no, more adamantly this time, but the clock above the bar told her it was nowhere near Cinderella time. Plus, the way Freddie was looking at her with those big, dark eyes meant she couldn't help herself.

"One more. But I'll get these."

It was probably a bad idea. The effects of the five double whiskies on an empty stomach were taking hold, but one more wouldn't hurt. It wasn't like she had anything to get home for other than Spook's tangy asides and disappointed glances. Freddie was sweet and funny and he smelt good. Plus, she was no longer swearing herself off men. Or women. Or, indeed, anything she desired. After the stress and pain of the last few years, she needed to learn to enjoy herself again. She'd be a long time dead and was done hiding from herself. Acid Vanilla had wants and needs, just like everyone else.

"Yes. Great stuff," Freddie said, beaming. "But I don't mind buying. I owe you."

"No. I insist." She held her hand up to the barman and gestured at him for two more of the same. He responded with a sage nod and reached for the bottles as she shifted her attention back to Freddie.

"You know, I've always liked the name Alice," he said. "You don't hear it as much as you used to."

She shrugged. "Depends on how you look at it."

"*Alice.* Yeah. I like it. Alice what?"

"My last name?" she asked, and he grinned eagerly. "Vandella. My name's Alice Vandella."

"*Alice Vandella.* Excellent."

She twisted her mouth to one side. "Yeah, about that, though. A lot of my friends call me Acid. It's my nickname. I prefer that. I think."

"Acid? Okay. I like that, too. Cool name. Why do they call you that, because of your acerbic wit?"

She laughed. "Something like that. It has been said." The drinks arrived and she picked up her glass. "Cheers."

They clinked their glasses together, eyes hooked on one another as they drank in unison.

Freddie brought his glass down, but the intensity of his gaze remained. "What did you say your agency did?"

Acid gave it a moment, placing her drink on the bar with care before regarding Freddie. Was this the face his interviewees saw as he grilled them for information? She sat back and flicked her hair over her shoulders, considering her answer. Giving away too much could get a person killed. And she wasn't talking about herself.

"It was my partner's concept. And it's hard to put into words."

Freddie frowned. "Your partner?"

"Business partner."

The frown faded. "Right. Well, I'm all for strange agencies that can't be easily explained. What is it, Ghostbusters?"

Acid chewed on her lip. He wasn't far off. "The best way I can describe what we are is private investigators. But that's not the entire story." She sighed, suddenly finding her drink very interesting. "The mission statement, if you can call it one, is that we 'help those who the authorities can't or won't help.' It sounds silly, I know. But it's early days."

She spat the words and stole a glance at Freddie. His bottom lip was sticking out, but he was nodding in a positive sort of way. "It sounds interesting," he said. "Not a million miles away from what I do. Giving a voice to those who don't have one. Telling their stories. Hey, you might be able to help me."

"What do you mean?"

Freddie, looking sheepish, scratched the side of his head, messing his hair up even more than it already was. "I've got myself into a bit of a mess with one of the people I'm trying to write about. A man called Axel Slater. He's an importer of fine art. Amongst other things, if you get my meaning."

Acid raised her head. "And what has he done?"

"Nothing. Yet. It started well. When I first approached him for an interview, he was fine. He couldn't have been more affable. But now he's leaning on me to tell his story the way he wants it told. I'm feeling uncomfortable about it, but I've no idea what to do or how to get him off my back. He rings me at least once a day about it. The last thing he said was that if I didn't write the book his way, then I had to pay him off. A release fee, as he put it, for wasting his time."

Acid blew out a long breath. "How much are we talking?"

"Fifty grand."

"Jesus. And if you don't give him it… what? He kneecaps you?"

Freddie's expression dropped. "He hasn't been explicit about that, but something along those lines, I imagine. It's extortion, but I've no idea how to get out of it. I know enough about Slater to know he's not bullshitting."

"You have got yourself in a bit of bother, haven't you?" she said. "I'm not sure what I can do to help. But I could have a word with the guy, see what comes of it."

"No. I can't ask you to do that," he said. "It's fine. I shouldn't have said anything. I'll sort it."

"You sure?"

"Yes. You could get hurt."

Acid very much doubted that. She finished her drink, seeing on the clock behind the bar that it was a few minutes to midnight.

"It's coming up to the witching hour," she said, leaning into Freddie. "I'm going to turn into a pumpkin soon and it'll be last orders here. But we could get a drink somewhere else, or…" She shrugged suggestively.

Or you could invite me back to yours?

She thought it but didn't say it. Neither did he.

Instead, Freddie finished off his drink and slammed the glass down on the countertop with some force. "Yeah, you're right. I'd best get on home," he said. "I've got a busy day tomorrow."

"Oh. I see." She couldn't hide the disappointment in her voice. Disappointment bordering on petulance.

Freddie lowered his chin and looked at her. "I would like to see you again, though. Could I get your number?"

"I don't have a phone, sweetie."

"What? Really?" He got to his feet. "Who doesn't have a phone in this day and age?"

"Me," she said, eyeballing him. Disappointment bordering on petulance, bordering on rage. "So, I guess I'll see you around."

She could feel his eyes burning into the side of her face as she turned to the bar.

"I'm sorry. I really do have a very early start," he said, finally getting the message. "But I'm in here most nights. If you ever want another drink and a chat. I'd like that."

"Maybe."

Out of the corner of her eye she saw his mouth flapping, but whatever he was trying to say, he decided against it.

Just go, mate.

I've scared you off. I get it.

She stared at the clock as it ticked around to twelve.

"Okay. Well, I suppose I'll see you later."

She didn't respond, and after a few seconds Freddie shuffled away. She waited until he walked up the stairs before spinning her empty glass away and huffing loudly. As she pushed off from the bar and got up, she caught the barman's eye.

"He didn't know what he had," he said, shaking his head.

"I know, right? Bloody men. No offence."

He grinned. "One more for the road?"

God, it was tempting. But her mood had dropped to an unrecoverable low and her bed beckoned. "Thanks, but I think that was my cue to get out of here. I'll see you again." She grabbed up her leather jacket and made for the door.

This was a good move, she told herself, as she hurried up the steps to street level. Freddie bloody Pearce wasn't the only one who had an early start tomorrow. Early for her, at least. She and Spook were meeting with Fiona Zoto at ten. A fresh case for The Avenging Angels.

Absolutely bloody wonderful.

But although it wasn't Acid's idea of fun, it would keep Spook from pecking at her head for a while.

At the top of the steps, she pushed the door open and the cool night air spiralled around her, chilling her skin and reviving her fatigued mind. As the chatter of the bats rose in her psyche, an idea hit her. Going straight home to her bed would have to wait. She knew exactly where she wanted to go. She headed for the street corner and hailed a black cab.

The witching hour had arrived.

It would be a damn shame to waste it.

Chapter Nine

Spook filled the machine with six scoops of coffee before clicking it on and sitting down at the pointlessly large dining table to wait. She considered it 'pointlessly' large because, despite there being six chairs and room for eight, they had never entertained friends here and never would. Hell, she couldn't have friends, period. Not anymore. Not really. She had acquaintances – Alicia from her yoga class who she occasionally met for brunch; Tom who worked in the local computer exchange who often reserved titles he knew she would like – but she couldn't call them friends. To do that would mean she'd have to divulge to them what she did, who she was. And that was out of the question. Spook Horowitz, despite her nerdy demeanour and diminutive size, had killed a person. She was an outcast from society. Someone who lived on the dark side of the street.

Yet this was the life she'd chosen four years ago when she'd thrown her dice in with Acid Vanilla. Back then, the idea of living like an outlaw appealed to the meek, by-the-book techie as nothing else had done before. Being newly present in Acid's orbit was thrilling, terrifying and fascinating all at once. For months she'd existed in a constant state of heightened emotions, shifting from panic to excitement to joy in a single minute. It was a new experience for Spook and she'd loved it.

But these days? It was hard to say.

She had faith in their agency, her dream ever since she and Acid had taken down Cerberix, her former employer, and achieved justice for Paula Silva, the prostitute viciously murdered by the firm's CFO. Acid, though, had made it abundantly clear her heart wasn't in it and that bothered Spook.

But that wasn't the only thing that bothered her about Acid...

Leaning across the table, she grabbed the box of cereal and poured a mound of bran flakes into the bowl in front of her. They looked like slivers of brown cardboard, hard to find appetising, but a healthy breakfast was important. Sometimes you needed to do what was right, not what you felt like doing. If only she could get that through to her wayward partner.

As the coffee machine bubbled and hissed on the counter, she caught sight of the digital clock above the cooker. The time read 8.55 a.m. She'd arranged for them to meet Fiona Zoto at her house in East Finchley at ten. It would take around thirty minutes in a cab to get across London, maybe longer at this time, and – what a surprise – Acid was still in bed after being out most of the night. Spook knew this because she'd heard her sneaking in at around four this morning. For someone who prided herself on a stealth-like approach, she could be incredibly noisy.

Spook picked up the milk and glugged a serving over the top of the cereal. She wasn't even surprised. There had been a time when Acid's free-spirited ways had appealed to her. But, over time, the erratic and dangerous elements of her character had begun to drag. The person Spook once viewed as brave and inspiring, she now saw as self-obsessed and distant. Spook got it. That was the persona Acid had constructed for herself in order to survive. First at Crest Hill, the home for psychologically dangerous girls, and then at Annihilation Pest Control. But there was only so much leeway you could give a person.

She glanced back at the cooker clock. 9.08 a.m. Her right leg was juddering uncontrollably under the table and she pressed her hand down on her thigh to stop it. She'd give Acid five more minutes, then go wake her. Today was important. They both needed to be on top form. She reached for her spoon before realising she didn't have one.

"Darn it."

She got up from the table and headed over to the cutlery drawer, dropping the carton of milk off at the fridge on her way. She was carrying a fresh spoon back to the table when she heard the front door open and then slam shut.

"What the hell?"

Acid! If she's sneaked out again, I'll—

"Hey, Spook. You're up then?"

Spook stared open-mouthed as Acid bound into the room. She was wearing black leggings and a black hooded top along with a pair of white trainers. Her hair was scraped back in a high ponytail and her cheeks were red.

"Where've you been?" Spook asked. "Out for a run?"

Acid brushed by her and opened the tall unit next to the sink. Grabbing a mug from the top shelf, she took it over to the coffee machine and poured herself some coffee.

"I can't get anything past you, can I?" she said, leaning with her back against the counter and taking the coffee mug in both hands. "I've been up since six. Thought I'd get in a bit of exercise before our meeting." She closed her eyes and smelt the coffee like she was in a commercial.

"You've been up and out already? I thought you were still in bed."

"And miss all the morning? Not a chance."

Spook frowned. She knew there were times when Acid didn't require sleep, but it was usually when she was in one of her manic episodes. Other than her energetic exuberance, she didn't seem overly frantic or out of control. "How far did you run?" she asked.

"Down Grosvenor Street, a lap around Hyde Park and back." She grinned and took a big gulp of the coffee. It must have been red hot, but she didn't flinch.

"Geez," Spook replied, still eyeing her with suspicion. "That's about twenty-five kilometres. How long did it take you?"

Acid shrugged. "Just under two hours?"

"Wow. That's fast."

"Is it?" She placed the mug in the sink and rolled her neck around her shoulders. "Right, Spook. We've got a meeting to get to, I believe, so why don't you get yourself sorted while I have a quick shower and we'll set off. I've already called an Uber, so we're all good."

Spook closed her mouth, which had fallen open again. She watched as Acid strode across the kitchen. At the door, she stopped and turned, clapping her hands together like an impatient teacher might do to a bunch of unruly kids.

"Come on, sweetie. Get with it. You're going to make us late."

And with that, she disappeared down the corridor towards the shower.

"Okay. Thanks," Spook called after her, but Acid was

already in the bathroom with the door shut. Muttering to herself, unsure of what had just happened, she went over to the unit and grabbed herself a mug for some coffee. She suddenly felt very lackadaisical next to her energetic friend.

———

FIFTEEN MINUTES later and they were in the back of a silver Ford Focus on their way to East Finchley. Acid had slipped the driver an extra fifty to 'not spare the horses', and as they sped through Camden Town, she pulled out a gold make-up compact along with a tray of black eyeshadow. Not being someone who ever wore make-up, Spook watched in awe as Acid jabbed the end of her finger into the dark mascara and rubbed it across her eyelids in a way that might have seemed haphazard if the result hadn't looked so good. Once done, she shoved the tray into the pocket of her leather jacket and pulled out a bright red lipstick. She applied this in two fast, fluid movements that covered her full lips perfectly. Rubbing them together, she pouted almost obscenely at the driver, who'd been watching her the whole time.

She turned to Spook and winked. "There we go. A bit of war paint never hurt the situation, did it?" Raising her head, she squinted out of the front windshield. "And here we are. East Finchley Tube station. By my reckoning, Baronsmere Road should be around the corner. I hope you've thought about what we're going to say to this Fiona woman."

"Yes, sure," was all Spook could find to say in response. The truth was, she'd been chasing her tail ever since Acid had burst into the kitchen forty minutes earlier and she was still struggling to get a handle on things. Whether Acid's renewed focus and vigour would last, she was unsure, but she had to see it as a good thing. She might be a loose cannon and prone to overkill in the worst possible way, but Spook needed her. While the Avenging Angels Agency had been her dream, her baby, she couldn't make it work without Acid.

Well, shit…

Spook stared out of the window as the car turned right and slowed halfway along a suburban street. They came to a stop and Acid flung open the car door. As she leapt out onto the street, she called back, but Spook didn't hear what she said. She was too caught up in her thoughts.

…couldn't make it work without Acid.

That was true of every aspect of her life, not just the agency. And that was what terrified her. What if Acid got arrested? What if she died? What if one day Spook came home and she was just no longer there?

"Are you coming, sweetie?" Acid asked, leaning into the car.

"Yes. Of course. Sorry."

She shunted across the back seat and got out the same side as Acid, who was holding the door for her. In front of them were rows of identical terraced houses stretching along both sides of the street for as far as they could see.

"What number is the house?" Acid asked, as the Uber pulled away, leaving the two of them standing on the pavement.

Spook pushed her glasses up onto the bridge of her nose and pulled her coat around her. It was a chilly morning and there was no one else on the street. It made her uneasy.

"Umm… Seventy-three."

"Okay, well, that's fifty-nine," Acid said, setting off

walking. "Sixty-one… three… five… There. The one with the red door."

Spook quickened her pace to keep up as Acid marched down the street towards Fiona Zoto's house. Pushing open the rickety black gate, she strode down the garden path and was banging on the door with the heel of her fist when Spook caught up with her.

"Please remember Fiona is a prospective client," she whispered. "She's not the enemy. She's not someone you're trying to assassinate."

Acid glared at her. "Yes, well, if I was trying to do that, I wouldn't be banging on the front door, would I?"

"No. But… be nice. Please." Spook looked down and fiddled with a button on her coat. Despite all the self-help books telling her that no one else had the power to make her feel anything if she didn't let them, it sure was a coincidence that it was always with Acid when she felt her most timid and clumsy.

They stood shoulder to shoulder, listening at the door. But other than the faint hum of traffic and the chirps from a row of birds sitting on a telephone wire above the street, there was nothing. Spook reached out and banged on the door herself, three sharp knocks that she hoped sounded less aggressive. Still nothing. She reached into her pocket and pulled out her phone.

"You sure it was seventy-three?" Acid asked, as Spook scrolled through her emails.

"I'm checking." She found the thread of correspondence between her and Fiona and scanned the messages. "Yes. This is the house. And the right time."

"Maybe she's deaf." Acid reached out and banged on the door again. The entire house shook. She stepped back and sniffed. "Come on. It's useless. She's not home."

She turned around, but Spook grabbed her arm as she heard movement behind the door. "Wait."

A second later, they heard a key in the lock and the door creaked open an inch. A woman peered at them through the gap.

"Are you them?" Her voice was deep and she spoke with an accent. "The Avenging Angels?"

Spook sensed Acid stiffen beside her. "Yes. That's us. Fiona, right? I'm Spook. We spoke on the phone."

Fiona Zoto opened the door fully and stuck her head out, scanning the area like a meerkat searching for a rogue jackal. "Come inside, quickly. It is not safe."

"Why not?" Spook asked, the hairs on her neck prickling as Fiona stepped back and ushered for them to come inside.

"It has gotten so much worse since last we spoke," she said. "My father. He has gone missing and I am scared they may come for me. Please, so I can lock the door."

Spook glanced at Acid, hoping to see an arched eyebrow or a smirk of reassurance. But instead she pushed past Spook and stepped into the house.

"It's okay," she told Fiona. "We're here now. Why don't we all sit down and you can explain what's happened?"

Chapter Ten

Fiona Zoto was what Acid would call a handsome woman. She had a long, slender nose and a well-defined jawline, and with her dark auburn hair and green eyes, she could have held a striking presence. *Could have.* Only, today her hair was unwashed and looked as though it hadn't seen a brush in days. In the gloom of the unlit house, her skin had a grey hue and her shoulders sagged as she led Acid and Spook through into the front room.

"Please, have a seat," she said, gesturing to a beige couch with a shaking hand. "Do you want a drink? I have tea, coffee, water."

"Not for me, thanks," Acid said, taking a seat on the couch and shifting up so Spook could sit beside her. And when she didn't sit straight away, Acid glared at her until she did. She was here. She was taking this seriously. It was only fair Spook pulled her head out of her arse and got with the program. For heaven's sake, this was what she wanted, wasn't it? For Acid to be full of glorious *purpose*.

She turned her attention back to Fiona as Spook

fidgeted beside her. For now, the screech of the bats had been subdued. A commotion of conflicting feelings bubbled on the cusp of her awareness, but she'd quietened the madness enough that she could present like a normal human being. Normal enough, at least. Deep breaths helped. The running as well. There was nothing like exercise and endorphins to silence the chaos inside of you. But then there were other times – like last night – when the only option was to give in to the chaos. She knew what she was doing was risky and without real merit. But she also knew it was the one thing that had given her the motivation and focus to get up early and be the person Spook wanted her to be. Even though her skin felt like paper and she was worried her teeth might shatter into a thousand pieces, she was attentive, ready, and determined to help this woman.

Until she gave in to the chaos the next time, anyway.

"I'm not sure if Spook mentioned me," she told Fiona. "My name is Alice Vandella. I'm the other half of the... of the agency."

Fiona sat in the armchair in the corner. "She mentioned there were two of you coming here today. Thank you." She clasped her hands together in her lap. "It is bad. I do not know where to start."

"At the beginning is fine," Spook said, leaning forward. "You said you were worried that your father had got involved in something dangerous. That he couldn't get out of."

"That's right. Only now it is worse. Much worse. He has gone missing." She turned her head as her voice broke with emotion. "I fear he may have been taken."

"Oh, you poor thing."

Spook placed her weight onto her feet like she was

about to get up and comfort her. So before she had the chance, Acid placed a firm hand on her knee to stop her.

Calm it down, kid.

Act professional.

Fiona wiped at her face with the curve of her finger and sniffed. "I am sorry. It is all very worrying for me."

"That's understandable," Acid said. "But we do need to know what we're dealing with. Can you go back to the start for me? Tell me about your father. Who is he? What does he do?"

Fiona placed her knees together, bony fists banging against each other on the tops of her thighs. "His name is Afrim Zoto. He is seventy-one and from Albania originally, a town called Kakavia on the Albanian-Greek border. He was born there. So was I. For as long as I can remember, he has had an import business. *A to Z International.* He has imported lots over the years, working in many different countries and industries. But for the last five years, he has specialised in premium leather goods. Bags, shoes, purses, belts."

"I see," Acid said. "And he was successful?"

"Yes, he has an expert eye, my father," Fiona continued. "I moved to the UK fifteen years ago and I finally convinced him to join me here six years later. The pieces he has been bringing over from Eastern Europe and Asia have sold very well in the UK. He had dreams of opening a shop in the city. I mean, he *has* dreams! Me vjen keq!" She made a noise like a barking seal and covered her mouth with her hand. "I am sorry. I haven't slept. Yesterday I was supposed to meet him for lunch but he never showed up. I rang him. Nothing. I went to his apartment and his office. He was nowhere to be found. No one has seen him or heard from him in days."

Acid gave Fiona's anxious disposition time to settle before she asked the next question. "What do you think has happened to your father?" She emphasised the word 'you', hoping it might convey to the already distressed woman that her worst fears might only be that. Fears. Not the truth.

"I know there was one person in particular who didn't like that my father, an immigrant to this country, was doing so well for himself. Some people can be brutal in their dislike of foreigners. Even more so for those trying to make something of their lives."

Acid leaned around the side of Spook. "Do you have a name for this person?"

"I am sorry, I do not know. My father didn't want me to be involved, for my safety. But he let slip that he is in the import business too, but involved in illegal activities. I do not know what they are. He has a warehouse in Woolwich on the same plot as my father's warehouse."

Acid and Spook exchanged glances. "He sounds like someone we need to talk to."

Fiona looked forlornly at the floor. "I should have asked more questions of my father, but he claimed he had it all under control. He has never been a man who talked deeply about his problems. He never wanted to worry me or have me involved in anything dangerous." She shook her head. "Yet, this is exactly what has happened."

"Is there anything else you can think of that might help us?" Acid asked. "Anything at all?"

Fiona pulled in a deep breath as if preparing herself to say something grand. "My father is a good man. But in Albania, in the business he was in, it was difficult to distance himself from criminal elements. He wanted his new business in the UK to be one hundred percent legal. He loved what he did, and when this man approached him he grew angry and unsettled." She let out a deep sigh and her shoulders wilted some more. "The reason I first searched for help and found your agency was because I hoped you might find this man and gather evidence of his illegal ways. So that the police would have no choice but to get involved. But now the situation has changed and I need your help in other ways. I need you to find my father. Or, at least, find out what happened to him."

Acid turned to Spook. She had that same glazed expression on her face like when she was watching one of those Japanese cartoons she so loved. An elbow to the ribs snapped her out of it. "What do you think, partner?"

Spook shook herself and sat up. "No... I mean, yes... I mean, don't worry, Fiona. We'll find your father, I promise. We'll—"

"Hey. Hang on a second," Acid cut in, shifting around to face Spook and lowering her voice. "Steady on, will you? Don't be throwing around promises we can't keep. And have we discussed a fee?"

Spook blinked. Up close, the thick lenses in her spectacles made her eyeballs look immense. "Not yet. I didn't think it was wise so soon."

"I see." She smiled and turned back to Fiona, who was dabbing at her eyes with a tissue. "Miss Zoto. You are aware that our services come with a cost?"

Fiona nodded. "Whatever you charge, I will pay. My father was a successful businessman. We have money. Just please find him. I won't be able to sleep until you do."

Acid narrowed her eyes, her jaw stiff with concentration. "How does a thousand pounds a week retainer sound to you?"

Spook let out a squeak, but Acid had anticipated as much and grabbed her knee again, squeezing her muscle as she held Fiona's gaze. A grand a week was a fair price. It showed the client they were a serious agency. It was also a fraction of what she used to earn working for Caesar.

"That sounds reasonable," Fiona replied.

Acid glanced at Spook. "Great. We'll start our enquiries straight away. I'm hoping we can find your father sooner rather than later."

Fiona wiped away another tear. "I just hope he didn't do or say anything that got him... That made someone..."

"Hey now. Don't be going there," Spook said. "We don't know anything yet other than you've been unable to locate your father. There might be a perfectly innocent explanation as to where he's been."

Acid swallowed a sigh. Spook, waxing lyrical again with her positive thinking bullshit. It wasn't helpful. "Did your father have an office?" she asked Fiona. "Somewhere he held his records? A computer?"

The woman replied with eager nods to all. "He has an office in Whitechapel. That is where the business is registered. He also has the warehouse in Woolwich."

"We'll start at the warehouse," Acid told her. "Are you able to give us access?"

"I can give you the keys to the office, no problem," Fiona replied. "But the warehouse might be a little more trouble. My father kept his business dealings private. He is strong-willed with a good brain. He wanted to do everything himself. I used to tell him he needed help, but he never listened. I wish he had. But the keys to the warehouse could be in his safe. I'm afraid I do not know the code. I was over at his office yesterday evening and tried lots of combinations, but I couldn't open it. I'm so sorry. I know it sounds pathetic of me."

"It's fine. And don't worry," Acid told her. "If you give

us the addresses of all your father's properties, that will suffice. And for now, don't mention to anyone that you contacted us or that we've taken on your case."

Fiona stiffened. "You think I am in danger!" Her voice rose considerably. "So you agree my father was involved in something illegal?"

Acid flattened her hands on her thighs and shifted her weight onto her feet. "I don't know, is the short answer. But until I do, I'd prefer to keep this between the three of us." Looking down at Spook, she gestured for her to stand. "Thank you, Fiona. We won't keep you any longer. If you get us the keys to your father's office, we've got enough information to get started on the case. We'll keep you informed of anything we discover."

"And don't worry," Spook said. "We won't stop until we find your father."

"Thank you." Fiona got up from the chair and did her best impression of someone who seemed optimistic. "I shall get you the keys right now. And is it okay if I write a cheque for the first payment?"

"Not a problem," Acid told her.

She offered them a meek smile and hurried out of the room.

"Thank you," Spook whispered, once she'd gone.

Acid didn't look at her. "Whatever for?"

"That you're here, taking the lead. Asking all the right questions. Acting as if you actually care about someone. It feels good, right?"

"Don't push it, sweetie." She inhaled sharply. "I told you I'd be involved. Let's leave it at that."

"But it feels good, no? To help people? I think finding Afrim Zoto is going to give us both purpose."

Jesus. This again.

She was all ready to tell Spook to stop it with the happy-clappy goals and purpose shit, but she stopped herself. Spook meant well and to reprimand her would be to fall back into old patterns of behaviour. Today she was in a good place. The bats were content, and whilst she could feel the distinct prickle of mania on the horizon, she was in control of it. Just like in the old days, when her condition was valuable for the work she did. The confusion and uncertainty that had plagued her since leaving Annihilation Pest Control were gone. Her thoughts were clearer than they ever had been. So, whilst the Avenging Angels – as a name and a concept – still bothered her, the thought of being in action, searching for clues and delving into a world of degenerate businessmen, excited her just as much. Zoto's world sounded both mysterious and dangerous and she was here for both of those things.

Whether they'd find the old man alive, however, was a different matter. Fiona appeared resolute and had kept herself together just now, but it was clear to Acid she was holding onto the hope of seeing her father alive. That wasn't good. Talk of the mystery man troubled her. Her mind wandered to Freddie Pearce. He was right with what he said; there were a lot of dangerous people in London who'd kill someone for far less than being a threat to their livelihood. The best-case scenario was that Zoto had realised his shadowy rival was gunning for him and was lying low. The worst-case – and perhaps most likely scenario – was that the poor old bastard was at the bottom of the Thames with a concrete block tied to his legs. Either way, some expectation management would be required in the coming days.

As Fiona returned with the keys, the addresses for her father's properties handwritten on notepaper, and a cheque for their first payment, Acid thought about saying something to her but decided against it once again. Caesar had always impressed on her how important it was to keep shtum in uncertain situations. Listening was a more valuable skill. Besides, Spook was much better at dealing with the customer service side of things. Empathy had never been one of her strong points.

There was no reason for them to outstay their welcome. So, once they had everything they needed, they bade Fiona farewell and told her they'd call as soon as they'd found anything. She saw them to the door, thanking them profusely and waving them off down the path.

As they walked along the street, Spook nudged Acid's arm. "Thanks for that."

Acid looked at her. "For what?"

"You know… Things have been strained between us recently, haven't they? But I'm glad you're here. I appreciate you showing up like you have done today."

Acid couldn't stop the instinctive eye roll; some patterns of behaviour were harder to shake. "Yes. You already said that."

"But it's true. I'm going to enjoy working with you again. I think you'll enjoy it, too."

She tsked loudly, but had an inkling Spook was right. Working this case – alongside her clandestine activities – could be the very thing she needed to get back on an even keel after the turbulence of the past few years. She even found herself grinning at the thought of it. "We'll see, Spooky," she said. "We'll see."

Chapter Eleven

Whilst Spook had been both impressed and thrilled with Acid's calm and considered behaviour in front of Fiona – and was overjoyed at how seriously she seemed to be taking the case – none of these feelings lasted very long. In the back of the cab on their way back to Soho, Acid had stared out of the window rather than engage with her. Every so often her nose would crinkle up and she'd mouth silent words to herself like she was going over plans in her head, but whatever they were she didn't voice them aloud. Spook had attempted conversation, asking her things about the case (things that could be asked in the back of a taxi with a civilian in earshot), but got nothing in return apart from vague, one-word answers. Once back at the apartment, she headed straight to her room and closed the door, muttering something about needing space to think over the case and how to go about it.

Well, fine.

That's what Spook needed as well. This was only their second case and it was important they did everything carefully, not rush in and screw things up. She was glad, at least, to see Acid was being thoughtful about it rather than her usual impulsive self.

After consuming a bar of Cadbury's Dairy Milk and soaking for forty-five minutes in a bath so hot it made her skin bright red, Spook got changed into fresh clothes and decided to make lunch for them both. It would be a nice thing to do, she thought. Plus, the ritualistic elements of sitting down to eat together would create a safe space in which Acid might open up a little more.

That was the hope, at least.

Now, standing over a pan of bubbling tomato sauce, Spook felt more stable than she had done all week, ever since they'd got back from Hastings. Why was it that when you had a lot of messed-up thinking going on, you weren't aware of it until you settled down enough that the shitty thoughts could clear? She smiled to herself as she stirred the twin pans in front of her, alternating the wooden spoon between stirring the spaghetti water and the now fully reduced pasta sauce. Acid had been so cold and unresponsive in the cab because she was putting all her energy into how to find Afrim Zoto. She was focused on the case. That was all.

"Are you expecting company?"

Spook startled at the voice and whipped her head around to see Acid leaning against the kitchen doorway. She'd got changed and was wearing a pair of blue denim jeans so tight they looked like they hurt, and a white Velvet Underground t-shirt with the faces of the original four members across her chest. Lou Reed plus... the other three. (Spook had tried immersing herself in Acid's interests at the start of their relationship, but gave up when she realised how much Acid's musical tastes clashed with her own sensibilities – and that her efforts were largely unappreciated anyway.) The fact that neither her top nor bottom half was decked out in the usual black could only be a good sign, Spook felt.

She grinned at Acid. "I'm making us dinner. Nothing fancy, spaghetti with tomato sauce. But I've got a decent block of parmesan in the fridge and some fresh basil that I was going to rip up and—"

"Not for me, thanks." Acid walked over and lifted a glass off the shelf by Spook's head.

"Oh?" Spook replied, trying not to sound surprised. Or hurt. "I thought you liked pasta."

"Why, because I'm half-Italian?"

"No. Because I've seen you eat it. And enjoy it." Spook struggled to keep her tone calm. "I thought we could eat together and talk about the case, discuss a plan of action sort of thing."

Acid went to the sink and twisted on the tap, waiting a few seconds for the water to run cold, then filling up her glass. Turning, she leaned against the counter and drank the whole thing down in three gulps.

Spook stirred her sauce, waiting for a response. But when Acid turned back around and filled her glass again, she couldn't contain herself. "What's wrong with you?"

Acid took another gulp of water and regarded her with a side-eye. "What's wrong with me?" she asked, lowering the glass. "Hell, kid. Where do you want to start?"

"You know what I mean," Spook said, biting a metaphorical tongue. "I thought you were amazing at the meeting with Fiona. Back there, you seemed keen to get going. But since we left, you've not said a word to me. Is it something I've done?"

Acid groaned. "Jesus, Spook. Why do you always make everything about you?"

"This is about the case."

"Is it?"

They glared at each other, a maelstrom of unexpressed feelings and unspoken words fizzing in the air between them. Like always, Spook looked away first. There was no beating that impenetrable stare, those enigmatic eyes.

"I thought it'd be nice, that's all," she mumbled, turning her attention back to the stove. "You haven't eaten anything all day. You must be hungry."

"Well, I'm not. I'll get something later." When the room fell silent, Spook looked up, thinking Acid may have walked out, but she was still standing by the sink. As their eyes met, a brief smile appeared. "But it smells good and I do appreciate the effort. I'm just not in the right frame of mind to eat."

Spook couldn't help but smile back. This was as close to an apology as she was ever going to get from Acid Vanilla. "So what's going on with you?"

The question was met with a sharp intake of breath as if Acid was preparing herself for one of her pointed, dramatic sighs. But she seemed to catch herself and it didn't materialise. "You know me, Spook. I've always got a lot going on."

"Yes, I know that. But you seem different this time. I don't know, you seem evasive. More than usual, I mean." She bit her lip, for real this time, not daring to look away. "I can't help thinking you're keeping something from me."

Acid flashed her eyes at her, the smile turning to a smirk. "Why would I do that?"

"I don't know. I'm confused. Today it felt like, for the first time in ages, we were on the same side. Both facing the same direction. I know you've been reticent about going full steam ahead with The Avenging Angels. I was surprised but pleased that you showed up today so involved."

Acid pushed off from the counter and walked over to the window. "I'm still not happy with that name, though. We need to come up with something better and we need to sit down soon and discuss our prices. Also, I was thinking, what if we started advertising on the dark web? You can do that easily enough, right? Maybe set up a portal the way we used to do it at Annihilation." She was pacing up and down, speaking fast, the words spat out without taking a breath. "How does that sound?"

Spook swallowed hard on a dry throat. As the words formed in her head, dizziness overcame her, but she fought it off and went for it. This needed saying. She had to know. "I'm worried you only want us to get involved in dangerous jobs, like at Thelmastone House. Jobs that involve killing people. We aren't going to be the new Annihilation Pest Control, Acid."

Acid stopped, her head snapping over to look at her. "Yes. I know. That's not what I meant. But if we are going to do this, we need to get the word out to people who need our help. Broken people, people on the edge of society, those dealing with life-or-death situations."

"You don't think those things apply to Fiona Zoto?"

Acid shrugged and continued her tour around the kitchen table. "I suppose. But it's not a particularly meaty case, is it? It's clear the old fucker has met his maker already. We aren't going to get her the outcome she wants."

"She wants closure."

"Did you not see the pain in her eyes today? She might have said all that about just wanting to know either way, but she didn't mean it. She wants us to find her father alive. What happens when we can't? When he turns up dead?"

"We don't know that will happen," Spook said. "And it won't be our fault."

"Yes. I know. But it's all a bit... I don't know... pointless. Isn't it? Sure, we'll no doubt find the guy who did it. We might even find evidence that we can pass on anonymously to the police. Well, whoopee. What a rush."

Spook turned the pans down to simmer. "I knew it. I knew this was it."

"You knew what? What did you know?" she demanded, prowling around the room like a person possessed.

No.

Like a caged animal.

She glared at Spook and jerked her chin forward as if provoking her for a response.

"I knew it was too good to be true." She turned back to the stove. She couldn't look at Acid when she was like this, bristling with unfettered chaos. "I thought we were cutting new ground. You'd agreed to the talk therapy sessions and seemed keen to finally establish the agency. I thought, great, she wants to do this with me. I was excited for us to be a team again. A partnership. But you don't work like that, do you?"

"Oh, Jesus. Here we go. Like what?"

"In the past, I've bent over backwards to help you. Done everything and anything I can. Even when I felt incredibly uncomfortable about what you were doing with the whole murderous vendetta business."

Acid snorted. "No one forced you to help me."

"No. They didn't. But I wanted to help because I saw how important it was to you. I also believed once it was over you'd calm down. I hoped we could move forward and create something worthy and important. The Avenging Angels. A cause for good."

"And you got your wish."

"Did I? Because it sounds like you only want to be involved if it involves death and bloodshed. That's it, isn't it? I get it now. I see what changed. You were all excited this morning because you thought the Zoto case might be more dangerous and fucked up than it is. Now you know it's not, you've lost interest." She caught herself waving her arms around and folded them tight across her chest. "Come on. Tell me I'm wrong."

Acid stepped forward, stabbing at the air with her finger. "You don't have a clue what you're talking about."

"Don't I?" Spook gripped her arms tighter in an attempt to halt the convulsions.

"Oh, for god's sake!" Acid yelled. "You really are an absolute pain in the arse. Fuck me!"

Spook had more to say, but Acid marched from the room and disappeared down the corridor. A second later, the door to her bedroom slammed shut.

Spook waited.

One, two, three…

And there it was.

Loud music blared through the wall.

She closed one eye and listened, but couldn't make out the song. It was fast and heavy and the bass shook the walls. She thought about going to her own room and losing herself in a game of Elden Ring for a few hours, but decided against it. One of them had to be the adult in this partnership. So instead, she took the pan of spaghetti over to the sink and drained the starchy water through a colander. Then she took it back to the stove and tipped the tomato sauce onto the dry pasta. It didn't look great, but it would do. The story of Spook's life.

She'd half-expected the front door to have slammed shut by now. There was no alcohol in the house as far as she knew, and Acid rarely spent too long without a bottle of something if she was in this type of mood. But as she dished out a portion of spaghetti and took it over to the table, she surmised that perhaps Acid was dealing with this one without her usual crutch.

That was something, at least.

Yet much later, after a wasted afternoon spent trawling the dark web for information on Fiona's father that threw up nothing, Spook lay awake in bed, unable to sleep. Acid had barely surfaced from her room all day, but at some point, in the darkness, Spook heard footsteps in the hall, then the creak and click of the front door as it opened and closed. Acid was on the move.

Rolling over, Spook lifted her phone to check the time. 1.28 a.m.

What the hell?

It was the second time this month Acid had sneaked out after dark. The first time, Spook had dismissed it as Acid not being able to sleep and wanting some fresh air, but now she wasn't sure. This was London. There were places open at this time of night. Seedy bars, nightclubs. But Spook worried it was worse than that. Suspicion and unease had been niggling at the edge of her awareness for too long and now they rose up to bite her. Throwing back her covers, she hurried over to the window and peeled back the curtain. On the street below, she saw a dark figure standing by the side of the road. They were wearing a black baseball cap pulled down over their face and had their hair up in a tight ponytail. But the silhouette was unmistakable, as was the way they jutted their hip to one side as they waited for a gap in the traffic. It had to be Acid. She was wearing a black turtleneck sweater and black jeans, and if her gait didn't give her away, the battered leather jacket certainly did.

But where was she going at this time of night dressed like that?

And more importantly – more worryingly – what was she doing when she got there?

Chapter Twelve

The bathroom reminded Acid of the one she used to have in her old apartment. It was grand and just the right side of ostentatious, with a spacious rain-effect walk-in shower and a freestanding bath in the centre of the room. The same slate tiles covered the walls and floor and, above her, a hanging ceiling concealed a border of LED lights that cast the space in a warm glow. Gold-plated metalware finished the look, from the door handles to the bath legs to the taps, to even the hinges on the dark mahogany toilet seat.

She removed her leather jacket and hung it over the side of the large sink unit. Pulling a plastic bag and a rubber stopper out of her jeans pocket, she placed the stopper over the end of the empty syringe she'd left in the sink and shoved the whole lot into the zip-lock. Once sealed she slipped it inside her jacket pocket. With one black-gloved hand, she lowered the toilet seat and sat down facing the bath, crossing one leg over the other. The hard porcelain of the cistern was cold through the thin material of her top as she leaned back. A few seconds went by. She gave a sharp cough.

Nothing.

"Bloody hell, wake up, will you?"

She waited another thirty seconds. Then, with a tut of annoyance, walked over to the bathtub. It was almost identical to the one she used to own, in fact; large enough to accommodate three people comfortably. She knew that because she'd done it. On more than one occasion.

Good times. Different times.

This bath only had one inhabitant, however. A scrawny man in his late fifties with a grey beard and pointed eyebrows that gave him a quizzical look even under the spell of the sedatives. Up close and naked, wet from the bath water, he looked very different from the photos she'd seen of him online. In one shot, taken outside of court on the day his sentence was overturned, he was looking straight down the camera lens with a sickening, supercilious smirk playing across his greying chops.

But not anymore.

Not tonight.

It was hard for anyone to look anything but vulnerable when they were lying naked in a bath and with their hands tied to the taps, but this wrinkled old goat looked particularly helpless. Well, good. Because that was likely how his victims had looked before he'd slaughtered them without mercy.

She leaned down and smacked him hard across the face. The harsh slapping sound she'd been expecting was dampened to a dull thud by the material of her glove. Annoying. "Come on, you pathetic prick. Wake up."

The flumazenil she'd just injected into his vein to counter the previously injected sedatives should have kicked in by now. She pulled the Glock 19 out of the back of her jeans as his eyelids flickered and he murmured something she couldn't make out. Stepping back, she aimed the gun at his forehead while his eyes opened. He glanced up at her, but it was like he was looking through her and his droopy eyelids fell closed again. She gave it a beat, adjusting her grip on the handle of the pistol and allowing his drowsy brain to catch up with what he'd seen.

"What the hell—" he cried out, water splashing over the side as he tried to sit up but found his hands were tied over his head and he was unable to.

"Calm it down," Acid told him. "There's no point struggling."

This was true. The knots she'd used would only tighten the more he pulled. But even then, she didn't want him pulling too harshly and causing lacerations to his wrists. Any sign that this was anything other than the last act of a desperate man and she'd failed.

Once he'd realised it was pointless trying to get free, the screaming arrived. Loud, terrified shrieks reverberated off the slate tiles and belied the man's slight frame. But even this was pointless. The large house stood in its own grounds with triple glazing on every window. In one of the most affluent areas of Hampstead, no one can hear you scream.

"Who are you?" he gasped, his saucer-eyes settling on her. "What do you want?"

"It doesn't matter who I am," she replied, raising her booted foot onto the side of the bath. She still had the Glock trained on him, but her finger was loose on the trigger. Tonight, the gun was a catalyst, not a tool. "But it does matter that I know who you are. And what you did."

"Fuck you. I didn't do anything. They let me go. Don't you watch the news?"

Acid stuck out her bottom lip. "No. I don't. But I do keep abreast of certain aspects of society. I'm interested in people who have done wrong, who have hurt others and got away with it. People who are guilty of their crimes but got let off on a technicality. Ring any bells, Doctor?" She lowered the Glock, waving the barrel over his chest and groin area as he whimpered to himself. "Four dead patients, two sexually assaulted, all whilst under your duty of care, after you'd convinced them to sign their life savings over to you. These were old women. One of them was in her nineties."

She narrowed her eyes at him.

Sick bastard.

"I didn't do it. Read the reports. The police in charge of the case planted evidence."

Acid nodded. "Yes. I believe that's true as well. But the thing is, you miserable prick, you getting let off on a technicality doesn't make the first part untrue, does it? It just means the police are as corrupt and pathetic as I've always known. And it's why, Doctor Sanderson, people like me are more important than ever."

She lowered her foot to the floor and walked over to the window. The glass was thick and mottled and all she could make out were vague shapes. The dark indigo sky that had hung over her head on the way here was now growing lighter. Dawn was around the corner.

Sanderson writhed some more, water splashing over the side of the bath as he grappled with his restraints.

"I wish you'd stop doing that," she told him. "You're going to tire yourself out."

She didn't need to tie him up. Not really. She could have simply injected him with a strong muscle relaxant – something like succinylcholine – which would have incapacitated him long enough to get him from bed to the bathtub. But unlike lorazepam, most muscle relaxants showed up on toxicology tests and that muddied the narrative. These things mattered. They were important. She didn't *need* to do any of this. Just like she didn't need to spend twenty minutes writing a suicide note, which she'd left on the open laptop in his office. But these were elements of her craft. She was an artist re-establishing herself in the role of mastery.

A modern assassin's greatest skill was how they constructed their hits so they didn't look like hits at all. This was what people paid top dollar for. A suicide, a freak accident, a burglary gone wrong. A gruesome murder brought with it far too much attention, but a man so racked with guilt over what he'd done that he took his own life? That was a few column inches in the newspapers, perhaps even a front page in some of the red tops, but then case closed within a few days. With someone like Sanderson – who the tabloids had named 'Dr Evil' and 'Sadistic Sanderson' during his original trial – the police wouldn't be looking too hard at the evidence. Indeed, they'd be glad to get rid of the evil bastard before he had a chance to sue them.

Yet despite all these factors, Acid cared about her work. If she was doing this, then she had to do it right. Like she used to. Every detail was important. Every aspect of the job mattered.

After another twenty seconds of thrashing and splashing, Sanderson ceased and glared over at her. "What do you want from me?"

"I want you to tell me what you did."

"I didn't do anything."

"Oh, come now, Doctor. We both know that's not true." She turned to face him, tilting her head to one side. "You murdered four of your patients. You did despicable things to them. I think you've probably guessed by now that you aren't going to be getting out of that bathtub alive. But your actual method of death, that's up to you. It can be quick and painless. Or very long and drawn out, and incredibly pain*ful*."

"Fuck you. Vicious bitch."

"Well, there we are. And people say doctors aren't as noble or as erudite as they used to be." She knelt and unzipped the side of her boot.

Sanderson craned his neck to watch her. "What are you doing?" he growled.

She stood and held up the fresh razor blade, twisting it in the light until Sanderson could make it out. He let out a shrill yelp.

"No! Please! I'm sorry. I didn't mean to do it... I was desperate."

"Desperate," she repeated, examining the razor blade with a lustful gaze, giving him the full sadistic killer routine. "So, you admit it. You did kill those women?"

She stepped closer and his eyes grew even larger. Glancing down his torso, she saw his miserable penis had all but retreated into his pelvis. It happened. In times of high stress, the body shuts down the parts that aren't needed. It was a throwback from caveman times. There was no cause to think about procreation when you were being chased by a sabre-toothed tiger.

Or being threatened by a she-wolf.

"Tell me the truth and I'll make it quick," she said. "I mean it, Sanderson. You don't want to know how long and drawn out this could get. There are places to cut a person, things one can remove that won't kill you straight away. You could be alive for days, weeks sometimes, but in tremendous agony and anguish. It won't be pleasant for either of us. But I'm prepared to go there."

"You wouldn't."

"Watch me. You see, I'm a professional. This is what I do. Now, did you kill those women?"

She glared at him, her eyes wide and unblinking as his flitted between her and the razor blade.

"Who sent you? Was it Helen Worksop? That witch. I knew she'd keep this going. Miserable bitch. She didn't care about her mother in the first place. She was only bothered about her pathetic inheritance."

"It wasn't Helen Worksop," Acid replied. "No one sent me. I heard about what you did and that they'd thrown out the case due to police error. I decided it was down to me to administer my own kind of justice." She smiled her sweetest smile. "I've been stalking you for the last week. I sat behind you in that Greek diner the other day, remember? That was where I took your door keys from out of your coat pocket and made a mould of them in dental clay before replacing them without your knowledge. Cool, huh? I mean, it's old school, but so am I."

Sanderson scowled at her. "You're crazy."

"Maybe." She raised her shoulders eagerly, but as she let them drop so did her expression, and for the first time she saw the shadow of acceptance fall across Sanderson's face.

He shook his head. "Fine. I killed those women. But so what? They were old, decrepit. Most of them didn't even know their own names."

An image flashed across Acid's memory. Her mother, Louisa, looking up at her with nothing but bewilderment on her sweet, innocent face. Regarding her daughter, Alice, as if she was a stranger. Because to her, she was. Especially at the end. And in many ways.

"They could have been one hundred years old and riddled with every disease and ailment known to man, that still doesn't give you the right to kill them."

"And it doesn't give you any right to kill me!"

Acid winked. "Touché, Doc. You have got me there. I did think I was pushing it a bit, going down the moral route." She giggled. "But, regardless, thank you for admitting what you did. Doesn't it feel a lot better?"

She breathed in pointedly and smiled as if his confession was a positive mantra for them both. She was playing a role, but she had also wanted to hear the truth. Before she killed him, she needed to hear him say those words. It proved she wasn't the merciless and unprincipled killer Spook thought her to be. She was an artisan, a highly skilled operative. And like in her days working for Caesar, she had a code. You had to have a code. Otherwise, you were just as bad as people like Sanderson.

The old man continued to glare at her, hatred twitching in the corners of his eyes. "You won't get away with this," he told her. "You pathetic, fucking c—"

"All right, Doc," she said, leaning over and holding the edge of the razor blade to his face. "I think it's time we parted company."

"I get it," he spluttered. "You're going to slit my wrists. Make it look like a suicide. Like morality suddenly overcame me and I couldn't live with what I'd done. Am I right? Well, go ahead. Do it. Get it over with."

The sneer stayed on his face but his eyes lit up. He blinked to try to hide the fact, but Acid spotted it.

"Oh, you're a wily one, aren't you?" she said. "But I like that. I do."

"What do you mean?"

"Well, that would be the obvious method, wouldn't it?"

she said. "I'd slice your wrists open, let you bleed out in the bathtub. It's what would happen in the movies, right? Only, I presume from your expression you know full well that deaths caused by a person slitting their wrists are incredibly rare. If you can get past the web of tendons and bone, you'll still struggle to sever anything important. Even if you do, it's going to take a lot longer than most people realise to die from those injuries. Plus, to make this look like a suicide, I'm going to have to untie your wrists. You're hoping when that happens you'll have enough strength to overpower me. Sure, I've got a gun, but you're willing to risk that." She flicked up her eyebrows. "Am I getting close?"

"Fuck you."

"Nice. The other option of course is that you feign death. There'll be lots of blood and it'll certainly look like you're on your way out. You're counting on me leaving you to it, and once I'm gone you'll have enough time to climb out of there and ring an ambulance. Yes?"

Doctor Sanderson bared his teeth but didn't respond.

"But alas, Doc. I know all this, too. Which is why we'll be doing things differently."

With one hand on the side of the bath to steady herself, she reached down under the water and with a flick of her wrist sliced the razor blade deep into Sanderson's inner thigh, an inch above the knee. It was so fast a movement he didn't even flinch, but a second later a pool of red coloured the bathwater.

"What the fuck?"

Acid blew out her cheeks as she got to her feet. "Yeah, sorry. That's your femoral artery I just sliced through." She placed the razor blade down on the side of the bath as the blood blossomed in the water like a red carnation. "Now, I don't wish to tell you what you already know, Doctor

Sanderson, but with your femoral artery sliced open, you're going to bleed out in... oof, under five minutes? Maybe less?"

"Please," he whined, the sinews in his neck bulging as he thrashed about. "I don't want to die. I'm sorry... I'm sorry."

"Bit late for that, Sanders." She threw him a wink. "But don't worry. As I say, it'll be quick. I imagine you're already feeling dizzy and like you're about to pass out. Nearly there. After you're dead, I'll untie you, place that razor blade in your hand and leave you in... peace. It'll be like I was never here."

"You bitch... I'll kill you..." Sanderson gasped. But his eyelids were growing heavy and all the colour had drained from his face.

"There we go," Acid whispered. "You have a good sleep. No one's going to miss you."

She watched him for another minute, until the life force left his body, and then finished reconstructing the scene, placing everything where it should be to leave the investigators in no doubt about what had happened here. There was no forced entry. The doors were locked. Tomorrow or someday soon, a friend or acquaintance (if he had any left) would realise Sanderson was missing. When the police broke down his front door, they'd find the bloated corpse of a man who'd come to terms with what he'd done. She walked into the bedroom and closed the laptop on his suicide note, smiling to herself as she surveyed her good work.

Yes. She was truly an artist.

One of the best.

Chapter Thirteen

The sun was making its presence known as Acid arrived back at the apartment in Berwick Street a few hours later. At the far end of the street, a van was parked outside Yang Sing, the driver offloading crates of fresh vegetables inside the restaurant's rear entrance. She watched him for a moment, before unlocking her front door and scaling the staircase up to the first floor. She had the time at around 5.30 a.m., and as she eased open the door to the apartment and locked it behind her, she heard Spook stirring in her bedroom at the end of the corridor. Acid froze, listening, but when no more sounds came she padded silently into her room. Once there, and with the door closed, she stripped down to her pants and pulled an old Black Sabbath t-shirt over her head. The heating timer had kicked in and the pipes were creaking as she climbed into bed and pulled the covers up around her. Tomorrow (or, rather, later today) she'd sit down with Spook and apologise for being such a rotter earlier. She may even suggest they head over to the warehouse in

Woolwich and begin work on the Zoto case. Despite all the shit Acid threw at her, Spook meant well and she deserved better. She closed her eyes. For once the bats were quiet. The job was done.

———

IT WAS past one in the afternoon when she finally surfaced. The sleep, although not extensive, had done wonders for her mood. As had disposing of that evil prick, Sanderson. She stretched and got dressed before brushing her hair and heading down the corridor towards the kitchen.

Spook was sitting at the table, nursing a cup of coffee as she entered. "You seem chipper," she said. "Sleep well?"

Acid glanced at her on her way over to the sink, assessing her face for tells. She appeared sincere enough.

"Yes, actually. I slept like a baby." Using an upturned mug from the drainer, she filled it with steaming coffee from the machine and carried it to the table, sitting down opposite Spook. "Everything okay with you?"

Her question was met with a shrug. "I guess."

Now who was the petulant teen?

"I was thinking we could go over to Afrim Zoto's warehouse today. See what we can find out."

Spook looked up. "Really?"

"Well… yes." She smiled. "You were right. This is still an important case, no matter what I think of the outcome. Fiona Zoto deserves to know what happened to her father. And we deserve to get paid handsomely to find that out for her."

Spook opened her mouth in theatrical shock. "Acid!"

"Oh, come on. I said I wanted to help, but don't expect me to become some pious sodding *angel*."

Spook sniffed, but couldn't hide her smile. "It's a good name."

"It's a terrible name. Totally bloody awful." She sipped at her coffee. It was strong and bitter and too hot to enjoy. Was there a metaphor in there somewhere? "But if it makes you happy…"

"You really are an infuriating person," Spook said, tilting her head back and peering down her nose. "Just when I think I'm finally getting a handle on you and how you operate, you flip those notions on their head."

"How do you mean?"

Spook winced, as if she was already walking down a street she didn't want to be on. "When I first met you, I thought you were terrifying and incredible in equal measures. You were like no one I'd ever met. You scared the living shit out of me, but I was prepared to follow you into hell if you'd have asked me to."

"I am rather incredible."

Spook waved her sarcasm away. "Then, once I got to know you better, I saw you were hurting, too. You weren't the impenetrable badass I thought you were. I mean, you were – you are – but now I know there's a human side to you."

Acid sat back and crossed her arms. "Is there a point to this bizarre character assassination? Or is this some weird nerd version of a roast?"

"It's not a character assassination – although, interesting choice of words. I'm simply trying to explain that I thought I knew you as well as anyone could. Yet lately I feel like you're a different person. Or rather, two different people." Acid opened her mouth to respond but Spook held her hand up. "I know what you're going to say but I don't mean Alice versus Acid. And I know you struggle with your condition, the extreme moods, the bats… but it's not even that. It's like one day you can be a pain in the ass – and I mean a real grade-A pain in the ass, to the point where I'm considering if we can even work together, never mind remain friends – and then the next day you're like this. Like today. Bright-eyed and dependable, eager to try new things and meet me halfway on matters. I don't get it. It never seemed so black and white before."

Acid didn't respond. But she knew the reason. Rather than fight against her base desires, like she had been doing for the past three years, she'd succumbed to them.

And wouldn't you know, it felt bloody great.

Ever since leaving Annihilation Pest Control, she had struggled with who she was in this new, civilised world and had mistakenly believed she needed to change if she was to get by. But that was never going to end well. Alice Vandella was transformed at the exact moment she smashed that empty wine bottle off the kitchen counter and stabbed it into Oscar Duke's neck. Thereafter, there was no changing who that person had become. She was strong and sassy, driven by chaos and rage. Despite being super intelligent and presenting herself as someone refined and fun to be around, there were demons inside of her that would not lay down and die. And so, when she'd first felt the pull of the night and the call of the blade soon after returning from Montana, she hadn't fought against them. She was done trying to defeat the demons. You didn't ever defeat them. You learnt to work with them. That's how you won. That's how you survived.

So, she'd started small. Whilst walking home one night, she'd stumbled upon a guy beating on a young girl in an alleyway. The lust in his eyes and the way he gripped at the girl's throat told Acid everything she needed to know about the useless waste of flesh. She made quick work of him. And as he bled out at her feet and the young girl ran for safety, she'd realised not only how calm and settled she'd felt, but how jubilant as well. Because this was who she was. Who she'd always been. She was an assassin. A killer. And yes, that didn't sit too well with her new role as a civilian, but it was important to be true to who she was, warts (and demons and guns and syringes) and all. She was certain the many self-help books Spook pored over would agree with her on that point. Maybe not the killing people part.

Since then, she'd begun to seek out new prey, spending hours on the mainstream web and its darker, more sinister equivalent. She read leaked police reports and researched cases, finding a long list of people who deserved to die for what they'd done. Simon James was first, a known killer of homosexuals who the police were unable to gather enough evidence to arrest. Then followed Maxim Volkov, a Russian agent with a potbelly and pronounced overbite who had poisoned a family of four in Bethnal Green. And Edward Singer, a paedophile child protection officer with alopecia who'd been abusing kids in his charge. With each hit, each skilful eradication, she felt herself growing in strength, both mentally and physically. After a while she began to have withdrawal symptoms between hits, which had never happened to her before. It was in these times that she found herself spiralling and unbalanced. It seemed the more blood the bats got, the more they wanted.

"Acid?"

She snapped out of her thoughts to see Spook leaning over the table. She shook her head. "Did you say something?"

The kid sat back in her chair and her wrinkled nose pushed the large frames of her glasses up her face. "Yes! I like it when you're focused and easy to talk to. Try to stay more like that."

Acid grinned. "I'll do my best. Now then, the Zoto case. Are we going exploring or what?"

Spook nodded. "I was thinking we could swing by the office in Whitechapel, try to find the keys to the warehouse and have a look around."

Acid shrugged. "Yeah, we could. But where's the fun in that?"

"How do you mean?"

She pushed her chair back, the legs screeching noisily across the tiled floor. "I mean, we don't need keys to get into the warehouse. I can get us in there, no problem. Plus, we don't want to show our hands too early. There could be people watching Zoto's office to see if he comes back. I want to know more about him and those in his vicinity before we alert anyone that we're looking for him."

Spook got to her feet. "Do you think he's dead?"

"I think it's likely. But we don't know, do we? And ever since we left Fiona's place, something hasn't felt right to me. I want us to keep our heads down for as long as possible."

Spook blew out a sigh, the realisation of what they might have got themselves into dawning on her finally. But that was a good thing. Acid needed her to take this seriously.

"Breaking and entering, Acid. That's bad. What if we get caught? We need to be careful."

"You know me, Spook," she said, walking over to the door and grabbing her leather jacket hanging off the back of it. "I'm always careful."

Chapter Fourteen

The conversation between the two women was good-humoured and easy as their cab drove along the side of the Thames before entering the Blackwall Tunnel, towards Greenwich. With the driver listening up front, they couldn't discuss the case, so they had some fun pretending to him they were tourists, 'oohing' and 'ahhing' at every bridge they went past, each time asking the poor man, "So is *that* one London Bridge?"

It was a rare moment of carefreeness that wasn't lost on Acid. It felt good to be out with Spook. Hell, she even felt optimistic about life, a rare emotion for her. The fact her bloodlust had been quenched recently helped. The fact she already had her next hit in sight helped even more.

The next one on her list was a man called Lucas Jelani, a small-time drug dealer who had recently made advances into the big league by killing a man known as Si Shinobi, his main rival and top boy of the Bringley Estate in Lambeth. Normally Acid would never have got involved in gang warfare, but the fact that this happened at a family meal and Jelani had murdered Shinobi's girlfriend and his three children put him top of her list. Besides, tracking down and eradicating a South London drug dealer was a departure for her. It could be fun.

The cab took a left onto Shooters Hill Road. Acid grabbed the handle above the door and shifted herself upright to watch out the window as they passed alongside the rows of suburban houses.

"I used to come to athletics club around here, you know," she said, not turning around.

"Yeah?" Spook replied.

"Thamesmead Athletic Club. I was good as well. Could have been a contender. It used to take me an hour to get to training each day after school. Two buses on my own. I was only a kid. All the way from Dagenham."

"That's where you're from, right?"

"Sure is. Alice Vandella was a Dagenham girl. Once." She scowled out the window. She had no idea why she was saying this. They never talked about her past. Or rather, she didn't. Spook, being Spook, had attempted to bring up the subject on many occasions, only to be shot down.

"Were you happy as a child?" Spook asked.

Acid's scowl deepened as she turned to give her a stern look. "Oh absolutely, sweetie. Until, you know, all the fucking shit happened."

Spook glanced at the driver with a worried expression. "Sorry. Dumb question. But I meant before... when you were younger. What was that like?"

Acid turned back to the window with a sigh. The last thing she wanted was an impromptu talk therapy session, yet she had brought this on herself. "I was happy," she said. "My mum and I were a good team. It was everyone else that ruined it."

"Yeah. I get that," Spook said. "Maybe we can explore that further in our next session."

Acid sniffed. "Yes. Maybe."

She shut up as the car went over a roundabout and she saw the waterfront for the first time since crossing over to South London. Another minute and they pulled onto a long road called Artillery Avenue.

"This looks to be the place," she said, eyeing the collection of immense steel-roofed warehouses over to her left. There were at least twenty, built in a criss-cross formation along the side of the Thames. The reason for this, she surmised, was so no warehouse had a direct line of sight into the entrance of another, thus no one could watch your comings or goings. These developers thought ahead. They knew their customer base.

The cab came to a stop and Spook paid the driver, apologising at the same time for their silliness. Trying not to let this bother her, Acid climbed out and breathed in the fresh air. She could taste salt from the river. As the cab drove away, they walked in silence towards the first set of warehouses, stopping where the tarmac turned to gravel and sand.

"Which one is it?" Acid asked, looking around and scrunching her face into the midday sun. It wasn't hot, the breeze coming in from the Thames saw to that, but it was bright.

Spook, who had called Fiona from the cab to confirm, counted along the row of buildings. "That one," she said, pointing. "Warehouse number twelve."

"Warehouse twelve," Acid said. "Sounds ominous, doesn't it?"

"Does it?"

She looked at Spook with a manic grin. "I don't know.

Just trying to inject a little excitement into proceedings. Come along."

Gulls shrieked overhead, unwittingly harmonising with the bat-chorus in Acid's head as she strode along the row of identical units until she reached the right one. With Spook following behind, she rounded the building and was met with two large double doors. A thick chain had been woven through the handles, fastened with a sturdy padlock.

"Geez," Spook exclaimed as she caught up. "You going to be able to get through that?"

Acid moved up to the doors and shook the chains, examining the padlock. It was rusted but shouldn't pose too much of a problem. Her old lock-picking kit was in the pocket of her jacket and she'd had plenty of practice of late. She got up on her toes and peered through the window panel at the top of the door. The glass was translucent with dirt and mildew, but she could make out a small reception area and a door through to what she presumed to be the main warehouse space.

Spook shuffled about behind her. "See anything?"

"Not really. We need to get inside." She lowered herself and turned around. "Ah, shit."

A man was walking towards them, and as she caught his gaze he pointed a stubby finger at her. He was huge in both height and width, with a thick black beard that made his gnashing teeth seem ridiculously white in comparison. Acid's initial thought was that he was a security guard – but not one affiliated with any official organisation. He was wearing khaki combat trousers and a thick black jumper that hung down over his immense leathery hands. In one of them he clutched a large monkey wrench and in the other a mobile phone.

"Who the fuck are you?" he yelled as he got nearer, his

voice more high-pitched than his size would have suggested. He stopped a few feet away from them. "This is private property. You can't be sniffing around here."

"We're looking for—" Spook started, but stopped as Acid hushed her down.

"We have a right to be here," she told the man. "Who do you work for?"

The man leered, exposing a row of mangled teeth. "Nah, missy. You don't get to ask the questions. Now, let me ask again. What purpose have you to be around here?"

Acid's gaze fell on the monkey wrench gripped in his hand. The oil smears on the backs of his fingers suggested this was a tool he'd been using prior to being disturbed, rather than a weapon. But it so easily could be both. She stepped forward, holding both hands out to him.

"Listen, mate. We don't want any trouble. We work for the owner of this warehouse."

The man's hands tightened around the wrench. "You need to leave. I'm not going to say it again."

"We will," Acid replied. "As soon as you give us some information. We're looking for Afrim Zoto. This is his unit. Do you know him?"

The man ground his teeth together with a growl. "Right, that's it. I'm going to ring my boss. He can come and sort this out. But, believe me, he isn't going to like being dragged down here to deal with you. And you certainly aren't, either."

He raised the mobile phone and began jabbing at the screen with an oily thumb. Acid glanced over her shoulder at Spook to see her standing stiff as a board with her hands by her sides. No help at all. She turned back. Whoever this meathead's boss was, he sounded nasty. Could he be the mystery man Fiona had alluded to? If he turned up now, the best result they could hope for was that their cover was blown. But unarmed and outnumbered (there'd be at least two of them and she could hardly count on Spook for backup), it could be a lot worse.

Decision made, Acid stepped over to the man as he waited for his boss to pick up.

"Look, mate," she said. "I'm very sorry we startled you. But I think there's been a misunderstanding. That's all."

"Too fucking late. We'll see how sorry you are."

He was staring off at something over to his left, focused more on the call than on her. Good enough. Pushing off from a standing start, she launched herself at the arm holding the wrench. Grabbing his wrist with two hands, she ran past him and twisted his arm around, digging her thumbnails into the pressure points on his wrists as she did. He cried out and let go of the wrench. His other arm, still holding the phone, swung back wildly, trying to swat her away. Keeping a tight hold on his wrist, she shoved his arm up into the middle of his back. At the same time, she stamped down on the back of his ankle with the heel of her boot. His cries grew louder and he stumbled over on that side, the phone toppling from his hand.

He was a big man but top heavy, and another hard stamp to the back of the knee sent him off balance. As he stumbled, Acid let go of his arm and grabbed onto his shoulders. Clambering up his back, she wrapped her legs around his thick neck. When he fell forward, she tightened her thighs around his head, gripping onto his ears as he hit the ground. She could feel the consciousness leaving him, but he continued to thrash around with all his might, leaning back and slamming her into the dirt in an attempt to shake her off. Sharp shards of gravel dug into the skin on her shoulders and upper arms but she held on, squeezing at his carotid artery with her powerful thighs.

"Hey! Spook," she shouted, gesturing at the dropped phone. "Grab it!"

Spook regarded her with wide, terrified eyes before running over and scooping up the dropped phone like it was a venomous snake.

"Kill the call and toss it," Acid snarled through gritted teeth, tightening her stomach muscles as the man hurled back enormous fists, pummelling at her torso. She sensed the fight was leaving him. Shifting her position to get a better grip on his neck, she continued to squeeze her thighs together while Spook ran over to the side of the river and tossed the phone. As it disappeared into the murky deep, Acid gave one last squeeze and felt the man go limp.

Gasping for air, she clambered off him and got to her feet.

"Are you okay?" Spook asked, running over.

Acid brushed herself down. "Just about. But I think it's best we get out of here before he comes round. We need to have a rethink. Maybe come back under the cover of nightfall."

"Or we could get the keys from Zoto's office and do it the proper way?"

Acid sniffed back and spat onto the ground. The phlegm had blood in it. Reaching up, she found her nose was bleeding. The big bastard must have caught her without her realising. Adrenaline mixed in with manic bat energy – it was one hell of a combination.

She patted Spook on the shoulder and set off walking. "Either way, let's get out of here. We can get a cab from—" She stopped as Spook screamed out.

"Acid! Help!"

The man had regained consciousness and had grabbed at Spook, clamping one of his large hands firmly around her ankle. With the bats now in control, she ran over and kicked the guy in the face before stamping down on his forearm.

"You fucking bitch!" he yelled, releasing Spook's ankle.

Acid grabbed her hand and pulled her towards her. "Come on, let's get out of here."

"I'm going to kill you. Both of you," the man growled, rolling over onto his front.

"Run, Spook," Acid yelled. "Fast as you can."

They sped across the gravel and didn't look back until they'd reached the main road. Once out of range of the warehouses, Acid slowed her pace a touch and stole a furtive glance behind her. Shit. The big man was giving chase. But as she upped her pace again, it became clear his sizeable bulk and the injuries meant there was no way he was going to catch them. His face was a bloody mess. They continued running down the side of a park before veering right onto a wide road with shops along one side.

"There you go, Spook," she called back. "This is what you wanted, wasn't it? Me and you working together, getting into scrapes. Just like old times."

"Go to hell," Spook replied, gasping for air. "That was scary."

"Ah, come on. With everything we've been through these last few years, that was nothing."

"Yeah, well, next time I say I want to work more closely on a case together, will you please slap me?"

"With pleasure." Acid smiled to herself.

Regardless of the fact they'd just wasted a morning and were no further forward in their investigation, she felt on top of the world. Finding Afrim Zoto might be a more difficult and dangerous task than she'd first realised, but that was a good thing. It was exciting. For the first time since she'd left Caesar's charge, she felt alive and complete and motivated to succeed. She wondered now whether it was simply the boredom of everyday life that had unsettled her these past years. She was different to normal people, had different needs, different thresholds of tedium and enjoyment. But now there was too much going on in her life for her to be bored and plenty to satisfy her desires, both physically and mentally.

Yes. This could be fun.

A lot of fun.

Dead or alive, she was going to find Fiona's father. Of that she was certain. Because one thing that was always true about the old Acid Vanilla – she always got her mark. And whether she called herself Alice or Acid, it didn't matter. That old persona was back. And she was here to stay.

Chapter Fifteen

In keeping with her renewed sense of focus and vigour, Acid set her alarm for 5 a.m. and was up and dressed and in her running gear ten minutes later. Heading into the kitchen, she filled a pint glass full of fresh water from the tap ready for her return (water was more easily absorbed by the body at room temperature) and padded as silently as she could towards the front door of the apartment.

"Acid, is that you?"

She was turning the door handle but stopped. Spook wandered out of her room, rubbing at her eyes.

"I'm going for a run," she whispered. "Go back to bed."

"What time is it?" Without her glasses, Spook squinted at her. "Are you seriously going for a run?"

"Yes. I am. I've been running for the last month. You know that."

Spook shrugged. She was still half asleep. "Yeah, I know. But I thought... Well, I wondered if you... Nah. Doesn't matter. Forget it."

She swayed in the doorway like a character from a zombie film who wasn't going to make it to the end credits.

"Go back to bed," Acid told her. "It's early. I'll be back in a few hours and we can have breakfast. We'll discuss what our next move is in terms of the Zoto case."

Spook yawned. "Yeah. Cool."

She didn't make any movement back to her room, but Acid wasn't waiting any longer.

"I'll see you soon." She opened the door and let it swing shut behind her before securing both locks. Then she walked along the short landing and down the stairwell to the front door of the building.

Outside, the streets of Soho were dark, but you could tell it was morning rather than night. There was a sense of expectation in the air, brought in by a cool breeze of rejuvenation. Acid stuck her earbuds in and selected her usual playlist on her phone. As the '1, 2, 3, 4, 5, 6...' of *Roadrunner* by Jonathan Richman echoed in her ears, she broke into a jog. It was an apt song. Lots of things seemed apt lately. She put that down to her positive outlook and lack of uncertainty. She was back, she was growing fitter and stronger by the day, and she'd made peace with the person she truly was. It was a good feeling.

Heading out onto Great Marlborough Street, she quickened her pace and leaned into her run as the long road turned into Grosvenor Street. She took a right onto Park Lane, the purple section of Monopoly, and what was once classically the most affluent area of London. There were many contenders for that title these days, but Acid had a soft spot for the Hyde Park area and Mayfair. It was where she'd first come with Caesar in the early days, where he'd wined and dined her, convincing her to give up her old life and join his organisation. She'd come a long way from being that young girl from Dagenham, but the more she relaxed into who she was, the more she found there was room for all sides of her personality. By allowing her direst cruelty and craving for bloody retribution to flourish, she'd also opened the door to the softer elements of herself, too. But wasn't that true of anything? There was no good without evil. No life without death. You had to allow both the yin and yang to breathe.

She scoffed to herself as she crossed over the road and entered Hyde Park via Speakers' Corner.

Yin and yang? Jesus.

She sounded like Spook.

Placing her focus only on the path in front of her, she ran on. By now, the inky sky had turned a lighter grey and a low mist hung over the park. It was eerie, but she liked eerie. She was a dark soul with a passion for life and a goal to eradicate all those who brought evil into this world. It felt good. If only she could monetise her exploits, then…

No.

She shook her head to remove the thoughts now entangling themselves around the more chaotic ideas she knew were lurking on the edge of her awareness.

Not for now.

Back to the moment, sweetie.

She opened her eyes wide and shifted into peripheral vision, taking in the vast expanse of green in front of her. In the morning light it looked washed out, like an Impressionist painting of a park rather than a real one. There were a few other people here, other runners mainly. She ran past an old couple power walking in matching Day-Glo outfits; a woman about her age running in the opposite direction; a younger woman wearing a baseball cap and pushing an old-fashioned pram; a middle-aged man walking his dog. She nodded pleasantly to each of them as she made eye contact, receiving the same back and feeling pleased with herself each time that she could present as a regular member of society when she wanted. There were no psychopaths here.

She sped on, pushing herself to her limit as she always did, relishing the stitch in her side and the fatigue in her limbs. Her lungs were tight and she could feel the machine-gun pulse in her carotid artery. She hadn't felt so alive in years. Later today she and Spook would get their teeth into the Zoto case and then later still – tonight, maybe tomorrow – she'd pay Lucas Jelani a visit. Feed the bats and her demons in the best possible way.

She ran past the Reformer's Tree memorial and headed down the wide path that would come out by The Serpentine. She'd do a lap of the lake up to the Peter Pan statue before heading for the north gates and back out onto Bayswater Road and on to Soho. It was her usual route and would take just under two hours if she kept her pace up. But as she ran alongside the parade ground, she saw someone in the middle of the path up ahead.

"Bloody hell."

It was the woman with the pram. She was leaning over the handle looking into the carriage with a heavy expression creasing her face. Acid slowed to a jog as she got closer. She hadn't thought anything of it earlier, but faced with the scene in front of her, she found it odd someone was out with their baby at this hour. Acid knew enough (as much as she ever wanted to) about babies to know that sometimes – often – they were grouchy little bastards and one had to walk them around to try to get them to fall asleep. But, still, it wasn't something she normally encountered on her morning runs. The woman was in the middle of an enormous park, a long way from any residential area. And then there was that weird Victorian-era pram, black and gothic in style, with an imposing concertina hood that hung over the carriage like a leathery bat wing.

Acid slowed to a walk, pulling back long breaths of cool air as she neared. "Is everything all right?" she called out.

The mother – or nanny, it wasn't clear – didn't respond. Along with the baseball cap, she was wearing black leggings similar to those Acid was wearing and a dark grey fleece top zipped to her chin. Up close, she appeared to be of Asian origin. Not Chinese or Japanese, but one of the smaller nations. Cambodia, perhaps, or the Philippines. Acid called out to her again, but she didn't look up or even react to her presence. Instead, she continued leaning into the carriage as if attending to whoever was inside. But there was no sound of crying, no baby noises.

The bats babbled feverishly as a prickly sensation blossomed in Acid's chest. Something was wrong. She was a few strides away from the pram when the woman snapped her head up to meet her gaze. Acid froze. She recognised the expression on the woman's face. Not her features, she'd never met her before, but the way she held her jaw rigid with concentration and the readiness in her eyes. The cruel twist to her mouth.

Shit.

Time slowed as the woman pulled two short tanto blades from out of the pram and stepped into a fighting stance. Acid glanced around her, scoping the area for a weapon or a way out. She could run in a variety of different directions, but she had no idea how fast this woman was and she didn't fancy putting her back to her. The woman swiped the blades through the air, making a swishing noise as a sly grin spread across her face. It told Acid she was a professional.

It also told her she was going to enjoy this.

The woman lunged forward and Acid ran at her, side-stepping at the last minute and twisting her torso away as a blade slashed through the air centimetres from her face. Acid grabbed the pram by the handle and positioned it between her and her attacker, shoving the metal frame at her as she came again. The woman let out a strange whooping sound as the twin blades slashed the air in front of Acid's face. Acid could now see the pram was empty. There never had been a baby, but there were no other weapons either. She was armed with a bloody pram. Against two Japanese fighting daggers. She'd been in situations where the odds were worse, but not for many years.

"Who sent you?" Acid said, as the woman circled her, stalking her, waiting for an opening. This wasn't an opportunistic attack or a mugging. This person was here to kill her. But why? As the rest of the world disappeared, she considered the woman's harsh features. She had thick, straight eyebrows that almost met over a slender nose. Her small mouth was pursed up tight, like a cat's anus.

Was she someone from her past?

An old adversary?

She didn't think so. But who was she? Why had she come for her?

Keeping the robust frame of the pram in front of her, Acid was able to dodge another attack, but there was only so long the already mangled pram would hold. She couldn't keep this crazy harpy at bay forever.

She raised her head and adjusted her grip on the pram handle. There was no point asking her attacker too many questions. It didn't work that way. Day one, lesson one, of any assassin training camp worth its salt: never reveal your identity or who was paying for the hit.

"I will kill you," the woman snarled in a deep, rasping voice. "I will kill you today."

She slashed at the hood of the pram but the blade got caught up in the thick rainproof material. Still gripping the pram, Acid stepped around the side of it and swung out with a classic roundhouse kick that connected with the woman's upper back. The blow knocked her forward but also loosened the blade from the cloth, which she was able to pull free. Seizing the momentum, Acid drove the pram forward, the hood and front part of the carriage crumpling as she shoved the mangled construction of steel into the assassin's centre mass. The sharp blades swung wildly in the air but couldn't find Acid as she drove the woman backwards. She was losing the battle and it only made her scream louder and spit out aggressive-sounding words in her native tongue. With the woman's lower body exposed, Acid ducked under the carriage and smashed her foot into her knee with everything she had. She didn't feel the joint break, but the woman screamed as if it had and the shock sent her stumbling to one side. At the same time, she lowered the blades to find balance.

That was Acid's opening.

She let go of the pram and smashed her fist into her attacker's jaw. As the woman's head snapped back she slashed out and the sharp blade sliced Acid's side.

"Fuck!" she screamed and leapt back, hand going to her side. She felt the flap of material and the wetness of blood as it flowed from the wound.

Shit.

Not good.

Holding her side with one hand, she raised her other, fist clenched and ready. The assassin had regained her composure, too. There were a few metres between them and a few metres more between Acid and the pram. It was no use to her now. The woman leered at her, teeth pink from the blow Acid had administered. Her baseball cap had fallen off at some point, but other than that she was unruffled. She still looked to be enjoying herself, the rotten cow.

Acid swallowed, consciously transferring her attention onto her adversary rather than the pain searing through her abdomen.

"I'm going to kill you," the woman repeated.

"Yes. You said that already," Acid spat. "But you know what? That goes without saying when you pull tanto blades on a person. I'd work on your banter if I were you."

The assassin screwed up her face. She was vibrating with intensity, readying herself for another attack. Acid remained still as the bat screeches grew louder. The pressure in her head was extreme. Her nerve endings rippled with heat energy. She felt strong and indestructible and like she was having an out-of-body experience all at once.

"Come on," she said, beckoning the assassin forward. "Let's dance."

The woman bared her teeth and with a grunt lurched forward, swiping the blades in a criss-cross fashion. At the same time, Acid leapt out of range and pushed off on her right foot to swerve her advance.

Everything was moving in slow motion.

She saw the woman stumble forward, saw her own foot kicking out at her. There was resistance, something hard but organic beneath her sole. She pushed against it, shoving the brutal bitch away and moving behind her. Capitalizing on her position, she grabbed the woman's shoulders and leaned into her, running her forward. As they approached the pram, she pushed off at the last second, jumping backwards as the assassin slammed into the mangled construction and tumbled over the top of it. The woman struggled to get up but was tangled up in the bent metal frame. Her arm got caught on a jagged part of the chassis, and in trying to free herself one of the tanto blades fell from her grip. As it clattered to the ground, Acid rushed over and scooped it up, the adrenaline in her system fuelling a fresh surge of indignation.

The bats screamed in her ears.

Finish her.

Acid swung the blade handle into her grip so the blade faced down and stabbed it into the woman's abdomen. As the sharp steel plunged deep into her belly, a terrible banshee wail burst from her throat and echoed through the early morning air, sending a grounded flock of starlings rising into the sky.

Acid leapt back to evade a counterattack as the woman lashed out with her remaining weapon.

"Fuck you," she spat, blood bubbling from her mouth and her hand wrapping around the blade handle protruding from her stomach.

Acid stood a few feet away, clutching at her side. The threat had been neutralised and, with that, her adrenal response began to subside. But now came the pain. She lifted her hand to examine her wound for the first time. The gash was about three inches long and about an inch deep. After a quick assessment, she surmised the blade had only severed muscle and tissue rather than any arteries or major organs, but she was losing blood and needed attention.

As her awareness spread to her surroundings, she noticed a person at the far end of the path. They were heading this way at speed and probably going to make this even messier than it already was for her. She glanced back at her attacker writhing on the ground in a pool of blood.

Another minute, two at most, and there'd be no more pain for her.

It was time to get out of here.

Still clutching her side, Acid turned and made a beeline across the grass. The nearest gate was a few hundred metres in front of her and from there she could get onto Grosvenor Street within a few minutes and be home in another thirty. As she got to the road, she pulled out her phone and scrolled through the names until she found the one she needed. This was the first time she'd had to call the number since she'd put it into her phone, but she was glad she had it.

The call rang and rang. Panic formed behind her eyes. Then, as she was about to give up...

"Song Shi, Chinese Medicine."

"Doctor Shi," she gasped. "It's Acid Vanilla. A friend of The Dullahan. We met a couple of years back when you operated on my friend after she was shot."

The line went silent for a moment, giving Acid time to recall the night Spook almost died. All because of her. She really ought to give the kid a break. Up ahead, she saw a man walking his dog and shoved her blood-soaked hand into the pocket of her jacket.

"What do you want, Vanilla?" Song Shi asked.

She passed the man and smiled her sweetest smile, but rather than greet her back, he frowned and stepped into the road to get away from her. As she hurried away, she leaned down to peer into the wing mirror of a parked car. Tiny spatter marks of blood dotted her cheeks and forehead. Not hers, but freaky all the same. She looked back to see the man scurrying down the street, dragging his small dog along after him.

"I need your help," she told Song Shi, setting off at pace

and breathing heavily through a wave of dizziness. "I have a deep wound in my side below my ribcage. I need you to stitch me up and I need blood. Type-A rhesus negative."

"That's going to cost you," came the stoical reply.

"Fine." She gritted her teeth as a gust of cool air found its way into the wound. It felt like another blade slicing at her guts. "My apartment is on Berwick Street, just off Wardour Street. It's a black door, number seventeen."

"Ah. Near to my practice." He cleared his throat. "Give me thirty minutes. Can you hang on until then?"

"I think so."

"Well, you'll have to, won't you?" The line distorted as the doctor burst out laughing. "I'll see you soon, Acid Vanilla. I'll bring two bags of blood, just in case."

He hung up and she slipped the phone back into her pocket before placing her hand over the wound. It hurt like hell, but she pinched the skin together as best she could to stem the bleeding.

Thirty minutes. It was enough time. That was, if she could make it back to her place before passing out. A flurry of questions invaded her thoughts as she pressed on.

Who was that woman?

And, more importantly, who'd sent her?

There was no doubt it was a professional hit. Yet as far as Acid knew, all her enemies were dead. The only explanation she could come up with was that the open contract Caesar had placed on her a year earlier was still online, on one of the many dark web forums used by the industry. It was possible the woman mistakenly thought the job posting was still relevant.

Or was this something to do with the Zoto case? Were they in deeper than she'd realised?

She hadn't spotted any cameras at the warehouse, but

that didn't mean there wasn't hidden surveillance. Someone could have followed them home. If Zoto had been hit – which was likely if he'd annoyed heavy people in the London underworld – then the mystery man Fiona mentioned would be tying up loose ends. Had he sent this trained killer to dispose of her before she delved into places she wasn't wanted? And if that was the case…

Bloody hell.

Her skin went cold at the realisation that Spook could be fighting off her own attacker right now. Either that or she was already dead.

Acid's hand went instinctively for her phone, but she decided against calling. Either Spook was safe and asleep or in dire trouble, and a phone call would help neither of those things. She shook the troubling thoughts away. She felt nauseous and weak and it was vital she put her energy into getting home.

Thirty minutes. It was enough time.

But it was going to be close.

Chapter Sixteen

Spook was fighting off a particularly stubborn early morning confusion and a bad case of bedhead when Acid burst through the front door of their apartment and fell into a heap in the hallway.

"What the hell?"

While her initial response was shock and horror, as she helped Acid to her feet and through into her bedroom and realised she wasn't going to die, her mood turned quickly to dismay, bordering on annoyance. For weeks she had been worried her errant friend was involved in something dangerous and this confirmed it.

As she struggled to get Acid out of her blood-stained clothes, she asked her the obvious questions – *Who did this? And why?* – but all enquiries were met with unhelpful grunts and dismissive shrugs.

"Jesus!" Spook exclaimed as Acid stood in front of her in sports bra and underpants. The way the exposed torn muscle pulsed with every sharp breath made her want to look away. "I'm not going to be able to—"

"Don't worry," Acid said, gritting her teeth as she flung her sheets onto the floor and lowered herself onto the edge of her bed. "Doctor Shi is on his way. He should be here anytime now."

"Doctor Shi?" Spook repeated. "We can't phone an ambulance?"

Acid tsked loudly. "We never use emergency services, Spook. You know that. Too many questions."

"What happened?"

"It was a hit," Acid said, her tone devoid of the usual flippancy. "A woman. I killed her. But it's certainly a worry."

There it was. That British way of ironically low-balling important situations that Spook had never got her head around.

"Yes, I'd say it is a worry," she snapped. "A big fucking worry."

Acid sighed and looked her in the eyes.

"Why do you think she attacked you?" Spook tried again. "Who sent her?"

"I didn't get a chance to ask," came the pithy reply, followed by a grimace of pain that knocked the sarcasm out of her. "But you're right. We should be concerned. I've got a few ideas about what happened, but nothing concrete."

"And…?"

"Afrim Zoto. It could be we've disturbed a hornets' nest taking on this case. Either someone doesn't want us asking questions about where he is, or he doesn't want to be found."

"You think Zoto could have sent someone to kill you? I thought you said he was probably dead."

"He probably is. My best theory is this is someone tying up loose ends. But I've no proof of that. Not yet."

Spook sat down on the bed before her legs gave way.

"I'm in danger, too," she whispered. "They could come for me next."

"Maybe."

"We need to drop the case," she said. "This is too much of a coincidence. We need to tell Fiona we're sorry but it's too dangerous."

"Don't be ridiculous," Acid said. "The whole point of what we do is that it's dangerous. That's why people hire us. Besides, we can't drop it, we need the money. Now more than ever if—" She shut up at the sound of footsteps ascending the stairs.

Spook shot Acid a look, searching her face for signs of panic. As her gaze fell to her bleeding side, a fresh surge of dread caught in the back of her throat. If this was another assassin come to kill them, she'd have to fight them off on her own. She couldn't do that. She wasn't strong or wily or trained in the art of killing. Sure, online she was unstoppable – put her behind a laptop and she could break through any firewall, crack any cyber encryption – but in the real world, not so much.

She yelped as a man peered around the bedroom doorway and lifted a leather bag in the air.

"Ah shit," she gasped. "Doctor Shi." With his Beatles haircut and surly expression, she recognised him straight away as the doctor who'd saved her life.

"I let myself in," he said, flashing what she assumed to be a skeleton key. "I didn't know who was here."

He pocketed the key and walked over to Acid.

"Here, Doc," she said, leaning back to give him a better view of the wound. "I'm going to need a decent patch-up."

Shi frowned, the rest of his face not giving anything away as he examined her injury. He tutted and shook his head before straightening up and turning to Spook. "Get me some towels, a bowl of boiling water and a chair." When Spook stared back at him, he stepped forward, shoving his round face too close to hers. "Now, please. I need to go to work. She has lost a lot of blood."

"Right. Yes." Spook hurried into the kitchen and filled the kettle from the sink. Switching it on to boil, she gathered up a stack of towels from out of the airing cupboard in the bathroom and a large porcelain mixing bowl that had been in the apartment when they moved in but never used by either of them. She filled this with the boiled water and, placing the towels on the worktop and the bowl on top, picked up the whole stack and carried it through to Acid's room.

Doctor Shi already had Acid hooked up to a bag of blood, which was hanging from a small metal tripod set up on her nightstand.

"Is she going to be okay?" Spook asked, placing the towels and bowl of water on the end of the bed.

Shi looked at her without expression; his dark eyes ran up and down her slight frame. She was suddenly very conscious of the fact she was wearing nothing but an over-sized Mandalorian t-shirt. "She should be fine," Shi replied. "But I need time and space to work. And peace. You leave us alone. I'll tell you when I am finished."

Spook looked at Acid for reassurance. She looked pale and tired, and when she nodded her response it seemed to hurt.

"Did you need anything before I—?"

Shi spun around to glare at her. "Get out!"

"Okay, fine. I'm going."

She closed the door behind her and went to her bedroom. The clock on her phone told her it was still early, a few minutes after seven. She climbed into bed. The recess from which she'd wrenched herself at the sound of Acid's blundering entry ten minutes earlier was still warm. She removed her glasses and placed them on her nightstand. Her heart was racing too fast to sleep, but at least here, cocooned in her bed, she could kid herself that she was safe. But for how long she could keep up the charade, she didn't know. Whoever wanted Acid dead wouldn't stop just because she'd foiled this first attack. There'd be more of them.

She grabbed the covers and pulled them over her head, shutting out the reality of her plight for a while longer. Despite all the self-help books she'd read and all the self-reflection she'd engaged in these last few years, Spook still had a fine line in disassociation. It wasn't a helpful move, she knew that. But for now it was the only move she had.

Chapter Seventeen

"Hey! We are done."

As the words echoed down the corridor, Spook lowered the covers from over her head. A few seconds earlier she'd been daydreaming that she was fighting off a string of assassins, cutting them down with her elite fighting skills. And a lightsabre.

"Can I come to see her?" she called out.

When no response came, she sat up and swung her legs onto the floor. The bedroom was cold, but the first rays of the sun were filtering through the blinds. She picked up her glasses and phone from the nightstand and squinted at the phone screen. 8.25 a.m. She'd been lying in bed for over an hour. It felt like minutes. She slipped on her glasses and walked over to her desk, where she grabbed a pair of jogging bottoms from the back of the chair, almost tumbling over as she dressed en route to the door.

Leaving her room and walking along the short hallway, she heard Acid's voice. It sounded even huskier than usual, like she was dehydrated. But she was alive and she was awake and that was what mattered. A heavy burden Spook hadn't even realised was weighing her down, lifted from her shoulders as she put her head around Acid's bedroom door.

Acid saw her and smiled. "Hey, partner. How are you doing?"

"It's me who should be asking you that question." She moved into the room but kept her distance. Doctor Shi was finishing dressing Acid's side and didn't acknowledge her.

"It'll take more than a nanny armed with a couple of kitchen knives to get rid of me," Acid said. But then she coughed and it looked like it was excruciating for her.

"Be careful. You'll split your stitches," Shi said, stepping away to inspect the dressing. "All done. Now you need to rest for a few days."

Acid glanced at Spook and the look on her face made Spook's stomach turn over. It told her that wouldn't be happening.

"You need to listen to what Doctor Shi is saying," Spook said. "You push yourself far too hard."

"We don't have time to rest." She hauled herself upright and regarded Shi with a pout. "I don't suppose you can find some information for us? About who might have put the hit out on me?"

Shi tutted theatrically. "Come now, Ms Vanilla. You know I can't do that. I stay neutral in these matters. Don't pick sides. Safer that way. And better for my bank balance, too." He laughed. No one else did.

"Yeah, I get it," Acid said. "And on that matter, how much do I owe you?"

He sniffed back, puffing his chest out as he did. "We'll call it five K this time."

"Five thousand pounds?" The words fell out of Spook's

I Am A Killer

mouth before she could stop herself. "That's a lot of money."

"Your friend's life not worth that?" Shi snapped. "You do know she paid more than that for me to save you, right?"

Spook didn't. She swallowed and shut up. Five thousand pounds. That settled it then. There was no way they could give up the Zoto case. They needed the fee.

"I can pay you in cash in a week or two," Acid said. "Would that work?"

Shi glared at her. "I guess so. Seeing as it's you. But any longer than two weeks and that becomes a problem. For me and you."

"I understand."

"Good." Shi checked the blood bag and removed the catheter from the back of Acid's hand before gathering up his leather bag. On his way to the door he looked over at Spook. "Try to get her to stay in bed for the next twenty-four hours at least."

"I'll try."

In the doorway he stopped and shook his head at Acid. "Yeah. Good luck with that. I'll see myself out."

Spook watched him waddle down the hallway and descend the stairs to the street. She waited until she heard the front door close before locking the apartment door and throwing across the bolts at the top and bottom.

Back in Acid's room, Spook ground to a halt in the doorway. "Oh no, come on. That's not cool."

Acid was already out of bed and examining the doctor's handiwork in the full-length mirror next to her wardrobe.

"He's given me some strong painkillers and a tetanus shot," she said, twisting around to see the back of her dressing. "I feel great."

Spook bit her lip. "Get back in bed. Please. The last

145

thing we need is for you to split your stitches and we end up owing that guy ten grand."

Acid laughed. "Oh, Spook. You are a worrier. I'll be fine. And you know as well as I do we aren't blessed with time to spare. We have to get to the bottom of this and fast. Whoever put out that hit on me isn't going to stop there. Until we know who sent her and why, we need to stay on our guard." She turned from the mirror, her derisive expression dropping to one of stern seriousness. "I think you should check into a hotel for a few days. Maybe even get out of London. Until we have more information, we're sitting ducks here."

Spook folded her arms, but it was less a show of protection and more to stop her hands from shaking. "Talk to me. What do you think is going on?"

"I've told you already. I have no idea." Acid swung open the double doors of her wardrobe. Reaching inside, she came out with a black leather holdall and walked it back to the bed, flinging it on top. "But that was a professional hit and our first step is to find out who was behind it."

Spook kept her arms folded but stepped back to allow Acid room as she returned to her wardrobe and grabbed a pair of jeans and a handful of creased up t-shirts. She threw the shirts on top of her holdall and sat down on the edge of the bed to pull on her jeans. Spook grimaced as she watched her yanking the waistband over the dressing. Once done, she pulled a faded black t-shirt over her head and marched over to her bureau, where she grabbed a handful of balled-up black knickers from the top drawer.

"What are you doing?" Spook asked. She had been waiting for an explanation but it seemed she wasn't about to get one. "Where are you going to go?"

Acid stopped. "I just told you. I need to find out who

put the hit on me." She zipped open the holdall and stuffed the underwear and t-shirts inside. "And while I do that, I need you to lie low. Book yourself into a small hotel some-where by the coast and wait for my call. Can you do that?"

"And you?" Spook asked, fingernails digging into the top of her arm. "Where will you go?"

Acid pulled a face. "Manchester, of course. There's only one man I know who can help me get to the bottom of this."

Chapter Eighteen

Acid booked the next flight out of Heathrow and was in Manchester by 6 p.m. From the airport, she took a taxi to Levenshulme and got dropped off on the main street. As the sun descended behind the rows of red-brick terrace houses, she stood on the side of the road and breathed in the dusk air. It always felt good to get out of London for a while. Away from the bustle and thrum of the big city and all the stresses and strains that came with it. She could breathe a little easier. Even if her reason for being here in Manchester was more business than pleasure. She slung her holdall over her shoulder and headed down the side of The Green Devil pub towards the large but innocuous thatched cottage that stood in its own grounds, set back a few hundred yards from the road.

As she entered through the main gate, she noticed the garden was more overgrown than the last time she'd been here. There were no lights on in the house, but that didn't mean anything. Beneath the benign Victorian façade was an impenetrable modern structure of reinforced steel and concrete. The leaded windows may have looked ordinary enough to anyone passing by, but they were made of high-density bulletproof glass, thick and strong enough to withstand anti-tank weapons. Both the front and back doors were made of six-inch steel with aged wooden frontages to fit in with the area and the overall look of the building. Acid got up to the front door, clocking the security camera poking out from the ivy that had encroached across the front of the house and around the large porch area. She gave the camera lens a wave before reaching up and banging her fist against the heavy door. The sound boomed through to the cavernous entrance hall beyond.

"Come on," she muttered to herself, holding her side as she rocked back on her heels. The painkillers Doctor Shi had administered had long since subsided, but the double G&T on the plane had helped in dulling the ache in her side. It was uncomfortable, but nothing she couldn't handle. "Where are you, D?"

She reached up to bang on the door again but heard the clank-clink of metal on metal. She stepped back and tossed her hair over her shoulders, shifting her expression into one of benevolent greeting as the door eased open.

"Yes, I know," she started. "I should have called first, but— Oh." She frowned. This was indeed The Dullahan's residence, but the man standing in the doorway was not the owner. For one thing, he was over a foot taller than her one-time rival and now friend. He was also wide where The Dullahan was wiry, and had a shock of bright orange hair.

"Where's The Dullahan?" she asked, gripping the strap of her holdall.

The man held his hand up. "You're Acid Vanilla," he said, in a sharp Irish accent. "Don't worry, he's fine. He saw ya on the security feed and asked me to come and get ya. He's inside."

The enormous man stepped back from the door to let her pass. After assessing the situation and concluding it was safe, she entered. "What are you, some kind of butler?" She took the door from him and let it swing shut behind her. It slammed home with a loud clang. "Do you want me to lock it?" she asked.

"If you wouldn't mind, that'd be grand," he said. "Hit three-one-four on the old keypad there."

"No problem." She turned and tapped the code into the electronic lock.

"I suppose you could say I'm a kind of butler," the man went on. "But you'd only say it once if ya wanted to keep any teeth in your head."

Acid turned back with a grin. "Point taken," she said. "So how do you know The Dullahan?"

He beckoned her down the hallway with a flick of his head. "My name's Seamus," he said, as they walked side by side. "Seamus Seacroft. And I met him about five years ago. I was in the industry, same as you, I believe, but I wasn't that good at it. I'm not made for stealth, as you can see. The Dullahan helped me out with my old boss. He pulled a few strings, which meant I could walk away without a target on my back."

Acid chuckled to herself. "It's all right for some."

"Oh aye, I've heard about you and what went down with your old firm. Quite the tale. And you were quite the assassin, too. One of the best, The Dullahan says."

"It's been a while since that was the case."

They got to the door to the kitchen and Seamus stepped to one side to allow her to go first. The lights were off and the blood-orange sunset cast the room in a dull glow.

"There she is," a gravelly voice resounded. "What a sight for sore eyes."

Acid moved her attention over to the far side of the room where a spindly figure sat at the large kitchen table, silhouetted against a window. Squinting through the gloom, she saw a version of The Dullahan she hadn't seen before. This one was gaunt and tired-looking and seemed to be on a smaller scale.

"Your eyesight going as well as your looks?" she replied. "Sight for sore eyes, my arse."

"Ah, come on now, Acid. Enough with the flirting. Have a seat."

She walked over to the table and pulled back a chair. Up close, she was even more shocked at how old and worn out her friend seemed. The lines in his cheeks and forehead that had always been there were now deep crevasses. His once intense blue eyes were sunken back into his head and had lost all their vitality. He'd already been in his fifties when Acid had first encountered him all those years ago, so by now he must be in his early to mid-seventies. But that wasn't so old, especially not these days. The last time they'd met, he'd been as sprightly and high-spirited as ever. Was he ill? Was something wrong? She sat down and faced him, working on keeping her thoughts from showing on her face.

"What brings you up this neck of the woods?" he asked.

"Nice to see you, too."

He laughed and she was glad to see the wicked twinkle in his eye was still present. "Now, Acid, you know full well I'm always glad to see you. These days, at least. But we also both know this isn't a social call."

She leaned back and glanced over her shoulder. Seamus was standing in the doorway with his arms folded. "Is he always this friendly?" she asked him.

Seamus laughed silently, his shoulders rising and falling. "He's all right, aren't ya, Jimmy?"

Acid arched an eyebrow as she turned back. "Jimmy? Still trying that one out?"

"Ya know. Trying it."

"You know, Spook's set up my old identity. Alice Vandella. She lives! She's got a passport, National Insurance number, the full shebang. I'm still not entirely comfortable with the whole thing. Likewise, with you, I'm not sure I can do it. You'll always be The Dullahan to me."

"I know, lassie. I get it." He closed one eye, his crooked smile rising to crease his face even more on that side. "But you're avoiding the question. What brings you to my kingdom?"

Acid cast her eye around the room, landing on a bottle of Jameson in the corner of the worktop. "How about you pour me a drink and I'll tell you all about it?"

He laughed. "Good to see some things don't change. Right y'are. Seamus, bring that bottle of whisky over, will ya, son? And three glasses."

Acid stuck out her bottom lip. "I thought you'd given up the sauce?"

"Ah, ya know…" he said with a shrug. "When in Rome…"

Seamus carried the Jameson over, along with three heavy-bottomed tumblers held in the palm of one hand. "What are we drinking to?" he asked, as he placed them down in front of The Dullahan.

"Do we need a reason?" The Dullahan asked. Then, winking at Acid, "How about old friends?" He poured out three decent measures and slid a glass across the table to Acid.

"Old friends," she said, picking up her glass and raising it in the air. "And old enemies."

"Meaning me?" The Dullahan asked.

Acid shrugged. "You. Caesar. Myself. Life."

They drank. The whisky was deep and with notes of black pepper that tickled the inside of her nose. The fact that she was picking up on such intricate flavours informed her that her senses were in a heightened state. It was weird. These days she didn't notice so much when she was in one of her manic episodes. The ups seemed to blend more seamlessly with the downs. Her personality and moods weren't so spiky that they threw her off. Either that or her whole life was now one long manic episode.

"How's Danny?' Acid asked.

"Danny?" The Dullahan frowned and ran his tongue over his bottom lip. "The lads doing all right. He's been over in Argentina recently. But don't ask. I don't. He still talks about ya. Clearly you left a lasting impression on the boy."

"Yes, well, he'll get over it." She finished her drink and returned her glass to the table. Glancing around, she saw Seamus sipping delicately at his.

"Why are you here, lassie?" The Dullahan asked. "Because I doubt it's to reminisce about how you broke my nephew's heart. Ya need my help with something?"

"Yes. I do."

"And there was me thinking you'd settle down once the big man was gone."

"Really?"

"Nah. I don't even know why I fecking well said that. Go on then, shoot. What's the story?"

She twisted her glass on the table in front of her. "I need you to find out if someone had put a hit out on me. Or I was wondering if there could be an historic one still online from Caesar's time. That's possible, right?"

The Dullahan swayed his head from side to side. "I suppose it is. After you took out Magpie, he opened the contract out to the wider community. But these people have their fingers on the pulse. Even if there is an old job post on one of those forums, I can't imagine anyone seeing it and not knowing it was outdated. No Caesar, no payment, no hit."

"That's what I thought," she said. "But this morning I was attacked." She lifted her t-shirt. The crisp white dressing now had a dirty brown stain on it in the shape of Australia, but otherwise she felt good.

"Looks nasty," The Dullahan said. "Who was it?"

"A woman. About my age. She looked to be from East Asia and spoke with an accent."

"And is she…?"

"Of course she bloody well is. I gutted the rotten cow. But I need to know who sent her. And why." She pulled her t-shirt down and sat upright. "Do you still have access to all the forums and your old contacts?"

"Aye. That I do." He pushed off from the table and got to his feet, taking longer about it than he used to. "I'll make a few calls. You don't have to get off straight away, do ya?"

Acid shook her head. "No. I'm safer here. I've moved Spook to a hotel on the coast. Just in case. You see, I've another theory why I was attacked."

"Which is?"

Acid sighed. How to tell him without sounding lame? "Spook and I have set up an agency. The aim is to assist people who are in trouble, people outside the law or who the authorities can't or won't help."

Seamus snickered. "Sounds like the A-Team."

"Yes. I know." She cleared her throat. "I'm wondering if the hit might have something to do with the case we're working on. A man called Zoto has gone missing and we think he was involved with some bad people from the London underground. My theory is he's dead and whoever killed him isn't too happy to find Spook and me sniffing around. Afrim Zoto is his full name. An Albanian. Can you find out if anyone has heard the name? And if anyone's put a contract out on him?"

The Dullahan nodded. "Zoto. Okay, I'll see what I can do." He gestured at the bottle of whisky. "Help yourself to some more of the ginger lady there. You might as well stay the night. Seamus here will make you up a bed in one of the guest rooms. That okay with you, lad?"

"No problem."

The Dullahan tapped the much larger man on the forearm as he shuffled past him. "It sounds like you've got yourself into a real mess with someone," he called back as he disappeared into the hallway. "I'll see what I can find out."

"Thank you," she replied. Then reached for the bottle.

A real mess.

Wasn't that the truth? But at least some things never changed.

Chapter Nineteen

Acid waited until The Dullahan had ventured upstairs and she heard him shuffling along the landing before she spoke again. When she did, she leaned forward to address Seamus, who was now sitting opposite her.

"When did he get so... old?" she asked him.

The big man grinned. "Ach, there's still life in the old bastard yet."

"Yes. I know. But still. He's half the man he was even last time I saw him." A sigh came at her from across the table. He was holding something back. "What is it? Is he ill?"

"Not that. But he had a fall. Four months ago now. Top of the stairs all the way to the bottom. Knocked him about something chronic. Ever since then he's kind of lost his nerve. But he's old. Happens to the best of us. And the worst, if we're lucky."

Acid blew out her cheeks. "Bloody hell. The Dullahan. An old man."

"You knew him in his prime?"

"I'll say. Although, he'd been in the industry for going on twenty years before I even came on the scene. People used to speak his name in hushed tones. And for good reason. The Dark Man. He was the best." She pulled up her sleeve to reveal the raised scar that ran down the underneath of her left forearm. "He gave me this. Back when we were less than friends."

"You were pitched against each other?"

"Oh yes. It seems like a lifetime away. Probably because it was. But even when he was a rival, I had a lot of respect for him. Everyone in the industry did. He was the best."

"He says the same about you. That you brought a new kind of creative genius to the role. A real trailblazer. The best in the business."

She couldn't help smiling. "I was."

Once, she'd have backed this statement up with a caveat – that she *still* was. Even now the words formed, but she swallowed them down. There was nothing worse than a has-been desperately hanging onto past glory.

"Do you miss it?" Seamus asked.

Now there was a question. She took a swig of her drink. Three long hours she'd spent with Spook in those ridiculous talk therapy sessions and all the kid needed to ask her was that question. She swilled the whisky over her tongue while she considered it.

She swallowed. "Do you?"

"Nah. I wasn't cut out for it. I'm more suited to protection work. Brute force over craftiness. But with you it's a different kettle of killers, right?" He fixed her with a hard stare. "It must be hard walking away from that life."

Acid gulped back the rest of the whisky and pushed the glass away from her. "Who says I've put it behind me?"

"Oh? I see. So you're still…?"

She shrugged. "Not entirely. I'm not an assassin. You can't hire me or anything. But lately, I've been… Well… put it this way, there are plenty of evil bastards out there. I can't help it if I happen to encounter some of them and they end up dead."

Seamus cleared his throat. "I see. Like a vigilante?"

"Eugh. No." She pulled a face. How she hated that word. *Vigilante.* It conjured up visions of middle-aged men with body odour and terrible social skills. "Let's just say I'm working a few things out right now. And at the top of that list is who sent the woman to kill me this morning."

"But you think it could be a historic contract?"

She reached for the bottle and poured another slug of the amber liquid into her glass. "The more I think about it, it seems doubtful. But that means it must be linked to the case we're working on. My hope is whoever ordered it has gone through the proper channels and I can get a name at least."

"Aye, well. If anyone can find out for you, he can." He finished his drink and reached for the bottle. "He thinks a lot of you, ya know."

"I know." She smiled as Seamus poured out more whisky for them both. "You don't have many friends in my walk of life, but I consider your boss to be one of them."

A silence fell over the table. They filled it by sipping their drinks until the atmosphere became too awkward.

Seamus spoke first. "Are you worried?" he asked. "About this hit on you?"

"Yes and no. I'm more confused than anything. Plus, my partner, Spook, she isn't cut out to deal with tanto-blade-wielding psychos. If whoever Afrim Zoto is mixed up with sent that woman to kill me, then Spook's in danger too. I need to know what I'm dealing with."

"I get ya," Seamus said. "If there's anything I can do to help, you let me know."

"You want to come and stand guard outside my apartment for the next few weeks?"

He laughed. "Anything but that. It's nothing personal, Acid. I like ya. But London brings me out in a terrible rash. Awful place."

She laughed too, but stopped at the sound of footsteps on the stairs. She raised her head as The Dullahan appeared in the doorway.

"Any news?" she asked. "Oh shit, what?"

It was the expression on his face that prompted the question. Like he'd come face to face with his younger self.

"What is it?" she asked again, getting to her feet.

The Dullahan held a hand up as if to calm her. "Don't fret, lassie. There's no official hit out on you, either current or historic, as far as I can see. But I did find out something." He padded over to the table and Seamus jumped up, pulling a chair out for him. Acid retook her seat as he settled himself. "It's probably not related. But does the name Kaan mean anything to you?"

She shook her head. "I don't think so. What is it? A person? An organisation?"

"Of that I'm not certain," he said. "I looked the name up. It means King of Kings in Turkish, which makes me think it's one person. They're a new presence on all the forums, but no one seems to know anything about them other than they're based in London."

"Have they posted jobs?"

"Not as such. They've been asking questions mainly. About fees, about the industry. Everyone is keeping them at arm's length, as you'd expect."

"You think it could be feds?"

"Possibly, but I doubt it. The last post from Kaan talked about a 'big assignment'. But as you know, no one in the industry uses that sort of terminology, so it's all rather curious."

"What about Afrim Zoto? Any mention of him? A hit?"

"I'm still waiting to hear from a few people, but so far not a dicky bird. I just wondered if you'd heard anything yourself about this Kaan person. A lot of people in the industry seem spooked. But as I say, it's probably nothing."

"But it could be something?"

"Oh aye, they could be the ones gunning for ya. But you can handle fecking Kaan, lassie. Especially as I hear you've been getting your practice in recent months."

Acid glanced at Seamus. There was no way The Dullahan could have heard their conversation. "Excuse me?"

The Dullahan's expression dropped. "Are you back in the game, Acid?" He glared at her, his famous stare still heart-stopping despite his diminished size.

"Why? What have you heard?"

"An open contract was put out a few months back on a retired gunrunner who fancied himself as an author. He was about to sell his memoirs and the contents of his little black book to the highest bidder. Called himself Eddie Dynamo. Ring any bells?"

Acid sniffed. "Maybe."

"It turns out a lot of operatives went for that job, as you'd expect. But before any of them got to Dynamo, someone else eradicated him. Someone outside the industry who hadn't applied for the job. Someone fitting your description." He shook his head. "Hell's teeth. You know the code, Acid. You apply for these things correctly. Even open contracts. You get on the list and you wait to be chosen. If you've taken some-one's pay check without going through the official channels, that's enough to get yourself on a gazillion hit lists. And to not even collect for the work done. What are you playing at?"

She looked away. "Eddie Dynamo. Little weaselly guy with dyed black hair and a bad comb-over?"

"Fecking hell. So it was you? Jesus, Mary and Joseph, Acid. I don't care what you get up to in your spare time, lassie, but don't be stepping on people's toes. Shite."

She stared down into her glass of whisky. "I didn't know there was a contract out on him."

"Acid, really, what are you playing at?" he repeated. It was a genuine question. "You killing people for kicks?"

She couldn't look at him. "I don't know. Yes. Maybe. I can't explain it very well. I just feel... compelled to do it. It's like an addiction." Finally, she risked looking up into the old man's eyes. The harsh intensity had subsided and she found only concern. "Shit," she whispered. "I just made the connection. Do you think this is what the hit on me was about?"

"It could be. But there's nothing on the forums, so I'm confused. How much do you know about this Zoto fella?"

"Not much. Not enough. His daughter talks about him like he's some bumbling old teddy bear, but that's daughters and daddies for you. I've got multiple theories. One is that he's got himself into a dangerous situation and is on the lam. Another is that he is in a dangerous situation and doesn't want the likes of me and Spook prying into his affairs." She cricked her neck to one side and Seamus winced as her vertebrae popped. "The other option, of course, is that he's dead, at the hand of a rival. Maybe even this Kaan person, who knows? But whatever the outcome, his daughter is paying us to find out what happened to him, so I need to keep going."

She pulled in a deep breath, realising she'd been talking ten to the dozen. It happened sometimes, especially when the bats were in flight. She lowered her chin. "But I get what you're saying about my extracurricular activities. I'll be more careful in the future, I promise."

The Dullahan frowned. "I strongly advise you to stop altogether. We both know you can handle yourself, but this is an unknown quantity you're dealing with. I'd hate to lose ya. Like I always say, I didn't get to take out the great Acid Vanilla, so I'll be damned if I'm going to let any other fecker do it." He laughed, but it turned into a harsh hacking cough, which appeared to drain him of energy. When he was done, he laid his hands flat on the table and let out a deep sigh. "Well, shite. I think I'd better get myself to bed. Seamus, can you see Acid is all set regarding a room and lodging for the night?"

"No problem."

Acid stood as The Dullahan got up from the table; it felt like the right thing to do. "Thank you," she said. "I appreciate you doing this for me. You're a good friend. And I will take on board what you've said."

He pointed at her with a bony finger. "Make sure you do."

"One thing. I don't suppose you've heard of a contract being put out for a man called Lucas Jelani?"

"Who is he?"

"Local gangster. East End. He's involved in all the usual stuff, drugs mainly, but guns and prostitution, too. He's not a nice man."

"Don't tell me. You think he should be eradicated and

you want to know that you're free to be the one who does it?"

"Something like that."

He shook his head wearily. "I'll ask around. And I'll keep my ear to the ground for you over the next few weeks regarding this Zoto fella as well. And Kaan. Jesus, with so many names, I can hardly keep up. But for now I'm off to my bed. Goodnight all."

He wandered away, waving his hand over his shoulder as he left the room.

Acid watched him go then looked at Seamus, then at the bottle of Jameson. But the moment had gone.

"I'll sort your bedroom out," he told her, getting up and following on behind The Dullahan. "Give me five minutes."

"No worries."

She sat back and drained her glass as a cacophonous chatter of bats buzzed across her nervous system. To say she felt relieved would be wrong, but if the attempt on her life was because she'd killed Eddie Dynamo, it meant Spook wasn't involved. That was one thing, at least. But it wasn't a certainty. She closed her eyes as the names Zoto and Kaan spun around in her head. Fiona had mentioned some man had approached Zoto and offered to buy his company from him. Could it be Kaan and his 'big assignment'? A hit on a rival who wouldn't sell up. If that was the case, it made sense he was now tying up loose ends by getting rid of anyone sniffing around. But it also meant Acid and Spook were both in danger. Fiona Zoto, too.

Bloody hellfire.

She shook the thoughts away. Her thinking was off-kilter. She was overtired and drunk from the whisky. Never a good combination.

"Acid. You set?"

"Coming."

She pushed herself up from the table and walked down the corridor to find Seamus waiting for her.

"First door on the landing," he said, gesturing up the stairs. "The bed's all made for you. Give me a shout if ya need anything else."

She gave a half-salute as she passed by and grabbed the handrail. "I'll be fine. Thank you."

While Seamus disappeared into the kitchen, she hauled herself up the stairs and into the guest bedroom, dropping face first onto the bed. What a day. Her head was spinning with chaotic ideas and far-flung notions, but she was too exhausted to concentrate on any particular one. She closed her eyes, allowing the night's warm embrace to cushion her bruised soul, with the hope that her thoughts might organise themselves into a more coherent arrangement between now and the dawn. Because whichever way she looked at it, she was still in danger. And the sooner she found out why, the better.

Chapter Twenty

Spook Horowitz was in Southend-on-Sea. Following Acid's insistence that she not remain in the apartment alone, she'd caught the afternoon train and booked into a small guest-house near the seafront. It was a pleasant enough establishment, run by two kindly old ladies called Bee and Dee who sported blue and pink beehives respectively and were either a gay couple or sisters.

Spook set herself up in their box room at the front of the house overlooking the road, and for the first twenty-four hours didn't leave her laptop other than to make herself far too many mugs of bitter instant coffee with the kettle provided, venture along the landing to use the communal bathroom, and toss and turn in bed in a useless attempt at sleep. So it was by mid-afternoon on the second day that her momentum waned.

Employing her superior hacking skills – and the ability to circumnavigate any security system ever created – she had planned to access Afrim Zoto's emails and cloud storage to help paint a richer picture of who and what they were dealing with. But she'd hit a brick wall. It didn't help that she was unsure what email program Zoto used or even what operating system. Her capability to crack even the wiliest of encryptions was the same whether he was using Windows, Mac or even Linux-based storage, but it helped to know which one. Going in blind as she was, it could take days rather than hours.

They didn't have days.

Then came the phone call from Fiona, who seemed even more antsy and eager for results than the last time they'd spoken. Reading between the lines, it sounded as though she was ready to pull the case and the rest of their fee if they didn't provide answers, and fast. It was not what Spook wanted to hear. After all this time spent around Acid, she thought she'd be better at dealing with feelings of fear and confusion. But not so. They still crippled her and made her want to throw up in equal measure.

The upshot of all this was that Spook realised lying low was not the answer. She had to do something. To get the information she needed, she had to get into Afrim Zoto's office and sit in front of his personal computer. That way she'd have what she was looking for in less time it took to drink six (maybe seven, actually) mugs of bitter instant coffee.

Decision made, she settled up with Bee and Dee for the remaining nights she had booked and caught the evening train back to London. The train from Southend stopped at Fenchurch Street, which she took to be a good sign as from there it was only a fifteen-minute walk to Zoto's office in Whitechapel. She had the keys in her rucksack, along with her laptop, a change of clothes and a bag of toiletries.

The streets of Whitechapel were peaceful as she walked from the station, but she kept her head down all the same, quickening her step at the mere suggestion someone might be following her. She reached her destination in less than ten minutes, inhaling deeply and exhaling large plumes of frosty breath as she stood outside the tall Victorian building that housed Afrim Zoto's office. In the moonlight it sure looked like an imposing place.

She shook her head.

Stay in the moment, Spook. Focus on what you need to do, not what you think might happen.

She glanced down at her phone screen where, in response to Spook's text, Fiona had confirmed the address. This was the place, all right. 11-15 Boyd Street, Whitechapel. The message also told her Afrim Zoto's office was on the second floor. Spook slid her rucksack from her shoulder to the crook of her arm and unzipped the front pocket. She removed a small pen torch and a bunch of keys, which she flicked into her fist so the largest key was sticking out through her fingers. It was something Acid had taught her in their self-defence sessions. What else had she learned? Which pressure points in the wrist made someone drop their weapon. How to headbutt someone in the groin if they were standing behind you. Acid meant well, but was Spook ever going to use these techniques?

Really? Her?

As the sessions had grown more complicated and the imaginary situations more threatening, she'd found herself disassociating in a bid to stay calm. There was no way she could do the things Acid asked of her, so what was the point? Even now, as she gripped the keys in her fist, it only made her worry about how effective she'd be against someone bigger and scarier than her who was determined to hurt her. Or worse...

Stop that.

Not helpful.

She stepped up to the building's main door and tapped the access code Fiona had supplied into the door's electronic keypad. The lock made a low whirring sound and the door clicked open. Spook didn't look around as she slipped inside the building. For now she was safe and she didn't want to know if anyone was following her. Once in the foyer, she grabbed the door and shoved it closed, making sure she heard the lock click home before finally allowing herself to breathe.

The reception area of the building was huge and with far too many dark recesses and gloomy corridors leading off from it. Spook switched on her torch, pleased with herself she'd had the foresight to bring it, but dismayed to see the batteries were low and the light dim. Following the dull circle of light, and trying to ignore the spiralling display of terrifying images her imagination was conjuring, she crossed the entrance hall towards a set of glass doors. They opened into a white room with a row of six-foot artificial trees along one wall and the metal doors of an elevator on the other. In the corner was the door to a fire escape, which she assumed would give her access to the second floor. But no thanks. She'd choose a brightly lit elevator over a dark stairwell any night of the week.

She called the elevator, bouncing from foot to foot as she waited for it to descend from the fifth floor. Her heart was racing and her hearing was on full alert for any sounds. There was no reason to believe she was in immediate danger, but in Spook's experience you let your guard down at your peril.

The elevator clanged to a stop and Spook stepped inside before the doors had even fully opened, jabbing her finger on the button to make them close again. A blue halogen bulb illuminated the elevator compartment, so stark in contrast to the rest of the building that when she looked out all she could see was blackness in the space beyond. Anything could be lurking out there… Anyone…

No! Stop that!

She rolled her shoulders back as the doors sucked shut and the metal box shuddered into action. The lights above the doors moved from 'G' to '1' to '2' then stopped. Spook waited. Every part of her body that could clench was clenched.

What the hell is going on?

The elevator had stopped but the doors hadn't opened. Had it broken down? Was she going to be stuck here all night?

As these disturbing thoughts seeped into Spook's awareness, bringing with them a rush of panic, the elevator doors shuddered open.

"Damn it. You're better than this," she told herself. "Stay strong. Stay logical."

Raising the torch, imagining it was a lightsabre, she stepped out onto the second-floor landing. As she swiped the beam around the space, the light landed on a switch on the wall in front of her and she rushed over to it, desperate to throw actual light on the situation. But as she got closer she stopped herself from flicking it on. A light could be seen from the street. If the evil men in her imagination were currently scoping out Zoto's office, it would send them a clear signal someone was here. Despite her anxieties, it was important to keep a low profile. That was what Acid would do.

"This is what you wanted, remember?" she whispered to herself as she took a left off the landing and crept along a wide corridor with doors spaced out on either side. "The Avenging Angels. Here you are."

Each of the doors had a number, starting at 200 on her right and going up to 220 on her left. She was looking for 206 and found it halfway along. With a shaking hand, she pushed the key into the lock and opened the door.

"The Avenging Angels," she whispered. "I'm an Avenging Angel."

It didn't help. As she stepped into Afrim Zoto's office, a wave of dizziness zipped through her and she had to grab hold of the door handle to steady herself. After taking a few moments to calm, she closed the door and shone the torch around, keeping the beam away from the large window opposite as best she could. It was a spacious office but with little furniture. Almost like a showroom. On top of the desk in the middle of the room stood an iMac and nothing else. Three black filing cabinets the same height as Spook stood against the adjacent wall, and on top of the one nearest the door was a small metal safe. She walked over to this first cabinet and tried each drawer in turn. They were all locked, so she turned her attention to the safe.

Fiona had mentioned her father had kept a safe, but Spook recalled that the code to get inside had so far eluded her. She stood on her toes to examine it. The lock was modern, with an illuminated green keypad rather than a dial. She squinted at the numbers, a part of her hoping the numbers on certain keys might have worn away, alerting her to which numbers comprised the code. But this wasn't a movie and she was out of luck.

She placed her rucksack down and walked over to the desk, sitting in Afrim Zoto's black leather chair. A flick of the mouse awakened the computer and it presented her with the login screen for AZoto's account. She needed a password to go in further, but this wasn't an issue. Opening a guest account from the main login screen, she bypassed the system and accessed the root account where she unlocked AZoto's profile and changed the password to Sp00ky22. Once done, she logged into his account with no problem.

As the desktop opened up, she removed her glasses and cleaned the lenses on her shirt. In the darkness, with the only light coming from the screen, it highlighted every smear and particle of dirt. Shoving the thick-framed spectacles back on, she clicked open Zoto's email program. It was desktop rather than web-based, but that wasn't unusual for a man of his age.

Once inside, she scanned the first bank of correspondence, skim-reading the preview text in the reading pane as she tapped on each one. Most of the emails seemed innocent enough. Fiona's father wasn't too big on words, sending back curt one or two-line responses to requests about stock and delivery dates. A lot of the emails included attachments, but mainly statements and invoices and nothing that caught Spook's eye, until a few rows down when she came across a message from a weird-looking email address. The sender's name stood out also, coming up as *2022DD2022*. She clicked open the message and leaned forward as the contents flashed up on the screen.

"Whoa."

At first glance, it looked as if someone had rolled around on a keyboard before hitting 'send'. But as Spook scanned the rows of symbols and letters, she realised she'd seen this type of encryption before. It was more sophisticated than she'd expected and without her trusty laptop and all its software she'd struggle to crack it. But there were a few English words in the jumble of random letters that she could pick out. *Morocco* was one. *Shipment* another. But ship-ment of what? Guns? Drugs? People?

She clicked open a new finder window to find a list of blue folders with innocuous names, such as 'Insurance', 'Accounts database', 'Contractor Information' and 'Visas'. As she opened each one, she found they held nothing unex-pected or out of the ordinary. But halfway down she got to a folder named 'Reconciliations', which had another folder inside named 'Custom Office Templates'. Inside this folder were seven spreadsheets, all with random numbers as titles.

"Curiouser and curiouser," she muttered to herself as she went through each one in turn.

The spreadsheets were encrypted. But unlike in the email, this was basic encryption – the sort offered by stan-dard home operating systems – that stood little chance against a hacker as skilled as her. In less than five minutes she had all seven documents positioned on the screen in front of her. Mostly they appeared to be Zoto's personal accounts – one was ins and outgoings, one was expenses, nothing of any interest – but the last spreadsheet was a different matter altogether. It was a basic database, with a list of websites in one column and what very much looked like corresponding usernames and passwords in two subse-quent columns. At the top of the page, someone had even titled the sheet, *Passwords and Logins*.

Spook chewed on her bottom lip as she considered the document. It seemed a little on the nose, but Afrim Zoto was in his seventies and it made sense someone his age might have created such a database. Especially seeing as every password listed was unique, the sort of thing you were told to do in every piece of advice on online security but most people never did. Herself included.

She scanned the list of websites, banks, trading accounts

and government access portals from both the UK and Europe. Nothing jumped out at her. Until…

"Shiiiiit," she exclaimed, drawing out the vowel sound until she had no breath to put behind it.

At the bottom of the list was a username and password for a site called Crypto Jones One Thousand. She recognised that name. And once she'd opened a new browser window and typed the name into the search bar, she remembered why. The search revealed no direct hits, but that was because most search engines only trawled the mainstream web. This particular site existed on the dark web. She spent a few minutes downloading The Onion Router and setting up a VPN before heading straight there, chewing on her lip as the site loaded.

Crypto Jones One Thousand.

This was the same site – posing as a crypto-trading forum – that Annihilation Pest Control had used to pass information to their operatives. The very same one through which Acid had received details of the individual who would turn out to be her last mark for the company. A mark who went by the name of Spook Horowitz.

It was a clever system, with users employing aliases and pre-determined codewords and terminology to post jobs and liaise with others in the murder industry. She'd been on there a few times since meeting Acid and it always gave her the creeps. She flicked back to Zoto's list of passwords and was readying herself to log in when she heard a noise out in the corridor.

Shit

She froze, fingers poised over the keyboard. There it was again. A shuffling sound, hardly audible but there all the same. She glanced back at the screen as the feeling of blistering panic erupted in her chest. It spread down her limbs and up into her throat. The noise was getting closer and she was now all but certain it was the sound of footsteps. Someone was out there. And they were heading this way.

With her body tense, as if readying itself for some kind of impact, she clicked open Zoto's emails and sent the list of passwords to herself. Then she put the computer in sleep mode, switched off her torch and got to her feet. Downgrading swiftness for stealth, she tiptoed her way over to the wall. She had no idea what she was going to do when whoever was out there entered the room, but it felt like the sort of thing Acid might do. Except before she could conceal herself behind the door, it swung open and crashed against the wall on the other side.

Spook let out a garbled scream.

The person in the doorway screamed back and the light flickered on to reveal a tall woman with auburn hair.

"Ms Horowitz," Fiona Zoto gasped. "What the hell are you doing here?"

Chapter Twenty-One

Spook's throat was so dry that when she went to speak, the words came out rough and scratchy. "Sorry… I was just… I couldn't sleep, so I came looking for some more information. But you knew I was coming. You replied to my message."

Fiona, who was pressing her long fingers to her chest, swallowed and shot her a stiff smile. "Yes, but I thought in the daytime. Office hours. You are sneaking around with the lights off as if you're robbing us."

Spook stared at her. "I didn't want to alert anyone to my presence. We still don't know the reasons behind your father's disappearance. And Aci—" She coughed. "*Alice* and I wanted to keep a low profile until we had more to go on…" She trailed off before she said too much. The last thing she wanted was to add to Fiona's worries.

"Did you find anything?"

"Umm… I'm not sure." She didn't want to tell her about the passwords. Not yet. This was her treasure, her piece of the puzzle. She smiled and raised her head, trying to sound breezy. "But what about you? What are you doing here so late?"

Fiona huffed out a breath but appeared to relax. She shut the door and pulled out one of the two chairs in front of the desk. "I couldn't sleep," she said, sitting and throwing one leg over the other. She reached into the pocket of her overcoat and pulled out a crumpled packet of cigarettes. "You want one?" she asked, offering the open pack to Spook.

"No. Thank you."

She watched as Fiona twisted a slim, all-white cigarette between her dark maroon lips and lit the tip with a gold lighter. Closing her eyes, she inhaled deeply before releasing a large plume of smoke into the room. Spook watched the cloud rise and dissipate before a loud sniff from Fiona captured her attention.

"I've hardly slept since my father went missing," she said. "The last few nights I've tossed and turned and put on meditation tapes, but tonight I decided to go for a drive. I was driving nearby and all at once a thought came to me. My mother's birthday. The twenty-second of February, nineteen-fifty-five. Twenty-two, zero two, fifty-five." She took another sharp drag and waved the cigarette at the safe. "I don't know why I haven't tried it before."

Spook grinned. With her interest piqued, it was easier to concentrate on the job at hand rather than her pounding heart. "Great, well let's see, shall we?" She walked over to the safe. "You want me to go for it?"

Fiona nodded. "Yes. Do it."

She repeated the numbers slowly and Spook tapped them in. Nothing happened.

"Did you press the star key?"

She hadn't. But when she did, the safe made a beeping

sound and she felt the air pressure on the door give way. Turning the handle, she felt something click and had to dampen a squeal of excitement as she pulled the door open.

"Yes! It worked." She was about to reach inside when Fiona got to her feet.

"Please. Let me." She strode over and Spook stepped aside. "This is what I was hoping for. The keys to my father's warehouse."

She lifted out the keys along with a spiral-bound notepad. There was nothing else in there.

"What's that?" Spook asked.

Fiona didn't respond, but her usual dour expression had perked up. She turned the notepad over and flicked through the first few pages. Spook watched as her eyes flitted over the contents but then the expectant expression distorted into a disgruntled frown. She curled her lip and shoved it at Spook. "It looks like nothing."

"Aww, shit, really?"

Spook took the notepad and leaned back, resting the top of her butt on the edge of the desk. The notepad was a standard-issue office ledger with a navy cover made of rough, recycled card. Inside, the first few pages were blank, but a series of faint blue lines ran horizontally across each page with a pink margin down the left-hand side. Spook flicked forward a few pages, eager to see more despite Fiona's reaction. They contained what she could only describe as doodles. Done in scratchy blue and black ball-point pen, they were the sort of mindless scribbles one made whilst on the phone. There were spirals and criss-cross patterns, drawings of arrows and stars and quite a few crucifixes. On another page someone had drawn out a very basic plan of a building. She held it up and turned it around but it didn't look familiar. Fiona peered over the top of the ledger.

"Anywhere you recognise?" Spook asked.

Fiona sighed and shook her head. She seemed deflated, but it was understandable. They had the keys to the warehouse, which was a step forward, but not much else. Spook, too, had hoped the safe would offer them more clues in the mystery surrounding Afrim Zoto's disappearance.

She kept going through the ledger, flicking past more doodles and pages filled with numbers. There was another badly sketched plan of a building and a page almost entirely covered in black hash marks. She stopped. In the centre of the page was a single word, eye-catching because it was written in large, thick capital letters. It was the first word featured in the ledger.

Spook raised her head and read it out loud. "Kaan."

"What?" Fiona had been extinguishing her cigarette against one of the filing cabinets but now spun around. "What did you say?"

"Kaan," Spook repeated, louder this time. "It says it here at the back of the notepad. Does that mean anything to you?" She turned the ledger around so Fiona could see.

"No. I've never heard that before," she said, her eyes widening. "Is it a name? A person? Do you think it means something important?"

Spook turned the ledger back around. "I'm not sure." But it was a start. She glanced out through the window, into the inky void beyond. "If you don't mind, I should probably get going…" She stood upright and faced the door, hoping Fiona would now take the lead. She didn't. "Could I get those keys off you?"

"Oh, yes. Of course." Fiona stepped forward with them at arm's length.

Spook took them and held them up. "Thanks. Alice and I will check out the warehouse as soon as possible. And in the meantime I'll look into who – or what – Kaan might refer to."

"Thank you," Fiona said, moving over to the door. "I have my car outside. Would you like a lift home?"

"You know what?" Spook replied, as a sudden wave of fatigue pulled at her soul. "That would be awesome."

———

FIONA'S CAR was white and sporty. That was about as far as Spook's car knowledge went. But she also assumed it to be an expensive vehicle, if the shiny wooden dashboard and tan leather upholstery were any indications. The interior smelt of strawberries and the engine made a purring noise rather than a growl, which she felt was another sign of quality.

"How long have you and Alice been working together?" Fiona asked, as they drove along Whitechapel High Street.

"Umm… off and on, around three years." It wasn't a lie. Not really.

"What did you both do before this? Before working as private detectives?"

Private detectives.

Spook peered out the side window as they drove through the neon streets, rolling the words around in her mind. It wasn't how she would have described The Avenging Angels and she knew Acid would detest that job title. Indeed, anytime Spook had been trying to sell her on the idea, she'd kept away from describing the agency in such terms. They were saviours, assisting those who needed them. Sometimes, yes, they would investigate disappearances and find missing persons like Afrim Zoto, but the work they did (in her head, at least for the time being) covered so much more than that.

She turned from the window to take in Fiona Zoto and their eyes met. She was waiting for an answer. "I was working for a tech company," Spook replied. "And Acid was… in the military." It was as good an explanation as she could come up with in the circumstances. It explained their complementary skills enough without going into too much detail. "She's very good at what she does."

"Acid?"

"*Alice.* Sorry. Acid is what I call her sometimes. A nickname."

"I see."

Spook returned to the window, praying the next words from Fiona weren't to ask her what exactly it was Acid did. Because right now she didn't know. Or maybe she did. Only she didn't know how to articulate it to herself. She was tired and confused and her body was craving at least a hundred hours of sleep.

The road they were on widened and she noticed a sign for Fenchurch Street. Was that one of the spaces on the UK Monopoly board? One of the orange ones? She screwed up her face to think. But it was the distraction rather than the answer that was of interest to her.

At the end of the street, Fiona took a left onto Cannon Street, past Monument Tube station. Now the area began to look familiar to Spook. Another ten minutes and they'd be in Soho. She inhaled a deep breath, conscious of the tightness in her chest. It had been a strange twenty-four hours since Acid was attacked, and Spook hadn't fully processed what had happened. That was one thing she had learnt being in Acid Vanilla's orbit over the years – you had to accept what happened without too much consideration. If she ever stopped to contemplate the swirling maelstrom of death and pain that was never far away, then it would cripple her. Best to look the other way, deal with things in her power, without thinking too much about the implications of the life she'd gotten herself into. It reminded her of a concept in a YouTube video she'd watched recently: she was better being like water, formless and adaptable, than a rigid oak tree that could break under high pressure.

That's what she told herself, anyway.

"What will you do now?" Fiona's voice pulled her from her thoughts and she looked up to see they were sitting at some traffic lights.

What would she do now?

The short answer was that she'd get inside her apartment, lock every single lock on every single door and try to get some sleep. But Fiona didn't mean that.

"As soon as Alice gets back from Manchester, we'll go to your father's warehouse and see if we can find any clues," she said. "I'm also going to create a program that will search the web for information on whoever or whatever Kaan is."

"I was thinking, what if it's the name of the man putting pressure on my father?"

Spook nodded. They were almost in Soho now and she didn't feel comfortable delving too deeply into her theories until she had more concrete intel. But the poor woman seemed frantic and she deserved something.

"I was thinking the same," she said, employing her most comforting smile. "You did well tonight, Fiona. With access to your father's warehouse and a name to go off, I'm hoping we'll make good ground in the next day or so."

"What is Alice doing in Manchester?"

Shit.

Why did she run her mouth off like that? Acid was always telling her about it.

"She was following a lead. Don't worry, we're both working on the case full time. We're going to find your father."

She grimaced internally, but the words had jumped out of her mouth before she'd realised. Yet it was true, she supposed, they would find him. Whether he was still in the same form as when Fiona had last seen him was another matter. The case was coming together a little more, but with that came new fears and added dangers. Despite calling Acid's phone three times today, Spook was yet to speak to her. So she was in the dark relative to any information she'd got from The Dullahan.

"Do you have anywhere you can go?" she asked Fiona. The last thing she wanted was to worry her more, but neither did she want another person's death on her conscience. "A friend or a relative who might let you stay with them for a few days. Until Alice and I investigate further."

Fiona frowned. "There is Maxine, a friend from university. She is quite close. Up in Cheltenham. You think I am in danger?"

Spook nipped her bottom lip between her teeth, wondering how best to say it without totally freaking her out. The fact remained, Acid had been attacked. Until they knew why, it was best to assume the worst. That someone out there didn't want Afrim Zoto's fate known and was ready to kill to keep it that way.

"Only to be on the safe side," she said. Then, glad to see the bright lights of Piccadilly Circus ahead: "You can drop me just here, if that's okay."

"You live here?"

"Nearby."

It was a five-minute walk to the apartment, but she had Acid's voice in her head, telling her not to divulge their address unless absolutely necessary. "Here is fine," she said. "I'd like some air and it's easier for you to turn around. Thank you." She sat up and stretched her neck to one side. The fact she was thinking this way pleased her. It proved she wasn't the idealistic oaf she often imagined herself to be.

"If you're sure." Fiona slowed the car and brought it to a stop outside the Lyric Theatre. The clock above the rear-view mirror read 01.52 and the streets were full of rowdy drunken people. But for once Spook was glad of their presence.

The interior light came on as she clicked off her seat belt and opened her door. "Please try not to worry," she said. "We've got the warehouse keys, that's awesome. As soon as I work out who or what Kaan refers to, I'll let you know. For now, go home, get some rest and first thing tomorrow drive over to Cheltenham. You've got my number and I've got yours. We can keep in touch." She stared at Fiona who nodded along with her instructions. "Try not to worry."

A surge of pride fought with a bristle of nervous energy as Spook grabbed her rucksack from between her feet and climbed out. As the car pulled away, she raised her hand in a farewell gesture, watching as the car disappeared from sight. Then she zipped her jacket up and ran as fast as her tired limbs would take her, all the way home.

Chapter Twenty-Two

"What the…?" Acid snapped her head up from the screen of her mobile phone.

Bloody hellfire.

She'd been so caught up in her thoughts that she'd let her focus slip. Instantly alert, she placed her phone face down on the table and raised herself upright, listening into the gloom. She heard footsteps in the stairwell, someone moving fast and without stealth. It was a few minutes after 2 a.m. Whoever it was didn't care for the element of surprise.

With a thousand invisible bats chattering across her synapses and a shiver of intense heat energy shooting through her veins, she shifted over to the side of the room to be out of sight from the door. A part of her hoped this was another attacker. She had the fire in her tonight and a demon that required sustenance.

Sliding her back along the bevelled edge of the kitchen worktop, she moved towards the door, fingers closing around the handle of a paring knife that was lying next to the sink. The piece felt flimsy in her grip, but it was the only weapon to hand. On reaching the far side of the room, she pressed her back against the wall, poised and ready as the apartment door creaked open.

"Acid?" a voice whispered.

Shit.

Up to this point she'd been working on regulating her heart rate – inhaling, holding, and releasing her breath slowly and steadily – but at the sound of Spook's voice, she let it go in one gasp.

"Hey, kid. I'm here." She stepped out into the hall to see Spook shuffling towards her. She looked like she had the weight of heaven on her shoulders. But that wasn't exactly new. "I thought I told you to stay in Southend until I called?"

Spook hobbled past her without response and flung her rucksack on the kitchen table.

"Spook! What the fuck?"

"Yeah, I know. Sorry." She slumped onto the chair facing the window. Her face said she wasn't in the mood to be reprimanded. "I went to Southend, but I was restless and felt useless and came back. I am an adult, after all. Remember?" Her eyes drifted to Acid's wounded side. "I'm glad you're back and safe. How is it?"

"A bit sore, but fine." She went to pat her injury but thought better of it. "And fair enough, I suppose, no harm done. Are you okay?"

"I just got a bit stressed walking home alone," Spook said. "You know how my mind gets."

"Why did you travel back so late?"

She shivered. "I came back earlier this evening."

"What? So where have you been?" Acid moved around the table and took a seat so they were sitting adjacent to each other. "Have you been out partying again?"

Spook humphed. She was definitely not in the mood for sarcasm. "As I say, I was restless. I knew I wouldn't sleep. I was worried about you. And me. And everything. I went to Zoto's office in Whitechapel to see if I could find any clues. Fiona was there doing the same thing. She was able to open his safe and we got the keys to the warehouse and—"

"You went there alone?"

Spook was startled at the ferocity of her tone. "Yes, and I was careful. But listen, I—"

"How careful? Jesus, Spook, what did I tell you? Until we know what's going on, we have to watch our backs."

"Is that what you've been doing?" Her eyes fell on Acid's hands, laid out flat on the table in front of her. There was dried blood under her nails and down the sides of her cuticles.

"I've been trying to figure out why the hell I was attacked," she said, sliding her hands off the table and letting them fall onto her lap. "So we can both rest easier."

Spook mouthed the word 'okay' but didn't look at her. Acid ran her tongue across her top lip.

"Let's start again, shall we? I apologise for getting in your face. I am feeling rather 'batty' presently." There was no verbal reply from Spook, but she gave a curt nod as if this statement had affirmed her suspicion. "Well done on getting the keys. Do you want to go over there now?"

Spook made a circle with her mouth. "Are you serious?"

"No time like the present. And I'd rather go back at a time when we stand less chance of running into that bearded wanker." The truth was, she was too strung out to sleep. A million thoughts fought for dominance in her brain and her skin felt like it was made of eggshell. She needed a release, a focus for her manic energy.

"Not tonight," Spook replied.

It felt like a punch to the guts. "But if we've got the keys…"

"Please, Acid. I'm exhausted and I'm still processing everything that's happened in the last couple of days – you getting attacked, the likelihood there're more assassins out there. I know we need to move fast on this, but everything will still be there tomorrow. We can wait until nightfall. It's only a few hours in the scheme of things and I'll be in a much better state of mind."

Beneath the table, Acid made a fist with both hands, cracking her knuckles. "Fine."

"Thanks." Spook yawned. "How did it go up in Manchester? Could The Dullahan help?"

Acid closed one eye and leaned back. She'd messed up by killing Eddie Dynamo, but there was no way she could tell Spook that. Experiencing The Dullahan's indignant tone and disappointed expression was bad enough. As they'd said their farewells this morning he'd been pleasant enough, but she could sense his frustration with her. She'd broken the code, gone off-book. He was right to be angry. It wasn't the way things were done; she knew that. Yet it wasn't the fatherly disappointment that cut so deep, as much as the fact that this could very well be the last time she saw the old bastard.

It was strange. In her youth she'd never thought about the last time with anyone. But that was because the last time was always just around the corner. Now she was out of the game – and The Dullahan was, too – life and death took on more meaning. She'd spent twenty years living in the moment because that was the only way she could stay sane, and now she had to worry about the future and people she cared about dying.

What an absolute bloody drag.

An image flashed into her mind's eye. A shadowy figure, standing on a hillside wearing a dark green suit. The first time she'd ever laid eyes on The Dullahan. She'd already heard the stories, of course – how he would drink his mark's blood after each hit, or how his stare could make a person forget their own name – but seeing him in the flesh was a whole other experience. He was ferocious and terrifying and graceful and erudite all at the same time. He was The Dark Man, The Blue-Eyed Killer, a master craftsman who deserved his mantle as the most feared assassin in the western world. That man was so different from the withered grey being she'd hugged goodbye earlier. But then she was a different woman, too, than the girl she'd been back when they first met. That version of Acid Vanilla was fresh off the shelf. She was as malevolent and brutal as she was energetic and intelligent. She soaked up every second of her training and tweaked what she'd learnt until she'd optimized her skills to the extreme. Her desire for greatness made her ravenous for power and status, eager to show the industry and then the world exactly who she was.

Bloody bollocks!

It was all so much easier back then, with only herself to worry about, and far too arrogant and conceited to give her own safety a second thought. She was young and impervious, full of ambition and sex and fury. She couldn't die. She wouldn't. She was Acid fucking Vanilla.

"Acid?"

She looked up. Spook had her arms folded and was looking at her as if she'd asked the same question at least twice.

"Excuse me?"

"I was saying – I found something else in Zoto's office. In his safe."

"Yes?" The bats gnawed at her nerves. She shifted her position on the chair, clenching and unclenching her fists. Her mind twisted back to what The Dullahan had said. If her killing Dynamo was the reason behind the hit on her, then she needed to face it head-on. She scowled into the middle distance, trying to remember her login details for the Crypto Jones One Thousand forum. If she took ownership of her mistake, then at least it was all on her. At least Spook was—

"…Kaan."

"What?" The manic, fractious haze that had been clogging her neural pathways dropped away. The room switched to high definition. "What did you say?"

Spook pursed her lips together. "Jesus. Listen to me, will you! I said I found a ledger with the word Kaan written inside. One word in big letters and underlined a bunch of times. I'm wondering if it might be the mystery man who threatened Zoto."

Acid looked at the ceiling, mouthing the name silently to herself over and over.

"What is it?" Spook asked.

"The Dullahan mentioned the name Kaan."

"No shit. What is it?"

"He didn't know. But someone calling themself Kaan has been posting on the Crypto Jones forum alluding to a job, a 'big assignment'. But those words aren't used on that forum. That's why The Dullahan took notice. He didn't think it was anything to worry about, but now…"

"…now this changes things."

"I'd say so, my clever little friend." Acid wagged her finger at Spook. "Good work, Sherlock."

Spook grinned. Her cheeks glowed red before her eyes fell on Acid's finger and her blood-encrusted nail.

Shitting hell.

She made a fist and placed it down on the table. "This is good," she said, levelling her tone. "It means we've got a lead. I take it you haven't found anything online yet?"

Spook's gaze lingered on Acid's hand. "I've not had a chance. I was going to move forward with a spider program first thing." She yawned again. "I'm wiped out. I need rest."

Acid remained at the table, keeping her face free from expression. Of the three principal traits of a good assassin – an alert presence, a clear mind, emotional balance – the last one was what she'd always struggled with the most. But over the years she'd mastered it.

"Yes. Get some sleep," she said. "But as soon as you wake up I need you on it. Everything you can find out about Kaan. Who they are. What they are. What their link is to Afrim Zoto. We'll lie low until nightfall and then visit the warehouse. My hope is there's something in there that will give us an indication of what happened. Papers, artefacts, maybe even a sign of a struggle. With the right piece of information, there's no reason we can't get to the bottom of this case and sign it off in the next day or two. Although, Fiona will need to prepare herself for all potential outcomes."

At the doorway, Spook turned back. Her face was solemn, but that pleased Acid. It meant she was taking the situation seriously, not acting like some real-life Nancy Drew in a hunt for the clues in a mystery novel, or a character from one of her online role-playing games. These were dangerous people they were dealing with.

"What about the woman who attacked you?" Spook asked. "If she was linked to the case, we're still in danger. Fiona, too."

Acid drew in a long breath and held it in her lungs for a

beat before exhaling. "I don't think the two things are related. Not anymore."

"Oh? What makes you say that?"

It could be argued that the fourth master trait of an assassin was the ability to read people's non-verbal signals. But Acid wouldn't have needed twenty years of experience to pick up on the distrust and annoyance coming off Spook at that moment.

"It was something The Dullahan said," she replied, and smiled. "But you're tired. I'll explain tomorrow when we're on a better footing. Okay?" She held Spook's gaze, willing her eyes to remain fixed on hers and not go exploring. Along with her blood-encrusted nails, she'd just felt the sting of a deep scratch running down the side of her neck. Michaela Starr must have caught her with a sharp fingernail while she was strangling her with a twisted-up bed sheet less than an hour earlier.

To the outside world, Starr was an experienced city trader, but Acid had recently discovered she was also known as Red One, top of the tree at The Red Scorpion Network, an underground organisation trading in drugs and human trafficking. Michaela was now hanging from one of the exposed steel girders in her modern loft apartment down by the river. A victim of suicide and the unrealistic expectations of the modern world (if you were to read the note on the glass coffee table below her feet). The blood on Acid's fingernails wasn't Starr's, though, but rather the remnants of a drunk who'd tried getting friendly in an alleyway as she'd made her way home. She hadn't gone looking for any more trouble. He was simply a bonus. And she hadn't killed him. She didn't think. But this was why she was hyper alert. A large colony of bats were flying high in her soul.

"Are you coming to bed?" Spook asked, flicking her head down the corridor. "It's late."

"You go. I'll be along soon."

Spook crossed her arms and scratched at the skin of her upper arm. "What are you going to do?"

Acid looked out the window. "I might get some air. I'm a little restless after all the travelling."

"Is that right?"

"Yes, it is. I can't sleep yet."

She'd also had a new lead on Lucas Jelani's whereabouts, thanks to the text message from her contact in South London, which she'd been considering when Spook arrived back. It could be nothing, but it could be exactly what she'd been waiting for. Two kills in one night. Maybe three. It made her tingle just thinking about it.

"Is that okay with you?" she asked Spook.

She was also harbouring the idea of calling into The Bitter Marxist. Just for one drink. To see if anyone she knew was in there. 'Anyone' being Freddie Pearce specifically. He'd been on her mind a lot since they'd met. Despite his nervy weirdness, there was something about the man that intrigued her. He was funny but unpretentious and came across like he didn't try. Plus, after all this time, she was still a sucker for a man with scruffy hair and good cheekbones. Killing evil bastards wasn't the only way to temper the manic energy swirling in her system.

But Spook wouldn't take her eyes off her and the look on her face was pure disappointment.

"I think you should try to sleep, Alice. We need to bring our A-game tomorrow. Both of us. Don't you think?" Acid opened her mouth to respond but Spook jumped in before she could. "Please. Stay home. Go to bed. For me?"

The way she said it, the pleading look in her eyes – even

with the bats screeching in her head, there was no other response to give.

"Fine," she mumbled. Jelani could wait. If they got the Zoto case tied up tomorrow, that would free her up to focus all her energy on him. She raised herself from the table. "I suppose I'm going to bed then."

Spook unfolded her arms and let them drop to her sides. "Awesome. I'll see you tomorrow."

She turned out the light and Acid followed her down the corridor to their respective rooms. One more night in the apartment wouldn't hurt. And now that it came to it, she was feeling rather weary. The bats wanted blood, but it was better to feed them when she could do it properly. And Spook was correct. They needed to be on top form. Something told her the next few days were going to be rather hectic, to say the least.

ACID SPENT the next day in a state of relative calm. She'd eventually fallen asleep around 5 a.m. and slept until noon. Once up, she ate a breakfast of oats and berries washed down with grapefruit juice and green tea and then went for a brisk walk around Hyde Park. After being attacked, some might have chosen a different route (and with stitches still in their side, not gone out at all), but if Acid had ever let a small thing like an injury or a near-death experience affect her, she'd be living in a padded cell right now. Besides, today she was there in bright daylight rather than the misty near-light of dawn. Every area in the park was heaving with tourists and dog walkers. There was no way even the most inexperienced and amateur assassins would attempt a hit under these circumstances.

By the time she got back to Soho and had double-locked

both the door to the street and that of their apartment, she was feeling more balanced than ever. After showering she'd feel even better.

Spook had surfaced and was huddled over a bowl of cereal at the table and scrolling through her phone when Acid entered the kitchen.

"You're crazy, you know that?" Spook told her, not looking up.

Acid side-stepped over the room so she was standing behind her and shoved two fingers against the back of her head. "Bang. You're dead."

Spook didn't flinch. "I knew it was you."

"Did you? For certain? You need to be more alert, Spook. This 'being careful' business works both ways. Come on. I'm standing behind you with a gun. What do you do?"

"Ah, leave it. I've just woken up. I'm eating breakfast."

"Oh, I'm sorry. You're right. Most killers would wait until you were fully awake before attacking you." She stayed put, pressing the ends of her fingers into Spook's neck. "Let's say I'm some shitbag who's about to execute you. What do you do? Like we went through."

Spook placed her spoon down. "I'd jerk my head back. Try to headbutt you."

"Then?"

"Then I'd run. As fast as I could. But you'd probably still be able to shoot me."

"Yes. But I might not hit you if I'm in pain and confounded from your surprise retaliation. Remember what I said, you've got the upper hand. Nothing to lose. Accept that you're already dead and act from that mindset."

"Yeah, I get it." Spook picked up her spoon and stuck it into a mound of soggy flakes, slurping them into her mouth.

Acid moved over to the sink and fixed herself a large glass of water from the tap. "You've not looked into Kaan yet, I take it?" she asked, turning back.

"That's what I'm doing now," Spook said, holding up her phone.

"Wow. Googling it on your phone? Hacker extraordinaire, hey? What would I do without you?"

Spook shot her a withering look over the top of her glasses. "It's always useful to start in the obvious places. Sometimes it's what you can't discover in the usual way that tells you where to dig."

"Fair enough. But nothing?"

"There's an import-export company called Kaan Global. But they're based in Norwich."

Acid downed the water as she considered this. "It's a start," she said, placing the glass in the sink. "I'm going to have a shower. You keep looking and then I was thinking we could get some food. My shout."

Spook pouted. "Gosh, you are in a good mood today."

"You know me, kid. I'm all about healthy living and having a positive outlook." She gave her a wink as she passed by on her way to the shower. She was only half-joking. More than likely it was the endorphins still in her system, but today the world seemed bright and full of possibility. There would always be a darkness in her soul, but she was making it work the best way she could. And so what if she had to hide her more nefarious and illicit coping mechanisms from Spook and the world at large? She'd spent her entire adult life hiding elements of herself. Nothing had changed. Right now the bats were at bay and she felt good. Leaning around the side of her bedroom door, she grabbed her towel and headed for the shower.

LUNCH COMPRISED an extensive selection of Dim Sum ('bring us the whole of this side of the menu') and a couple of bottles each of ice-cold lager. They ate and drank well and even shared a few laughs as they walked back to the apartment. Regaining her appetite was always a sure-fire sign for Acid that her moods were settling. With this balance came a clearer head and a renewed eagerness to find Afrim Zoto and collect the rest of their fee from his daughter. They'd agreed to eight-grand minimum on the retainer (enough money to pay off Shi and make rent) and the case had already dragged on longer than she'd have liked. It was time to grab the bull by the balls.

She spent the afternoon in her room, listening to music and keeping her head clear of any thoughts other than those that were relevant. It was a process she'd sharpened over the years and involved closing her eyes and visualising her entire being fading away until she was nothing but spectral light. Then she'd imagine herself being rebuilt, piece by piece, using only the specific characteristics she'd need for the job. For her, it was a similar practice to stripping a gun and oiling the elements so it was more effective and deadly when put back together. She wouldn't have ever described her process as meditation, but by sitting quietly without distraction and deconstructing her persona, she could better deal with the chaos in her head and reach a point where she felt at peace.

Although, peace wasn't the correct word. Peace implied a certain serenity and an acceptance of the world that had always evaded Acid, even as a young girl. Still, going through this timeworn ritual helped hone her manic disposition into something of value. Back in her early days in the killing industry she'd thought of herself as having superpowers, and when the situation was right it certainly felt that way. Her awareness and focus were so intense she could almost see things before they happened. Her thinking was super-fast and creative and her muscles burned with powerful energy. The best part was she often felt invincible, and that was also the worst part as well. It was the one aspect of her condition she had to always remain on top of. Going into dangerous situations with confidence and drive was one thing. Going in thinking nothing could kill you was a guaranteed way of getting killed.

Once rested and ready for action, Acid dressed in a pair of black jeans and a black turtleneck sweater. Checking herself in the full-length mirror by the door, she scraped her hair back in a high ponytail and secured it at the base with a hair tie she rolled off her wrist. Pulling her hair tight, she grabbed her jacket from the bed and headed down the corridor towards Spook's room.

"Hey." She knocked the crook of her index finger on the door. "Did you find anything?"

A rustling sound came from the room beyond and a second later the door opened to reveal a bedraggled Spook. She took her glasses off and cleaned a lens on her t-shirt as she squinted at Acid.

"Not really. I've spent most of the afternoon working on a spider program that will crawl both the mainstream and deep webs, focusing especially on non-indexed sites. It's not finished yet but it'll be comprehensive when it is. If Kaan is out there, we'll find him."

"That's great," Acid told her. "How much longer do you need?"

"Another hour? Then I can set it running while we go to

the warehouse." She placed her glasses on and looked Acid up and down. "Are you ready to go?"

"Yes. It's almost dark out. Get ready and as soon as your program is done we can leave."

"Gotcha. Will do."

Acid ran her tongue across her front teeth. She was eager to get out there and see what Zoto's warehouse had in store for them.

"I'll be in the kitchen," she said, remembering there was a quarter bottle of vodka in the freezer. A bit of Dutch courage never hurt. "Be as quick as you can. We've got work to do."

Chapter Twenty-Three

Once Spook's spider program was set up – crawling the internet for any mention of Kaan in relation to London, Afrim Zoto, and six other parameters – Acid booked them a cab to Woolwich. With a new crescent moon providing little light, they had the cover of darkness but asked the driver to drop them a few blocks from the warehouse district all the same. This way they could approach laterally rather than via the obvious route, and hopefully avoid any more bothersome security guards.

As the cab's taillights faded into the distance, Spook felt a rush of something close to excitement. The night air was cool but not cold and it tickled the skin on her neck in a pleasant way.

"Hey, wait for me," she said, skipping along after Acid, who had crossed over the road and was striding purposefully down the street. To their left was a high iron fence, painted dark green and with sharp razor wire draped across the top. On the other side stood the first collection of warehouses, numbers one through six. There were thirty buildings in total, and the plan was to walk around the perimeter and approach from the opposite side. This would provide better cover than last time, allowing them to access Zoto's warehouse without using the main access road.

"Do you think anyone will be around at this time of night?" Spook asked, catching up.

"I'm hoping not."

"Are you?"

It was a loaded question and even asking it sent a shiver down Spook's back, but she couldn't help herself.

Acid didn't look at her when she responded. "Why would I want to deal with the same pathetic prick as last time? This is a covert mission, in case you've forgotten. We get in, we see what we can find, we get out."

"Good. I'm glad," Spook said, feeling brave. Or stupid. It was a fine line sometimes. "It's just... I get the impression you're enjoying clashing with people at the moment."

Acid skidded to a stop and turned to glare at her. "Do you have something you want to say to me?"

Spook stopped, too. Neither of them blinked as they stared into each other's eyes. Absolutely, she had something she wanted to say. She'd heard Acid sneaking in and out at all hours and had seen the blood under her fingernails. Something sinister was going on and she wanted to know what. And how worried she should be about it.

"Come on, Spook. Spit it out."

"It's nothing," she mumbled and looked down. "After the excessive force demonstrated at Thelmastone House, the high body count, I worried you were starting to... I don't know... enjoy killing people."

"Don't forget who those people were, Spook. And what they did. Jesus. *Excessive force*? Every single one of the bastards that I killed at Thelmastone House deserved what they got."

She set off walking, head held high and chest out, giving the impression of someone completely unabashed and unrepentant. Whether she was either of these things, it was hard to say. But wasn't that always the way with Acid? She'd spent so long hiding her emotions, and even her humanity, that she couldn't bring herself to admit she was wrong. Or that Spook might have the semblance of a good point.

"Wait," Acid rasped, holding an arm out across Spook's chest as they got to the far side of the lot.

She stood in silence as Acid peered down the fence that ran alongside the first building and then gestured for her to carry on. They shifted over to the fence, where a eight-foot metal gate stood between them and warehouse number twelve.

"Do you have the keys?" Acid asked, reaching back but not turning around.

Spook stiffened.

Shit. No. Had she…?

Please no…

Her hand scrambled into the pocket of her jacket, her heart doing a backflip as her fingers touched on metal. She pulled out the keyring with its collection of six keys and handed them over.

"Fiona thinks the large brass one fits the main gate," she whispered. But Acid ignored her, going through the keys in turn and opening the lock silently on her third try. From where she was standing, Spook couldn't see if it was the brass key or not.

Acid pocketed the keys and eased open the gate enough that they could both slip through. The old metal creaked and groaned, but there was nothing they could do about it.

Once on the other side, Acid shut the gate but didn't lock it. They'd already gone through their entrance and exit plans at the apartment. It was important to keep your routes clear and open in case a swift withdrawal was required.

Keeping to the shadows, they doubled back on themselves, walking down the narrow passage between the fence and the length of the first warehouse, which was the last one numerically, number thirty. Once they were behind it, they edged along the rear of the buildings, counting in twos until they reached what Spook surmised was number fourteen.

"That's it, then," Acid whispered and pointed to the one in front of them. "Number twelve." She strained her head to one side and closed her eyes.

Spook remained stationary, waiting for the verdict. When Acid still hadn't spoken ten seconds later, she leaned in. "Anything?"

Acid's eye twitched. She shook her head. "No. We're clear." She opened her eyes. "Come on. Stay close."

They padded down the pathway between the two warehouses until they reached the front. Each building had a single security light above the main entrance that illuminated the ground before it in a three-metre radius. Squinting through the gloom, Spook saw no movement, no shadows. They were alone.

Acid slipped the keys from her pocket and moved around to the front of the building. Spook gave the lot a brief inspection, left and right, then followed her up to the double doors at the entrance. Acid was already trying the keys in the lock as she neared. She held off from telling her Fiona thought it was the large silver key with '101' engraved on the base that she needed. On the second attempt, the lock clicked open and Acid raised her head and gave her a manic grin. Spook was used to it by now, but it was still unsettling.

"Here we go." Acid pushed the door open and waved her inside. "After you."

"Erm… okay."

Spook stepped through the door and looked around. The security light filtering through the window illuminated the reception area, but there was nothing of interest in it. No filing cabinets, no cupboards, nothing that might hold clues. Acid closed the main doors and was over to the internal door in two strides, selecting a new key as she went. This time she got it the first time and stepped through into what Spook presumed to be the main ware-house space.

"What the fuck?"

"What is it?" Spook gasped, hurrying after her.

Her breath was tight in her chest as she pushed through the door and let it swing shut behind her. She couldn't see anything except for the dark shape in front of her, which she hoped was Acid.

Cool, stale air enveloped her, invading her nostrils with a dank earthiness. The smell reminded her of the outbuilding her father had built at the end of their garden. Back when Spook was young and innocent and free from the evils of this world.

"Acid? What is it?"

She felt something move past her and the lights flickered on above her head. She shot a look over her shoulder, comforted to see Acid standing next to the switch by the door. But when she turned back into the room any relief she'd felt dropped away, replaced by a fog of confusion.

"What the fuck?"

The room they were in was vast and took up the entire

footprint of the warehouse minus the tiny reception area. It was also completely empty.

"I don't get it," she muttered. "This was Afrim Zoto's main warehouse. Why is it…? Has someone…?"

She trailed off. It didn't make any sense for it to be empty. She moved further into the space, examining the floor for shapes in the dust and dirt, a sign of boxes or crates recently removed. But there was nothing. It was like a shell. An empty showroom. She spun around to face Acid, her mouth flapping but unable to form any words.

In response, Acid raised her eyebrows and shrugged. "No idea. What did Fiona say exactly, last time you spoke to her? Had she been here?"

"No. She didn't have the keys, remember?" She looked up, scowling at the corrugated iron roof and the steel girders above her head. "That was why she was at her father's office the other night. She had an idea what the code for his safe might be. And she was right. She gave me the keys from inside. That's where I found the ledger pad with the word Kaan in it."

Acid nodded in remembrance, her deep scowl wrinkling her brow and the top of her nose. "It doesn't look like it's ever been used," she said. "Not any time recently, at least."

"That's exactly what I was thinking," Spook said, self-conscious of the enthusiasm in her voice. She coughed. "What do we do now?"

"Right now we go home," Acid said, walking towards the door. "After that I'd like to speak with Fiona again, see what she thinks of this development." She stopped with her hand on the door handle. "Did you get the impression she was legit?"

"Fiona? Yes. She's worried to hell and back about her

father. I can see it in her eyes every time she talks about him. Why do you ask?"

Acid didn't budge. "We have to be open to all possibilities, Spook." She yanked open the door. "For now let's get out of here. Beresford Street is a ten-minute walk from here. We can get a black cab from there."

She disappeared into the reception area, letting the door swing shut behind her and leaving Spook standing alone in the empty warehouse.

"Hey, wait for me."

Spook opened the door and, keeping a tight hold on the handle, leaned over and switched off the light, making a swift exit before the darkness ignited her unhelpful imagination. The reception area was empty, but that didn't surprise her. Acid was acting particularly tenacious this evening and was impatient at the best of times. As Spook opened the front door, she found Acid standing in the dull orange glow of the warehouse's security light, looking towards the main gates of the warehouse lot.

"Acid? Everything okay?" Spook asked. But she didn't answer. She didn't even turn around.

Spook stepped into the light. That's when she heard the rumble of a car engine. She shot her attention to where Acid was looking. Three men were walking towards them. And while it was hard to make out their faces in the darkness, it was less difficult to make out the assault rifle one of the men was carrying. Behind them, a large van the same colour as the night sky was parked with its back doors open and facing into warehouse number eight. Spook couldn't see into the van or what was being loaded or unloaded.

"What you doing here?" one of the men called out. "Who are you?"

Spook side-stepped over to stand shoulder to shoulder

with Acid. As the men got closer, she could see they wore loose fitting jeans and hooded tops. They each had afro hair, trimmed short and with sharp fades on the sides. The one talking also had a neat beard. He glared at her and Acid with dark eyes full of hate.

"I asked you a question, innit," he said, coming to a stop a few metres away. "Who are you?"

"We're nobody," Acid replied. "You don't have to worry about us."

The man glanced at his colleagues. The one holding the rifle sneered and adjusted his grip. "Oh, but we do, darling," he said. "We can't have birds snooping around our ends this time of night. You might see something you shouldn't."

Spook stifled a yelp. This was not going well. The man with the gun looked like he was waiting for any excuse to employ his lethal toy. Resisting the urge to grab onto the sleeve of Acid's jacket, she instead rocked her weight on her heels, readying herself to make a run for it.

"We haven't seen anything," Acid said. She glanced at Spook with an intensity in her eyes as if giving her a sign. But what she meant by it, Spook didn't know.

Damn it!

Why didn't she know?

Had this been covered in their assault training? Maybe on one of those occasions when her mind had wandered?

Acid placed her hands into the pockets of her jacket. "Listen, we're going to turn around and walk away," she told the men. "We haven't seen anything or anyone. Okay? We don't want any trouble."

The man rolled his shoulders back and stood up to his full height. "Nah. I don't think so," he said. "Boss man won't be too happy if he finds out you were here snooping and I let you walk away. It's his decision what happens next, ya get me?"

Acid raised her head and sniffed. The small muscles at the side of her jaw quivered, accentuated by the deep shadows cast by the security lights.

"We weren't snooping," she said. "But fine."

"Acid..." Spook started, but stopped as Acid nudged into her.

"It's no problem, Spook. We'll go with these men. Yes?" The words came out in a soft monotone. "Are you ready to go?"

Spook tensed. This time she'd picked up on the cues. "Yes," she heard herself say.

The bearded man made a grab for Acid's arm, but she pulled her hand out of her pocket and flung the bunch of keys in his face. He reeled back as they hit him in the eyes.

"Run!" Acid yelled, and Spook pushed off from the ground to follow after her.

Acid reached back and grabbed her wrist, pulling her along beside her. As the three men erupted in an explosion of shouted expletives behind them, they took a right down the side of the nearest warehouse. With heads down and not looking back, they raced to the end of the passageway. Once there, Spook risked a furtive glance over her shoulder. The men were giving chase, running in single file, with the gunman taking the lead.

"Get those fucking bitches now," one of them cried.

The man raised the rifle, but Acid grabbed for Spook and yanked her to safety around the corner as the crack of gunfire echoed between the two buildings.

"Who are they?" Spook yelled, as they ran along the narrow channel between the rear of the warehouses and the perimeter fence.

It was a dumb question and Acid didn't respond. Why would she? It didn't matter who they were. They were armed and angry and involved in something illegal. Spook had enough experience of the shadowy underbelly of the world by now to know that the specifics of their illegal activities, along with the risk attached to what she and Acid had interrupted, were massive deciding factors in whether the two of them lived to see tomorrow.

"This way," Acid rasped, cutting a left that took them down between warehouses twenty-two and twenty-four.

They got to the far end and burst out into the open. The gate was in sight. Another fifty metres and they'd be clear. Another hundred and they'd be safe.

With lactic acid burning her insides, Spook pressed on, matching Acid stride for stride as they raced for the exit. Behind her, the shouting from the men was growing louder and clearer. They were getting closer. More gunshots echoed through the air. Spook let out a high-pitched squeal but didn't allow the shock to slow her down. She knew by now that if you felt no pain by the time you heard the gunshot it was a good sign. You never hear the bullet that kills you.

They were at the gate. Acid slammed into the steel bars to stop herself and grabbed the handle. The gate didn't move. She let out a grunt and tried again. Nothing. As Spook got up to her, she was jiggling the gate frantically but it wasn't opening. So much for leaving a clear getaway.

Spook grabbed Acid's hand to help force the damn thing open, but it wouldn't budge. It was locked. Someone had locked it. As the realisation dawned on her, she heard laughter over their shoulders.

"Ah shit. Were we supposed to leave that gate open?" the bearded man said, as the two of them turned around. "I wondered, ya know. Thought it was odd it had been left unlocked. Was that you, was it?" He reached up and wiped at the blood seeping from the cut above his eye. His smile grew more sinister as he lowered his hand to see the damage. "Dumb bitch. You'll regret that. Not least cos now you've got no keys."

He and his cronies laughed in unison, like a bunch of slavering jackals closing in on their prey.

"But the fact remains we haven't seen anything," Acid said. "Let us go. We never saw you. We aren't going to tell anyone we were even here."

Spook chewed on the inside of her cheek. Was this another play by her fiendish partner? Did she have a plan to get them out of this?

Both those questions were quashed as the bearded man lunged forward and smashed his fist into Acid's stomach. She doubled over with a groan. Spook made to go to her, but before she did, the man kneed Acid in the face.

Someone screamed.

Spook realised it was her.

She screamed again as Acid stumbled against the fence.

Shit.

No.

She wanted to move, to help her friend, but her feet were stuck to the ground and her muscles weren't responding. As Acid struggled to get up, the man with the rifle stepped forward and pointed it at her head.

"Don't be silly now," he told her.

The bearded man looked the two of them up and down, shaking his head in apparent disgust. "Stop fucking around, all right?" he said, pointing a heavily ringed finger at Acid. "Any more of this and you're going to really piss me off. You don't want to do that."

Acid looked up at him and grinned. Her teeth were stained with blood.

"Fuck me. You've got a death wish." He tsked loudly and began to walk away.

Spook held her breath.

Was this it?

Were they done?

But as the man reached the edge of the nearest warehouse, he called back over his shoulder. "Grab them, fam," he said. "These bitches are coming with us."

Chapter Twenty-Four

The inside of the van was grimy and stank of petrol and body odour. Acid was sitting with her back to the driver's cab and Spook was over to her left, leaning against the side panel. In front, to her right, the man with the rifle was perched on a metal flight case. Every so often a beam of light would shine through the two small windows in the rear doors, illuminating the inside of the van, and each time it did, she glanced between Spook and the man, making eye contact with both but saying nothing.

No one had spoken since she and Spook had been bundled into the rear of the Ford Transit ten minutes earlier. The gunman kept grinning at her, perhaps willing her to speak so he could reprimand her in a way of his choosing, but she wasn't going to give him the satisfaction. Besides, she had to conserve her energy until she knew what she was dealing with at their destination.

The men hadn't tied them up, which was a mistake. She reached up and felt at her face. Her nose wasn't broken and there were no obvious cuts that would need attention. Her bottom lip was split open and she'd bitten a chunk out of the inside of her cheek when the prick had kneed her in the face, but the mouth healed fast and other than that she was unscathed. For now. It didn't mean she'd remain that way when they got to wherever they were going. Whoever this boss man was, it was clear his foot soldiers viewed him with the utmost respect, bordering on fear. That said a lot.

A few minutes later and the van slowed before coming to a complete stop. As lights flooded in through the windows, Acid sensed Spook trying to get her attention.

Calm it down, kid.

Show no fear.

A few seconds went by. Acid shifted all her attention into her hearing, listening for noises outside the van that might indicate where they were. But there was nothing. Just silence. They'd been travelling for less than thirty minutes, and thirty minutes in any direction from Woolwich was still inside the London Orbital Motorway. Where was the sound of traffic, the police sirens? She glanced out of the windows. The light coming in was too bright for streetlights. *Shit.* They were in some sort of lock-up or a garage.

She looked over and gave Spook a stern look, which she hoped conveyed everything she needed it to.

I'll handle this.

Let me do the talking.

They had one chance of making a first impression with the boss man and if they blew it they might not live to see the morning. After tracking Lucas Jelani's movements for the last month, researching his methods and methodology, she had some idea of how South London gangs operated. If this lot were anything to do with them, it'd be an execution rather than anything rash and in the moment. If they were taken to a second location tonight, it would be a very large possibility they were about to die. That's when her 'nothing to lose' mindset – the one she'd been trying to instil in Spook – would come to the fore. If you knew you were going to die, you had carte blanche to try whatever you could to turn the tables. It had worked out for her before, many times. But she was younger back then and fitter – she felt invincible even when the bats weren't filling her with manic energy.

The back doors of the van opened on the two men who'd been riding in the front. The man with the beard beckoned them with one finger. "Out."

Acid shuffled along the floor of the van until she reached the lip of the vehicle, where both men grabbed hold of her and yanked her out.

"Hey, calm it down, hands!" She struggled to get away, but the bearded man gripped the tops of her arms as his friend pulled Spook from the van.

As she'd thought, they were in an enormous hangar, similar in size and structure to Zoto's warehouse. The man with the rifle clambered out of the van and walked past them, slamming the heel of his hand on a red button on the wall next to the entrance through which they'd driven in. A large metal shutter lowered to the ground with a clang. As the concertinaed metal sealed itself, the atmosphere in the hangar shifted. The fresh, cool air at once was gone, along with their chance of escape. The man strolled back to join his cronies, holding the rifle at waist height aimed at her feet.

"This way," the man with the beard said, heading for a door that was cut into a wall of corrugated iron opposite the shutters. "And don't try anything stupid, yeah?"

Acid felt a hand on her back, shoving her forward. She followed the man over to the door, lowering her head to demonstrate obedience but not enough she couldn't scope out the space. Her dry eyes searched for inspiration, a weapon, a way out. There was nothing.

The man opened the door and stepped over the raised lip into the next room. He waited there, holding the door open for the rest of them to follow. Acid went next, stepping through into a space the same size and similarly lit as the last. Long work benches spanned the length of the room on both sides and someone had swept a gigantic pile of sawdust and rubble into one corner. At the far end, a stair-case led up to the next level. The men hustled them over to it and they ascended the stairs in silence, the man with the beard going first, followed by Acid, then Spook, then the other two men. The one with the rifle took the rear and this formation suggested the men were well seasoned in this sort of thing. There was no way she could overpower the two nearest to her without catching a round or two somewhere lethal. She hadn't had a proper look at the weapon, but she assumed it to be an AK of some description. A 47 or 74. It might have even been supplied by good old Lucas Jelani.

At the top of the steps was another door and, beyond this, a long metal corridor that fed into another building joined onto the hanger. The metal walls turned to brick and then plasterboard as they traipsed along in single file. Acid could sense the unease coming off Spook and willed her to keep it together. Their lives depended on what happened in the next few minutes.

They reached the far end of the corridor and the bearded man stopped at another closed door. He turned to Acid and Spook, wagging an extended finger between the two of them.

"All right, listen, yeah? We're going in to see our boss. I've told him you were snooping around where you shouldn't have been. So we'll see how he wants to handle this. No funny business, yeah? Ya get me? Otherwise…" He raised his finger and made a slicing motion across his throat.

Acid held his gaze, resisting an eye roll with everything she had, but also feeling slightly relieved. The cutting-the-throat action was a hackneyed move and it revealed the guy's inexperience. He might well have had a few bodies under his belt, but this was all still a pose for him.

"What's your boss's name?" she asked.

The man sucked air through his teeth. "You're going to see him now, innit. Ask him yourself. Don't worry, I called him from the van. He's looking forward to meeting you."

He pushed open the door and ushered the two of them to go first. Acid adjusted her posture, pulling her ponytail tight before stepping through.

The room beyond was made out in a luxurious style, massively contrasting the raw iron and exposed plaster of the rooms leading to it. The walls and ceiling were painted bottle-green, and an enormous white fur rug, which probably cost more than the furniture in Acid and Spook's entire apartment, all but covered the dark wooden floorboards. There were no windows, but a series of ornate brass uplighters filled the space with enough light. In the centre of the room were three green leather sofas set out in a U shape. On the middle one, facing the door, a man was reclining with one leg resting on the knee of his other.

As they entered, the man looked up but made no move to stand. He was wearing dark blue baggy jeans and an oversized black mohair sweater with white flecks. Around his neck was a thick silver chain, and when he smiled at Acid a silver tooth glinted in the light.

"Bless. Come forward," he said. His voice was deep but

gentle, despite the South London accent. "My bro Kofi here tells me they found yous snooping around. Is that correct?"

Acid felt a hand on her shoulder. It guided her forward until she was standing in front of the couch. She let it happen; it wasn't the time for heroics. Not yet.

"No, that is not correct," she replied. "I can see how it may have appeared to your men, but we didn't even know they were there. We were about to leave when they saw us. We didn't see what they were doing. We didn't see *anything*."

She made this last statement sound as resolute as she could. But the boss man blew out a sharp sneer. "What do they call you?"

"They call me Acid. They call her Spook." She remained still, but every muscle in her upper body was tense. She drew in a breath to make herself relax. At times like this, it was important to stay loose. "And you are?"

The man laughed. "Acid? Spook? Are you taking the piss?" He looked past them at his men. "Are these bitches for real?"

A ripple of snickers erupted from behind her. She ignored it.

"We are for real," she said. "Those are our names."

The boss man crooked his head to one side and frowned, but she remained stoic and after a few seconds he laughed. "Have it your way. *Acid. Spook.* My name is Malachi Moses. And despite all this… upset tonight, the first thing you need to know about me is that I'm a legitimate businessman. You understand me? Only, I don't like people sniffing around in my business. I guess I'm funny like that."

"But we weren't sniffing around your business, I promise," Spook blabbed. "We don't want any trouble. We're working for Fiona Zoto. Do you know her? Or her father?

Afrim Zoto? He's gone missing. We were checking out his warehouse and—"

Acid coughed and glared at her friend, hoping she'd pick up on the subtext.

Shut the fuck up.

She had planned to keep the reason for them being at the warehouse to herself until it was pertinent. Spook had just blown any leverage they might have had.

"An American lady," Moses said. "Nice. How you liking it in London, darling? We got it all here these days. Money, guns, razzamatazz. The whole lot."

Spook looked down and mumbled something into her chest, eliciting more laughter from Moses.

"What she says is true," Acid butted in. "We are looking for Afrim Zoto."

"Zoto?" Moses repeated, attacking the 'T' in the name with menace. "Not heard of any Zoto. He owns a warehouse in the district, you say?"

Acid nodded. "Number twelve. But it's a shell. Nothing in there. I don't suppose your men have seen anything suspicious over the last few weeks?"

"What the fuck?" Moses uncrossed his legs and placed both feet on the ground. Leaning forward, he regarded her with irate eyes. "Do you think you're the one asking me the questions?"

Acid swallowed but didn't take her eyes off him. "I apologise. I didn't mean to overstep the mark. We just want you to understand that our motives for being there tonight had nothing to do with you or your business."

"And I told you I've never heard of no Zoto. What about you, fam? Ring any bells?"

The bearded man, who she now knew was called Kofi, stepped forward. "Nah. But warehouse twelve has changed hands a lot over the years. He could be the new guy."

Acid turned to Spook. That didn't seem right from what she remembered of their meeting with Fiona.

"I don't suppose you go by the name Kaan, by any chance?" she asked.

"Kaan?" Moses sat back, mouth open and exposing his silver teeth. "This bitch still asking the questions? Shit. No, I don't go by the name Kaan. Or any other names. Why would I? Like I told you already, I'm a legitimate businessman."

She didn't believe that for one second, but neither did she care. She rolled her head from side to side as if she was stretching her neck, but scanning the room for exits. There was a door over in the right-hand corner, but it would be risky to go for it. The last thing she wanted was to grapple her way past these fellas, only to run into the store cupboard.

She shifted her attention back to Moses. He didn't look to be carrying a piece, and neither of the other two men had drawn a weapon when it would have been apt for them to do so. That meant only one of them was armed. One assault rifle versus the push dagger concealed in her belt. She'd triumphed over worse odds.

"Does the name Kaan mean anything to you?" she asked. "Have you heard it recently? Someone's name maybe, or an organisation?" She was pushing her luck, but by leading the conversation in this way, she also hoped to prove to Moses she had zero interest in whatever illicit schemes he was involved with.

"Listen to me, yeah? I don't know anyone calling themselves Kaan." His tone had shifted. He was irritated. But this wasn't the worst outcome. Irritation was rarely a threat.

"We think he may be a business rival of Zoto's and has had him killed."

Moses sucked air through his teeth. "Why are you telling me this? Why would I give a fuck about some wasteman called Zoto? I keep telling you—"

"Yes, you're a legitimate businessman. I understand. But I'd appreciate it if you didn't mention this – or us – to the police. We aren't exactly one hundred percent by-the-book in terms of how we conduct our own business."

She smiled and held her ground as Moses looked between her and Kofi with an open mouth. "Have you heard this, fam?" He laughed. "Fucking hell. We've got a real live bird on our hands here, boys. Listen, Acid, we may be legit now, but we don't talk to the fucking feds, ya get me? Ever."

"That's good to hear. I appreciate that. And you need to believe me when I say we have no interest in you or your business."

"Is that right?" Moses tsked and shook his head. "Kofi, come here, fam."

He beckoned him over and Kofi sat beside him on the couch. They faced each other and talked in hushed tones for a few moments. When they were done, Kofi stood and Moses sat back, rubbing his palm down his face.

"We can all walk away from this without any issue," Acid told him. "You don't need to worry about us. Let us go. You'll never see us again."

Moses laughed. "Ya know what, fuck this. Get these dickheads away from me. They're starting to piss me off. Ghelan?"

Acid leaned into Spook as the man with the rifle stepped around the side of her. "Yes, boss?" he said.

"Take these two freaks back to the warehouse."

"And?"

"And let them go." His words said one thing, but the intense way he was staring at his foot soldier sent Acid's bat sense tingling.

"Thank god," Spook whispered.

"All right, you two," Ghelan said, lowering the rifle but keeping his finger on the trigger. "Let's go."

Spook shifted around and shuffled towards the door they'd entered through. Acid gave Moses a nod of thanks and then walked after her.

"Open it," Ghelan snarled as Spook got to the door. With a shaking hand, she eased it open and stepped through, closely followed by Acid.

"Have a pleasant night," Kofi shouted after them, and a rumble of deep laughter carried down the long passageway after them. The way Ghelan was jabbing the end of the rifle into the small of Acid's back as they walked down the stairs told her everything she already suspected. They weren't being released. They were being taken somewhere to be eradicated. Tomorrow their bodies would wind up in the Thames, or in the boot of a beat-up car waiting to be crushed at the nearest yard.

At the bottom of the steps, Spook stopped to let Acid and Ghelan catch up. She smiled as Acid got closer, her round face a picture of relief. Acid returned the smile, but then looked away. The next few seconds mattered.

"Outside," Ghelan said, shoving Acid with the rifle butt.

Spook made to leave also. But as she turned towards the door, Acid stood on the back of her heel.

"Ouch! Shit! What the…?" Spook cried out. She stumbled over and Acid stepped back, knocking into Ghelan.

It was the distraction she needed. She spun back and grabbed the end of his rifle, twisting the muzzle into the air.

With her other hand she reached around and flicked the push dagger out of her belt, stabbing it into the man's arm below his wrist. He screamed and let go of the rifle. Feeling its release, Acid chucked it to the floor before leaping up and smashing her elbow into his face. She felt the cartilage in his nose buckle with the force of the blow. As the bats screamed their approval and Ghelan groaned in pain, she regained her balance and kicked his legs out from under him. He hit the hard concrete floor head first, knocking himself out. With her mind free from thought, driven on by instinct and an overriding yearning for blood, she pounced on him, yanking the push dagger out of his arm and holding it aloft. Grabbing his head she rolled it to one side, exposing his neck and jugular vein. The bat screams grew louder...

Do it.

Kill him.

She tightened her grip on the dagger...

"Acid! No!"

She froze, the dagger in her hand poised and ready. Shooting a look over her shoulder, she saw Spook standing by the door holding the assault rifle. She was aiming it at Acid's head.

"What? Are you going to shoot me?"

Spook sniffed. "Don't kill him. Please. Let's go."

"No. Go on then. Shoot me." She opened her eyes as far as they could go. She was on the brink. "If you're that bothered. Shoot me."

She knew full well there was no way Spook was going to kill her. Even if she pulled the trigger, the way she was standing meant she'd knock herself on her arse and empty the mag into the ceiling before she caught Acid with a lucky stray.

Spook lowered the gun. "Please, Acid. He's out cold. Let's get out of here." She let go of the rifle and it fell to the floor with a clatter. "You don't need to kill."

Acid adjusted her grip on the handle of the push dagger. Her hands were sweating. She looked at the man on the floor beneath her. Then back at Spook. Then she lowered the dagger.

"You're a bloody pain in the arse, you know that – *fam*?" She climbed off the man, housing the dagger in its concealed compartment in her belt. "And I really need to show you how to hold a rifle properly. Remind me to—"

Shit.

Voices echoed down from the level above. It was Moses and Kofi.

Spook whimpered. "What do we do now?"

The rifle was lying a few metres from Acid's feet. She could grab it and mow the rotten pricks down before they got halfway down the stairs. But would Spook ever forgive her for that? More importantly, could she bear to listen to any more of her moralistic whining this evening? Besides, for now the moment had passed. She grabbed Spook's arm and they headed for the door. It was time to get out of here.

Chapter Twenty-Five

Once out of the hangar, Acid and Spook raced down a long tarmacked slope that curved through an open gate at the bottom of the incline. On the other side of the gate, Acid could see a wide road that cut through the middle of an industrial estate. She and Spook were side by side as they ran, but didn't look at each other or speak. For now, Acid trusted Spook knew what to do. Mainly, get away from the dangerous men as fast as possible. As they reached the open gate, loud shouts could be heard behind them, then the distinct pop-crack of gunfire.

Legitimate businessman, my arse.

And why the hell had she let Spook's pathetic whining sway her? She should have slit the bastard's throat and opened up his friends' chests with the AK as soon as they appeared at the top of the stairs.

Acid gritted her teeth and quickened her pace. No use beating herself up about it. She'd fucked up. She wouldn't again.

They continued on into the industrial estate. Large

buildings like the one they'd left behind stood on either side of the long, newly surfaced road. At the end of it were lights and the steady hum of traffic. If they could reach the main road before Moses' goons caught up with them, they had a fighting chance. But as they raced for the lights, Acid heard the loud revs of a car engine. Or, more likely, a van engine. The one they were brought here in. A second later came the screech of tyres as it pulled out of the hangar lot. They weren't going to make it to the main road.

"Over here," she gasped, shoving Spook and guiding her into the shadows down the side of one of the buildings. With no streetlights and only the thin crescent moon in the sky, it was hard to see where they were putting their feet, but it was soon clear that the narrow street was a dead end.

Shit.

Shitting hell!

They'd run themselves into a trap. Slowing her pace, Acid darted her head left and right, searching for inspiration. Down the side of the adjacent building, at the bottom of a shallow concrete trench, someone had dumped a pile of filled industrial rubbish bags. There were about thirty in total and even from this distance the smell coming off them was vile. But it was all she had.

"Spook. Down here."

She jumped into the trench and dived over the top layer of bags before reaching for Spook and helping her to clamber over.

"Oh my god. That's disgusting." Spook gagged as Acid dragged her down behind the stinking pile.

"Shut up. Stay down."

The reek of rotten food and ammonia was intense. They leaned against each other, releasing long slow breaths and then inhaling fast through their mouths to best deal with the ferocious stench.

They'd had enough of a start on the men that it was unlikely they'd been seen veering down this side street, but there was always a chance. Acid held Spook's wrist, squeezing it tight, conducting the moment, not ready to let her go until she was certain they were safe. The sound of an engine cut the night air. But as soon as it was heard, it began to grow quieter. As if it had driven past them.

Thirty seconds went by. A minute. Acid's eyes watered. A harsh metallic taste pricked the back of her throat. After another minute she released Spook's arm and raised her head over the stinking pile. The street was empty and, other than the low buzz of the city, there was no sound.

"I think we're clear," she whispered.

"Yeah?" Spook got to her feet, screwing her face up as she peered down towards the end of the street. "That was close."

"It was stupid is what it was." Acid grabbed the handles of the two bags immediately in front of her and flung them to one side before clambering over the top of the pile. Once on firmer ground, she rubbed her hands on the front of her thighs. "I should have killed all three of them."

"Then you'd have been just as bad as they are," Spook said, as Acid helped her climb over.

"Who says I'm not?"

"I do," Spook answered when they were stood facing each other. Acid tsked and set off walking up.

"Well, you're wrong. And I can't believe you were going to shoot me." She turned and walked backwards a few steps, checking Spook was following her. "I didn't think you had it in you, my oh-so-moral friend."

"I wasn't actually going to pull the trigger."

"No shit!" she scoffed and spun back around.

"But I didn't want you to kill that man," Spook added, running to catch up.

"Whyever not? He was going to kill us. You know that, don't you?"

"We agreed – *you agreed* – that if we started this agency, there'd be no unnecessary killing. You looked me in the eyes and said 'fine'. I remember it clearly. There are plenty of other ways you can utilise your skills without resorting to… that! The Avenging Angels aren't assassins. We're a force for good."

"Sometimes killing people is a force for good."

"Really? You believe that?"

"Fuck me." Acid stopped at the end of the short street. Down to their right was the main road, with streetlights and cars and the buzz of signage from a Chinese takeaway. She turned back to Spook, ready to say more, but decided against it. She wasn't getting dragged into her moral maze. It was a trap. Instead, she headed for the main road and to the nearest bus stop. The sign nailed to the back of the shelter told her they were on Coldharbour Lane in Camberwell and a short walk from Brixton Tube station.

"Do you have any cash?" Acid asked, as Spook appeared beside her.

"Nope," she replied, staring at the sign. "I haven't carried cash for two years."

Acid clicked her teeth. "We've got two options. We walk all the way home. Or we jump the Tube." She knew which one of the two she'd prefer.

"How long will it take to walk?"

"Too long."

Spook pushed her glasses up her nose. "I guess the Tube it is."

"Not going to have a problem with that, my little do-gooder?"

"Go to hell." Spook set off walking, calling back as she strode away. "If you think killing people and dodging a fare is the same level of wrong, then we really do have problems. I thought you were cleverer than that. *Alice!*"

Acid cricked her neck to one side, fighting the smile twitching at her lips. She liked this side of Spook. The part she always took the credit for cultivating. The part of her with bite. It gave her hope.

———

BRIXTON TUBE STATION was still busy despite the late hour, which meant they could slip through onto the platform without hassle. A sleepy-faced attendant leaning against the wall made eye contact with Acid when she pushed in behind a tall, skinny male before the barriers closed, but he said nothing. He didn't even react. Either he didn't care or was so entrenched in the mundanity of his job that it didn't register. Spook, in turn, hunkered down and slid under the larger barrier used by wheelchair users, springing up a moment later with red cheeks and a wide grin splitting her round face.

"Good work," Acid said, pulling her close as they moved into the milling crowd towards the escalators. "See? Being bad can be fun."

Spook didn't respond, but her smile was slow to fade as they made their way down to the platform and jumped on the Victoria line. The train was crowded, mostly with night-time drinkers heading home, but Acid and Spook were able to get seats, and to Acid's relief their fellow passengers gave them a wide berth. Not because they looked scary or unapproachable, but rather because the two of them reeked like the devil's arsehole. She hadn't been able to smell herself outside, or she'd got used to it, but in the confines of the stuffy carriage, the stench coming off the two of them was overpowering.

But they weren't the only things that stank. Something wasn't right in the Zoto case. Acid closed her eyes. Her mind turned over at one hundred miles an hour as thoughts of Afrim Zoto and Kaan collided with those of begrudged assassins and open contracts. She went over what The Dullahan had said, seeing his disappointed face in her mind's eye. He was right, she was stepping on some pretty dangerous toes doing what she was doing.

But would it stop her? She didn't think so. Tonight the bats had smelt blood and they were restless.

Alighting the Tube at Oxford Circus, they vaulted over the barriers and raced for the exit with the station attendant's yells echoing off the tiled walls behind them. They jogged along Oxford Street and took a right down Wardour Street, slowing halfway along when it was clear no one was in pursuit. Then they trudged the last ten minutes of the journey back to their apartment in relative silence. Spook appeared to be exhausted, but that suited Acid perfectly; with any luck, she'd head straight for her room when they got in and sleep through until morning. That way, she didn't have to come up with ridiculous excuses about why she was going out again. She couldn't rest now even if she wanted to, even if her body would allow it. Her nervous system fizzed with manic energy. Her mind was a storm of chaotic thoughts and ideas. She had to do something. She had to quell her needs. Having come so close but then denied her kill, it was all she could think about. The bats were in flight, screeching their distaste in every synapse in her brain.

They were angry. They craved blood.

Chapter Twenty-Six

Acid double-locked the door of the apartment and followed Spook into the kitchen. Why wasn't she heading for her bedroom? Or a shower at least, they both still stunk from lying on the rubbish heap. As Spook sat at the table, an image of choking out the diminutive American flashed in Acid's mind.

"It's pretty late," she said, shaking the image away. "We should get some sleep. You look exhausted."

Spook leaned back in the chair. "Don't you think we should talk about what's going on?"

"What is going on?"

"What do you mean? Everything is going on. We've got about a million threads to follow in the Zoto case, plus we still don't know why you were attacked. Aren't you at all concerned that someone tried to kill you and we don't know why?"

Acid pulled out a chair but didn't sit. "What if it's nothing? An isolated incident."

"It was a professional hit. You said it yourself." Spook sat back, scowling as Acid chewed on her top lip.

To tell her the truth would be to admit to everything she'd done over the last six months. She knew the kid had her suspicions, but if Spook knew the extent of her activities she'd lose her mind. This wasn't Acid falling off the wagon a few times. She'd carefully researched her victims and meticulously planned out each hit. It was professional assassin work she was engaged in. Albeit without a client and a pay check at the end of it

So what was she?

A vigilante? An exponent of justice?

Neither of those explanations felt correct because they implied the hit was for the greater good. As it was, she would never have killed anyone who didn't deserve it – that's where the extensive research came in. But she'd started on her killing spree because something inside had compelled her. The bats, her condition. Or maybe more than that. Killing these corrupt, evil people quietened an ache in her. It made her feel alive. It connected her to her past. To the young girl who had taken Oscar Duke's life. She was a killer. An angel of death. By accepting this, she'd become free again.

She gripped the back of the chair. Spook was staring at her. "If it'll make you feel better, I'll ring The Dullahan. Find out if he's heard anything."

She removed her jacket, slipping her phone out of the inside pocket as she placed it over the back of the chair. Swiping the screen open, she tapped on the last called numbers and selected the top entry. To get away from Spook's prying eyes, she walked over to the window and looked out onto the street below. He answered the call in two rings.

"You're still alive, then?"

"For now. Did I wake you?"

"Me? Not a chance. I'm awake most nights. Do all my sleeping in the day."

Acid smiled into the receiver. "And you used to call me a vampire."

"The Lipstick Vampire. Aye. I'd forgotten about that." A clatter of phlegmy laughter resounded down the line. "But you're doing okay down there?"

She rested her forehead on the windowpane; the cool glass felt good against her skin. "Yes and no. I don't suppose you've heard anything."

"Sort of. I was waiting for confirmation. But seeing as you've called, I might as well tell you what I know. See, I've been asking around. Mentioning the names Zoto and Kaan on the off-chance one of my contacts in the industry knows anything…"

Acid leaned back. Anticipation clenched at the muscles in her stomach and chest. If she had a name, she had a goal. She had a mark.

"Before I tell ya, let me be clear. I've not got any evidence this is linked to a hit on your good self," The Dullahan continued. "But someone I know thinks Zoto and Kaan might be the same person."

"What?"

She spat the word out with such surprise she heard Spook startle behind her. "Acid? What is it?"

She waved her away without turning around. "Are you serious?" she asked The Dullahan. "Who told you this?"

"Come on, lassie. I can't and won't divulge that information. But that's not all. Kaan hired an assassin a few weeks back. It wasn't done through the Crypto Jones site, but I know a man who knows a man who brokered the under-the-table deal. The person in question is a freelance operative going by the name Lamia Loveless. A woman. From what I hear, she's first class. *Or was.* I'm wondering if she was the one who attacked you."

"Lamia Loveless? Okay." She peered out the window. Below her, a line of people swayed and strutted along the neon-lit streets, but she didn't pay them much attention. She was too busy considering this new piece of information. "Do you have a photo? Or a description?"

"Not yet. But I'm presuming the name is an alias. Seamus tells me Lamia was a character from Greek mythology. A demon with the head and breasts of a woman and the lower half of a serpent. She also ate children and babies. That was her thing, apparently. I thought it fit in with the fact she was pushing a pram."

Acid stepped back, her focus shifting from out the window to her reflection in the glass. Her eyes were wild and her hair unruly. She looked unhinged, filled to the brim with manic intensity. But that made sense. That was how she felt.

Knowing the name of the person who'd tried to kill her was one thing. But if Zoto and Kaan were the same person, that changed everything. From what she already knew, it sounded as if Kaan was setting something up, creating himself as a force to be reckoned with in the London underworld. To do that, he'd need to crack some pretty heavyweight skulls and remove any rivals in his way. Doing so put him and those he loved in danger. At least until he established himself. So if Zoto was Kaan, then it made sense he'd want to stay hidden at all costs, to keep his only daughter away from his affairs.

"You still there, lassie?"

Acid cleared her throat. "That's quite a lot to take in."

"Aye, I bet."

"If Kaan is Zoto and he sent someone to kill me, that puts us in rather a tricky position with our client, Fiona, though."

"It certainly does. But then you've got to ask yourself, does she really want to know who her daddy is?"

"Acid?" Spook rasped. "What is it?"

She shushed her away again. "Probably not," she told The Dullahan. "But if that prick did send someone to kill me, I still need to find him."

The Dullahan laughed. "I thought you might say something like that. But keep in mind, I've not had confirmation on any of these theories as yet. You know as well as I do how the industry works. You've got to question everything you hear. Because people will tell you anything to protect themselves and their interests. Or to throw a person off course. I still think my original theory has weight, that the hit on you was payback."

"Because I stepped on someone's toes? I don't know, D. If Zoto is Kaan and knows we're looking for him..."

"Aye, but there's a third option, too. That it's both those things. There's another rumour in the industry that this Kaan fella is trying to set up an assassin network linked to a larger organised crime enterprise."

"Jesus." Acid spun on her heels to see Spook leaning over the table, listening intently. She mouthed 'what?' at her, which Acid ignored. "But Zoto is in his late seventies," she said. "Doesn't that strike you as odd? Why wait until now to set this up?"

"Listen, kiddo, I'm reporting everything I've heard up to now. I'm not saying it makes total sense or that it's even the truth. I'm still waiting on a few people getting back to me. When they do, you'll be first to know."

Acid turned from Spook's watchful gaze. "What about the other thing I asked you to look into?"

"The drug dealer fella, Jelani? Not a dickie bird about him in any of the forums. I'd say you're free to do what you want as far as he's concerned. But I'd still advise against it. Not that my opinion will sway you in any way."

Acid closed her eyes. "Thank you. I do appreciate this. You're a good friend."

"Oh feck off, ya big softie," he scolded, but she could hear the warmth in his voice. "You be careful now. Ya hear me?"

"I will be. Speak to you soon." She hung up and turned to Spook who was standing a few feet away.

"Well? What the hell was all that about?"

Acid puffed her cheeks out. "All right, kid. Let's sit down. I'll fill you in."

It took her all of five minutes to relay everything The Dullahan had said. Almost everything, at least. She brushed over the part about her stepping on people's toes and The Dullahan's theory that her illicit nocturnal undertakings could be one reason for the hit. When she'd finished, she rested her arms on the table.

"So?" she asked. "What do you think?"

To her credit, Spook had listened for the whole time she'd been talking rather than butting in with questions, but now the way she was staring off into the middle distance was perturbing.

"Spook?"

She didn't shift her gaze. "I think... what the fuck is going on? I think we can't tell Fiona. Not yet, at least."

"Agreed on that one. But Zoto and Kaan the same person?"

Spook blew out a long breath. "It sort of makes sense. I

think. I mean, there was the name in the ledger pad and the fact that his warehouse was empty. Could just be a front?"

"It's starting to look that way."

Acid got up and walked over to the sink. Her limbs were tingling. She felt restless and claustrophobic. She wanted to scream, to hit something, to run at the wall as fast as she could. Instead, she picked up a glass from the draining board and filled it with water from the tap.

"It's a total headfuck is what it is," Spook said, while Acid gulped down the water. "But it is getting late. I think we should sleep on it. Tomorrow we can sit down and come up with our next move. If there is one!" She stretched her arms above her head.

"Yes. Absolutely," Acid said. "You should sleep on it. Good idea."

Spook let her arms drop onto the table with a thud. "You too, I mean."

"I don't think I can sleep. Not yet. You know how I get. I think I might go for a walk. The fresh air might help me relax." She grabbed up her jacket and moved over to the door. "I'll be fine. Don't worry."

"Don't worry? There are people out there who want us dead. We should stay here together, with the doors locked. If Zoto or Kaan or whoever they are wants to stop us, then we aren't safe. Please, I just think—"

"Spook!" Acid snapped. "You'll be fine. I'll lock both sets of doors. And you've got the pistol I gave you. Please. I need to get out of here for a while. I need some air. I need to clear my head."

She stared into Spook's pleading eyes. The poor kid was terrified, but Acid couldn't help her. She needed to leave. The little action she'd had tonight stirred something inside of her and this new information only deepened her resolve.

The bats were in flight and the intense pressure in her head was growing unbearable. She needed a release.

Spook sighed. "Whatever I say, you're going to go out anyway." She looked into her hands, sadness and disappointment drooping her features.

But Acid didn't care. She was on the edge. "Thanks, Spook," she said, already hurrying down the corridor to her bedroom. She grabbed a can of deodorant and sprayed herself liberally from head to toe. That should cover up most of the smell. Satisfied, she headed for the front door, yelling as she went. "You get to bed. I'll see you in the morning."

"Please be careful," Spook called after her.

As Acid unlocked the front door and swung it open, she thought about calling back, telling Spook what she always told her in these situations.

I'm always careful.

But she didn't. It didn't need to be said. And right now she couldn't promise that she would be. All she cared about was silencing the screeches echoing in her head.

She knew just how to do it.

Chapter Twenty-Seven

Acid walked to Regent Street and found an available cab in minutes. She gave the driver the address for The Bitter Marxist and settled herself in the back seat, noting the time on the digital display next to the meter showed it was eleven minutes past the witching hour. At this time of night, it would take them around twenty minutes to get over to Chelsea, but that didn't mean her drinking time was scant. Despite most establishments closing around midnight, especially mid-week, The Bitter Marxist stayed open until four most nights. Later, if the mood took. This was unheard of in London and flouted all British licencing laws. But that was The Bitter Marxist for you and the reason why it had always been Acid's first choice of drinking den. However, the guarantee of a late-night drink wasn't the only thing that had tempted her across town. Freddie Pearce had mentioned he drank there most nights. Her hope was tonight would be no exception.

She was already feeling calmer as the cab pulled up

outside the street entrance to the bar, and by the time she was halfway down the stairs the stress and confusion that had plagued her were all but gone. Anticipation crackled in the air, and as she pushed the door open, a wave of hot air brought with it the demonic doo-wop sounds of *Sunglasses After Dark* by The Cramps.

Perfect.

Letting the door swing shut, she threw her attention around the room as surreptitiously as she could. Two of the round tables had been pushed together and were occupied by a group of men with slicked-back hair and shady features who looked as though they were planning a job. Of the five stools spaced out along the bar top, only two were free. The others were taken up by a thin woman with grey hair dressed all in black, who could have passed as an older version of herself, and two Middle-Eastern men laughing hysterically about something. But no Freddie Pearce.

Gritting her teeth through the frisson of anger pulsing its way down her torso, she wandered up to the bar. Maybe she'd have one drink here and head over to Lambeth. See if she might find Lucas Jelani on the off-chance. Or anyone who deserved her wrath. Something had to happen tonight to relieve the intense hum of frenzy threatening to consume her. The bats nibbled at her nervous system as she waved the barman over. It was the same guy as last time.

"What can I get you?" he asked.

She smiled, looking him up and down. He was still too muscular and clean-cut, but she might make an exception. She let her eyes linger on his lips for a moment before fixing him dead in the eye. "Do you know what? I can't decide. What would you recommend?"

The man glanced over at the bottles on the back wall.

"That depends on what you're into? Do you like something strong? Something fruity? A bit spicy?"

"Yes. To all the above." She let her eyes crinkle up just the right amount, pouting enough that her intentions were obvious but not grotesque.

The barman smiled, but he wasn't taking the bait. "So…?"

It was futile. He might have been pretty, but he was also stupid. Or gay. Or maybe he was terrified of her. It happened sometimes with the young ones. And there seemed to be a lot of young ones around these days. She sighed. "Give me a Chivas Regal, double. Thank you."

"I'll get that," a voice said over her shoulder. "If you don't mind a bit of company, that is."

She spun around, catching herself in time and swallowing down any outward show of excitement. "Freddie," she said, tilting her head to one side to take him in as lurid thoughts flashed across her mind. "Fancy seeing you again."

He moved around the back of her and sat on the remaining stool. "Is anyone sitting here?"

"I don't think so. I've just arrived."

"I know." He rested his forearm on the bar and leaned over to get the barman's attention.

"You know?" She frowned, watching as he raised two fingers to the barman and waved them between him and her, indicating he'd have the same drink. "What do you mean?"

"I mean, that I've been here since eleven," he said. "That was my stool you're sitting on. I was in the bathroom."

"I see. I wondered if you might be here."

"Really?"

She snorted. "Calm yourself. I was in the neighbourhood, that's all."

"But you hoped I'd be here."

"*Wondered.*"

They both looked up in unison as the barman appeared with the two double whiskies. Freddie handed over a twenty and told him to keep the change.

"That's not going to cover it," the barman said, waving the twenty at him.

"Oh, right. Sorry."

Acid smirked as he scrambled into his blazer pocket and came out with a tattered brown wallet. Flipping it open, he pulled out a credit card. "Can I put it on here, please?"

He was flustered, but the lights from within the glass-fronted fridges behind the bar cast deep shadows across his face that accentuated his fine bone structure. She hated him a little for being so gawky and looking so good, but she hated herself more. She was horny, that was all, she told herself. She was searching for a release. Some relief from the nagging torment inside her soul.

She looked away as Freddie tapped his card on the machine and gathered his wallet back into his pocket.

"Sorry about that," he said. "Total amateur, aren't I?"

"It's fine." She shifted around to face him and picked up her drink. "Cheers."

"Yes. Cheers."

They chinked glasses and Acid took a long drink. It was so needed. Placing the heavy-bottomed glass down on the bar top, she noticed Freddie was watching her every move.

"Stop it," she told him.

"Stop what? What am I doing?"

"Looking at me like that."

"How am I looking at you?"

"You know."

"Well, it is good to see you tonight, Alice."

She tensed at the sound of her name, but let it go. "I suppose it's nice to see you too, Freddie."

They drank, eyes meeting over the tops of their glasses, smiles forming as they took each other in. Freddie was nervy and awkward and didn't sit still for one second, but there was something about him she liked. He reminded her of a stray dog, a lost soul who needed care and attention. Not that this meant she saw him as a project, like some women might; she didn't do relationships. But despite his nervous mannerisms, his eyes were bright and intense and filled with pain. She sensed he was someone like her, someone a little broken, making the most of life as best he could.

"Listen, Freddie," she said. "If anything happens between us tonight, it will only be physical. Do you understand?"

He raised both eyebrows. They were thick and dark, but a good shape. Similar to her own when she didn't spend time with the tweezers. "Wow," he said. "You don't mess around, do you?"

She shrugged. Maybe it was forward. But she was a forward person. She didn't have time to pussyfoot around situations. Caesar had always taught her that if you wanted something in life, the best way to get it was to ask for it straight out.

"I'm just saying..." She lifted her glass and took a big gulp of the fiery liquid.

"*If* anything happens..." Freddie repeated.

"Oh, come on. Let's not play games." She lowered her chin. "We both know where this is heading. But it's just sex. That's all it ever is for me. Besides, you're too young for me." This was a lie. She'd guess at there being about five years between them and she'd had much younger. But she wasn't giving it to him on a plate, either.

"I'm not sure about that," Freddie replied. "How old are you?"

"Excuse me. One never asks a lady—"

"Now, now, Alice. Let's not play games." He grinned. So did she. "I'd say you're... what, thirty-five? Thirty-six?"

"Close enough." She baulked internally as she did the maths. She was thirty-eight in December. Jesus. How the hell had that happened? Almost forty. Some days she felt it.

"When's your birthday?" Freddie asked, and took a sip of his drink.

"Why? Are you going to buy me a present?"

"Maybe."

She shot him a half-smile and narrowed her eyes. "First of December."

This seemed to liven him. He rolled his shoulders back with a grin. "So, you're a Sagittarius."

"Oh god. Are you into all that shit?"

"Not really, but I've always thought Sagittarians were cool. I've never met one I didn't like."

She curled her lip but couldn't keep it up. "Yep. That's me. Half woman, half horse. With a licence to shit in the street."

He laughed, almost losing a mouthful of whisky. "Good line."

She tipped her head to one side. Was it? It was hardly sex talk, but it was true. Her entire life she'd been unencumbered by the petty morals and laws of society. She did things her way, on her terms.

"I can't take the credit," she told him. "It's a Keith Richards line. Another Sagittarius."

"You're in good company."

"I guess so."

Freddie nodded at the sounds drifting from the speaker over his shoulder. The Velvet Underground doing *Rock & Roll*. It was one of Acid's favourite songs, but she hadn't even noticed it was playing until now. "You like the Velvets?" Freddie asked. When she nodded in the affirmative, he waved his finger at her outfit, the black jeans and leather jacket. "Of course you bloody do. I love them, too. The Velvets, The Stooges, The Doors. All that sort of stuff..."

She fought against a smile. "Me too. Plus the New York Dolls, Bowie..."

"God, yeah. Amazing."

They were nodding along eagerly to each other, almost in disbelief, like disillusioned teenage freaks who had spent years surrounded by jocks and had finally bumped into another of their tribe.

"My mum got me into music," she said, before taking a large gulp of her drink. Where the hell that had come from? She hadn't spoken or even thought about her mother in over a year. It was easier that way.

"She sounds like a cool lady," Freddie said.

"She's dead."

"Ah, I'm sorry."

"It's fine. It was a while ago."

"What about your dad?"

She sniffed. "I never knew him."

The poor bastard. He was two for two in the clumsy question stakes. At least now he'd hopefully change the subject.

But it seemed not. "Both my parents are dead as well," he said.

"Oh. Shit." It was the best she could do. She didn't do sympathy. She didn't do feelings at all if she could help it. Yet the crumpled expression on Freddie's face compelled her to continue. "I'm sorry about that."

"I was only nine when my dad died. It was hard growing up without him. My mum died a few years ago." He shrugged, but there were tears in his eyes. "It is what it is."

Acid remained still, resisting the urge to hold his hand. All at once, he'd switched from a nervy man with amazing cheekbones to a little boy.

Come on, Fred, pull it back.

This was not what she had come here for. This was supposed to be about carnal desire. Sex. She lowered her eyes to his groin, hoping to reignite whatever fire had been burning between them. It was forward, even for her, but she was done with talking.

"Listen, Freddie. Do you want to get out of here? Maybe go to your place?"

"What?"

She leaned forward and lowered her voice. "Let's go back to yours. All this talk of dead relatives is making me horny."

He laughed at her inappropriate joke, which was something. But as he lowered his head to look into her eyes, she could tell this wasn't going to go the way she wanted.

"How about we have dinner first?" he said.

She sat back as the warm haze she'd been wrapped in dropped away. For the last thirty minutes she'd been in a bubble, fixated only on Freddie Pearce. Now she heard the chink of glasses and the murmur of voices, the boom of the jukebox. Her nose picked up on the smells of liquor and body odour and the hint of ammonia coming from the bathroom in the far corner.

"Dinner? Are you serious?"

He grabbed her hand. "Not now. Obviously. But I like you, Alice. I'd like to talk more before we… you know. Have dinner with me one night this week. I want to get to know you properly."

"No. You don't. I'm bad news."

"Are you?"

She pulled her hand away and sat upright. "I don't do dinners. I'm too busy."

She felt like picking up her glass and smashing it into his face. This foolish little boy. Did he not see what he had in front of him? She sucked in a deep breath. The bats were circling overhead. Their screeches of displeasure reverberated through her soul. Leaning forward, she fixed Freddie with a stern look.

"This is a now or never situation for you, Freddie boy. We go to your place, we have wild, freaky, amazing sex – the best sex you've ever had, I promise you that – or you never see me again. What's it going to be?" She bit down hard on her bottom lip. The pain helped her to focus.

"Wow," Freddie exclaimed. "No one's ever propositioned me like that before."

"No point in dancing around the matter. I'm a busy woman."

"Clearly." To his credit, he maintained eye contact. But the way his Adam's apple rose and fell as he swallowed gave him away. "I do want that. I bet it would be fantastic. But I do like you as well. I want to find out more about you before we jump into bed. Because something tells me we're going to spend a lot of time in bed once we get there."

She shook her head but couldn't hide her smile. "Either

you're more self-assured than you seem or you're just stupid."

"Can't I be both?"

She laughed and looked away. Damn it if the man wasn't intriguing. Despite herself, she found herself asking, "Where would we go, for this dinner?"

He gestured with his thumb over his shoulder. "There's a great fried chicken shack around the corner." When she laughed, he played at being hurt. "Not good enough? Jesus. Expensive taste, hey? Fine. I know a good place. It's nice. Intimate."

"Fucking hell, mate. If it's intimate you want—"

"Dinner first."

She stuck out her bottom lip. "Okay. I'll let you buy me some food. But you're right, I do have expensive taste."

He grinned and placed his glass down. "Not a problem." He slipped off his stool. "I need to use the bathroom."

"You've got a weak bladder, Freddie boy."

"In my defence, I have had a few more drinks than you. Back in a tick." He walked past her. She waited enough time as she felt reasonable before twisting around in her seat to watch him. A large, heavy-faced man opened the door to the bathroom as Freddie went to push and he stumbled into him.

Jesus.

What a fucking klutz.

She turned back to the bar and finished her drink, telling herself the warm feeling in her stomach was down to the whisky. Nothing else. She was gearing up to order another round when two men bustled up to the bar beside her and called the barman before she had a chance. She shifted in her seat, observing the pair without making it obvious. They were in their late twenties, a black guy and a white guy. Both had a few days of stubble growth around their chins and their hair was cropped short. Their attire was what one might call urban wear: loose-fitting clothes, branded trainers and lots of gold jewellery. It was rare to see men of this ilk in The Bitter Marxist, but not unusual. If you needed to talk business, away from the ears and eyes of the civilian world, it was the place to come.

"I can't believe the man is being so blatant," the black guy muttered. "So much heat on him right now after Si got taken out. The Pharaohs want him gone, ya know. And the feds are all over him. If it was me, I'd be lying low for a time."

"Yeah, but that's him all over, innit," his friend replied. "Lucas fucking Jelani. Man thinks he owns the whole city."

Acid's attention had been waning since they started talking, but at the mention of Jelani she perked up. Lucas Jelani. The name on top of her kill list. The man she'd been looking for. Her mark.

She remained still, listening intently as the two men continued.

"But you're right," the white guy said. "I'd be lying low, too. Or maybe even get out of the country for a while. Man is crazy, like I say. You know Jamal saw him walking around the Bottomley Estate tonight?"

Acid stiffened.

"What the fuck, you serious?" the guy's mate said.

"His fam lives there. His mom and his little bruv are in the first block near the park. Jamal said she's not been well. Jelani is probably risking it to see her before she pops, innit."

"Jesus, fuck!" Acid gasped when a hand landed on her

shoulder. She'd been listening so intently that Freddie's reappearance startled her.

"Shit, sorry," he said, sitting down and holding his hands up. "I didn't mean to make you jump."

"It's fine," she told him. "Listen, I'm going to have to get off."

She got up, holding onto the edge of the bar to stop herself from shaking. It wasn't fear or tiredness or even lust causing her body to vibrate now; it was excitement. Excitement mixed with powerful bloodlust. She finally had the mark in her sights.

"You're leaving?" Freddie said. "But I thought... we could maybe..."

"My friend texted me while you were in the bathroom," she said, going for the first thing that came to mind and not caring how lame it sounded. "She needs my help. I said I'd go over to her house right away."

"Oh. I see."

"Next time," she said, placing a hand on his shoulder. "Dinner, yes?"

He smiled. "I'll look forward to it. Oh, here you go."

She was pushing off from the bar, heading for the exit, when he pulled out his wallet. Bouncing from foot to foot, she waited as he flipped it open and removed a business card from one of the compartments.

"My number's on there. Give me a text or a call tomorrow – or whenever – and we'll sort something out."

She glanced at the card as she took it from him. "Yeah. Maybe."

"We'll have fun, I swear it. You choose a time and a place and I'll be there."

"I might."

"Good enough. I guess." He went to get up but Acid stepped away.

"I really have to go." She stuffed the card in her jacket's inside pocket "I'll see you later."

She raced up the steps and pushed through the door. Her mind was already on other things. She had to silence the chattering voices in her head. Freddie Pearce had blown his chance to help her. Now it was Lucas Jelani's turn. She wasn't going to let this one slip through her fingers.

Chapter Twenty-Eight

The night sky was overcast and not one star was visible as Acid hunkered down behind a raised flower bed in the courtyard of the Bottomley Estate. It had taken her thirty minutes to get over here from Chelsea. A twenty-minute taxi ride and another ten minutes of walking time. She'd chosen to approach the area on foot, knowing the night air would rouse her senses and clear any cognitive fog that might cause her issues. This was the closest she'd come to Jelani ever since he'd made it to the top of her list. She couldn't mess this up. He might have been visiting his sick mum, but he was a violent and dangerous man. Killing him wasn't going to be a walk in the park. But that's why she was so excited about this one. Jelani was a challenge.

She raised her head over the edge of the flower bed. A stairwell led down from the mezzanine courtyard, where she was waiting, to a car park below. She could hear the rumble of voices drifting up the steps. Two people. Males. They seemed to be arguing about something, but their voices were growing quieter as they walked away. It was nothing to concern herself with. She heard the ping of an elevator and took cover once more behind the flower bed.

Like the rest of the estate, the crumbling structure – comprising three raised flower beds with a bench seat built into the brickwork on the other side – would have been installed in the late seventies and was probably a nice enough feature back then. But, as if acting as a fitting microcosm for the rest of the estate, it had fallen into disrepair in the subsequent years. The bricks were chipped and broken. Spray-painted tags and obscene graffiti covered every surface and the flower beds themselves were a dumping ground for takeaway wrappers, empty cans and crumpled cigarette packets. A few dozen rose bushes had once fought for life but had long ago lost the battle. The bush's sinewy remains did, however, provide enough cover that she could observe the stairwell of Jelani's mother's block of flats without being seen.

The elevator doors opened and an old man shuffled out. He was stooped over and carrying a cardboard box under his arm. It looked like every step hurt the poor old sod. It must be hard spending your life living somewhere like this. There was no future to be found here in these concrete tower blocks. Acid tipped her head back, taking in the tall tenements. For people like Jelani, growing up somewhere like this, it was almost inevitable they'd fall into a life of crime. But then, a lot of people had it hard. It was no excuse for killing innocent women and kids. No excuse for...

Bugger.

She realised the bitter irony too late. It could have been Spook's voice in her head.

No, she told herself. It wasn't the same. She wasn't the

same as him. Lucas Jelani was an evil man. He did bad things to innocent people. He had to die.

On her way over to the estate earlier, Acid had happened upon a group of three young girls, all in their early teens and full of attitude. It had taken her a minute to calm them down and get past the barrage of insults thrown her way (at her attire, mainly; they thought she was a goth) but after that, fifty pounds each and the promise that nothing would come back on them got her the information she needed. Jelani's mother's flat was on the first floor, number seventeen. From where she was hiding, she had a good view of the front door, and through the rippled pane of glass in the centre of the wood she could see the hall light was on. She pulled out her phone to check the time. 1.46 a.m. The mother really must be on her last legs if Lucas was visiting her at this late hour. The other possibility, of course, was that he was staying the night, but Acid didn't want to consider that just yet. If that was the case, her plans were out the window. She needed the cover of night.

She'd formed a basic plan, to make the hit appear as though it was a random mugging gone wrong. It meant the kill could be messy, the messier the better. The more it looked like a professional hit - perhaps by a rival gang in response to Shinobi's death - the more likely she would ignite a gang war. That wasn't her intention. She wanted Jelani, that was all. It was he alone who had to pay for what he'd done.

She closed her eyes, playing the scenario over in her mind. Once Lucas left the flat, he'd take the stairs or elevator down to the courtyard level. She'd approach the stairwell and as he stepped out into the open she'd barge into him as if by accident, checking his waistband to see if he was carrying (there was no way he'd be wearing a shoulder rig or any kind of holster). If so, she'd grab the weapon and shoot him in the heart at close range. It would be over before he realised the unassuming woman who'd just knocked into him had also sent him to hell. She was wearing gloves and if she used his own gun there'd be no link to anyone else. She'd toss the weapon nearby and get gone before anyone saw her.

The other possibility was that he wasn't armed. This would make the job harder and more dangerous, but with the push dagger in her belt and surprise on her side, she'd manage it. Leaving his sick mother's flat in the middle of the night would mean his guard was down and his mind elsewhere. It would be enough to…

Shit.

She froze at the sound of movement over her shoulder. With her hand instinctively going to the dagger in her belt, she spun around. Just in time. A dark figure lunged at her from out of the shadows. She darted out of the way as a knife blade flashed by her ear. The man grunted as he stumbled forward and she grabbed him around the back of the neck and ran him into the flowerbed. He was tall and muscular, but he hadn't anticipated her reaction and was now on the back foot. She smashed his head against the crumbling bricks and jumped away, unsheathing the push dagger. Her vision zoomed into sharp focus as the man righted himself and turned around, a vicious sneer spreading across his face.

"Fucking bitch," he growled in a heavy accent.

He was white, with a shaved head. He looked to be in his mid-forties and was wearing dark jeans and a black polo-neck shirt. A heavy gold chain hung around his neck.

"Who are you?" Acid rasped. "Who sent you?"

The bats, her guts, her instincts, they all told her this

had nothing to do with Lucas Jelani. This was about her. It was another hit.

"Fuck you, bitch." He raised the knife, jerking it at her, forcing her back.

"Is that all you've got?" she replied, raising the push dagger and lowering herself into a fight position. If this was a professional hit, then whoever wanted her dead had gone for the cheap option. This idiot was inexperienced and sloppy. She sucked in a slow breath, ready for his next move.

He lunged at her and she stepped to one side. His knife blade slashed the air in front of her, and as his arm finished its trajectory she struck out with the push dagger. There was a flash of light and a cry of pain, and he fell against the flower bed. He still had hold of the knife, but blood gushed from a deep cut on his arm. It looked like she'd sliced through his flexor muscle.

"Fucking bitch," he gasped.

"Change the record, mate."

She was getting bored with this prick. For one thing, he was ruining her cover. And if someone had paid this amateur to kill her, they'd very much underestimated her. She was insulted.

With a grunt, the man brought up the knife and moved on her again, but with his arm carved up and bleeding, his grip would be poor. She let him approach, skipping back like a prize fighter, tiring him out as he stumbled after her leaving a trail of blood in his wake. He bared his teeth, a bitter snarl twisting a long scar on his cheek into a backward 'S'. But he was faltering with each step. Her response to his attack and the wound she'd inflicted had knocked his confidence.

"Keep it together, sweetie," she taunted, beckoning him

to follow her. "What are you waiting for? I'm right here. Come for me."

"I will kill you," came the mumbled response.

"Do it then. Kill me."

He flipped the knife around so the blade was pointing down. Lifting his torn, bleeding arm over his head, he lurched towards her.

Straight into her trap.

As he moved forward, she ran at him, grabbing his arm and digging her thumbnail into the exposed, bleeding flesh. At the same time, she stabbed the push dagger into his chest in a flurry of sharp punches, pummelling his torso with the lethal blade. He let out a desperate groan that sounded almost comical, like the noise a cartoon dog might make on realising its wily feline nemesis had outsmarted it. The man dropped the knife as she punctured his chest and abdomen with the short, wide blade. Finally, she grabbed his collar and held him at arm's length, slashing the blade across the skin of his neck with a sharp backhand. A jet of warm, sticky crimson spurted into her face and she let go of his collar, wiping her hand across her eyes as he slumped to his knees and then toppled forward. Before he came to rest, she grabbed his shoulders and rolled him onto his back. He stared up at her, eyes wide with fear.

"Who sent you?" she asked.

He tried to swallow as blood bubbled out of his mouth.

Bugger.

She should have probably demanded an answer to that question before slicing his throat open. That was messy of her. Not in keeping with her sense of artistry at all. But this fight hadn't been about skill or technique.

She leaned over the top of the man as he let out a low wheezing sound. "Who sent you?" she asked again.

But it was too late. His eyes bulged and turned to glass and he released his last breath.

"Fuck," she muttered, quickly checking him over but finding nothing. No ID, no jewellery inscriptions or tattoos of names or symbols that could point to who the hell he was and where he had come from.

She sheathed the push dagger and cast her attention around the courtyard and up to the first-floor landing. No one was around. But as her adrenaline levels lowered and her manic frenzy waned, she heard sirens. They were off in the distance and this being South London they could be heading anywhere, but her guts told her they were for her. She scanned the tenements, spinning around to take in all three buildings that faced each other in a triangular formation. She couldn't see anyone, but someone up there must have seen the fight and called the police.

"Bollocks," she spat, returning her focus to Jelani's mother's front door. "Pissing shitting hell."

The sirens were getting closer. She couldn't risk it. She zipped up her leather jacket and fled the scene.

Chapter Twenty-Nine

Acid stuck to the back streets until she reached Lambeth Bridge, keeping her head down as she crossed, avoiding looking at the cars as they passed by. Once over the river, she walked the rest of the way back to Soho via a series of parks and green areas; Victoria Tower Gardens, St James's Park, then cutting through Green Park and on to Berkley Square. It took her twice as long this way, but gave her more thinking time in the fresh air and helped her come down from the immense high she was feeling after slicing up her attacker.

The fact the man was so ill-prepared and undertrained bothered her. Why would a person hire someone so pathetic? It made no sense. And if it wasn't a professional hit, then what the hell was it? Zoto was still a factor. As was Kaan, his possible alter ego. But even this confused her. If Zoto was Kaan, and was gearing up to start a crime organi- sation, it made sense he'd want to get rid of her and Spook before they exposed him. But then why had no one attacked Spook? Surely she was the easier target? None of it made sense and her head swam with conflicting ideas and dark thoughts. So much so that she'd walked to her front door on autopilot before she realised where she was.

She unlocked the door, turning the keys slowly in their prospective locks so as not to wake Spook. Once inside, she locked up and slid the bolts home, still taking great care not to make a sound. Padding her way up the stairs, she leant her weight on the handrail to avoid the creaking steps before taking the same care with the locks on the door to the apartment. She could feel her pulse in her neck and inner thigh as she eased open the door and slid inside, closing it behind her. Kneeling, she bolted up and was sliding her key into the main lock when she heard someone cough behind her. The hallway light came on and she turned to see Spook leaning against the kitchen doorway.

"You've been gone a while," she said coldly. "Long walk, was it?"

Acid got to her feet and Spook jutted her chin out as if evoking a response. When none was forthcoming, she tsked dramatically and disappeared into the kitchen.

"Bloody hell," Acid whispered to herself. This was all she needed right now.

She wandered along the corridor and peered into the room. Spook was sitting facing the door with Acid's laptop on the table in front of her. She didn't remember leaving it there.

"Have you had fun?" Spook asked.

Acid rested the side of her head on the doorframe, trying to get a read on her. The question seemed innocuous enough.

"I went for a drink," she said. "A few drinks, actually. Got talking to a guy. You know how it goes; one thing leads to—"

"Do you know you're completely covered in blood?" Spook said, cutting her down. "I'm assuming it's not yours."

Acid dropped her shoulders and stepped into the room. "I got jumped. Another attacker. I think it's safe to say they're connected."

"Really?"

"Yes."

"Where did this happen? The Lambeth Estate? Elephant and Castle?"

"Excuse me?"

Spook opened the laptop and spun it around to show her the screen. A browser window was open on a local news report about Lucas Jelani. As she was looking, Spook clicked off the browser window and onto the 'Notes' app, where Acid had logged a list of locations where Jelani had been sighted, along with ideas on how she'd carry out the hit.

"Oh."

"Is that all you can say? For god's sake, Acid. I knew you were up to something and I suspected you were falling back into your old ways. But I didn't think for a moment it had got this extreme."

Acid pursed her lips but pulled back from falling into surly teenager mode. She wouldn't give Spook the ammunition. Besides, it was Spook who had made her that way, with her stupid rules and petty morals. Why couldn't she understand that Acid didn't see the world the same way as her, or anyone? She had different DNA from most people and different ethics and codes (although, admittedly, she had broken most of those too, recently).

"I know you've been going out in the middle of the night and killing people."

Acid sighed. There was no point denying it. "Yes. Bad people," she countered. "People who deserved to die."

Spook closed the laptop. "So, what? Are you a serial killer of bad guys? A real-life Dexter Morgan?"

Acid frowned. "Who?"

"Never mind. I'm right, though, aren't I?" Spook glared at her. "I've been all through your laptop. Even those folders you thought you'd encrypted. This isn't just some flash-in-the-night thing. You're planning it out, doing the research and everything."

"Yes. And? You're not the only one who can use a computer." She dragged the nearest chair out from under the table and sat, resting her arms on the table. "That's how you ensure things go according to plan and you don't get caught. It's what I always used to do. No difference."

"Yes, there is! You used to get paid for it, at the very least."

Acid leaned forward. "I'm doing the world a service."

Spook laughed. It was one of those bitter, put-on types of laughs that people thought were empowering, but just made them sound whiney and pathetic. Acid lifted her head, catching sight of herself in the chrome metal surround of the oven door. The reflection was warped, but she could see her face was all but covered in blood. Only a streak across her eyes was clear, where she'd wiped at them with her hand.

Oh, shit.

In all the chaos she hadn't realised it was that bad. And there she was thinking she might get past Spook by telling her she'd been out for a drink. The thought brought a smile to her lips.

"Ah, cool. You find this funny?"

She returned her attention to the red-faced American. "No. I don't. But nor do I see what your problem is. I know it's rather unconventional, but I'm doing society a favour.

I'm only killing total shits, criminals, traffickers, those who hurt others and deserve to die. The same way I always have done."

"That's total crap. What about me? I was one of your marks. I didn't deserve to die."

Acid sneered, not totally swerving the surly teenager act. "The way it was told to me you did."

"Exactly," replied Spook, banging her finger on the table for emphasis. "Don't you see? Caesar told you what you wanted to hear and now you're telling yourself the same thing. But it's bullshit. What you're doing isn't for the greater good, Acid. It's wrong. There are laws and officers of the law out there who deal with these people. And before you say it, I know the cops can and do get it wrong, but so do vigilantes. And so do assassins, no matter how highly trained or knowledgeable they are." She sat back and stared at Acid. Her expression said she thought she'd made the winning point. "You're better than this, Alice. It's not who you are."

"It is, Spook."

"You're a good person. I know it."

"I am a killer." She got to her feet, stabbing her finger at Spook, which was also caked in dried blood. "Why can't you get it through your silly little head? That's all I've ever been good at. It's all I've ever known. I thought I could change, but I can't."

She wavered, wanting to say more. But from the way Spook had her head tilted to one side and her tongue stuck in her cheek, what was the point?

"I'm going for a shower, then I'm going to bed. I'll see you later."

She strutted out of the room before Spook could come back with anything, muttering wicked protestations to herself on the way to the bathroom. Once there, she hung her jacket on the back of the door, stripped naked and threw her blood-stained clothes into the laundry basket. Habit had her step in front of the mirror above the sink and she couldn't help but laugh once more at her gory reflection.

What a fucking mess.

She blew herself a kiss before stepping into the shower and twisting the dial all the way around. Shards of icy cold water speared her skin, but she rode it out, relishing the attack on her senses. As it grew warmer, she put her head under the jets, letting the water cascade through her tangled hair and turn red, then pink, and finally clear as it swirled around her feet. She washed with soap and, after rinsing, turned the dial off. But rather than reach for a towel, she remained in the cubicle, leaning against the glass and letting the water drip from her body. It had been a long night, but she sensed a tingle of manic desire under her skin. She was still restless. But wasn't that always the case?

She got out of the shower, grabbed her jacket and walked naked to her room, leaving a wet trail along the hallway. Once in her lair with the door closed, she went to hang up her jacket when she felt something in the inside pocket. She pulled it out and saw it was Freddie's business card.

She turned it over and read the front.

Freddie Pearce
Journalist

She ran her finger over the digits of his phone number, wondering if he might have changed his mind. Her eyes shifted to her wardrobe, knowing there was a beautiful floor-length fur coat hanging inside (real fur, naturally, with the scent of death in every stitch). She had visions of herself turning up at Freddie's door wearing the coat, a pair of killer heels, and nothing else. Let's see the uptight fucker refuse her then.

No.

Fuck that.

She crumpled the business card in her fist and chucked it on the floor before walking over to her bed and slumping face down onto her pillow. Sleep felt close now, and tomorrow was another day. She could deal with being alone for now. Hell, it was all she'd ever really known.

Chapter Thirty

Spook splashed a measure of milk into her mug and stomped over to the fridge. Flinging the door open wide and letting it hit the wall on the other side, she shoved the milk carton on the shelf and slammed the door shut. Stomping back to retrieve her mug from the counter, she carried it over to the kitchen table, placing it down with all the grace of a bar-room thug. Coffee sloshed over the side as she scraped a chair out from underneath the table and sat down. As she did, she noticed the digital radio next to the bread bin and wondered about switching it on and turning the volume up to full. But, no, that would be too obvious. The radio was ornamental rather than functional, having never been used since they bought it.

She lifted her mug of coffee, savouring the aromas of citrus and cocoa that turned bitter as she took her first sip. The clock above the oven read 9.08 a.m., but she'd been awake since just after seven. A heady mix of excitement, nervousness and rage had woken her, and once she'd remembered why she felt that way, there was no way she was going to get back to sleep. She'd tried reading her new book (a rather dry account of the future of AI, unimaginatively titled *Rise of The Machines*) to diffuse the feelings of trepidation pricking up the hairs on her arms, but it had been useless. After reading the same paragraph three times, she'd admitted defeat and dragged herself into the shower.

Now, washed and with her hair blow-dried and straightened to the nth degree, she felt ready for the day. Ready to face whatever trials and tribulations would show themselves.

"Jesus. Can you make any more noise?"

Spook looked up to see Acid standing in the doorway.

"Sorry, was I being noisy?"

Acid shook her head. "What time is it?"

"It's gone nine," she replied. "Time to get up, anyway."

"Is it?"

She shuffled into the room. She was wearing a black t-shirt with the sleeves cut off and a pair of old worn leggings that were so sheer Spook didn't want to look at them too closely. Acid headed for the coffee machine via the cupboard and poured herself a mug of black coffee. Sipping it as she walked over, she pulled out a chair and sat. After a few more sips of coffee, she tossed her hair over her shoulder and fixed Spook with a grin.

"So? What's the plan for today?"

Spook huffed out a breath. "Seriously? You're going to act like last night didn't happen?"

"No point going over it again, is there? You made your point very clear. I take that on board."

"So, you'll stop?"

"I didn't say that." She drank more of her coffee, smacking her lips in such an annoying way Spook had to turn away.

She shook her head at the oven, contemplating not

telling Acid what she'd discovered. But what good would that do? This was important. She took off her glasses and rubbed at her eyes with the thumb and forefinger of her right hand.

"We've had a hit," she said.

"Excuse me?"

Spook placed her glasses back on and turned back to her.

"The spider program I wrote to search for Kaan. We've had a hit. A few hits, in fact, all from the dark web. Mostly from underground forums, but also in a conversation between an informant and his handler. They were using messaging software with cast iron encryption, but I managed to crack it. Kaan sounds dodgy as hell. And dangerous." She paused for Acid to respond, but she only placed her mug down and waved her hand for her to continue.

"He's new on the scene, as we suspected, and is getting people riled up on both sides of the law. There are already a couple of deaths linked to him as he encroaches on the more nefarious edges of the underground. And get this, the informant told his handler in one exchange that Kaan is an alias. So it could be Zoto." She whispered this last part as if Fiona might be listening. It was silly, but she felt bad for the poor woman. If their theory was correct, it would destroy her.

Acid chewed on her bottom lip, thinking. "Good work, Spook," she said. "Really. I mean that. What you can do with that laptop is very impressive."

Spook fiddled with the handle of her coffee mug, trying to ignore the warm tingling sensation spreading across her cheeks. "It's easy if you know how."

"For you it is. And listen, I know what you're doing

comes from a good place. You care about me and what we're doing. I need to remember that. And I will be more considerate in the future." She looked her straight in the eyes with an intensity Spook almost felt in her bones. "You're a good person, Spook."

A shrill giggle escaped her throat. She coughed to cover it. Was this just Acid manipulating her? Kissing her ass so she'd give her a break? She wrinkled up her nose, trying to make sense of the conflicting emotions. Even the most robust bullshit detectors faltered when they were being told what they wanted to hear.

"But it makes sense, right?" Spook went on. "If Zoto and Kaan are the same person? The warehouse is clearly a front. But probably for Fiona's benefit rather than ours. To keep her thinking her father was on the straight and narrow. From what I understand, Kaan has interests in a multitude of businesses, all as bad as each other. Guns, human trafficking, murder for hire."

"But if that is the case," Acid said, "why didn't he tell Fiona he was going away for a few months on business or whatever? Ghosting her as he did was bound to throw up a lot of questions for her."

"Maybe he wasn't planning on it. Maybe something happened and he had to go dark quickly. If he was making moves on people and knew there'd be blowback, he could have purposefully blanked Fiona's attempts at contact so as not to put her in danger. When he found out she'd hired us, he had to get rid of us before we discovered the truth. Hence the woman who attacked you."

Acid frowned. "Yes. Good point."

The warmth in Spook's cheeks spread to her whole body as another compliment landed. She hated herself for it, but with Acid Vanilla you took what you could get.

268

"Yet there's something else," Acid went on. "Something I haven't told you."

Spook looked up, the warm tingling feeling turning to pure ice and dripping down her spine. "What?"

"I may have pissed someone off in the industry," she said. "The Dullahan thinks that my... nocturnal pursuits might have led me to take someone's mark without realising it. That's not on. Not on at all. There's a possibility that hit on me was payback."

"But I told you, Kaan is trying to get into the murder for hire business. What if it was him who put out the hit? Not only are we looking for him, but you're taking his business, so we've doubly pissed him off." She sat back in her chair, realising she'd been leaning further and further over the table with each word.

Acid twisted her mouth to one side and rocked her head from left to right. "It's not beyond the realm of possibility, I suppose."

"No, you're right. It's too much of a coincidence." Spook sighed and pushed her coffee mug away. Too much caffeine left her feeling deflated. "I got carried away and I—"

"No. You might have something there."

"Really?"

"You spend enough time in the seedy underbelly of a city, you run into the same people. The criminal underworld isn't as extensive as you might think. And I know you think that what the Avenging Angels are doing is worthy and on the side of good, but ask any lawman and they'd disagree. Our agency is part of that underbelly. It's underground. Off-book. There were a lot of high-profile shits at Thelmastone House. Our involvement there alone could put us on the radar of some very heavy people. Kaan. Zoto. Whoever.

And then they find out I've been taking out marks without going through the proper industry channels. We could have the whole of the London underworld wanting us dead." She smiled and threw up her eyebrows. "It'll be just like old times."

"Don't, Acid. Please. I'm not finding any of this amusing. I think we should pull out of the case. Tell Fiona we're sorry but we can't find her dad."

"What and return the fee? We need the money, sweetie. I don't know about you but..."

She stopped as a sharp ringtone cut through the air. Spook glanced around, remembering she'd placed her phone on the worktop. She moved over there and scooped it up.

"Shit. It's Fiona. What shall I say?"

She answered it before Acid responded, putting on a professional voice. "Hey, Fiona. How are you?"

Despite shifting her tone down an octave, there was still a nervous vibrato under the surface. It didn't help that her heart was playing a cover version of one of Acid's more frantic punk rock songs on the inside of her chest.

"I'm worried," Fiona said. "I don't suppose you've heard anything?"

Spook looked at Acid for help and got nothing but a shrug. "Not really. I did say I'd call you straight away if I did. We went to your father's warehouse, but there was nothing there of note." Acid pulled a face at this, but what could Spook do? How did you tell someone you believed their father was potentially gearing up to become the new face of organised crime? "Has he not been in touch with you?"

"No, of course he hasn't." Fiona practically spat her response down the phone. "Don't you think I'd have told you? I've heard nothing. From anyone. And every day that goes by, I am growing more and more worried. Please. You must find him."

Spook exhaled heavily down her nose, not taking her eyes from Acid. Why was she the one shouldering this and not her? "Maybe he's trying to protect you," she tried. "Maybe he doesn't want you to know where he is."

"What do you mean?"

"Well... I don't know... What if he's involved in something dangerous and doesn't want you to get hurt? That could be it."

"But I'm his daughter. Why has he not been in contact?"

"I don't know," Spook replied. "But on that same note, myself and Alice, we were talking and we don't think it's fair to take any more fee from you. We've exhausted all our resources and he's not showing up. I wonder if maybe you should go to the police." She turned her back on Acid as she said this. She already knew the sort of look she was going to get.

"Please, Spook. I need you to keep going." Fiona sounded as if she was crying. "I hired you because I believe you are good people and will not give up. Please keep searching. If anyone can find my father, I believe it is you. You are kind and brave and clever."

Spook puffed out her cheeks. What was it with all the manipulative tributes this morning? "Okay, we'll keep up the search. Please don't cry, Fiona. We'll keep going."

"Thank you, Spook," she said. "I appreciate this. I appreciate you."

"No problem. We'll speak soon." She hung up and let her head drop. "Don't say it," she called out. "I know..."

"It's fine," Acid said. "We can't walk away from this now

even if we wanted to. Besides the fact we still aren't a hundred percent sure why someone put a hit out on me, something still doesn't feel right with all this Zoto and Kaan business. I can't quite put my finger on what it is, but there's something iffy and I need to know what it is."

Spook placed her phone back on the worktop. "Okay. Tomorrow we reignite our investigation in earnest, maybe widen our search. Fiona said her father had premises in Folkestone. Maybe we could—"

"Tomorrow?" Acid interjected. "Why not today? There's no time like the present, Spook."

Spook lifted her head and stuck her chest out. She waited a moment before turning around. "No. You need to take today off and sort your head out. I don't want to work with you any longer if you aren't going to be honest with me – and if you're going to carry on killing people just for the hell of it."

"It's not *just for the hell of it*. Jesus."

"Regardless. This is not what we agreed. It's not what I signed up for. Please, Alice, I beg of you, have a good think about what you're doing."

"You do know you calling me Alice isn't going to miraculously alter my personality, Spook? Alice is Acid. Acid is Alice. We've always been the same person." She stood up from the table. "What you don't seem to appreciate is that you need me to be this way. Now more than ever until we know what the hell is happening and whose hit lists we're on."

"You could get yourself killed," Spook shot back. "Or arrested."

"I won't."

"You might. The agency was supposed to be a fresh

start for you. For us both. A way of moving away from our past."

"I don't want a fresh start. I don't want to move away from my past." Acid yelled the words and glared at her. The gravitas of this statement was not lost on either of them. "I am a killer. It's who I am. Deal with it." She turned and headed for the door.

"Oh, that's right," Spook shouted after her. "Run away, like you always do. Go out and get drunk or kill someone, why don't you?"

Acid stopped, one hand on the doorframe. She turned around and lowered her chin. "I was going to get dressed and then perhaps do what you suggested, have a think about things. But you know what? Fuck that. I think I will go out. I need to get away from you for a few hours." She raised her head. "Because quite frankly, Spook, all this holier than thou bullshit is pathetic."

With that, she spun around and disappeared down the corridor, leaving Spook to snarl silently at the space where she'd been standing. Her hands were twisted up into tight fists, but who was she kidding? She didn't have it in her to hit anything. She sat and picked up her mug of coffee, taking a large gulp. Great. It was cold. She lolled her head back against the chair and sighed into the ceiling. That had not gone the way she'd hoped, but screw it. And screw Acid Vanilla, too. Let her go on a bloody rampage across London. Let her get herself killed. Spook didn't care anymore. She was done. Finally, she was done.

Chapter Thirty-One

Acid had walked from Soho to Westminster Bridge before
the red mist parted and she slowed enough to think about
where she was heading. Up to that point, she'd just
wanted to move, to escape the confines of her apartment
where the air was stifling with Spook's disappointment in
her. Her muscles were taut with nervous energy and her
head filled with the chaotic chatter of the bats. If anyone
had got in her way or tried to stop her as she marched
through Leicester Square and along Haymarket, they
would now be nursing a black eye or a bust lip at the very
least.

Yet despite being caught up in claustrophobic mania,
with wet hair sticking to her face (she hadn't bothered
drying it after showering, she just needed to get out of
there), and an expression of stern resolution tightening her
jaw, she found some enjoyment in her march down White-
hall. Passing Churchill's Old War Office, The Ministry of
Defence, New Scotland Yard and then Downing Street, she
felt the same sense of mischievous pleasure she always had

done when in the presence of these noble institutions of law and civility.

She wasn't like other people.

She never had been.

And that was okay with her.

She crossed over the bridge and took a left along The Queen's Walk, finally coming to a stop near the London Eye, where she looked out over the river. She took in Big Ben and the Houses of Parliament on the other side. Two renowned symbols of London. Her home. She breathed in the salty river air. It didn't feel like home. But nowhere felt like home to Acid. It hadn't since that fateful day when the authorities ripped her from her mum's loving embrace and her last chance at a normal life. She closed her eyes, relishing the cool breeze on her face.

Bloody hell, Acid.

What was she doing here? Her mind drifted from her mum to Caesar, then to Spitfire and even Davros, her old partner in crime at Annihilation. Everyone she'd ever cared about was dead. Most of them by her own hand. Spook was all she had left. She shivered and, without considering it too deeply, pulled her phone out of her jacket pocket, along with the screwed-up business card she'd rescued from her bedroom floor. She tapped in the number and held the phone to her ear, gazing into the murky depths of the Thames as the dial tone kicked in.

"Hello, Freddie Pearce…"

She stuck out her chest. "Freddie. It's me. It's Alice. From The Bitter Marxist."

She let the words hang in the ether between them. This was unfamiliar territory for her, calling a boy up out of the blue. It was maybe the first time she'd ever done it.

"Alice. Wow. I didn't think you'd… you know. But I'm

glad you did." His voice was warm and full of energy. "How are you?"

"Not too bad." She grimaced. "Listen, are you busy?"

"Tonight?"

She gritted her teeth. "Like, right now? The next hour or so?"

"Oh, right." Freddie sounded surprised, but why wouldn't he? It was midday on a Wednesday. He was probably at work like most normal people were. Acid leaned over the side of the river wall, contemplating throwing her phone into the Thames.

What an idiot.

What a bloody idiot.

"Yes! Why not?" Freddie said. "I've got a few things to finish here, but I can meet you around one-thirty. How does that suit you?"

Acid released the breath that had been stuck in her chest. "Perfect. I'm on the South Bank at the moment, but what about St James's Park? Next to the café by the lake?" She knew it sounded lame and the stuff of pathetic romantic comedies, meeting in a park, but it was safer out in the open where she could see any would-be attackers coming. It was unlikely a professional assassin worth their salt would strike in daylight, especially when she was with Freddie, but she couldn't be too careful.

Well, shit.

The idea had barely formed in her mind when she felt a sinking feeling in her stomach. And just like that, she knew this relationship was doomed. She couldn't bring a civilian into her world. It wasn't only unfair; it was impossible.

But she'd said it now. And here they were.

"One-thirty in St James's Park," Freddie said. "I'll be there. I look forward to it."

"Okay, cool. I'll see you then."

She hung up and yelled a silent 'fuck' at Big Ben. The famous clock tower looked back at her with an aloof indifference. At least it would pass some time, she reasoned, as she set off walking back the way she'd come. There was no way she could go home yet and Freddie was good company. As long as she kept him at arm's length, all should be well.

———

AN HOUR later and she was sitting on a wooden bench overlooking the river, holding a tray containing two cardboard cups of coffee. She'd arrived early on purpose, to allow herself time to scope out the area beforehand and settle into her surroundings. At times like this, when entering unknown territory (and meeting a handsome man in a park was as unknown and dangerous a concept for Acid as infiltrating a drug baron's stronghold or a corrupt government official's underground bunker), it was important to get the lay of the land, familiarise oneself with all exits and entrances and consider each eventuality.

But what were these eventualities? Really?

That she and Freddie might have a laugh, like they had done the last two times, maybe even enjoy each other's company?

If she'd been the type of person who got embarrassed or wound herself in knots of self-reflection, she might have worried she came on too strong the other night. But Acid didn't do either of those things. Worry to her was a negative and destructive concept. And why shouldn't she be honest if she wanted something? Most people danced around their desires, never facing them head-on, or asking for what they truly wanted. It was an awfully limiting way to be, if you asked her. But then, we all had our foibles. Our own crosses to bear.

She saw Freddie before he saw her, and couldn't help but smile at his awkward gait and the way his head jerked left and right, like a baby bird searching for its mother. Though, a baby bird with a good body and a handsome face nevertheless. He was wearing black jeans and a black t-shirt with a tight-fitting dark tweed blazer over the top, and damn it if she didn't feel a familiar stirring in her own black jeans.

Placing the tray of coffee down on the bench, she adjusted her position so she was facing away slightly, giving him her best side. She pursed her lips into a perfect pout and was just raising her hand to wave when her phone vibrated in the pocket of her jacket.

Shitting hell.

She slid it out, half-expecting to see Spook's name on the caller-ID. She'd be wanting to know where Acid was. Or perhaps even calling with a torrent of apologies and anaemic explanations as to her behaviour. But it was The Dullahan.

Shit.

What did he want? Was this about the Zoto case? There wasn't an answering machine linked to her account, but if it was super important he'd call back. Besides, she felt pissed off and manic and she wasn't at work right now. Also, Freddie had seen her and was waving. She placed the phone back in her pocket and smiled as he got closer.

"Fancy seeing you here," he said, nodding at the bench. "Is this seat taken?" It was a cringeworthy comment, but she let it go.

"Here you are," she said, lifting the tray of coffees. "Do you want cream and sugar?"

"Oh. Thank you very much. No. Black is fine." He took a coffee and sat down. "This is nice."

They smiled and nodded at each other as a bubble of awkwardness swelled between them. Acid sipped her coffee. It was the sort with real teeth, but cool enough to drink.

"Thank you for meeting me," she said, twisting on the bench to face him. "It's good to see you."

"Thank you for calling. I didn't expect you would, to be honest. But I'm glad you did. Are you okay? You sounded a little strung out on the phone."

"Did I?" She exhaled a long breath. "I guess I am. It happens sometimes."

"Is there anything I can do to help?"

She crooked her arm, placing her elbow on the back of the bench and resting her head on her hand. *Yes*, she wanted to tell him. *Take me back to your place and fuck me until I don't remember who I am.* But staring into his big brown cow eyes, full of concern and care, helped as well. "Not really," she said. "But thanks."

He sipped his coffee, his benign expression only faltering a little as the bitterness hit his tongue. "Talking helps, you know."

"Does it?" She laughed. "Maybe, Freddie. But it also gets you into trouble. You don't want to hear what's going on for me."

"Try me." He wasn't letting up. He leaned in, his eyes searching hers. "Alice?"

Talking helps. He sounded like Spook, but they both probably had a point. She ran her tongue across her front teeth, assessing how much she could, and should, say. "I told you my friend and I were setting up a new consulting agency, yes?"

"That's right. How's it going?"

"Not good. Let's just say we have very different ideas about how the company should be run and how we should conduct our work. It's becoming a problem." She looked away, blinking into the sun, wishing she'd brought sunglasses. "We're very different as people, my partner and I. She thinks I'm too heavy-handed. I think she's too by-the-book."

"I see. What is it exactly you do?" he asked, and as she turned back, his eyes found hers once more. They were full of compassion and interest. "The term 'consulting agency' always sounds vague to me, a bit dodgy. It hides a multitude of sins…"

Acid coughed out a breath and laughed. "Is that so?"

"Shit. Sorry, I didn't mean that you were dodgy… I meant other people. Agencies. I was just… Oh shit…"

"Freddie. It's fine." She tilted her head to rest it on her hand again and smiled. "You're fine."

"Okay. Thanks." He tilted his head the opposite way to her so they were staring into each other's eyes. "You know you have such an amazing way about you."

Jesus.

The compliment caught her off-guard, but she remained unmoved physically.

"Your eyes are stunning," he went on. "They're so cat-like. In the best possible way. Plus, I've not met anyone in real life with heterochromia before. It's very cool."

Acid smiled. She'd heard almost every possible comment about her different coloured eyes – one blue, one brown – but the fact he knew the term for it was impressive. As was the way he was gazing into them. His expression wasn't one of lust entirely, but of satisfaction. Contentment even. It was rather unsettling for someone like her, though not unpleasant. And maybe this was what she needed in her life. Someone to look at her the way Freddie was doing right now. She'd never looked for safety in others. Physically she could take care of herself, and mentally she at least had it under control (most of the time). As far as her emotional safety she didn't need protection, because ever since Spitfire she'd kept her heart locked away. But time passed and things changed. Maybe she didn't need Freddie to ravish her to get her out of her head. Maybe she simply needed to know he cared. And that he saw her and didn't judge her.

She stiffened at the thought.

Could she do it?

Really?

Could Acid Vanilla be in a relationship? She was surprised to find the concept didn't make her feel sick. But a proper, grown-up relationship? With a civilian? It wouldn't be normality exactly, but it would be something close. Yet, if it was on her terms, maybe she could at least—

Damnit.

Her phone was ringing again, vibrating against her ribcage. The bloody Dullahan. He could certainly pick his moments.

"Excuse me," she said, sliding the phone out of her pocket and seeing it was indeed him on the line. "Just an old friend," she told Freddie, putting it back without answering. "I'll call him later. Where were we?"

Freddie smiled. "I was blowing it by getting all gushy and pathetic, I think. Sorry. I'm not very good at this sort of thing. I always come on too strong, or not enough, or I say something stupid that only I think is funny but everyone else finds offensive." He trailed off and looked down, shaking his head at his coffee cup.

Acid laughed. "Freddie, it's fine. You were being sweet. I liked it." She smiled as he raised his head. "I'm just not used to it, that's all. Not when it's sincere. I suppose we're both a little rusty when it comes to interpersonal interactions."

"Interpersonal interactions?" Freddie repeated. "Stop it, you're getting me all aroused with that dirty talk." He laughed, but his jaw stiffened almost immediately. "Sorry, that was awful."

"No. It wasn't," she told him. "It was funny. You're right. I have an odd way of looking at relationships, I guess."

"We're all a bit odd, I think," he replied. "The best people are, at least. To paraphrase the Mad Hatter."

She got the reference. A warm feeling rose in her belly. Her gaze dropped to his lips. They looked so full and kissable.

"You were saying… about your agency…"

"Oh. Yes." She leaned back and shook her head. "What was it I was saying?"

"You were telling me what sort of consulting agency it was."

"Ah. Right. Was I?" She bit her lip. "There's nothing much to tell. We help people who need help but who can't get it from the obvious sources for whatever reason. For instance, at the moment we're working for a client whose father has gone missing. Trying to locate him for her, or at least find out what happened to him. She doesn't want the police involved, as she thinks he's caught up in something dodgy."

"Woah. I wasn't expecting you to say that. So, you're like private eyes?"

"I suppose so. It's the closest way of describing what we do. Although we aren't very good at it. The father's where-abouts are still unknown."

"Was he into something dodgy?"

282

"It's looking that way. He was in the import and export business, or at least that's what he told his daughter. But the more we discover about him, the more elusive he becomes."

"What's his name?" Freddie asked. But on seeing Acid's expression shift, he held up his hand. "Sorry, that's bad of me. Data protection and client privilege, all that business. I get it. But I also might be able to help. I've spent a lot of time researching the London underground scene, especially in the import and export world. I might have heard of the guy. I probably have. I might even have interviewed him for my book."

Acid rolled her head back. Speaking to someone – anyone – about a mission was a huge no-no. But, as Spook was at pains to point out, she was no longer an operative at Annihilation Pest Control. She wrote her own rules now. Still, it was important to keep some things to herself. If she harboured designs on building a relationship with this man, she could never tell him the truth of who she was. Or what she did.

And that right there was the reason her stomach was in knots.

She smiled as she watched him staring at her, waiting eagerly for a response. Screw it. They'd hit a brick wall with the Zoto case. What harm could it do?

"I can't say too much," she started. "But I don't suppose the name Kaan means anything to you?"

Freddie mouthed the word to himself, and a look of acknowledgement spread out across his face. He smiled. "Kaan. Yeah, I've heard of Kaan. Goes by that one name? He's new on the scene. From what I heard, he's got fingers in a lot of pies."

Acid was sipping at her coffee, but now lowered the cup and rested it on her thigh. "Yes. That's right. Go on…"

"I've not met the guy, but I've seen the look in people's eyes when they talk about him. He's shaken a lot of people. And these are bad people I'm talking about. Dangerous men." He swallowed and then frowned, eyes darting everywhere else but towards Acid, as if he was unsure whether to go on.

She leant over and put her hand on his arm. "It's okay. This is in strictest confidence. None of this will come back to you."

"Yeah, it's… It's not that… Well, it is, I suppose. You see, the last I heard, Kaan was working with Axel Slater. The man I told you about. The one who threatened to kill me. I was trying to set up an interview with Kaan for my book, and Slater found out. He got very heavy. I had to cancel."

"You did the right thing. No shame in that." She squeezed his arm in encouragement to continue.

"He's got a place over in Bethnal Green," Freddie said. "Kaan, I mean. It's where he does most of his business, where I was going to meet with him."

Acid let go of his arm. "What? Seriously? Do you have his address?"

"I think so," he said, reaching into the inside pocket of his blazer. "I keep bits of research and stuff like that on my phone. Hang on."

She sat up as he produced his iPhone and began swiping at the screen. The frown creasing his forehead grew deeper and more pronounced. "Yeah, here we are. I think it used to be a dodgy strip club, but now it's just a dodgy members-only club with a lock-up and office out the back." He showed Acid an address on the screen and she committed it to memory. "But, Alice, he's an incredibly dangerous man. You shouldn't go there alone or unannounced. I've got his number if you want to speak to him. It's best if you call first. Do it respectfully. Turning up there unannounced is going to be like waving a red rag at a very angry bull."

Acid rocked forward, placing her weight onto the balls of her feet. "Yeah, maybe."

"You're not going to do that, are you?" Freddie said, leaning forward to try to establish connection. "Shit. You're worrying me. I shouldn't have said anything. Why don't you sleep on it? We could go get that dinner. How about that? I can tell you more of what I know about—"

"No. I'm sorry." She got to her feet. "I have to see him. Find out what the deal is. We believe Kaan is intrinsically linked to the man we're looking for. He might even be the same person."

She had to see him, to speak to him. She had to go over there today. Now. This case had gone on long enough without any leads.

"But it's risky, Alice. He could get spooked. He could hurt you."

"I'll take my chances." She shot him a smile. "Don't worry, Freddie. I can handle myself."

"I don't doubt that. I saw what you did to that guy in The Marxist. But I can't let you go over there alone. I'll come with you."

"No, it's not a job for…" She almost said civilians. "… Someone without prior training. Don't worry, I'll be careful. And thank you. I'll ring you. We'll do dinner. I promise." She grabbed his face and kissed him hard on the lips. He seemed surprised at first, tense, but then kissed her back. It lasted only a few seconds before she pulled away and fixed her eyes on his. As she did, she felt the familiar prickle of manic energy filling her system.

The bats were awake and they wanted blood.

"I'll see you soon," she said, before walking away and breaking into a jog as she headed for the nearest gate. *An incredibly dangerous man.* She hoped so. It would make this a lot more fun and give the bats what they craved. But either way she had him. She knew where Kaan was and perhaps Afrim Zoto, too. She left the park and headed for the taxi rank on the corner, hailing the first one as she approached. She had Bethnal Green in her sights. It was time to put this case to bed.

Chapter Thirty-Two

The address Freddie supplied took Acid to a neglected side street alongside Regent Canal, a short walk from Mile End Park. On the corner was a run-down kebab shop and next to this was a strip club called Girls on Film, which professed to be open twenty-four hours but was closed. As Acid walked, she could hear music drifting out from somewhere, but no sign of life. On the other side of the street were the rear entrances to what she assumed was a row of food establishments, the stinking bins of overflowing slop by their back doors giving them away. The height of the buildings on both sides cast the street in an ominous shadow and left the air cold.

As Acid neared Kaan's place, she slowed her pace to a saunter, distorting her expression into one of curiosity and confusion for any cameras that might be watching – playing the role of someone who had lost their way. There was no signage on the building except for a small brass plaque with the legend 'Members Only' next to a door painted with black gloss. She walked straight past it and onto the street at the far end, which ran perpendicular to this one and parallel to the main street a few blocks over.

Here she stopped, her eyes burning from the brightness of the sunlight after becoming accustomed to the gloom. It was certainly apt that Kaan's nefarious business dealings were being conducted on a seedy street and from inside such an ominous-looking building, but something about it felt off. The man was supposedly trying to make a name for himself in the industry. He was already feared and seemingly successful. Why operate out of somewhere so run-down and grotty?

She stepped aside as an old woman shuffled past, dragging a tartan-covered shopping cart. Looking up and down the street, which was busy despite despite dusk already approaching, she didn't feel any clearer about Kaan's set-up. Bethnal Green was a working community, full of normal working people. If she were establishing a crime empire, would she choose this area?

But then, it provided excellent cover. Perhaps that was the point.

Caesar had always operated as if he was above the law, but mostly that was because he was. Acid had never been privy to who had actually hired her to do their dirty work, but taking into account some of the marks she'd killed over the years, it was safe to say the UK and US governments were on Annihilation Pest Control's client list.

She stood on the corner for a while longer, not sure exactly what she was waiting for. Inspiration, perhaps? But the reality was she had to get inside Kaan's place and see for herself what the deal was.

Though not yet.

Something had her reach into her jacket and pull out her phone. She now had three missed calls from The Dullahan. That was unusual, to say the least. She scrolled to his name and hit 'call', lifting the phone to her ear as she retraced her steps into the darkness of the side street.

"Come on, Dullahan," she muttered down the line, as the engaged tone beeped in her ear. "What are you up to?"

She tried again but got the same thing. It would have to wait. But now she had her phone in her hand, it would be savvy to let someone know of her whereabouts. She scrolled down to Spook's name and her finger hovered over the call button.

No.

She couldn't do it.

She couldn't deal with the irritation and disappointment in Spook's voice. Besides, she'd want Acid to wait for her before going in and that wasn't happening. The bats were eager to get their teeth into whatever was waiting for them inside that members' club. Instead, she tapped out a quick message, giving Spook her location and letting her know she was following up a lead on Kaan. She wrote that she would report back as soon as she knew anything, switched off her phone and then pocketed it.

By this point, she'd wandered back down the street and was standing in front of the club. Up close, she realised the door had been painted a dark navy blue rather than black and it appeared to be recently done. Scanning her attention up and around the entrance, she saw no security cameras or intercom system. There was no bell, no buzzer. The door didn't even have a handle. Reaching up, she banged on the door with the underside of her fist, surprised when it creaked open an inch.

"What the… Hello?" she called out.

There was no response.

She pushed at the door, opening it to reveal a narrow

corridor. From the minimal light filtering in from outside, she could make out another door at the far end. There were no pictures on the walls, no carpet even. Just exposed white-washed brickwork and uneven wooden floorboards. She stepped inside and held the door open while she looked around for a light switch. There wasn't one. Instead she used the failing light from outside to guide her down the corridor.

At the second door she stopped and, holding her breath, shifted all her awareness into her hearing. The sound of traffic drifted in from outside, but it was hard to pick up any noises coming from the room beyond. She placed her ear up against the cold wood. It was plywood and painted an off-white colour. Was that scratching she could hear? Mice, maybe? Or rats? If this was the place Kaan conducted his business, he didn't care too much about people's opinions of him. Or, again, maybe that was the point. Maybe this grim, dingy club was the perfect setting for how he wanted to be perceived. It was certainly disconcerting.

Acid gripped the door handle, her other hand moving to her belt, ready to unsheathe the push dagger if needed. Her instincts told her there was no one on the other side of the plywood door, but it was important to prepare oneself for all possibilities. Twisting the handle, she eased it open. Light shot out from the other side, illuminating the wall beside her. But no sound, no angry voice asking her what the hell she was doing here.

She stepped into a large room that was a far cry from the grotty entrance and corridor. Three walls were painted a rich teal colour and decorated with abstract artwork, whilst the fourth was all but covered by a large batik of a tiger's face. In the centre of the room were two black leather couches on either side of a glass coffee table and, on the floor, an enormous fur rug that could only be bearskin. The light came from three gold-plated lamps on the wall to her left, about the same height as her and in the shape of palm trees. The metal fronds of the trees each held a bright LED bulb and, as she examined them, halos of light leaked out across her vision, making her blink. The room was extravagant and lush and everything in it appeared to be brand new. And more like how she'd imagine a crime lord's pad to look.

"Hello?" she called out, taking tentative steps further inside and casting her gaze up to the corners by the ceiling, looking for cameras. But there were none in sight and, other than the furniture, the place was empty.

Across the room was another door, this one closed but solid wood and painted teal like the walls, the handle and hinges made of brushed gold. She was over to it in three strides and listening carefully. Again no sound could be heard from the other side. Without pause, without taking a breath, she grabbed the handle and pulled the door open.

The next room had the same teal walls and another door in the same position on the other side. But rather than couches, there was a long table leaning against the wall in front of her, on which the light was coming not from lamps this time but from a bank of monitors.

Acid moved around the front of the table, eyes wide, flitting from screen to screen. There were four monitors, each of grainy black and white security footage. She saw the outside of the building, the main door (there must have been a hidden camera somewhere). She saw the corridor entrance and the room she'd just vacated. Each screen had a time stamp and date, showing it was live footage, and the fact she could see herself staring at a collection of monitors confirmed this. As she moved, the image on the screen moved with a split-second delay. She glanced around, but could see no camera. It had to be embedded in the wall opposite. These days all you needed was a hole the size of a pinprick. Technology moved faster than she could keep up.

She turned back to the screens, her muscles tightening as another person appeared on one of them. She leaned in for a better look. They were wearing dark clothes and had long hair. She assumed they were female, but she couldn't see a face or any distinguishing features. The room they were in was a similar size to the one she was in, but empty except for a single chair. As Acid watched, the person moved towards the doorway.

Shit.

She straightened up as the door on the other side of the room creaked open. Back to the screen, she saw the person moving into another room. This one. Acid looked up. There they were. Standing in the doorway facing her.

She was right, it was a woman.

A woman she knew.

"Fiona?"

Fiona smiled, but her eyes told a different story. "Hello, Acid Vanilla."

The skin on Acid's arms rippled with goose bumps. Fiona had only ever known her as Alice.

"What the fuck is going on?" Acid asked. "Why are you here? Did you know all along? Is your father Kaan?"

Fiona's eyes flashed with malevolence and she chuckled to herself. "So many questions. But don't worry, we shall enlighten you. Just not yet."

Acid's hand drifted around her back, fingertips poised on the latch of the push dagger. "We?"

Fiona raised her head and Acid sensed someone behind her. A sharp pain stabbed at the side of her neck.

"Shit, what the—"

She spun around, about to draw her weapon, when the sight of the man in front of her knocked all reason and consideration from her mind. "You?"

Freddie Pearce sniffed. "Yes. Me." He was holding a syringe in the air, his thumb depressed on the plunger. The vial was empty.

Acid clutched at her neck. As she stepped back, her legs gave way and she stumbled. "Freddie, what the fuck are you doing?"

She sounded like she was underwater. She couldn't focus on anything. A shiver of ice-cold fear ran down her spine.

"Why are you...? I don't get it... You're Kaan?"

She staggered back and felt someone grab her under the arms. She struggled, but her limbs didn't work. Hands grabbed her, laying her down as a black cloud descended. She could hear Fiona's shrill laughter in her head, but couldn't tell where it was coming from.

"That's the way, Alice. Rest for now." Freddie's voice was booming and distorted. It filled up the room and the entire world.

She tried to respond, but her mouth was a wet circle of limp muscles and too many teeth. "Whun... mun... Gaa..."

Freddie tutted. "Best not try to talk for now, Al. The propofol I injected you with is making you sound like an absolute moron." He let out a cackle of laughter. "Don't be alarmed, though. It's not poison. It won't kill you. Though you probably know that already. Hell, what am I telling you for? You've probably been on the other end of a syringe of propofol regularly over the years."

Acid struggled to open her eyes, hanging onto the precipice of consciousness with everything she had. Nothing made sense, and it was futile anyway. The fog in her head was distorting her thoughts and she could sense herself slipping under. She fought it for a few seconds more, but her body was numb and she couldn't move. The last thing she saw before she drifted into the abyss was Freddie shaking his head and smiling as if watching a rambunctious puppy.

"It's understandable you're confused, Alice. But please don't worry. I will reveal all once we get to our destination. And do you know what? I think you're going to love what I'm going to tell you. I honestly do."

Chapter Thirty-Three

Spook lifted her head up from the pillow, listening intently in the darkness of her room for whatever it was that had wrenched her from sleep. As dreams faded from her awareness and her physical body flashed online, she heard it again. It was coming from downstairs. A sharp banging on the front door of the apartment.

Her hand scrambled at the nightstand for her glasses and she shoved them on her face, almost piercing her eye with one of the arms, before switching on the bedside light. A sudden stab of worry that her phone was gone disappeared quickly as she remembered she'd left it in the kitchen. She twisted her old alarm clock around to see the display. The time was 9.33 p.m. Still early. After the drama and upset of the last few days, she'd been exhausted and gone to bed at seven. She had intended to read for a while, maybe even watch Netflix on her laptop. Yet once in bed, sleep had wrapped its warm arms around her almost immediately.

The banging went again.

She had to do something. But what? Where was Acid when she needed her? She climbed out of bed and shuffled over to her bedroom door. Maybe it was Acid that was banging. She could have gotten drunk and lost her keys. Spook tiptoed out onto the landing. No one knew where they lived, so that was the most likely explanation, but the thought only made her angry as she approached the top door to the apartment and slid back the heavy bolts. As she twisted the key in the lock and yanked open the thick wooden door, a rush of cool air wrapped itself around her, rousing her some more. Peering down the dark stairwell, she heard more banging and someone yelling.

"Acid? Are you in there? Open this fecking door!"

Shit. She knew that voice. Grabbing onto the handrail, she hurried down the stairs and up to the main door. "Who's there?" she whispered.

"Spook? Open up, will ya?" the voice barked. "It's The Dullahan. I need to speak to Acid."

"Wait a second."

She leant down and unlocked the bottom bolts and locks before doing the same with the top ones. Stepping back, she switched on the light and hauled open the heavy metal door to reveal the wiry old Irishman. He was wearing a long tan leather overcoat with a large fur collar and a green trilby pulled down over his face. He glared at Spook and his craggy, clean-shaven face looked deathly white in the hallway light. His pale blue eyes seemed paler than the last time they'd met and this made his intense stare even more daunting.

"Where is she?" he asked, stepping inside. "I need to see her."

"She's— Oh!"

Spook was startled as she noticed the man in the shadows. He was huge, almost seven feet tall and wide too. With his orange hair, bushy sideburns and thick scowl, he reminded Spook of the giant from a picture book of fairy tales she'd had as a kid. But then he smiled and his eyes danced with warmth and she felt bad for making that connection.

"That's Seamus," The Dullahan said, standing next to her and gesturing at the man. "He works for me. He's a good lad. You okay, son?"

"Aye," Seamus replied, in a voice that didn't fit his size. "I'll wait outside for you. Just in case."

"Just in case?" Spook whispered. "Why? What's happened?"

As Seamus turned around in the doorway, placing his back to them, The Dullahan shut the door. "Upstairs."

"But I was trying to tell you. Acid isn't here. I don't think so, anyway. We had a row and she stormed out. I've not heard her come in since then and…" She trailed off as The Dullahan trudged up the stairs, drawing back deep breaths and clinging onto the handrail as he went.

"What's going on?" Spook asked, following him. "Is Acid in trouble? Am I?"

"What do you think, if I'm here?" came the gruff reply. "I've been calling her but she hasn't answered her fecking phone. So I got Seamus to drive me down here."

They got to the top of the stairs and The Dullahan pushed on through into the corridor beyond. Striding down towards the kitchen, he glanced into Spook's room and then threw open the door to Acid's bedroom. Spook joined him there, lifting herself up on her toes to peer over his shoulder. The room was indeed empty and the bed, whilst not made, didn't look to have been slept in recently. Through to the kitchen, they found this empty as well. Acid wasn't here.

"She's probably at some bar," Spook said, flicking on the light. "Do you want a drink of anything? Tea? Something stronger?"

The Dullahan paced around the table, eyes narrow and disdainful as he took in the messy worktops and unwashed plates stacked up in the sink. "Not for me. Can you contact her, get her back here?"

"What is it?" Spook asked, her concern for her and Acid's safety overriding the edginess she always felt in the hoary assassin's presence. "Is she in danger?"

He stopped pacing. "Aye, you could say that. She asked me to find out if anyone in the industry had mentioned the attack on her and to look into the names Kaan and Zoto."

"Yes. That's right," Spook said. "They're part of our case."

His stare intensified as if he was trying to turn her to stone. He began pacing once more. "I've now heard back from all my contacts," he continued. "No one has put an official contract out on Acid – or you, if you were worried about that – but someone has been recruiting. And outside the usual networks."

Spook opened her mouth to respond, but the look The Dullahan gave her made her shut it right away.

"I don't have a name yet," he said, as if reading her mind. "But from what I do know, I'd bet this is that Kaan fella you've been looking for. I spoke with an old contact. Someone he knows got approached by a man using the name Kaan. He said he was recruiting assassins and mentioned he wanted to take out someone who used to be in the industry. From what my contact said, it seems Kaan didn't want to go through the usual channels in case this ex-assassin got wind of his intentions. Clever of the fecker, really. But no prizes for guessing who the ex-assassin is."

Spook wilted onto one of the kitchen chairs, slumping against the wooden back. "But why now?"

"My contact couldn't get to the bottom of that. But Acid has been stepping on a few toes recently, if you didn't know. Going after other people's marks. She didn't realise, so she said. But that was no excuse. My guess is this Kaan had some big contracts she took away from him."

"But we think Kaan and Zoto could be the same person. And that he knows we're trying to find him. Isn't that too much of a coincidence that Acid has doubly pissed him off?"

The Dullahan let out a low grumble that might have been a laugh. "If you said that about anyone else, I'd say maybe. But with that woman... You know as well as I do that she lives to piss people off. If she hadn't been such a good operative, Beowulf Caesar would have got rid of her years ago. But she was too good for that. Plus, he had a real soft spot for the young lassie. She can be bloody charming when she wants to be. But you know more than anyone, I suppose. She gets away with things." He stopped walking and took a seat opposite her. "Or at least, she has done. Up to now. But from what I hear, this person – Kaan or whoever it is – means business. We need to find her. Now. Before he does."

"There's this bar she keeps going to," Spook said. "We could try there and— Oh, shit. Wait a minute." She got up and walked over to the counter, scooping up her phone. As the facial recognition kicked in and the screen flashed up, her heart dropped into her guts. She'd had a message. From Acid. She looked up. "Bethnal Green," she said.

"What's that?"

"Acid messaged me two hours ago. I was in my room and, to be honest, I was in a stinking mood with her so I left my phone in here. I've only just seen it." She held it up. "It says she got a lead on Kaan. She went to Bethnal Green to check it out. Hang on."

She tapped the call function on the screen and held it up to her ear. The Dullahan watched her as she waited for the ringtone, but none came. "She's switched her phone off."

"We hope *she* has," he said, rising from the table. "Do you have an exact location?"

"Yes. There's an address."

"All right, come on. My car's waiting outside. I'll get Seamus to drive us." He was striding over to the door, showing surprising agility considering how twisted and frail he'd appeared walking up the stairs a few minutes earlier. "Fecking well come on, Spook. Time is of the essence."

"But…" She looked down at her baggy t-shirt and sweatpants, her bare feet. But The Dullahan was already heading for the front door. Spook chased after him, reaching for her sneakers and stepping into them as she hurried down the corridor. She grabbed the keys and locked the door before catching up with him halfway down the stairs.

"Do you think she's okay?" she asked, biting her lip as soon as she'd said it. It was a dumb question, and when The Dullahan didn't respond she didn't push it.

At the bottom of the stairs, she overtook him and opened the door, shrieking as a heavy weight pushed against it as she released the catch.

Shit.

What the…?

Was someone breaking in?

Was it Kaan, come to kill her?

The Dullahan growled. "Ah no. Feck."

Spook stumbled back, knocking into the old man as a

figure fell through the doorway and landed with a thud on the floor. She saw right away it was Seamus. His head was facing her, with his feet hanging out the door and his big blue eyes staring up at her. His big blue, lifeless eyes. Between them was a perfect red circle where someone had shot him in the head.

Spook squealed, hands going to her mouth to stop herself as she looked up to see two men standing on the other side of the door. They were both dressed in black and looked to be twins. Both had the same tanned, clean-shaven complexion, with dark hair and eyes, and the same chin. They carried matching pistols.

"Who the feck do you think you're dealing with?" The Dullahan barked, gesturing at Seamus' body. "That's my man right there."

One of the men shrugged, the other smirked.

"We *know* who *we* are dealing with," the shrugger uttered, in a French accent. "It is you who are in the dark, no?" He jerked his gun at them. "But don't worry, you'll find out soon enough. If you don't want to share the same fate as your friend here, I suggest you shut up and do what we say. Get in the car. Now."

Chapter Thirty-Four

Bloody hellfire!

It felt like there were a million bats inside Acid's skull, desperate to break out. She blinked, but her vision was blurred and she couldn't make out anything except shapes and light auras. A herd of floaters swam through the vitreous humor in her eyes, causing her to blink some more.

"She's awake," a woman's voice boomed.

Acid jerked her head up as consciousness spread through her body and the remembrance of what happened flashed in her mind. She found she was sitting in a wooden chair. Her arms were around her back, with her wrists bound together. She yanked at the restraints. They felt like plastic cable ties. They weren't impossible to break, but with her arms behind her back and unable to create momentum it would be tricky.

"Don't even think about it."

She felt something hard and cold press against the back of her neck. The muzzle of a handgun, no doubt.

She blinked some more, and as her vision cleared she

saw she was in a dark room. Two huge halogen lamps illuminated the space in front of her, ten feet by ten feet. Two empty chairs sat facing the one she was sitting on, and to her right was a wooden desk on which was a closed laptop and a metal box about the size of a shoebox. Beyond the square of light, the room could have gone on forever, wide and long, like an endless dank abyss. All she could see was the area she was in and then nothingness. However, despite this, the room seemed familiar to her somehow and looking up at the roof she realised why. She'd been here before. This was Afrim Zoto's warehouse.

Footsteps in the darkness snapped her attention to a space beyond the lights as Freddie appeared through the gloom. He was wearing the same black jeans as earlier, but was now wearing a sheer black shirt that showed off his lithe, muscular torso underneath. On seeing Acid, he smiled.

"There she is. Sleep well, did you?"

She didn't reply but stared him out, trying to get a read on him.

His manner was still awkward and his movements nervy – especially in the way he jerked his head to one side as he considered her. But what was once endearing was now edgy and disturbing. Not surprising, considering he'd injected her with a strong sedative and tied her to a chair, but it was more than that. He'd given up trying to be cool or erudite and was letting a darker and more twisted physicality take over. His eyes burned with passion.

"I asked you a question, Alice," he said, stepping over to her and shoving his face into hers. "Did you sleep well?"

"I've had better," she said, turning her face from his as he loomed over her. "What the fuck is going on, Freddie?"

"I told you. All will be revealed." His voice rose a few

octaves as he spoke, saying the words in a sing-song fashion. It was like he was play-acting a deranged person and hitting all the right tropes. "But first I need something from you."

He walked over to the desk and opened the metal box. Not taking his eyes off hers, he pulled out another syringe and held it up, flicking his eyebrows as he did so. This time, the needle was attached to an empty vacutainer bottle, the type used for taking blood. He returned and nodded at the person holding the gun, who she presumed to be Fiona. She felt a tugging at her arms and then a release as her ties were cut.

"Don't try anything stupid," Fiona snarled, stepping around the side of her and holding the gun to her temple. "Believe me, it would give me great pleasure to put a bullet through your pathetic brain."

"Arm, please," Freddie sang, grabbing her right wrist and pulling it towards him. He placed the syringe between his lips and yanked up the sleeve of her jacket. She watched him for a moment before turning her attention to the woman.

"I'm going to take a wild guess and say you're not called Fiona Zoto."

A smirk spread across her strong features. "You need to do better research on your clients. You and your little friend were so keen to take the case you didn't even check my credentials. But don't feel bad, it wouldn't have mattered if you had. We took care of everything. Like true professionals should."

"Let me introduce the great Lamia Loveless," Freddie said. Having revealed the crook of Acid's arm, he was now placing the needle against the most prominent vein. "You might have heard of her."

Acid rolled the name around in her head. Lamia Loveless. The new operative on the scene that The Dullahan had mentioned. The one he'd thought was her attacker from the park. She looked the woman up and down. With her hair slicked back the way it was, and dressed all in black, she looked the part. A far cry from the timid woman she'd met a week ago.

"But I don't understand," Acid said. "Why hire us if this was your intention? Why not just kill me if you're as good as they say? *Unf.*" She bit her teeth together as Freddie drove the needle into her vein.

He chuckled to himself as he drew out a vial of blood and then licked his lips. "Perfect. Thank you for that."

He straightened up before Lamia grabbed Acid's wrist and pulled her arm around her back. Her gut instinct was to fight, but she was woozy and ungainly from the effects of the sedative and the woman's grip was strong. Without too much effort, she grabbed the other wrist and tied her hands tight with a new cable tie.

"Hey. Careful."

Freddie popped the vacutainer filled with her blood out from the syringe casing and walked back to the table, placing it carefully inside the metal box. Tossing the needle into the darkness, he turned back to Acid and grinned. "Isn't this fun?"

"Why the blood?" she asked. "Are you planning on framing me for something?"

Freddie tsked and rolled his eyes camply. "Can you imagine? But no. Not that."

She sniffed. "All right, Freddie. You've had a laugh. Tell me what's going on. Are you Kaan? Or Axel Slater maybe?"

"Don't be ridiculous." He cackled. "Kaan doesn't exist. None of them do. Kaan, Axel Slater, Afrim Zoto. They were all made up. All fabrications. Well researched and planned out to help create a credible narrative that you'd find plausible, but fabrications nevertheless."

Lamia stepped aside as Freddie walked past Acid's chair and disappeared from view around the back of her. A second later, she felt his hands on her shoulders.

"You're very tense," he whispered in her ear. "You need to learn to relax. It's not good for you, all this stress."

She shrugged him off as he massaged her trapezius muscles, but it did nothing but elicit more cackling.

"I'd be a lot less stressed if you explained to me what the hell is going on," she told him. "What do you want from me? Who are you?"

"Ahh! Now there we go!" He let go and moved around the front of her, wagging a finger in her face. "Now you're asking the right questions. Who am I? Who *the hell* am I? Because whilst Kaan and Axel Slater and Afrim Zoto don't exist – neither does Freddie Pearce, I'm afraid. Good old Fred. Such an affable chap. You were starting to like him, weren't you, Alice? I could tell. What a shame."

She looked at him with eyes like slits and a sneer crippling her lips. He was playing with her and she wasn't going to give him the satisfaction of asking again. She adjusted her position on the chair, rotating her hand so she could reach her fingers to her belt. Excitement rippled through her as she discovered the push dagger was still in its home. They hadn't noticed it. But no one ever did.

"Okay, fine, here we go," he said, rolling his head back before shaking out his shoulders as if limbering up for a fight. "Let me introduce myself properly, Alice. My name – my real name – is Darius Duke. I think you knew my father. Oscar Duke."

Chapter Thirty-Five

The room spun as Acid's vision zoomed from micro to macro and back again. She swallowed, but it was hard with a dry throat.

What.

The.

Fuck?

She opened her eyes as wide as they'd go to chase the last of the sedative from her system. To deal with what she'd just heard, she needed all her faculties.

"You're Oscar Duke's son?"

Freddie – or rather, Darius Duke, if he was to be believed – bowed at the waist. "The one and the same." He straightened up and stuck his bottom lip out. "And I've got a few bones to pick with you, Alice Vandella."

"How did you…? When did you—?"

"Do you know, I've been obsessed with you since I was nine years old. Ever since you murdered my father." His face dropped and the mischief drained from his eyes. He raised his chin. "Do you have any idea what you put me and my mother through, Alice Vandella? She was broken. She never got over it. To find out her husband had been murdered and by the fifteen-year-old daughter of some tart he was screwing."

"Fuck you," Acid spat, squeezing her fists together so tightly the tendons in her wrists rubbed painfully at the cable ties. "Don't call her that."

"Hmm. But that's what she was." He grabbed one of the empty chairs, placed it in front of her and sat down. There was less than a metre between them. "She tried to keep it from me, dear old mum. Didn't want me to know the truth about what had happened. But I found out. It was all over the bloody papers, for one thing. Then everyone at school learned about it. Kids can be so cruel."

He stared off into the middle distance for a moment, as if reliving something from his past. When he returned his attention to Acid, his eyes looked to be jet black. The windows to his soul. "I followed your case from the start. I kept a scrapbook of newspaper clippings. I even tried to write to you when you were in remand and in Crest Hill." He looked up at Lamia and smiled. "A home for criminally dangerous young girls. You'd have loved it."

"I never received any letters," Acid told him. Her mind was racing, but none of the thoughts were useful or pleasant. "I didn't even know you existed."

"No. You didn't. And why would you care anyway, right? There's no doubt hundreds of children have grown up missing one of their parents because of you."

"Is that so?" She cleared her throat, at the same time moving her fingers to the latch on her belt concealing the push dagger. "So I take it you know all about me. Who I was, who I am..."

Darius leaned forward. "That was the puzzling thing.

You were at Crest Hill, doing your time for my father's murder, and then all at once they released you and you vanished. It was like one day you existed and the next you didn't. I mean, I read the reports that said you'd committed suicide after a fling with your doctor. But they were rather inconclusive, and the older I got, and the more I investigated, I found a lot of holes in those reports. They recorded no autopsy for one thing. And many of the people who'd signed off on your death were either dead or missing. So, you see how it looked."

He placed his hands on his knees and pushed himself upright so he was standing over her. She tensed, ready for him to strike. But instead he laid his palm on the side of her face, cupping her cheek tenderly. She'd have rather he hit her.

"Don't!"

She moved her head away, eliciting another piercing cackle from Darius. Seizing the opportunity, she eased open the latch on the back of her belt. Moving slowly, careful not to reveal what she was doing, she began coaxing the dagger from its holster with the tips of her fingers. Lamia was standing to her right a few metres away. She still had the gun pointed at Acid's head but her focus was on Darius and, from the angle she was standing, she couldn't see Acid working the blade free and gripping it in her fist.

"For years I thought they'd given you a new identity. I press-ganged the relevant authorities, but no one would tell me anything. I was right, though. In a way. You did have a new identity, Acid Vanilla." He leered at her with eyes so wide she could see the whites around his dark irises.

"But forgive me, I'm jumping the gun." He eyed Lamia's weapon and his lips twitched. "If you'll excuse the pun. You see, Alice, I never gave up hope that I'd find you. I didn't know what I was going to say or do when I did, but I kept hold of the fact I would. My father was a rich man, with lots of savings, and after my mother died of brain cancer it all came to me. It's such wonderful stuff, money. You can do all sorts with it. I played the stock markets and did rather well for myself. I made enough that I never had to find a normal job. Which was lucky, because my full-time job was finding you. Finding the person who killed my father."

Spittle flew out of his mouth and hit Acid on the chin. She wiped it on the collar of her jacket as Darius closed his eyes and muttered to himself.

"Your father was attacking my mum," she said, purposefully keeping her voice low and soft. "I was only fifteen. I just wanted him to stop hurting her. I didn't intend to kill him."

"The police report said you practically decapitated him with a broken bottle. One copper said it was the most frenzied attack he'd ever seen."

He had her there. "I'm sorry," was all she could find to say. "I know how hard it can be to lose someone."

"Do you? Do you, Alice?"

She lowered her head. "Yes. I do."

It was a good move, playing subservient at times like this, but she was also playing for time while she sawed through the thick plastic cable ties without alerting them to what she was doing.

"I've been looking for you for twenty years," Darius said. "High and low. I'd almost given up hope I'd ever find you. Eight months ago your name pops up in a deep search program I'd had created by some tech-wizard over in India. Alice Vandella is alive and well and living in central

London. We could have walked past each other and I wouldn't have known. Imagine that?"

Pissing hell.

Why had she let Spook convince her that restoring her old identity was a good idea? Alice Vandella had been dead and buried. She should have remained that way.

"So I hired some more clever tech people," Darius went on. "After a bit of digging – using facial recognition software and the like – one of those glorious geniuses discovered your profile on the old Annihilation Pest Control database. It was a tricky bit of software to infiltrate, of course, but nothing's impossible these days." He shook his head at her. "Alice Vandella. A top assassin. Wow! But it makes sense, I suppose. It also inspired some very creative thinking in my pretty little noggin, I can tell you. The more I found out about you and your old boss and what you all did, the more it got me thinking... I wanted a piece of that action. It sounded fun. And lucrative. I mean, the names alone! Brilliant! I was wondering about Dastardly Doom. What do you think?"

"Yeah. You should go for it," Acid told him. She could feel the cable ties giving way. Another minute or two and she'd cut through them.

"You sound like you have it all figured out," she added, hoping to appeal to his ego. Like she'd told Spook in their last fight training session – one thing about power-hungry maniacs, they loved talking about themselves. "But a few things don't make sense. I presume you were behind the woman who attacked me in Hyde Park. Why send someone to kill me if you wanted to confront me with your big secret? She could have succeeded."

Darius moved over and stood beside Lamia, the two of them smirking. Acid's jaw was so tense the muscles below her ears throbbed. The bats screeched at her to hurry, to free herself, to leap forward and open up the bastard's neck with the push dagger.

"It's true. She could have killed you. But I wouldn't have let that happen. And I needed to be certain you were the person I suspected you to be. I'd been following you for weeks, but I wanted to make sure you were the infamous Acid Vanilla I'd heard so much about. You disposed of Sagur so effortlessly that I knew I had the right girl. Also, I wanted to watch you in action. I was there that morning, you see. We both were, Lamia and me. We wanted to see you perform for us. Very impressive, I have to say. Down in Lambeth, Klaus was only supposed to capture you and bring you to me. So that was rather annoying when you killed the poor chap, but what do you know? It was charm and clever planning over brute force that won out in the end. I'll have to remember that, going forward."

"All this rigmarole, the Zoto case, the warehouses, Fiona, Freddie, you set it all up just to get to me?"

"I did it because it was fun!" Darius yelled. "Because I could. A few months' lease on a lousy warehouse. Some breadcrumbs and red herrings placed around the darker corners of the web. It didn't take much."

Acid kept on at the cable ties, going slower now with both sets of eyes on her. Her wrists were raw and the skin was torn where the hard plastic had rubbed, but she didn't feel any pain. The pain would come later. In a warm shower, if she was lucky. For now, it was about channelling this fiery mix of rage and manic energy into a useable force.

"You said you were following me for weeks. Why not snatch me earlier? You could have overpowered me with enough people. Yet you plan this wild goose chase, have us running around the city looking for people who don't exist.

Just so you can bring me here to kill me? Because that's what you're planning, right? To make me pay for taking your father from you?"

It was a bold approach and a bolder question, but she needed to know. The chaos in her head was clouding her judgement. If she knew what her fate was to be, she could act from that point. If all was lost, she was free to try anything.

"I've told you already. It was a bit of fun. And a way for me to explore this new world. It was exciting and god knows we all need excitement, Alice, Acid." Darius grinned before his expression darkened once again. He walked over to the table. "And I don't want to kill you. Not yet, at least. I want you to suffer. Like I did. Plus, I wanted to get to know you. Find out who you were. And what a treat that has been." He glanced at the metal box. "But more so – this is about revenge. I had to bide my time. Keep you dangling on a string while I finalised my master plan."

"What are you talking about?" Acid asked, leaning forward and yanking her wrists against the ties. "What master plan?"

Darius turned on her, his voice rising in volume. "Will you stop bloody well butting in?! I've not finished!" He screwed his eyes up and pinched the bridge of his nose with his free hand. "Now where was I? Ah… yes, excellent." He drew in a deep breath and opened his eyes. "Perfect timing, boys."

Acid froze at the sound of movement from the depths of the warehouse. Squinting past the hot lamps into the darkness, she could see four figures coming towards her.

"No," she muttered under her breath, as a flurry of dark thoughts smashed into her brain.

It was Spook and The Dullahan. Their hands were

bound in front of them and they had gags around their mouths. Two men with wide shoulders and stern faces dressed all in black shoved them forward. As they got closer, Acid glanced between her two friends. Spook appeared to be in shock and her eyes were puffy and red behind her glasses. In turn, The Dullahan's face was hard and unflinching. Deep anger burned in his eyes. Neither of them tried to speak. They knew it was useless.

Darius waved his hand at the two chairs in front of Acid and his men marched Spook and The Dullahan forward, shoving them onto the seats. Acid locked eyes with each of them in turn.

Don't worry. I've got this.

She turned back to Darius, who had been watching the exchange with an eager grin. "What are they doing here? They're not a part of this."

She asked the question but already suspected what the answer would be. It was this dawning realisation that pricked up the hairs on the back of her neck and sent a shiver of icy indignation shooting down her spine.

"They're an essential part. Don't you get it? That's another reason I had to keep you strung along for so long. I needed time to do my research." Darius' eyes flashed with eagerness as he opened the metal box again. "I needed to work out how best to get you three – that's you and the two people closest to you – together in one room. It wasn't easy when this old fucker lives at the other end of the country. But as I hope you're already appreciating, I'm rather good at coming up with a plan. Somewhat of an out-of-the-box thinker, I've been told. Useful for times like this. So I invented Kaan and the Zotos. I posted things on the dark web that I knew this leprechaun chap would see. I even paid off some of his friends to give out false information. All for this moment."

He looked inside the box with the excited air of a kid peeping into his Christmas stocking. Reaching in, he pulled out a ten-inch knife. The steel blade shone in the light as he held it up and regarded it lustily.

"Come on, Alice. I did this all for you. You've got to give me some credit. And it's all worked out so beautifully. I'm a fucking genius." He grinned and tapped the knife against the side of his head. "Upstairs for thinking, downstairs for dancing."

"You don't have to do this," Acid told him. "It's me you want."

"It's you I want to suffer!" Darius screamed, grabbing Spook's hair and yanking her head back. The kid's eyes bulged and she wailed behind the gag. Acid lurched forward in her seat, arms yanking at the half-sawn cable ties. But they held tight.

"You bastard. Let her go."

"I want you to grieve as I did," Darius snarled, spittle flying out into the air, illuminated by the bright lights. He tightened his grip on Spook's hair. "So here it is, Alice. This is where I return the favour. Where I take away everything that you care about."

Chapter Thirty-Six

"Darius! Don't do this!" Acid pleaded, trying an alternative approach. "It's not her fault your dad died. It was me who killed him. Kill me if you have to."

"Don't worry, we'll get to that," he said. "Eventually."

"Eventually?"

He let go of Spook's hair and appeared to mellow slightly. "There's still lots for us to discuss, Alice. I need to keep you alive. For a while, at least. You have to know the truth before you die."

"The truth about what?"

He pointed the knife towards the open metal box. "Did your mother ever tell you about your father, Alice?"

He glared at her, a supercilious smile spreading across his face as the realisation of what he was implying showed itself on hers. "No. I'm guessing not. Which is why I took a vial of your blood just now. You see, there's a big chance you could be my half-sister. Imagine that?"

"You're talking shit."

"Am I? We'll find out soon enough. Once my people test

your blood." He closed the metal box and picked it up, handing it to the men who had brought in Spook and The Dullahan. "Do you know where you are taking this?"

The men nodded in unison. "Shall we go now?"

"Yes, leave us. We've got it from here. I'll be in touch soon." He watched as the two men disappeared into the gloom and then spun around. "Isn't... this... all...SO... exciting?"

Acid stopped sawing at the cable ties and glared at him. Half-sister. Was he serious? Or was it part of his twisted game? His face gave nothing away.

"You're lying," she whispered. "Oscar Duke is not my father."

"*Oh, but he could beeeee,*" Darius sang. "Sorry, Al. And believe me, I was as shocked as you appear to be when I found out. Yet it seems my dear old dad had been seeing your mother off and on for years. Long before I was born. And long before you were born, too. Did she not tell you that? Tut tut. And the two of you being so close as well. It turns out she was on the game long before her supposed accident meant she couldn't dance anymore."

"That's not true." Acid's body felt numb, as if her soul was floating away from her. Except it wasn't the drugs. "You're sick."

"No. I'm not. I'm a genius. I've told you that already." He sighed and shook his head. "Me and you, hey? Siblings. Lamia can't see it, but I can. We've got the same jawline, the same shaped eyebrows. But it's more than that. I think we're very alike. We've got the same cynical worldview; the same taste in music – that wasn't a fabrication – the same drive. Although I'm not referring to sex drive. That's all you. Just think, you wanted to bone your brother. Sicko."

Acid drew in a long breath, holding the oxygen in her

lungs and slowing her heart rate in the process. When she exhaled, she did it slowly, relaxing her limbs at the same time. Now calm, she put the push dagger to work once again. By now she could cut the ties in one sharp movement, but Lamia still had the gun on her and was watching her intently. The sudden movement would give her away and she couldn't risk it. But another half-minute and she'd have sliced through the tough plastic; another minute and the situation would look very different.

"If we are related," she said, "what then?"

"Nothing changes. I kill everyone you care about, then you find out I'm your long-lost little brother – or not – then I kill you." He shrugged. "The results of the DNA test will change nothing, I'm afraid. Either I kill my sister or I kill a stranger. But you have to die for what you did. This way, it means we get to draw out the agony and the pain a while longer. That's the point here, sis. The only point."

He stepped back and positioned himself between The Dullahan and Spook. Spook strained at her ties, squealing pointlessly over the material in her mouth. Next to her, the staunch Irishman remained still.

"Okay, you two," Darius said. "On your knees."

Spook's eyes bulged wider and her squeals grew in volume. She shook her head frantically.

"On your knees! Now!" Darius screamed. "Or I'll have Lamia empty that magazine into Alice's face."

Lamia stepped forward, adjusting her grip on the handle of the gun. It was only a nine, but if she was using hollow points, one round would turn Acid's brain to mush from that distance. There'd be no need for the full mag.

"I swear to god I'll slice you open right now," Darius spat, grabbing Spook by the back of the neck and provoking more muffled squeals.

"Spook, do as he says," Acid said. "It'll be okay," she lied.

Darius shoved Spook forward and grabbed the chair out from under her. She stumbled onto all fours before pushing herself upright and kneeling in front of Acid. Tears were running down her face. Darius moved over to The Dullahan next, but the old man growled and stood up off the chair of his own accord. Fixing Acid with pale, unblinking eyes, he lowered himself onto the concrete floor. Once there, he gave her another nod of reassurance. It didn't help. The bats were in a frenzy. Her eyes darted over to Lamia. If she looked away for one second, she'd rip through the ties and launch at her.

If she looked away…

But she wasn't, and acting rashly would get them all killed.

"That's more like it," Darius boomed, the rage gone from his voice. "You know, Alice, I was thinking earlier… If it wasn't for my father, then you would have grown up very differently. You'd probably have six kids right now with three different baby daddies. I imagine you'd be on benefits if you weren't on the game. Like your dirty slut of a mother."

Despite a million chattering voices in her head urging her to act, to destroy, to slay this prick, she remained still. Emotional control might have been the hardest of the assassin's traits for her to master, but master it she had. Darius was trying for a reaction. He wasn't going to get one.

"Oscar Duke might have made us both," he went on. "But who we are now, who I am, who you are, that's all on you, Alice. When you killed my father, you changed both our paths. You made us both into killers." He frowned and stuck out his bottom lip as a small child might. "Isn't that awful? Yet at the same time rather beautiful, too."

She didn't respond. She was almost through the ties and only had one go at this. Her eyes darted from Darius to Lamia to Spook and The Dullahan and back again. If she flung the dagger at Lamia, she'd incapacitate her at best; at worst, throw off her aim. At the same time, she could launch herself at Darius, barge him away from Spook and follow up by diving on Lamia and getting the gun. That should give Spook and The Dullahan time to get to their feet and to safety while she finished off the two cretins with the nine. She exhaled. It was going to be messy, but these things usually were. From the calm intensity in the The Dullahan's eyes she could tell he was ready, that he knew she was planning something. That reassured her.

"Okay, Alice. Enough talking," Darius said. "Choose."

"Excuse me?"

"You heard," he said, lowering the knife, waving the tip between Spook's throat and The Dullahan's. "Choose which one of your friends I kill first?"

"Fuck you. I won't do it." She was so close now. Another ten seconds.

"Choose!"

Spook and The Dullahan both yelled, but the gags muffled their protestations. They shook their heads and glared at her.

"Choose!" Darius screamed. "Or you'll all die right now."

"No," she yelled back. "I won't. I can't."

Five seconds...

She was ready. It was time to finish this.

Three seconds...

"Fine," Darius said. "I'll choose." He stepped behind

The Dullahan and grabbed his forehead. Acid stopped what she was doing, frozen in time as she saw the knife come down with a violent swish. All she could do was stare in disbelief as Darius wrenched her old friend's head back and sliced the long blade across his throat. As his neck opened, a spurt of his blood hit her in the face.

No!

Fucking hell, no!

This wasn't happening. She was so close. She was ready to go. He was too. One second more. They could have over-powered them and escaped.

Like she always had.

Like he always had.

He was The Dullahan, for Christ's sake.

The Dullahan.

She tried to shout, but the noise got stuck in her throat. The Dullahan's eyes bulged as a wave of shock and terror shuddered through him. The blood spurted out of his neck like a grisly fountain. Darius had severed his carotid artery and that was it. The old man's icy blue eyes met Acid's and at that moment they both knew there was no coming back from this one. He was dead. The great Dullahan was dead.

Chapter Thirty-Seven

The bat screeches filled Acid's head as Darius Duke let go of The Dullahan and he slumped to the ground face first. He was already dead, but the blood continued to gush from his neck, pooling out over the concrete floor in front of her. Acid watched for a moment, then gritted her teeth and looked up. There'd be time to process her friend's death later. If she survived.

"Good choice," Darius said. "I'm one of those people who prefers to save the best until last. What about you, Alice?" He moved behind Spook and yanked the gag from around her mouth. "Do you have any last words, Spook? Anything you want to say to your wonderful friend here? She does get you into some scrapes, doesn't she?"

Spook gulped back air, almost dry heaving as she did. "Acid... Please... I—"

"It's okay, kid," she said, locking eyes with her. "Keep it together."

Tightening her grip on the push dagger, she cut through the last millimetres of plastic, feeling a rush of adrenaline as the cable ties gave way. She tensed her triceps and held her position, arms still behind her back. Her heart felt like it had been torn to pieces, but to lose her mind now was to lose everything.

"You two are so sweet together, aren't you?" Darius said. "The killer and the tech-nerd. It's almost like you're in a sitcom. A really unfunny one."

He raised the knife to his face and scratched his chin with the tip despite it being covered in The Dullahan's blood. But this was his shtick, Acid realised. Going from affable clown to unhinged psychopath in the blink of an eye. What wasn't clear to her yet was whether it was an act to freak her out or if he was truly unbalanced.

"Who would you play?" she asked, hoping the latter was true and she might distract him. "In this sitcom, I mean."

Darius frowned. "Why, the murderer, of course. Who else? I thought you were supposed to be smart."

He was waving the knife around as he spoke, playing with them, relishing his moment in the spotlight as Spook sobbed on the floor in front of him. Directly in front of him…

"Spook," Acid said, as a thought came to her. "Do you remember our training?"

The kid looked up and sniffed. "What?"

"The training we did. In the flat. You know – if all is lost, you might as well try anything. Do you remember?"

Darius sighed loudly. "For heaven's sake. Give it a rest, sis. No one's trying anything. All that's going to happen now is you're going to watch me slice open your little chum here. But this time we'll do it nice and slow. Make it last longer. So where do you want me to start? Eyes? Ears? Ooh, nose maybe?"

"You're talking bollocks," she said, flicking up her eyebrows at Spook. "Yes?"

Spook scowled and shook her head.

Come on, kid.

"How dare you," Darius growled through clenched teeth. Back to the unhinged psychopath. "I'm a fucking god. After I remove the likes of you from this world, I'm going to—"

"Bollocks!" Acid yelled.

And Spook got it. Finally, she got it. She looked at Acid with terrified eyes, but she held her gaze and gave her the firmest nod she could offer.

Come on, Spook.

You can do this.

She nodded again, more intensely. It had to be now. With a whimper of fear, Spook leant forward and Acid held her breath. Spook made a weird groaning sound and then swung her head back with a loud grunt. The trajectory was perfect and the back of her cranium smashed into the fleshy mound of Darius' genitals, knocking all the air out of him. He cried out in a voice at least two octaves higher than normal, bending over as the pain spread through his nether regions. Instinctively, his hands went to his groin and the knife clattered to the floor.

That was all Acid needed.

Leaping up from the chair, she launched herself at Lamia, arcing the push dagger through the air. She intended to bury the stubby blade in the assassin's sinewy neck, but despite being distracted by Darius' cries, her reactions were sharp and she saw Acid coming, raising her arm to block the attack. With a grunt, Acid stabbed the blade into her shoulder instead. Leaving the dagger embedded in the muscle, she grabbed Lamia's wrist and dug the thumb

of her other hand into the pressure point under her bicep.
She cried out but released the gun and, as it fell to the floor,
Acid let go of her arm and elbowed her in the face. The
tough assassin stumbled back, yanking the dagger out of her
shoulder and chucking it at Acid. She swerved it and side-
stepped Lamia before delivering a swift roundhouse kick
that connected with the side of her head and knocked her
over the table.

Turning her attention to the commotion to her left,
she saw Spook barge into Darius as he went to pick up
the knife. The force knocked him over but he was now
close to the fallen gun. He noticed it at the same time as
Acid did.

No.

Not a chance.

She dived for it, scooping it into her grip as she hit the
ground. Twisting her body, she aimed at Darius, but the
bastard had grabbed Spook. Holding her by the neck and
the top of one arm, he swung her in front of him, using her
as a human shield.

Shit.

She couldn't take the shot. Darius danced around for a
few seconds, then shoved Spook at her before running away
in the opposite direction.

"Bastard!" Acid scrambled to get upright, leaning
around Spook as she fell into her. She fired a couple of
rounds at the disappearing Darius, but the angle was bad
and she couldn't find her mark.

"Bastard! Bastard! Bastard!" The rounds whizzed wide
and over his head as he ran for the exit. Getting to her feet,
she was ready to go after him when Spook yelled.

"Acid, wait."

She spun around to see the kid lying on the floor. She

looked broken and was covered in blood. The Dullahan's blood. His lifeless body lay next to her.

"Come on," she told Spook. "You have to get up. We have to— Uh!"

Something like a wrecking ball smashed into the side of her. She hit the hard concrete with a thud and lost her grip on the gun. She reached out to grab it but it spun away, coming to a stop at the base of one of the lamps. Before she could stand, the same wrecking ball in the shape of Lamia jumped on top of her.

"You fucking loser!" she shrieked, grabbing Acid around the neck. "I am Lamia Loveless. You are nothing. You are no one."

Acid tensed the muscles in her neck and smashed her fists into her attacker's kidneys as hard as she could. But it had little effect. As Lamia's grip tightened around her throat, Acid raised her hands, grabbing the bitch's face.

"Fuck you," she snarled. "I'm Acid Vanilla."

She shoved her thumbs into Lamia's eye sockets and pressed hard. She had every intention of popping her eyeballs if that's what it took. The assassin cried out and let go of her neck, leaning back and jerking her head free from Acid's clutches, then lunging forward and thumping Acid in the face. The blow knocked her head back and the room spun. She tasted blood in the back of her throat as bony fingers clasped her face on both sides. She tensed her neck muscles, knowing what was coming, but she couldn't counter Lamia's brute force as the evil bitch lifted her head and smashed it onto the concrete floor. The crack reverberated through Acid's skull but she remained conscious. Just. Lamia lifted her head again, readying it for another meeting with the hard floor. The first blow had been a test run, but now Acid was dazed and Lamia had a better grip. Another blow and it could all be over. Cracked skull. Unconscious. She'd never wake up.

"Time to die, Acid Vanilla," Lamia whispered in her ear. "You were no match for me."

"Go to hell," Acid spat. But it was no use. She was done. She was—

"Yeah, go to hell, you fucking bitch!"

Lamia grunted and let go of her as the room turned upside down. Acid heard a thud and felt a heavy weight on top of her before being rolled onto her side. As her vision righted itself, she saw Lamia lying on the floor with Spook on top of her, legs bicycling in the air like a turtle that had fallen on its shell.

Acid pushed herself up onto all fours, scanning the vicinity for a weapon. Where was the damn push dagger? It had to be around here somewhere…

"Shit, Spook." She'd spotted it lying next to the kid's foot.

But so had Lamia. She shoved Spook off her and grabbed it, slashing the weapon wantonly through the air. Spook screamed and recoiled, giving Lamia time to get to her feet as Acid did the same. While Spook crawled under the table, whimpering to herself, the two assassins faced each other. They were both covered in dirt and grime and at least three different people's blood. Their chests rose and fell in unison as they fought to catch their breaths.

"Now we finish this," Lamia gasped, gripping the push dagger in her fist.

Acid's hand dragged across her mouth. "One way or another."

Lamia smirked and rolled her shoulders back, but Acid's attention had fallen some way behind her. To the base of the furthest lamp stand where the gun was wedged.

She made to lunge at Lamia but at the last second dummied the move and stepped around the side of her. The world zoomed into tunnel vision as she concentrated her attention on the small grey pistol. She saw now that it was a Sig Sauer P226. The gun of choice for the US Navy Seals. It didn't matter what it was. It was a gun. It had bullets in it. Enough to kill this sour-faced twat. She grabbed it, finger already a quarter way down on the trigger as she spun around. But before she could take the shot, Lamia rushed her, knocking her into the lamp and sending both her and it clattering to the floor.

"Acid!" Spook yelled. "She's getting away."

With the gun still in her hand, Acid pushed herself upright. Lamia was already disappearing into the black void of the empty warehouse. Raising the gun, she fired off a few rounds in what she assumed to be the right direction, but with only three lamps left to illuminate such a vast space, she was shooting blind.

"Shit. Shitting hell."

She jumped to her feet, ready to give chase, only to see Spook on the ground, clutching at her arm, which was covered in blood. Her once grey top was now red and sticky.

"No!" Acid rushed over to her. "Did she get a vein?"

Spook looked up at her, her face was white and her eyes glassy. "I don't know. It doesn't hurt. Is that a good thing?"

Acid placed the pistol on the ground and took her wrist, rotating her arm into the light to inspect the damage. The wound was deep, almost to the bone in one part. But the blood, although plentiful, was seeping rather than spurting.

"Acid?" Spook said. "Is that a good thing?"

"Yes, sweetie. It is." She rested Spook's arm on her lap and let go of her wrist. "Hold it together to stem the bleeding. It's not fatal, but it will need a few stitches. We'll get you over to Song Shi as soon as I'm done."

"As soon as you're done?" Spook gasped. "It's done, Acid. It's over. They've escaped."

"No, Spook. This is far from over." She picked up the gun and got to her feet. "That prick killed my friend."

"No, what if they're—" She shut up as Acid glared at her. "Fine. Go. But be careful. Please."

That was all she needed to hear.

"You know me, sweetie," she called back as she ran for the exit. "I'm always careful."

Chapter Thirty-Eight

Acid burst through the heavy double doors and found herself outside the warehouse. Night had fallen and the benign stillness in the air was a shock to the system. A chill wind whipped through the passageways in between the long buildings, turning the sweat on her skin ice cold. She licked her lips, tasting the blood seeping from her nose, and gazed around the wide corridor of concrete and rubble that led to the gates at the far end of the site. Off in the distance, she saw the red glow of a car's taillights. A person was running towards the waiting vehicle. In the moonlight it was difficult to make out features, but their ungainly bearing told her it was Darius.

She raced after him, raising the Sig Sauer and firing off two shots. One of them went wide of the mark and the other punctured the ground to the left of him, sending up a mini-explosion of concrete and dust. Darius leapt into the air and glanced back before veering behind a metal industrial waste bin as she fired and missed once more.

Bloody shitting bastard.

He was getting away.

She stopped next to a cluster of empty oil drums and sucked back a sharp breath. She'd never get a kill shot while she was running. Not at this distance. She had to do this properly. She had one chance.

Adjusting her stance, she gripped the Sig Sauer like Spitfire had taught her all those years ago: arms outstretched; both hands on the handle; eyes open but aiming with the dominant one; body leaning forward to manage the recoil. She had him. Darius was almost at the car as she got the back of his head in her sights. Tensing her finger on the trigger, she relaxed her upper body, waiting for the space between breaths.

Take it! the bats screeched.

Take the shot.

Kill him.

Kill…

A loud screech invaded the manic chatter in her head. She squeezed the trigger as something hard and heavy battered into her side. A sonic crack echoed through her body as the gun was knocked from her hands. She doubled over, her body reacting to the searing pain in her arms.

No!

What the fuck?

She straightened up in time to see Lamia swinging a metal bar at her head. Shifting out of the way, she punched her in the side of the head as the weight of the heavy bar carried the vile cow forward. The blow seemed to rattle her but she remained upright, and the punch only exacerbated the pain in Acid's arm. She stepped back and into a fight stance as Lamia turned to face her. Off in the distance she heard the car speeding away, no doubt with Darius inside. It only made her more determined to kill the woman in front of her. She sniffed back and spat a mixture of blood and phlegm on the ground between them.

"Come on then, Lamia Loveless," she hissed. "Let's see what you've got."

The woman laughed. "You still think you're something special, huh? You know, I read all about you. Everyone said you were the best. But to see you in action makes me think people didn't know what they were talking about." She wrinkled her long nose, flaring her nostrils at the same time. "I'm going to kill you now. Do you understand? I'm going to kill the great Acid Vanilla. The great phoney."

Acid raised her fists in readiness, eyes searching the ground for the lost gun. It was nowhere in sight. Back to Lamia. She was holding the metal bar in both hands like it was a baseball bat. A lucky strike in the right place and she would be a goner. Acid rocked up on the balls of her feet, swaying left and right, ready to evade the attack. Dodge and strike. That was the plan. Get her on the back foot.

That was how she'd win this.

With a screech, Lamia struck out, swinging at Acid's head. Already sensing the play, Acid ducked under the metal bar and slammed her fist into Lamia's bony chest. A grunt of air left her body, but she hadn't winded her enough to slow her down. Acid was backing away when the heavy elbow ploughed into the side of her face, knocking her into the cluster of oil drums. They were rusty and old, and as she hit them they toppled over and she landed on the sharp edge of one of them, letting out a cry as the ragged metal tore through the stitches above her hip.

She held her side. The pain was so intense she could feel it in her teeth.

"I am everything they said you were and more," Lamia

snarled as she walked over to her. "I am Lamia Loveless and you are nothing."

"Jesus. You think a lot of yourself," Acid replied, grimacing in agony as she tried to stand.

"Perhaps that's true," Lamia said. "But unlike you, I can also back it up with action." She booted Acid in the ribs, knocking her down.

It felt as if all the life force had been kicked out of her. Acid rolled onto her back. The pressure in her head was unbearable. The bats were going insane. She lifted her shoulders off the ground to get up, but Lamia jumped on top of her.

"Now you will die."

Hands clasped once more at her throat, and a tremendous weight pressed down on her windpipe. She kicked out, bucking her hips to throw her off, but it did no good. As Lamia's hands tightened their grip, she held her breath, fingers scrabbling around in the dirt, searching for a weapon. It felt like her head was about to pop. She tried to grab Lamia's face, but the assassin had learnt her lesson from before and lifted her head, making her long arms rigid-straight so Acid couldn't reach her.

Shitting shit.

Was this it?

After everything she'd been through, all the marks she'd killed, all the operatives she'd faced off against, it was this miserable bitch that would be responsible for her demise.

No. It wasn't going to happen.

The Dullahan was dead. These rotten pricks weren't getting the pleasure of eradicating both of them.

Not today.

Not ever.

She clawed a handful of gravel into her fist and flung it

into Lamia's face. It wasn't the most elegant or stylish of moves, but fights to the death rarely happened that way. Lamia cried out, her hands instinctively going to her eyes, and Acid bucked her hips again, this time destabilising her enough that she was able to shove her off and scramble away.

"Acid!"

She looked up to see Spook running towards them. She was still gripping her wounded arm tight with one hand, but the other was holding Darius' knife.

"Quick. Give it here." Acid got to her feet, staggering backwards and screwing up her eyes as a spiral of dizziness overcame her. Lamia, too, was on her feet and rubbing her eyes.

"You're pathetic," she hissed. "Is that all you can do, throw stones?"

Acid reached behind her. As Spook got closer, she shoved the wooden handle of the knife into her palm.

"Not entirely, sweetie," she said, fingers closing tight around the knife. "You see, what you need to realise is that you never write me off. I might not be as skilled or as fast as I used to be, but I've always got something extra up my sleeve. Or, in this case, behind my back."

She ran at Lamia, bringing the knife around and holding it out in front of her like a makeshift lance. Barging into the tall woman at full speed, she drove the sharp blade deep into her belly up to the hilt. Lamia coughed and then gasped as Acid twisted the sharp steel into her guts, jerking it to one side, slicing her stomach open. She stepped back and yanked out the blade, bringing a torrent of blood and intestines with it. Lamia bent over, shaking with the shock. Her arms hung loosely by her sides and her head bobbed up and down, giving her the look of a macabre marionette.

"Y... You..." she stammered.

"Yes," Acid said, giving her a winning smile. "Me!" She crossed her arms and shifted her weight onto her right hip, delighting at the sight of blood spluttering from Lamia's mouth as the fucked-up mare dropped to her knees.

"Don't worry about our fee," Spook called out, as the one-time Fiona Zoto fell face first into the dirt. "We'll waive that. Seeing as we never found your father."

As blood pooled out from beneath Lamia's body, Acid turned to Spook and arched an eyebrow. "That was a good one for you. Very droll. We'll make a hardened cynic out of you yet." She laughed, then stopped as the recall of what had happened hit her like a brick to the chest. "Bloody hell," she whispered, reeling back. "The Dullahan."

Acid brought her hand up to her forehead. She could hardly take it in. A shudder of emotion ripped through her, an unhelpful mix of remorse, rage, guilt and sadness.

But mainly rage.

Spook came up beside her and placed a sticky, blood-stained hand on her arm. "I'm sorry. He was a good man."

"I'm going to find that bastard," she whispered, her voice full of venom. "I'm going to crucify the fucker. He won't get away with this."

She set off walking. It was a long way to The Bitter Marxist on foot, but so be it. Someone there had to know something about Darius Duke. She'd find him and make him pay. For killing her friend and for what he'd put her and Spook through. The other stuff – her mum, Oscar Duke, her and Darius' possible relationship – she couldn't deal with any of that right now. Her lips curled into a sneer as she walked on, pushing the troubling thoughts down inside of her. The sooner she killed Darius, the better. Not only would she get revenge for what he'd done, but she wouldn't have to deal with the headfuck of what he'd just told her. Two birds with one stone.

"Wait, where are you going?" Spook caught up with her and grabbed her arm. "I need to get my arm stitched up. We need to go to Doctor Shi. You're bleeding as well. We both need attention."

Acid yanked her arm away and carried on walking. "He killed The Dullahan."

"Yes and it's awful, but neither of us is in any sort of state to do anything about it. It's over, Alice."

"It's not over."

"Yes!" Spook yelled. "It is. For now, at least. It's over."

Acid stopped and stared off into the distance. The car Darius had left in was no longer in view. She breathed heavily down both nostrils. Damn it. Spook was right. Her arm was a mess and the longer they left it, the less chance it would heal properly. She looked at her friend. The only one she had left.

"Fine," she said. "But I am going to kill that mother-fucker. I promise you that. Darius Duke is a dead man walking."

Spook smiled. "Yes, I thought you might say something like that."

Chapter Thirty-Nine

FIVE DAYS LATER...

Acid peered through the trees at the house opposite. Standing on its own in a leafy area of Highgate, the three-storey residence was a far cry from what she'd expected, but her lead had been adamant this was the place. She checked her phone. It was a few minutes after seven and the sky was turning a deep orange colour. The downstairs lights had just come on, but her guess was they were on a timer. Through the large picture window, she could see an open-plan living area with expensive furniture and a television screen bigger than anyone needed. But not him. Not yet.

She lowered herself into a sitting position. It was important to be patient at times like this. On some jobs for Caesar she'd had to wait for over twelve hours before she got any action, sometimes in spaces more confined and uncomfortable than the grove of bushy evergreens where she'd been squatting for the past three hours. She narrowed her eyes, casting her attention up and down the quiet street, alert for the sound of cars. Three hours. But she was pleased with herself. She'd kept her guard up and stayed alert. Because whilst patience was key, being vigilant was more important. Lack of focus lost you the mark, lack of focus got you killed.

She sat up as a sharp pain seared into her side. Falling badly on the oil drums had opened her old stitches as well as providing her with a new scar. Shi had been good about it, however, doing a two-for-one deal for her and Spook and putting them on the road to recovery. But it could have been so much worse.

Acid shook her head.

In the centre of the storm, one didn't consider the implications of what was happening. But once back in the safety of her apartment, the demons had set in. She'd been led on for weeks, controlled and manipulated by Darius' twisted narrative. If he hadn't been such a dramatic, egotistical prick, so desperate to stage his big revelation, things could have been very different. He'd had the upper hand from the start and was always a few steps in front. He could have slaughtered her, Spook and The Dullahan many times over before they even realised what was going on.

He was shrewd. She had to give him that.

But whether he was her half-brother she couldn't be sure. A part of her wondered, but whenever those thoughts popped into her head she busied herself with other things. In the last few days, she'd arranged for a crew from Manchester to collect The Dullahan's body and clean up the mess. They worked in the industry and were close allies of the great man. She trusted them. They'd do right by him.

And so would she.

Because even if Darius was her half-brother, it didn't change a damn thing. He was going to die for what he'd done.

And wouldn't you know it? Spook was right all along.

Acid did need a purpose. And now she had one. A mission bigger than her. She was going to find and kill Darius Duke. Hell, even Spook was behind her and ready to help find him. But that's because she had no choice. As long as Darius was still out there, he was a threat to both their lives. Especially as Acid had heard from one of the Manchester crew that someone fitting his description had recruited a whole team of assassins over the last six months.

So, for the first time in a long time, Acid and Spook were in agreement. They had to work together to find Duke before he found them. It would be good for the two of them, Acid thought. They needed a shared enemy, something else to focus on rather than their fractious relationship. Hell, she'd even apologised, and meant it, for being such a bloody cow these past six months. Who said she couldn't change her ways?

"Oh. Here we are." Her attention snapped back to the present at the sign of movement across the street. "Bloody hell."

She parted the trees in front of her to get a better view. A figure had appeared in the window. He was wearing a crisp white tracksuit rather than his usual black streetwear, but she'd know that face anywhere. The heavy brow, the straight nose and full lips. Lucas Jelani. He was on his phone, talking animatedly.

She waited a few minutes, watching, making sure there was no one else at home. Then she got to her feet and slipped the small rucksack off her back. Inside was a Glock 19 and a rail-mounted suppressor. The perfect combination for a gangland-style execution like the one she had planned for him. Plus, she had her trusty push dagger in her belt.

She smiled to herself. After all the runaround this evil prick had given her these last few months, it was almost going to be too easy. But that was fine. Sometimes easy was good. She could take him out and still have time for a drink in The Bitter Marxist before heading home. Spook would still be up and the smell of liquor on her breath would help her alibi.

Because whilst she and Spook were getting on better, there were still things Acid would have to keep from her. Things she had to do alone. The bats were still greedy and their bloodlust was as strong as ever.

She fitted the suppressor onto the barrel of the Glock and placed the weapon inside her jacket before zipping it up.

Alice Vandella would always be a part of her, but Acid Vanilla was here to stay. She couldn't change now, even if she wanted to. She stepped out from the cover of the trees and strolled across the street towards Jelani's house. Acid Vanilla was a killer. That was what she did. It was who she was.

And that was fine by her.

A Note From The Author

As this is the first book I've written since going full-time as a professional author I felt it was an apt time to say some big thank yous to everyone who has helped me get to this point.

Suzanne & Alba - my wonderful wife and daughter. You're the reason I do this. Knowing I get to spend more time with you as a result of being a full-time writer is what drives me on when things aren't going to plan. I love you both very much. Thank you.

Mum & Dad. For always believing in me and supporting me in my sometimes madcap, sometimes clearly stupid, creative endeavours over the years. You've always championed me and had my back. I love you. Thank you.

Tina - my amazing editor. You 'got' what I was trying to do with Acid from day one and always steer me (and her) in the right direction even when I might get a bit lost myself. Thank you.

The Hit Squad - my wonderful advance copy reading team. Your help in honing each book into the sharpest, best version it can be is always invaluable. Thank you.

And finally I want to say thank you to YOU. For buying my

book and supporting my writing career. I really would be nothing without my readers and I appreciate every one of you. Thank you.

Matthew Hattersley

July 2022

Next in the Acid Vanilla series

vinci-books.com/badblood

A deadly game begins...

Ex-assassin Acid Vanilla faces her darkest fears as she confronts the aftermath of her friend's brutal murder.

A heart-pounding thriller that will keep readers on the edge of their seats until the final page.